DISCARDED

SHIFTER'S VAULT BOOK 1

MAGGIE ALABASTER

1

VIVA

INSIDE THE TRAIN car was stifling. Either the aircon was fucked, or there was none. The small space pressed in on me. Sweat beaded on my brow. I needed to breathe. Not just inhale and exhale, but draw a clean, clear breath that didn't smell like piss.

I rose from my rock hard seat, grabbed the bottom of the windowsill with the tips of my fingers and pushed upward. I grunted and strained. The window opened a whisker.

"Come on, motherfucker," I growled out loud. There was no one nearby to hear. I didn't care if they did. If they didn't like it, they could sit somewhere else.

I growled in frustration and wiped sweat away before it trickled down my nose.

They put the oldest carriages on the cross-city line. Out of sight of anyone important and out of mind. Don't like it? Too bad, you can walk. The city probably thought we should be grateful. When—okay *if*—they thought of us at all.

Assholes.

Teeth gritted, I shoved at the window again. It didn't budge. It wasn't nailed down, it was just stiff from years of disuse. Or misuse. Whatever.

I glanced toward the carriage door before I took the three steps toward my suitcase. As old as the train, and at least as worn-looking on the outside, it opened with no effort.

Because I take care of my shit, I thought.

From the pocket In the side of the case, I pulled out a bag. Simple, plain, black cotton, the bag was obviously handmade. The stitches looked rough and uneven. What can I say? Sewing is not my thing.

Inside the bag were several small pouches, each much better made. Not by me. Okay, I bought them off the internet rather than try sewing again. One day I would replace the bag, but for now, it did what I needed it to do.

I drew out one pouch, opened it and lifted it to my nose. Eyes half closed, half alert, I inhaled the smell of cinnamon and nutmeg. The combination had a small amount of potency, but it should be enough.

I breathed in and the power crept into me, like the warm sensation that comes from smelling a fresh cup of coffee.

Power soon scratched at my skin, itching to get out. I held it firm.

I stepped back to the widow and pressed the tips of my fingers to the sill. Power wanted to gush away, but I forced it to trickle out of me, down through my fingers and into the gap. I let it sit there for a moment, then levered the window up enough to squeeze my fingers underneath the frame. I now had enough purchase to give it a last shove. Breath ground out of me, sweat trickled into my eye, but the stiff window opened one, two centimetres. There, it stopped; stubbornly jammed in the warped sill. No amount of power would move it further.

I pressed my face to the small opening. The breeze caressed my skin and dried the worst of my sweat. The air from outside was warm and sticky, and smelled like fuel and something dead. Still, it was better than the air inside.

Once I cleared my head, I took in the view. It hadn't changed much in the last hour, but something *felt* different. My skin tingled. Anticipation, or was it something more?

The train slid into a tunnel, rattled through in a flash of shadows, then clattered out the other side.

The blur of concrete became buildings, each one covered in graffiti. A tag here, a face there. Several dicks and balls hastily painted between passing trains. The usual inner city shit.

I tilted my face back to look above the towering, worn facades. Striking blue sky stretched overhead. If I looked at it long enough, I might forget the rest of Sydney existed.

I watched for a while, half mesmerised. I could swear I smelled the scent of lavender. Clear and fresh.

I must have imagined it. Wishful thinking, maybe, because I'd rather be in a garden, or on a beach. Somewhere a long way from here.

I turned from the open window. My nostrils flared. The stale smell inside the carriage lingered, but the heat was less oppressive. A little bit at least.

I flopped down on the seat and leaned against the window, head back, booted feet beside my suitcase. Through half-lidded eyes, I stared up at the ceiling. I knew every knot and flaw; a scratch here, a gap there, several pieces of well-aimed gum and the gods knew what else. I had counted and memorised them to pass the time. Sitting still wasn't a skill I had mastered.

My eyelids fluttered shut. A soft breath escaped from between my lips. Maybe I would indulge in a sleep—

"Next stop, Copper Square station." A male voice sounded across a loudspeaker. A recording.

The train began to slow.

My eyes flew open, gaze instantly drawn back to the window.

A bird wheeled past, little more than a dark blur with wings outstretched. It let out a squawk as though outraged to find a train in its part of the city.

I have news for you, bird, I thought. *A train is the least of your problems.*

I rose, eyes on the greasy window pane. My gaze was drawn to the east and I forgot all about the bird.

With barely a clatter on the tracks, the train slid into another tunnel.

Immediately, daylight, overhead light, *everything* was gone. I was plunged into absolute darkness. The train sounded louder now, or maybe it was my heart.

I blinked and searched for even the smallest pinprick of light to break the endless, oppressive black. I found nothing but the start of my own panic.

Just before I groaned or screamed, a glow finally appeared.

The light of a yellow lamp, then another. They illuminated the tiles of a tired, deserted station. Apart from being illuminated by what looked like flood lamps from a previous century, there was nothing notable about it. Anyone who passed through would forget it a moment later, just like all the rest on the long line.

"Shit just got real," I murmured. I almost wished it hadn't. Another day, another week...

I shook my head. I was ready. As ready as I could be, anyway.

The smell of lavender hit me again, stronger this time. I closed my eyes and sucked in the scent. It smelled like peace and calm. It was an illusion designed to make the unwary lower their defences.

Not gonna happen. I shook my head. Fuck, it already had, I'd almost been lulled to sleep. I pushed all my walls back up, all my vigilance. I couldn't let my defences down again, not today.

Gradually, the train slowed further.

A chill passed through from my lower back to the top of my spine.

Copper Square. That was what it said on the maps. At least, maps that showed it at all. To those who knew, it was simply known as the Vault.

I wanted to stare. I forced myself to step back from the window. I would have time for that soon enough.

I have to be ready.

I glanced toward the carriage door before I reopened my suitcase. I felt around at the bottom of the chest, under jeans and shirts. Beneath the folds of denim and cotton, my fingers touched something hard. I grabbed hold of the leather sheath and pulled it out. The pattern on the side was worn to nothing but a line or two. It was anyone's guess what it had once been. Maybe a dragon, or a griffin. Something the knife was made to kill.

I slid the knife out to check the blade and sent a quick prayer to Hades it would be enough.

Idiot, I told myself. The knife was made by the best blade-smith in the country. It could slice through the iron-like ribs of a griffin. It would do for what I needed.

I replaced the knife in the sheath and tucked it down the side of my jeans.

The train drew to a stop as I closed my suitcase and clicked it shut.

Not a minute passed before the doors between the carriages slid apart. The car I was in wouldn't open to this station. I'd been warned about that. That was one reason I chose it. They would find it harder to take me by surprise. At least in theory.

The man who stood in the doorway was a head taller than me, and half again as wide. Every inch of him looked like muscle carved out of rock. Even his face looked made of stone, all hard angles and chiseled lines. I bet he was chiselled underneath his black t-shirt as well. His biceps certainly bulged to the point of straining the seams. On another day, I might use my power to tease them loose, just to watch them break.

Dark hair cut close to his scalp revealed a long scar on the right side of his head. Full lips were set in a line. He looked like he never smiled, or scowled. Shame, I bet he could do a few fun things with his mouth.

"I guess this is my stop," I said, my voice even, thank the gods.

'Treat other people like they're wild animals,' my mother told me when I was barely old enough to walk. 'Show them fear and they'll tear you to bits.'

I didn't think she meant literally, but I wasn't going to let myself be torn. Except in a good way. I presumed this guy was big under his jeans, but I didn't take my eyes off his face and chest.

"Yeah, no shit," he replied. His voice was a rumbly baritone that probably melted panties on an hourly basis.

I breathed in his scent—sandalwood and spices. I couldn't smell lavender anymore, but he smelled even better. I exhaled. A tingle of power tickled at my skin. I reminded myself to stay on guard. I didn't need my panties melted. At least not today.

"I'm Bain." His deep voice was as emotionless as his face.

I cocked my head at him. "Is that your real name?"

He didn't answer. Instead he asked, "Where is Izzy?"

"The chick who's watched me since I left my place this morning?" I asked. He didn't seem surprised I noticed. I didn't care. I wanted him to know I had seen her. "Fucked if I know," I added, shrugging one shoulder.

Bain looked at me like I might have killed her and thrown her body out the tiny sliver of the open window. Yeah, right, like that was possible. The opening was far too narrow to fit a whole person. Bits and pieces, sure, but that was messy and messy wasn't my thing.

"She was here for a while, then she left. That was about an hour ago. Maybe she got off somewhere else."

Bain gave me a sceptical look, which I met unflinchingly.

I would watch him carefully, and not turn my back on him. If he thought for a moment I posed a risk, he would probably slit my throat and leave me beside the tracks for the birds to eat.

Hard pass.

My hand almost twitched near the blade, but I forced myself to keep still. Bain would be looking for signs of aggression. I wouldn't let him see any, at least until it was too late.

If he noticed anything, he gave no sign. Either he didn't, or he had the best godsdamn poker face in the city.

Note to self, don't play strip poker with him, unless you're ready to lose. Which I might be some day.

He turned to a man behind him, who was hidden by the wall until now. "Go and find Izzy," he ordered. Without waiting for a response, he turned back to me.

"Come on. Follow me." He took in my neat outfit and frowned slightly. Did he disapprove? Too fucking bad. I could have worn a cocktail dress, but I didn't own one. I wasn't the feminine kind. Jeans and t-shirts did me fine.

I drew myself a little taller. "Right. After you then." I couldn't have squeezed past him anyway, he was too big.

He nodded and backed out the doorway. "This way."

"Thank you, Bain." I flashed him a smile.

A slight quirk of his eyebrow suggested he was surprised I used his name.

Why wouldn't I? I might need him at some point. Besides, it didn't hurt to be friendly, right? Just because he'd shown no sign of being amicable doesn't mean I shouldn't try. I wouldn't lower my guard, but I might get him to lower his. Yeah, probably not, but it was worth a try.

He nodded, turned sharply and walked away down the short corridor toward the stairs off the train. His scent trailed after him, leaving behind several drops of power, which dissolved quickly when it mixed with the stale, disgusting carriage smell.

I wrinkled my nose. The dank air suppressed my senses and made my stomach heavy.

I gave myself a shake and picked up my suitcase. I stepped through the door and let it close behind me.

Just before I stepped off the train and onto the brightly illuminated platform, Izzy hurried through the carriage toward me. Her face looked flushed, hair pulled free from her neat plait.

She smiled brightly and spoke with no sincerity at all. "I'm so sorry, I got sidetracked."

I smelled man, and sex, all over her.

"Who were you screwing?" Bain asked bluntly.

Izzy's face flushed pink. "No one. Just some guy." She shrugged, unapologetic.

Bain nodded. "I see."

I suspect she might get into trouble later for not keeping a closer eye on me. I put that in the 'not my problem' basket and moved on. Although, I admit I was a little envious. I didn't need the distraction right now, but I hadn't had a good fuck in... Too damn long.

"Maybe you can keep an eye on our guest?" Bain suggested. He directed a vague wave toward me.

Izzy pulled a stick of gum out of her pocket, unwrapped it and tossed the wrapper back into the train. She shoved the gum into her mouth and smiled. "Sure, Bain." To me, she smiled with mock sweetness. "Sorry, I'm supposed to guide you and stuff."

"Yeah, whatever." I smiled back with the same amount of sincerity. "I didn't need a nursemaid and I'm sure he was cuter than me." Not that I wasn't pretty fucking cute. I was, but she was not my type and vice versa.

"Yeah, well, I wasn't paying much attention, except to his size. If you get my drift." Izzy grinned.

"We get it," Bain said. "Let's get going. We've dicked around here long enough." He stomped off toward a set of stairs at the end of the platform.

Strange.

Now I was able to look more closely, the station didn't look as worn as I'd first thought. In fact, the railings shone and the concrete under my boots looked as though it dried the day before. Even the benches looked like they'd only just been painted and bolted into place.

The train rumbled and pulled away from the station. Before it picked up speed, it wound around a bend and was gone. Not just from sight; I could no longer smell or hear it. I strained for a moment, but it was absolutely gone, as though it had never been.

Fucking strange.

"First time in the Vault?" Izzy asked. In spite of the question, she didn't seem interested in the answer. She glanced over her shoulder at me, then away.

"Yeah," I said, sure neither she nor Bain heard me.

Izzy gave a soft laugh, an edge of bitterness to the sound.

"Don't worry, we're mostly harmless. Well, I am. Bain is known to kill people for no reason."

He regarded her from under heavy brows, but said nothing to confirm or deny it.

Well, that's reassuring.

"If the rumours are true, I do the same," I said.

Izzy glanced back at me again, surprise on her face this time. She looked me up and down and clearly decided I was joking. She gave an awkward laugh. "Well, I'm sure you'll have an interesting time here then."

"I'm sure I will," I agreed. "Someone had to accompany the artefact." I nodded toward my suitcase.

"We could have sent a courier," Bain said. He seemed to think all of this was a waste of time.

"Apparently the Covener doesn't trust couriers," I said. The head of the Witches' Council didn't trust anyone, especially Bain's boss, the current Keeper of the Vault.

Bain shrugged. "Suit yourself. I'm sure he knew what he was getting you into."

He was right, the Covener knew. That was why he sent me. Him and his asshole of a son.

I followed Bain down the stairs, to a street which was almost dark at the tunnel. I drew in a deep breath and let my mind sift through the smells. There was lavender again, the sandalwood scent of Bain, a peach perfume from Izzy, the faint smell of a normal city, and something else I couldn't place.

A black car waited for us by the side of the road. At least, I assumed it was for us, since Izzy led the way right to it.

"Come on, Jaq charges by the hour," Bain said with a grunt. He opened the boot of the car and reached for my suitcase

"Thank you." I hefted it high enough for him to grab hold and swing it into the boot before he slammed it shut.

Slamming doors; that was the perfect metaphor for my life right now.

I wanted to turn away, to leave the artefact with them and go home. I could trot back up the stairs and sit on the platform until another train came.

I set my lips in a line.

That would be pointless. Even if I had a home to go to, the train only stopped at Copper Square when the Vault ordered it to. They could easily leave me waiting on the platform forever.

I opened the door to the back of the car and slipped in behind Bain. With his back to me, I was able to draw in his scent. The sandalwood infused me with enough power to force my body and mind to calm. With a jar of whatever he washed with, I could sink the Vault and half the city into the harbour.

I couldn't leave, but I could take them all to the bottom with me if I wanted to.

Which I didn't. In spite of what I'd said to Izzy, I wasn't homicidal, or suicidal. The small dose of his smell was all I needed to get through these next few hours. Alive, with any luck.

Izzy sat in the seat beside me and loudly chewed her gum. She flashed me a smile, then leaned forward to talk to the driver.

I sat back and looked out the window as the car moved away from the sidewalk.

We travelled through darkness broken here and there by streetlights. Shapes of buildings appeared at the edge of each circle of light, but not enough to show more than neatly dressed stone and black recesses that might be doorways.

Where there might be sky, there was nothing. No stars, no moon.

"We're here," Izzy said.

I realised we'd stopped. For a minute or two at least, by the look of it.

While I had admired the city, Bain and the driver stepped out of the car and now stood waiting. Bain handed my suitcase to another man, who curled his lip at the ragged state of my case.

I gave Izzy a nod and opened her door.

"Do you need help?" Bain opened mine and looked at me as though I'd deliberately sat waiting for him.

"Thank you, I've got this." I gave him a brief smile.

He grunted and moved away.

Unless the goddess of bad luck heard and made me trip, I could get out of a car by myself. The bitch listened at the worst possible times, but I managed to step on the sidewalk without falling on my face.

Win.

Only after I closed the door behind me did I look at Bain again.

He stood with a couple of other men, speaking to them in a low voice. Both looked as cheerful as he did. One nodded and hurried away. The rest fell in behind me and Izzy.

I turned to take my suitcase from the man who held it. He looked like he might argue, but Bain gave him a sharp nod and he released the handle.

Damn right, bitch, I thought. *My clothes are in there.*

Not just that, of course. I gripped the handle a little tighter, aware of the eyes on me. Not on me, I reminded myself, on my suitcase and the box inside.

I heard the Covener's words in my mind. "Guard that box as though it were worth a lot more than you." To him, it was. I was nothing. Less than nothing. An escort, and a scapegoat if it went missing.

"Perhaps you should take it yourself?" I had told him.

"Then how would I be rid of you?" Covener Denis Crane

looked at me from under his bushy eyebrows. His mouth curled downward behind his thick beard.

"I'm sure you'd find a way," I retorted. I shouldn't taunt him. My power was stronger than his, but if he ordered me dead, I wouldn't survive the day. Still, I wouldn't show him I was beaten.

"Yes, I would." He nodded. "In fact, I have." He looked smug.

I wanted to wipe the expression off his face, but no one touched the Covener without his consent.

"The artefact isn't that important, is it?" I guessed. "This is about Max." His brat of a son would be Covener one day, and he never let anyone forget it. Max Crane would give us a shit reputation amongst paranormals, if we didn't already have one. Denis hated anyone who wasn't a witch, particularly me. My power was at least part shifter. My blood was tainted, according to them. As if I fucking asked to be different.

I sure as fuck didn't ask to be paired with Max during the coming of age ritual at midsummer three years ago. The memory alone turned my stomach.

Every witch within a hundred kilometre radius turned up at the Council's Ritual Chamber. There, anyone over eighteen would ask Hades for guidance. Or a lesser god if you were brave enough. And Hades, if he felt like screwing with us, would force the girls to kneel at the feet of the mate he chose for us.

I don't know who was more horrified when I knelt at the feet of Max Crane; me, him or his father. God-given or not, the Covener and his asshole son turned their backs firmly on me and encouraged everyone else to do the same. He must have worked in this plan to send me away since the moment my knee touched the ground.

"The artefact is vital to the shifters." His lip curled. "But *everything* is about the future Covener. You'll do well to remember that." He crossed his arms and looked at me with eyes full of disdain. "I won't have him, or any witch, tarnished by tainted blood."

And that was that. After three years of being avoided and ignored by people I thought were my friends, I'd rather take my chances with the residents of the Vault. They were a hundred times worse, if I believed my mother, but I couldn't see how. The worst they could do was treat me like crap, and was more or less used to that by now.

"Fine, I'll go." I sighed loudly like he'd twisted my arm. He would never see me flinch, no matter what it took.

"Yes, you will." He turned away and I was forgotten.

My mind was drawn back into the present at the thud of Bain's boots. He trotted up steps which led into a tall building.

This one was lit better than the others. Gargoyles leaned over the doorway, glaring at anyone who dared to come close. Intricately carved shelves of stone supported their weight. Did I see gems sparkle in their eyes, or was that a trick of the light?

I blinked, but whatever I saw, or thought I saw, was gone.

Bain stopped and nodded to another man, this one older and smaller than Bain, but with shrewd eyes. He looked at me with disinterest; his eyes lingered longer on my case. Like Bain, he was dressed in black; jeans and a coat too heavy for the heat of the day.

I presumed he knew what my suitcase held. For a moment, I thought he might take it from me and dismiss me. Instead he moved away, leaving Bain to open the doors.

"Thank you." I gave the other man—Bain's superior, I assumed—a dark look for not having the courtesy to address me himself. I mentally slapped myself.

Shit, Viva, don't make enemies unless you have to.

The man's eyes narrowed and his mouth drew back, but he said nothing.

"Don't mind Tevan," Bain said, speaking near my ear. "He's always grumpy."

I forced a smile. "I'm sure he's anxious to have the artefact delivered."

Bain's eyes suggested something more, but he said nothing and moved away before I could interpret the look.

He ushered us inside out of the darkness and the doors closed, shutting us in.

2

I HATE ELEVATORS.

I squeezed the handle of my suitcase and pretended to be calm. The walls were too close, especially with five of us inside. The smell of sandalwood, peaches, sweat and old carpet mixed like several radio stations at a rock concert. My senses were overwhelmed.

I could take power from Bain and Izzy, but I couldn't use it before it sank into my belly and made me nauseous.

I really *fucking* hate elevators.

Pull yourself together, I told myself. Once I did what I came here for, I could relax. Until then, I would have to fake it until I made it. That didn't sound right. Whatever.

The door finally slid open on level five.

Izzy's face was pale, lips drawn into a line so firm they looked bloodless.

What does she have to worry about?

"Are you good?" I asked. Partly to deflect from my own

nerves, partly because I'd be pissed if Izzy puked on my boots. I might puke on hers if she did. My belly felt like a fully grown dragon settled in there.

Izzy turned to me and shrugged. "Yeah. This place freaks me out." A flush brought colour back to her cheeks.

"I suppose it would." I looked past her to Bain, whose expression hadn't changed, except a slight frown on his brow.

"We get out here," he said, a growl in his voice.

Izzy stepped out first, Bain on her heels. He turned and gestured for me to follow. The other two men, both dressed in black like almost everyone else here, stayed close to me. Or rather, my suitcase.

Bain headed down a wide corridor.

I gripped my suitcase handle until my knuckles turned white. Some of my nerves came from carrying the artefact. If the package wasn't intact, there wasn't anywhere in the world the Witches' Council wouldn't find me.

I would be rid of the bloody thing soon, thank Hades.

The corridor stopped.

I almost ran into Bain. I caught myself at the last moment and swore under my breath.

He turned to give me a dark look, which I ignored.

"Ummm." When I said the corridor stopped, that's exactly what I meant. We stood facing a blank, white wall.

Bain snorted and even Izzy grinned.

Yep, apparently they'd both lost their minds.

Bain pressed a spot in the wall and it disappeared like it never existed.

Okay, I should have known magic was involved. Duh.

I stepped out into a wide, sunlit courtyard, and blinked at the sudden light.

The courtyard was neatly paved and edged with flowers. To one side, a huge fountain rained down a tinkle of water. A number of creatures were carved into the base of the black stone. A dragon, several griffins and others I didn't know, flew in a frozen battle, wings spread, mouths open to attack. I wanted to walk around it, to see who they fought, but Bain cleared his throat.

"This way." He gestured, palm up, toward a doorway on the other side of the courtyard.

I gave the fountain a last look, nodded and followed. I managed not to gape at the grandeur of the gardens, and the variety of trees and flowers.

The trees were all fruiting ones, and harmless, and the flowers were all fragrant.

I kept my lips apart and breathed through my mouth to keep from drawing in too much scent. Still, power crept in, danced under my skin and into my blood.

The sensation was like a drug. I forced myself to maintain control, even though I wanted to draw it all in and drown in it.

I concentrated on Bain as he spoke. "The Keeper's residence is quite small," he began.

I turned a surprised look on him. "Small?" I echoed.

He raised an eyebrow at me. He almost looked as though he might give me a mocking smile, but only managed a twitch at the corners of his mouth.

"Compared to other places in the Vault it is. The Alpha's residence, for example. This building is still twice the size of the Witches' Council, as befitting the Keeper of the Vault." He looked smug.

I shrugged. "The Council has to hide out in the open." Like I gave a fuck if the buildings in here dwarfed anything of the witches'. As far as I was concerned, they could all go to Hades.

"Indeed." He nodded once.

I followed him through the doorway and into what looked like a residence. Once my eyes grew accustomed to the abundance, perhaps *overabundance*, of red and gold, Simple furniture, albeit well-made, was placed to make the best use of light from wide windows. Every table bore a vase of flowers, all fresh as if picked only moments before. The scent of the room would have overpowered even normal folk, but Bain didn't seem to notice. Perhaps he was accustomed to the cloying smell.

"Ah, this is Viva." An older woman stepped from a corridor and moved toward us with an easy grace. Her grey hair was tied in a neat bun, but she wore loose pants and a blouse in bright turquoise, which matched the casual way she spoke. A choker in the same shade sat at her throat, unadorned apart from light embroidery in the shape of vines.

"Calista Breakwater." Bain gave the woman a nod. "This is Viva Taylor. Calista is the Keeper's aunt."

I smiled, awkward and lopsided with anxiety. "Nice to meet you, Ms Breakwater." I had heard Calista was a formidable woman. She radiated power in her bearing and the steel in her eyes.

She gave me a shrewd look before her face melted into a warm smile which drew me to her immediately.

In the next moment, I reminded myself to be on guard. A friendly face could still mean a blade in my back.

"Just Calista." She seemed unruffled. "Is Bain trying to intimidate you? He was always like that, even as a boy. He's mostly harmless." She gave me a conspiratorial wink.

"Viva," Bain said as though he hadn't heard her, "I'll leave you in Calista's capable hands."

Calista clicked her tongue at him as he walked off. "That boy, always so uptight." She shook her head.

I snorted before I could stop myself. I already had my

family's reputation to contend with, without making myself look foolish. Snorting like a dragon hunting its prey…

Oh well, take me or leave me, I guess.

Calista smiled, snaked an arm around mine and led me in the direction she'd come from.

"I would assume you've heard many things about the Vault," she said without preamble. "Most of it is probably true, but we don't bite. Well, most of us." She gave a soft laugh. "At least, not in human form."

"I've heard many…interesting things," I said. Calista smelled of lilacs, the soft scent a welcome change from train air and sandalwood.

Calista gave me a look, but said nothing. It seemed she'd already made up her mind about me. She probably thought I was no better than the average witch. I might be offended, but she had a point. I would have to try to prove we weren't all assholes.

She opened a door near the end of the corridor.

"I'll leave you here to freshen up and rest for a few hours," Calista said graciously. "You must be exhausted."

"A little bit," I said. Honestly, I wanted to rid myself of the damn artefact as soon as I arrived. For something so small, it began to feel heavy. I considered demanding to see the Keeper, but thought better of it. I was in no position to make demands.

If he wanted to see me immediately, then I would be in front of him now.

My mother always said those who lived in the Vault liked to play games. This was probably one of them.

The Covener was no better. Many times I saw him leave less powerful witches to sweat before he allowed them an audience. The Keeper might do the same to me. It was was possible, even understandable, but as annoying as fuck.

"Thank you, Calista." I felt uncomfortable addressing her

by name. "I should sit down for a little while." *And clear my head.* The smells in this place were overpowering.

"Why do you look scared?" Calista asked.

For a moment I thought she was speaking to me. I glanced back toward the door, ready to respond.

A reply died unsaid when I saw Izzy standing outside. The other woman had followed so quietly, I forgot she was there.

"No reason," Izzy said lightly. She wouldn't meet Calista's gaze, but she certainly *looked* scared. She smelled it too, like sweat and fear.

"So you say," Calista said. "Come with me. We'll let Viva rest."

Panic threatened to claw at me, but I soon realised it was coming from Izzy. What had her so terrified? Surely it wasn't just her getting busy for an hour while I was on the train unsupervised? Maybe she'd fucked the wrong guy. She wouldn't be the first person to do that, and she wouldn't be the last.

My godsdamn 'tainted' blood was evidence of that.

I forced an insincere smile. "Yes." The word squeaked out, higher than I intended. I cleared my throat. "Izzy should have a rest too too, after watching over me so well."

To her, I said, "Thank you for helping me find my way. I would have been lost without you."

Not. I just didn't want her to end up feeding the birds. For some reason, that mattered to me. Maybe I just objected to a senseless death.

Izzy looked surprised, but grateful. She still stank of fear. Whatever was going to happen to her was going to suck. Her eyes said as much.

I knew I couldn't do any more, without making trouble for myself.

"Yes, Calista," Izzy said meekly and followed the older woman out of the room.

I turned away from the door after it closed behind them. The smell of coffee greeted me, reminding me I hadn't eaten since breakfast.

Steam spiralled from a black, porcelain cup which sat on the table. Witch made porcelain, created with power. Either the Keeper wanted to taunt me, or they appreciated the stuff. It was virtually unbreakable after all. Or rather, it could break, but the power would bind it back together again until it wore out. Even power had its limits.

My mother had a teapot made of witch porcelain, but no one was allowed to touch it. The pot was worth more than most people made in half a year.

Yet here was a pair of matching cups and saucers. The other one was empty.

Decadent bastards.

Beside those, a plate held a small cake, the top dusted in sugar.

At least, I presumed it was sugar. Several known, unscented poisons could be ground down to powder form. Hades only knew how many *unknown* poisons could as well. Not to mention ordinary, everyday drugs like cocaine.

"Idiot," I whispered to myself. "Stop jumping at shadows." If they wanted me dead, I would have fed the sea serpents a few kilometres off the shores of Australia by now. Yeah, my imagination often centred around being eaten by any number of animals, including guys like Bain.

There are several ways to be a tasty snack.

I reached for the cake, but stopped with my fingertips suspended above it. I shouldn't assume everyone here in the Vault wanted the Keeper to have the artefact, especially one the witches had in their possession for so long. Here, away from Bain's watchful eyes, someone might think they could get rid of me and take it. Hells, they were welcome to the bloody thing. They didn't need to kill me to get it.

I shook my head.

The Keeper's eyes would be even more vigilant here than on the train. Or Calista's eyes. Nothing would happen here without either of them being aware.

And yet, I couldn't shake the wary unease which settled around my shoulders like a blanket. Not the kind I could use to make a blankie fort and hide, but the itchy kind that irritated my skin.

I pulled out a chair and sat at the table, my eyes still on the cake. I was hungry, but I couldn't bring myself to eat.

Forget the artefact, I told myself. *Remember why you're really here.* I rested a hand lightly over the knife to reassure myself it was still there. I couldn't lose my nerve, not when I was so close.

An hour or two and this would all be over.

I moved my hand away from my hip to pick up the cup and sniff the coffee.

A surge of power flooded into me, but dissipated almost immediately. I twitched involuntarily.

Even though I expected it, the sudden jolt of power always took me by surprise. The scent of coffee, however strong, never lasted long enough for me to use it. Presumably because it was diluted in boiling water. Fortunately, the taste more than made up for it.

The coffee could also contain poison, but at least I would die happy.

I sipped.

It had gone a little cold, but still tasted amazing. How did they know my favourite blend?

I snorted. I didn't bother to hold it back this time. There was no one else in the room to hear.

The idea any shifter would bother to learn a witch's preference was ridiculous. The choice was obviously coinciden-tal; the combination was popular amongst witches, shifters and ordinary humans.

I gave in to hunger and broke the cake in half. Lemon and rose was *not* my favourite, but I took a few mouthfuls before nerves made my stomach rebel.

I placed the half-eaten cake back on the plate and took a few more sips of coffee.

The cup in my hands, I stood and stepped through a doorway which led out to a small balcony.

I marvelled at the clear air. I could be forgiven for thinking we weren't deep in the heart of a city. The Vault existed in a power-wrought bubble, or so I was told. It certainly seemed to be in a place away from the rest of the world.

The balcony overlooked a garden, one with different plants to those in the courtyard.

Honeysuckle vines draped over lattices; their sweet, tiny white flowers flowed like water. Roses in every shade imag-inable grew between the lattices, pops of vibrant colour and more fragrance than I dared to inhale.

I held my cup under my nose. The coffee counter-acted the flowers, at least a little. The temptation to lower the cup and suck in more power than I could hold was strong. The things I could do with all that power…

Before I could give in, I hurried back inside.

I walked around the room, taking in the art on the walls and appreciating the huge tub in the bathroom. A glance in the mirror on the wall showed my face was flushed, but I was otherwise presentable.

If the Keeper deigned to see me.

I wandered back to the table and took another couple bites of the cake.

A knock on the door made me jump and almost choke. The cake might kill me yet.

I coughed and swallowed my mouthful before the door swung open. Hopefully my face wasn't too red. I could have used more coffee, or even water to wash the cake down the rest of the way. Since I had neither, I fell back on the usual method of pretending nothing was amiss.

I was close now. Hades willing, nothing else would go wrong.

Bain stepped inside and stopped.

His eyes looked weary and wary, but the stoic set of his mouth was unchanged. He gave me a long glance, which started at my feet and swept up my body. He lingered at my breasts before finally looking at my face.

"It's time," he said simply.

"Time for what?" I asked with a smile. Before I could stop myself, I touched his hand with the tips of my fingers. A trickle of power passed from me to him. A jolt of fire shot the other way, right up my arm and into my core.

He responded with the slightest jerk and a flash of surprise as the fatigue lifted from his face.

I drew back. I could kick myself for acting so rashly. What had I *thought* would happen? His scent gave me energy, but I didn't have to use it on him. The fire I got back from him was a complication I didn't need.

I was a Hades-cursed idiot.

"The Keeper is ready for you." Bain's voice was tight. He didn't seem angry, but he didn't look grateful either. If he felt a hint of the lust I did, he gave no sign whatsoever.

Yep, I really would have to avoid playing poker with him. He was good. Too good.

"You mean he's ready for the artefact." I let a hint of bitterness sneak into my tone. Not because I was frustrated at not being able to read him. Okay, not *just* because of that.

It was easier, safer, to let him think I knew I was unimportant. That I was resigned to what was to come.

He would know the truth of it soon enough.

I turned my back on him and opened my suitcase. If he was going to slide a knife between my ribs, he would do it now.

I half hoped he'd grab me from behind, undo my jeans and... But even if he wanted to, we shouldn't keep the almighty Keeper waiting. I couldn't keep the sarcasm out of my thoughts.

I pulled out a small wooden box from inside my suitcase and held it in the palm of my hand.

Bain made no move to take the box.

I made no move to give it to him, even though I felt as though it might burn through my skin.

Not literally. If it was, I would have thrown it through the balcony doors and into the garden. An artefact that burns is a dangerous thing. I wouldn't put it past the Covener to make a last minute switch in the hope of destroying the Vault from the inside. And me with it. Two birds with one, small stone.

Bain gestured for me to walk beside him out of the room and down the corridor.

I moved into step beside him and tried not to look like I had to walk quicker to keep up with his long strides.

I took mental note of the direction we took and the turns we made. Hades only knew if I might need to make a quick escape later.

I was soon completely lost in the labyrinth of windowless passages.

I glanced at Bain, but his face still offered nothing. For all I knew, he was leading me around in circles.

Finally, we stepped into a corridor twice as wide as the rest. At the end was a set of double doors, glistening black in the low light.

Guards stood to either side of the doors. Chatter came from within, low but steady.

It stopped abruptly as I stepped inside. Every eye turned to me.

I lifted my chin and focused my gaze on the man seated at the far end of the room.

He was handsome, but in a totally different way to Bain. Where Bain was tall and solid, this man was slender and wiry. His sleeveless tunic showed muscles beneath skin a shade or two lighter than Bain's tan. While Bain might beat him in a wrestle, this man looked like he'd leave him in the dust in a footrace.

The most striking difference between the two was that this man was smiling.

"Keeper." Bain walked forward. "Viva Taylor." He said my name like a grunt. A hint of disapproval, maybe?

Too bad. I'm here now.

I smiled. "Hey."

The Keeper rose and gave me a bow. He kept his eyes on my face, apart from a flicker toward my breasts. "Viva. I'm sorry to have kept you waiting. I know you must have had a long day, but there were matters I had to attend to."

"I understand," I replied. "It's all good. I'm sure you have many more important things to do."

"Not more important than this." The Keeper moved closer, almost close enough to touch and held out his hand.

Mine trembled, but I managed to hand him the box.

"Thank you." He took the box and retreated to his chair.

The hush that filled the room when I entered hung heavily now. The anticipation was thicker than smoke.

The Keeper eased the lid open and tipped it up over his palm. A small stone dragon fell out, along with a narrow scroll.

A mutter passed through those watching.

The Keeper placed the scroll on his lap and admired the stone dragon.

"Small, but incredibly powerful," he said. "It's past time this was returned to the Vault. Our gratitude to the Witches' Council for its return."

His eyes narrowed slightly. The artefact was a point of contention between the Council and the Vault for at least a hundred years. I doubted he felt much gratitude for its return. More like, 'it's about fucking time.'

"The treaty between the Vault and the Council is finalised," the Keeper said for the benefit of everyone present. "The Witches will reinforce the power which protects the Vault. In return, shifter kind will offer what protection the witches need to keep them safe from humans."

A ripple passed through the room, some approving, others not. Apparently they'd prefer to lose the safety of the Vault than help any witches.

I lowered my eyes before anyone could tell I thought they were stupid to even think of refusing help. The hate ran deep from both sides.

I looked back up as the Keeper handed the artefact to another man and picked up the scroll.

He frowned and read aloud.

"I, Head of the Witches' Council, Denis Crane, trust you are well. This artefact and treaty should be of great benefit to the Vault. The treaty will bring peace and prosperity to all our people. I wish, however, to give a gift to show my good faith. I offer you—"

"Keeper," I interrupted. I reached inside my jeans and pulled the knife free.

The room echoed with the sound of drawing knives and extending claws, including Bain's.

From the corner of my eye I saw him step toward me, naked blade in a hand now closer to a paw.

I dropped to my knees.

With trembling hands, I placed the knife on the floor in front of me, the blade pointing toward me; the ancient sign of supplication or surrender.

"I beg for asylum."

The Keeper lowered the scroll and stood. "There's a little known law amongst paranormals," he said slowly, "that if anyone asks for asylum before being offered as a tribute, asylum must be granted."

I let out a breath. I had gambled on him knowing this. However, he had no obligation to adhere to it. He was well aware of that, I saw it on his face.

"It's a rarely used law," he continued, "since apparently witches, or the Keepers of the past, have little desire to give away their people." He picked up the scroll and finished reading.

"I offer you the artefact's escort, Viva Taylor, to do with as you please." He raised his eyebrows.

"What do you expect from a witch?" someone muttered.

"It seems you know the Covener well," the Keeper remarked. He looked down at me, his expression guarded.

"Yeah, just a bit," I replied.

"Well enough to not only anticipate his actions, but to do something about it. How long did it take you to find that law?"

"About a year," I admitted.

"Clever and persistent," he said approvingly. "Put your claws away." He crouched and picked up my knife.

He smelled of spices. Something similar to cinnamon. I couldn't quite place it. Either way I let a sliver of power draw and soothe my racing heart.

"Fine steel, nicely made. Did you steal it?" His mouth was turned up at the side as though teasing, but his eyes were shrewd like his aunt.

I flushed. "No, I did not. It was a gift from my sisters." Some of whom I had been tempted to use it on at times. I might use it on myself if I failed here.

He nodded, turned the knife and offered it to me, hilt first. "If you really want it, asylum is granted." He looked me in the eyes, firm and unwavering. "Please, join me for dinner. I'm sure we have a lot to talk about."

"Thank you, Keeper," I said softly. If I was the kind to cry, I might do it now. I had secured my freedom. The Covener and his asshole son were going to be furious.

To Hades with them, I was safer here in the Vault than anywhere near the Council.

"Please, call me Dex." He gave a bow to those gathered, tucked my hand into the crook of his arm and led me from the room.

3

VIVA

"HOW DID you know about that law?" I asked. I propped my elbows on top of a round table as thick as my arm. All around the side, carved dragons and griffins battled each other.

Witch made, I presumed. Otherwise the work would have taken a master craftsman years to complete. It wasn't something bought at the local furniture place, or IKEA.

Worn sections on the surface suggested it was old or well used. Possibly both.

Dex sat back in his chair and smiled slowly. "I read a lot." He seemed to be teasing.

"It's true." Calista swept into the room. She wore the same style of wide trousers and blouse as she had when I met her. Instead of turquoise, she now wore bright, intense pink. A matching clip held back the side of her long hair. The rest tumbled free, almost to her waist.

She slid in the chair beside Dex with the grace of a cat and gave me a wink.

"Anything he could get his hands on since he was three," Calista continued. "It didn't matter what it was, he would read it. Naturally, we kept some things out of his reach until he was old enough." She chuckled.

Calista was easy to like. So was Dex. Now that I had asylum, I might begin to lower my walls, but not immediately. Not tonight. I was still on edge, waiting for the condition of my place here. There would be one, there always was. No matter how subtle.

"That's what *they* thought," Dex said in a loud, conspiratorial whisper clearly designed for Calista to hear as well. "I was good at putting things back where I found them."

Calista shook her head indulgently and gave a hand signal to one of the servants, a pale skinned woman with short hair and similar clothes to Calista, but in a subtle, pale yellow.

Dragons chased themselves around bands she wore on her wrists. Other servants who hovered near the door wore the same. A symbol of their rank and service, perhaps? It was a relief from all the black everyone else wore.

"Yes, sir." The woman nodded, gave a half bow and hurried away.

Calista turned back to me. "Now you have asylum, what do you plan to do with it?" she asked.

I hesitated. That was a good question. One to which I had no immediate answer.

"I don't know," I admitted. I hadn't dared assume the Keeper would accept. A thousand scenarios had run through my head, but most ended up with me dead, or sent back to the Covener.

So, dead.

"I can offer you the freedom of my residence," Dex replied easily, as if he made similar offers to witches on a daily basis.

"The Vault itself is another matter. That will take some time. Witches are…not common here."

His dark eyes watched me closely. I sensed he took in every nuance of my words, expression and posture, and committed them to memory.

"Mmmhmm." Calista looked from him to me. "There is room in the sanctuary."

I hesitated. "Sanctuary? Do you have a harem of some kind?"

Shifters, according to my mother, were little more than animals, who hunted and mated in packs. "Don't believe them when they pretend to be civilised," she said. "Pretty words hide their bloodthirsty ways."

They didn't seem much different to witches, as far as I could tell.

Calista snorted. "Not exactly. Women's sanctuaries are exactly that; a safe place for women and their children to reside. Some may be consorts, if they want." She shot a glance toward Dex.

He smiled and inclined his head slightly. "Others prefer to spend their time working, or with each other."

"Oh," I said. "That would be nice. Staying here, I mean," I added. I wouldn't object to spending more time with Dex. I had sharp eyes and he was as much a feast for them as Bain.

Honestly, though I hadn't expected to be offered a choice. I still wasn't convinced I did. I was more or less his prisoner here, in this very fancy cage.

I cleared my throat slightly. "What is the alternative to the women's sanctuary?"

"Do you want to leave so quickly?" Calista's tone was light, teasing, but her eyes were as intense as Dex's.

Only an idiot would underestimate either of them. The artefact probably benefited the shifters in a way the Covener never could have anticipated. One of my top ten rules of survival was to never underestimate even the smallest artefact.

Of course, it wasn't just the artefact they were after. Undoubtedly Dex accepted my request for asylum because it would benefit him in some way. How, I didn't know. I might be a prize, or they may assume I would keep the bubble of power in place.

Whatever the reason, it didn't matter. I needed the Keeper for my own safety. He wouldn't withdraw asylum without raising eyebrows, but Hades only knew what debt I had to him and when he'd call on it to be repaid.

It would be. I had no doubt in my mind of that.

I answered carefully. The wrong words now could tie knots around me that would outlast my great grandchildren. Paranormals had long memories. "I don't know what I want. Except not to be sent back."

"Take your time." Calista leaned over to pat my hand.

Dex's smile showed a dimple in his cheek which made him look boyish.

Oh yes, I would have to watch him closely. He reminded me of the veil flower in my mother's garden. Their fragrance was sweet, but their petals would draw blood from any creature, human or insect, which touched them. Their scent put me in a bad mood, as though it wanted me to use my power to kill.

Needless to say, I avoided them and was relieved when my mother ordered them all pulled out of the gardens.

"Thank you," I said as easily as I could. I wanted to roll my shoulders to relieve the tension which built up there. With some effort, I kept myself still. Best to appear as confident, but as grateful as possible. If I didn't seem like too much of a threat, I might be safer. At least for now.

The conversation paused the moment a servant set an empty plate in front of each of us. Platters of food were placed in the centre of the table. Bread, some kind of meat in sauce, fragrant rice and a bowl of steaming vegetables all made my stomach rumble.

A bottle of wine, one of water, and glasses were placed near Dex.

A small man with a shining head bowed and gestured toward the food. He wore form fitting clothes like Dex, but his shirt was the pale yellow of the other servants. His black trousers looked slightly loose, but the dragon-covered bands seemed tight around his wrists.

"Baffor doesn't speak." Dex gave the man a nod. "Just tell him what you'd like and he'll put it on your plate." He waved toward Calista, who addressed Baffor with a smile.

"A little of everything."

Baffor nodded. Evidentially he could hear perfectly well. He picked up Calista's plate and stepped around the table, closer to the food. Tongue between his lips, he spooned food onto the plate. He arranged everything so nothing touched, then lowered it for Calista to see. When she nodded, he carefully placed it back in front of her.

"Thank you, Baffor." Calista's hands rested in her lap. It seemed here they waited until everyone was served before they ate.

In my family, everyone started immediately, as if the food might run out before we finished. So much for shifters being animals.

"The same for me please," I said when Baffor's eyes settled on me.

As he had done with Calista, he showed me the plate, laden with food in neat piles.

"Um, that looks fine, thank you," I said uncomfortably. What would happen if it didn't?

Baffor beamed. He placed my plate in front of me before

he moved around to Dex. Only once he left did we pick up our fancy, silver forks.

"In case you're wondering," Dex said, a forkful of food halfway to his mouth, "if he didn't put the food on the plate properly, it would be thrown away."

"That seems like a waste of food," I said without thinking. "I mean—"

Calista snorted and her eyes narrowed. For the first time, she seemed annoyed.

"It behooves the servants to do their jobs right," she said, her voice tight.

Behooves? I presumed that meant they expected the job to be done right, every time. "I guess you don't want half-assed servants."

"Certainly not." Calista looked offended at the idea.

Great, I would get thrown out because of the tidiness of their dinner plates. Maybe my mother was right after all.

"She didn't know, Aunt," Dex said. "Things are different here from the way witches do things. It will take her time to understand shifter ways." He didn't speak like I was a lesser being, as the witches would.

I was used to being treated like I was the dirt under people's shoes. This made me uncomfortable and on guard. Why was he being nice? He had to have some kind of agenda

"I suppose so." Calista shrugged and looked at me like a mother would a kid covered in mud. Not hostile, but like I should know better. She lowered her eyes and began to eat.

Dex nodded for me to do the same.

Determined not to make an idiot of myself again, I stuffed a piece of a green vegetable, a pepper of some kind, into my mouth. If I kept it full, my mouth couldn't run away with me. At least in theory.

For a moment, the pepper tasted benign, if a little over-spiced. Slowly, heat leached from the spices and flooded into my mouth until it started to burn. My eyes watered. I reached for a glass of water and took a gulp. It barely took the edge off the fire which burned down my throat and into my stomach. There, it singed my insides, until I felt like I might burst into flame.

I sucked in a breath through my nose, but the spices had dulled my senses. I couldn't breathe enough of the fragrance from either the food or my company to soothe myself. On the verge of panic, I drank half the glass of water, until finally the sensation faded.

"Oh dear, are you all right?" Calista asked.

Someone slipped a handkerchief into my hand and I wiped my eyes. "Witch's food is a little…blander."

Hades, if all their food is this hot— Great, I made a fool of myself again, without meaning to and so soon after the last time. Maybe the sea serpents weren't so bad.

"I think the cook went a little overboard." Dex pierced a chunk of potato before he ate it. Around his mouthful, he said, "Should I have them executed?"

I wasn't sure if he was serious or not, until Calista laughed.

"We do like our food hot." Calista gave him a look, then turned a sympathetic smile to me. Apparently she'd forgiven my judgment of their waste of food. "Try the rice. It should be easier on the palate."

I licked my lips and started on that instead. It was flavoured with something floral, which I couldn't identify, but was much more lightly spiced. I watched carefully to make sure I wasn't making another mistake before I mixed some of the meat in with it. I couldn't rule out the idea that the meat might be hot, and that mixing food together on the plate might be a capital offence.

No one looked disapproving, and Dex did the same with his rice, so I figured I was good. Or I'd be in a cell beside him.

Either way, I tucked into what I assumed was chicken. Apparently at least a dozen things taste like chicken, but I wouldn't think about it too much. After all, I hadn't seen Izzy in a while.

In the end, I ate most of my meal and a swallow of wine when Dex poured some and passed me a glass. It was probably expensive, but I hardly knew Chardonnay from Cabernet. I would have killed for a bourbon and cola, but no one offered one and I didn't bother to ask.

Dex took a sip from his wine and watched me over the rim, dark eyes on mine. The look he gave me was unreadable, but made me nervous. I sensed he was considering how I fit into some political plot, or maybe what size lingerie I might look best in. I didn't want to play his games, or anyone's.

Whether or not I had a choice was another thing.

I gripped the stem of my glass and looked into it to avoid looking at him.

"Is the wine acceptable?" Calista asked.

Was this a test of my sophistication? I would fail miserably, surely they knew that? Of course they did. Maybe Calista wanted to see if I could hold on to my dignity.

"It's very nice, thank you." I took a larger sip than I intended. It warmed me all the way down to my toes and left a sweet, berry flavour in my mouth.

"We trade with the shifters in Caran Valley," Dex said. "They make the best wine in the region."

"So I understand," I replied. "I've heard they produce a bubbling wine which is becoming sought after." Okay, it might all taste the same, but I paid attention to the news. "I've yet to try any," I added, as though I had any intention of doing so.

"Perhaps I should get you some, so you can try it." Dex said. Of course, he would have the resources to get any number of things regular people, paranormal or otherwise, couldn't.

I didn't know how to respond to that, but Calista saved me from having to.

"Do either of you want dessert?" she asked.

Dex's eyes flicked over to her. "No, thank you," he replied.

He had better manners than the rest of my family put together, at least in addressing his aunt. Was this how they usually behaved, or was it for my benefit?

"Not for me either, thank you." The meal had settled in my stomach. Hopefully it wouldn't burn a hole through it.

"Very well, I'll see you both later then. I'll take tea in my room." She leaned to kiss Dex's cheek, gave me a nod and slipped out with a casual grace that made me feel clumsy.

"I have to check over some cargo which arrived by train," Dex said, "would you like to come? You might find it interesting." He gave me another direct look. He clearly expected me to say yes.

I didn't remember seeing anyone take anything off the train but me and Izzy, but I hadn't paid attention to the back of it. They could have carried off a dozen crates while Bain and I talked and waited for Izzy.

"Okay. Sounds like fun." I swallowed and tried to clear my head, half drunk from wine. I would need to find some flowers and draw a little power. The wine might loosen my tongue until I said something I would truly regret.

"Good." He slipped his hand into mine and pulled me gently to my feet.

Just when I thought he wouldn't let go, he released my hand and stepped toward the door.

He led me through labyrinthine corridors into a different part of the residence. Two guards accompanied us; men I didn't know. Both wore the same form-fitting black trousers, and dark green shirt under a leather jacket. They both looked like they knew how to use the knives at their hips.

One of the guards stepped forward to open a door and moved aside, expression as stony as Bain's. Evidently he wasn't alone in being a cold, unsmiling bastard.

The room beyond was large and decorated with gold and blue, and dark, rich wood. A table stood in the centre. A desk to one side suggested the Keeper used the room for work rather than leisure.

"Can you read?" he asked. He headed toward an open crate left near the table.

"Of course. I couldn't have found that law if—" I stopped short. "You're teasing me."

He flashed a smile and handed me a sheet of paper. "I'm sorry, I'm told it can be irritating."

"Oh, who told you that?" I scanned the page, a manifest of items which should be in the crate.

"Oh, a few people." He made a vague gesture with his hand. "I don't suppose you know what's supposed to be in here?"

"I have no idea," I replied. "More artefacts?"

"Let's see, shall we?" He removed the lid and started to pull out a variety of taped up, bubble wrapped items. He put each aside.

"Don't you have people to do this?" I asked.

"Yes," he replied, "us."

I frowned. "Other than us."

"Well, yes," he agreed, "but I like to do these things myself. It's good practice."

"For what?" I cocked my head at him over the paper.

"When the Alpha has an heir," he replied easily. "They might need a regent, or a steward. I'll be more accustomed to the role if I have to step into it. That makes me more useful."

"Indispensable?" I suggested.

He pointed a finger at me. "Exactly."

"I see. I suppose that is more useful than decrepit old uncle." I bit back a smile.

He glanced at me in surprise and then laughed. "Yes, it is. Now, I count ten items."

"That's what you should have."

"All here." He grabbed a knife out of the drawer and started to cut at the tape. "Ten artefacts. And you." He regarded me with his intense gaze. "Why did he want to give you away?"

"I don't know when to keep my mouth shut," I replied dryly. "Witches like their women quiet and well behaved." And not tainted with shifter blood, or god-chosen for their beloved son.

"Ah. Fortunately shifters are outspoken folk and proud of it. I think you'll fit right in."

I favoured him with an ironic smile. "The Covener would be mortified. I think he wanted me taught." And broken.

"Oh, I can teach you a few things." Dex grinned. "I'd like to show you something."

"I bet you would," I said under my breath.

4

VIVA

"THE MOON LOOKS CLOSER HERE." I looked up into a sky beautifully decorated with twinkling stars. The moon hung above the roof and cast a silvery glow over the residence.

Dex's balcony was wide and dotted with chairs, tables and a chaise. The fragrance of honeysuckle and moon roses filled the warm night like a perfume.

I inhaled lightly and sighed. The power washed away the lingering effect of the wine and cleared my head. If not for that, I might have thought this was a dream.

"Everything in the Vault is bigger." Dex's tone was deadpan.

I glanced at his face.

Moonlight illuminated his grin.

I gave a snort of laughter and turned my face back toward the sky.

"When I heard the head of the Council was sending an

escort, I didn't expect her to be anything like you," he said thoughtfully.

I turned to look at him sidelong. "We witches are full of surprises."

"Maybe I didn't give it enough thought?" he suggested. "I do that sometimes. Make assumptions. Not think things through."

I didn't believe that for a moment. He might have anticipated someone older, or meek, but he wouldn't have presumed anything until he laid eyes on me. Even after that.

"Really?" I asked. "You don't strike me as the rash type."

He shrugged. "I have my moments."

I nodded and stepped over to place my hands on the rail. "The same has been said about me."

"I can't imagine them saying that about anyone who worked for a year to find a way to avoid ending up in virtual slavery." He leaned his back against the rail and crossed his arms over his chest.

One side of my mouth pulled back. "No, they'd put that down to my stubbornness," I replied.

He laughed softly. "You say that like it's a bad thing."

I turned to face him. "Are you honestly saying it's not?"

He hesitated for a moment. "You've met my aunt. I admire women with strength and persistence. And intellect. She'd have my head if I didn't."

I bit back a grin. "I suspect you're right. I would imagine she's not a woman to be crossed."

Interesting that Dex found her intimidating.

"No, she isn't," he agreed. "I'm sure the same can be said about you." His head tilted back slightly as though watching for my reaction.

I shrugged with one shoulder. "Is that why you granted me asylum?"

"Because I'm intimidated, and scared you'd stab me if I didn't?" he asked. His dimple showed again.

I laughed softly. "I'd be dead right now if I even tried."

His smile faded. "You would have if I'd refused, wouldn't you? Used the knife on yourself, I mean."

I paused. "Maybe," I admitted. "Or provoked Bain so he'd have no choice." That was a last resort, but something I factored into my plan. "I just—"

"Couldn't bear the idea of being a slave?" he finished for me.

"Would you?"

He responded with a surprised look. "I've never given it any thought, but I don't think I would care for it too much either. However, at least I would be alive."

I had no reply to that. "You wanted to show me something?"

"In a manner of speaking," he said. "I want to know what your plans are."

"I have no idea. I can't go home." I didn't want to. Home was the past.

Something in my tone drew a chuckle from him. "Let me guess, you can also use a knife, sword or maybe a bow, and you can talk politics like a senator."

"Well—"

He took my hand and ran his fingertips across mine. "Did your parents know you have calluses?"

"My father died when I was three." I shrugged. "My mother taught me sometimes power isn't the right weapon." When Dex didn't reply, I added, "I practiced with a bow, and knives, well out of sight."

Dex threw back his head and laughed. The sound echoed through the deepening dark.

"And the head of the Council gave you away like you're

not worth a dozen crates of artefacts. I hope you don't mind me saying so, but I think he's a sand-headed fool."

"I find I can't disagree with that." I exhaled through pursed lips. I could tell Dex so much more, like how I practiced using my power out of sight of anyone, and that perhaps once in a while used it to guide arrows in the right direction. "Do you need an archer in your army?"

"What makes you think I have an army?" he asked.

"Men like you always have armies," I said easily.

"Do we?" He seemed amused by the line of conversation.

I shrugged. "Are you saying you don't?"

"Possibly, but I suspect they would object to a witch in their midst."

"Ahhh, shifters aren't as enlightened as I thought," I said ironically.

Rather than be offended, he just laughed. "Seeking asylum and fighting beside shifters are an entirely different den of dragons. Not even the Alpha would send witches to battle."

"Is he like you?" I asked. "And your aunt?"

"Oh, Hades's tits no," he replied. "He's a hundred times worse. The gods never put a more stubborn bastard on the face of the world. Or so I had thought." He gave me a sidelong look.

"I'm sure he's not that bad," I muttered.

"Perhaps, but you and he are alike, I think. You'd probably hate each other."

"Remind me not to get on his bad side either then," I said dryly.

"How could you possibly do that?" he asked, a hint of irony in his tone.

"Because I'm a rebellious, difficult witch?" I suggested. "Who couldn't deal with the idea of doing whatever you tell me to do for the rest of my life."

He chuckled. "It happens I like exactly that."

I rolled my eyes at him. "Disobedience doesn't bother you?"

He smiled. "You are forthright, aren't you?" He hesitated for a moment. "I don't need a slave. I prefer people to think and act for themselves. Within reason. Besides, apparently you're a lethal archer."

Now he was teasing.

"Oh, absolutely. I've slaughtered a good many apples in the past. As it happens, they were all rotten." Typical for the Council. There were a few rotten apples I'd like to pick off there.

"The moment I saw you, I knew you were an apple-killer." His teeth flashed white while he spoke.

"Now there's a title to stir fear into the hearts of men," I said grandly. "Viva Apple-Bane, destroyer of fruit."

He laughed aloud and long at that. "Remind me to keep you from the orchards."

"Indeed you should. The oranges and limes would not be spared." I couldn't keep from laughing. I couldn't remember how long it had been since I had.

Once I composed myself again, I asked, "Did the Covener offer you anything else?" Or anyone else?

Dex sighed and drew back, evidently not pleased at the change of subject. "Yes. I declined. Why? Are you offering yourself?" He tilted his head speculatively.

"You're persistent," I told him.

"It's another fault of mine," Dex agreed. "Does that mean you're saying no?"

"I didn't say that," I replied. Honestly, it was so long since I'd been fucked, and he was both hot and attentive. I could just as easily fall into his bed as Bain's.

The next thing I knew, Dex's hand was on my hip. His tongue plunged between my lips. He tasted of spices and wine.

I barely had a chance to catch my breath before he pulled away. The look he gave me was as clear as if he shouted the words. He meant to have me. Asylum was a courtesy, because in the end he would own me anyway.

Hades, it was everything I fought against, but in that moment it seemed inevitable. Fuck me, even desirable.

"We should take it slow," he said.

"Right." I licked my lips. "Yes." I stepped away, once again to clear my head.

Dex nodded. He turned and spoke to a guard in a low voice. The guard saluted with a fist to his chest, turned on a booted heel and left the balcony.

"I've arranged for a servant to take you to the woman's sanctuary. You can have a nice long bath and spend the night there, then decide later what you want to do."

"Okay," I said, barely able to put one word together, much less more.

If my reaction bothered him, he gave no sign.

What had Calista said? Some of the women in the sanctuary became Dex's consorts? I would probably be one of any number of women.

"A bath sounds great," I replied slowly. "Any chance of a map of the place?"

"No," he said a little too quickly. "You'll soon learn your way around. In the meantime, you'll be accompanied at all times. I would hate for you to get lost."

Of course, he didn't want me wandering around the place in case I went somewhere I shouldn't. That was fair, why should they trust me? I sure as Hades didn't trust them.

I was somewhat outnumbered though. At least if I avoided using my power.

I didn't assume the shifters didn't have power of their own. My ability to convert scent to witch power came from somewhere. For all I knew, Dex could throw me all the way back to the Council without a thought.

Not literally. Even full of the strongest scent, I couldn't hurl a fully grown person more than a few metres.

I murmured agreement. "I wouldn't want that either." If I was honest with myself, I probably couldn't find my way back to the room I was allocated in the first place, much less anywhere else.

"I'll come and check up on you tomorrow." He gestured for me to precede him inside as the door opened to admit a young woman in the familiar pale yellow and dragon wristbands.

"Ah, here's—" Dex cocked his head at her.

"Czari, Lord Keeper." The servant gave him a nod. She had long, wheat-coloured hair and bright green eyes. I presumed she was also a shifter. No human had eyes that colour.

"Ah, of course," Dex said, as if he'd known her name all along, but just forgot. "Take good care of Viva, and don't make her angry. She knows how to use weapons."

I grimaced. "I'm harmless," I told the servant. I was anything but harmless, but the whole place didn't need to know that, did they?

"If you say so," Czari replied, her tone respectful but wry.

I smiled and shook my head.

Dex didn't seem even slightly annoyed. Clearly his description of his people as outspoken was accurate.

Czari led the way out the door. "I'll show you to the sanctuary."

REFRESHED, with my skin tingling from the scent of bath oils, I followed Czari deeper into the sanctuary.

I asked after Izzy, not because I was overly worried, but it seemed the right thing to do.

Czari had no answer for me.

"Those who serve see a lot but are not told everything." Her dark eyes were half-lidded. She must know a thousand secrets about her employers, but she wouldn't share a word.

I understood. Servants loose with their words didn't remain servants for long. If they were lucky, they would be thrown out of the residence with their lives. Those not so lucky would serve as a reminder to the others.

"Not even about other servants?" I pressed gently.

"We know what our employers wish us to know," Czari replied simply, her expression unchanged.

I snorted, but didn't push any further. Servants, if the Council's were anything to go by, usually knew more about the goings on in any place than the employers. However, I sensed Czari genuinely knew nothing about Izzy.

I would ask Dex or Bain when I saw either of them next.

Czari stopped outside a tall door, squares inset into the shining wood from top to bottom. Every crevice was polished to the highest sheen. She opened the door and I stepped inside.

Or outside.

The courtyard was the biggest I ever saw. As wide as it was long, it was lined with trees and bushes covered in roses, honeysuckle, moonroses, starlillies, dragonblossoms and Hades knew what else. Benches were scattered here and there, in places which would give shade during the day.

Right now, the gardens were lit by a row of globes, which danced lightly in the slight breeze.

In the precise centre, a small fountain tinkled as water flowed from the hands of a stone carving of Hades, into a bowl at his feet.

Although recognisable as the god, the shifter's version

had wider shoulders and a penis way too big to be normal. The witches would also never depict him naked. Nor with Persephone kneeling, mouth open to take in his cock. Another god, one I didn't recognise, crouched behind her, cock erect and aimed to slide into her. His hand gripped her hair. The stone was carved into intricate strands which wound around his fingers.

They looked so real I almost expected them to moan and sweat.

Doors lined the sides of the courtyard, at least thirty of them, each as intricately carved as the next. The globe light picked out women, and a variety of animals, all in similar poses to the statue. I was almost certain that bull's dick wouldn't fit into any hole on the woman he leaned over.

That was fiction for you, I suppose.

Several doors stood open. A few women reclined on couches nearby, glasses in hand, speaking in low voices. None gave me more than a glance.

"Please, this way." Czari led me across the courtyard to a closed door near the end.

I stepped lightly into a reception room lit with smaller versions of the globes outside. They gave just enough light to illuminate the small, hexagonal blue and white tiles which covered the floor. Larger tiles adorned the walls all the way to the ceiling, giving the space a sense of being under water. It was disconcerting, but pretty. Certainly fancier than anything I was used to.

Czari nodded toward an open door and I peered inside. The light didn't penetrate as well here, but I spied a large bed and what looked to be a sitting room to one side. My suitcase sat against one wall.

Open curtains framed a small window. All I saw through it was darkness.

"How many women live here?" I asked

"Maybe twenty," Czari replied. "This suite is yours."

How many was he screwing? I wondered. "Wait, all of this?"

"The Keeper insisted. You don't like it?" Czari looked confused.

"Oh, it's very nice." Was I surrounded by shifters? Did they know what I was?

She smiled. "The tailor will be here in the morning."

I blinked. "Tailor?"

Czari looked sideways at my clothes. "You'll want the latest fashion. The Keeper insisted."

Of course he did. What else did he insist on? How I wore my hair? Who I spoke to? I suspected the answer to both of those was yes.

"Ah." I said finally. "I guess I could do with some new clothes."

Czari inclined her head. "If I can do anything—"

"You can call me Viva," I said firmly. I wasn't much for formalities unless the occasion called for it. "Maybe we can be friends."

"Of course." Czari's expression was guarded, promising nothing.

"Just do the best you can," I said. I resisted the urge to sigh.

"Right."

"I think I'll get some rest." I paused before I realised why Czari looked expectant. "You may go. Thank you."

Czari nodded and smiled. "I will be in the servants quarters, across the corridor. You only have to push this." She pressed a button beside the door, which I hadn't noticed before. A buzzer sounded somewhere distant. "I will come."

"Ah. How…convenient." And much easier than shouting for her, or wandering around lost.

"Indeed. Rest well." Czari lowered her hand from the

button and stepped out the door, which she closed behind her and left me alone.

~

I WAS awoken shortly after dawn when what sounded like a horn blasted out, then again. A few seconds passed before another double blast.

"What is that?" I leapt off my comfortable, if overly soft, bed and threw jeans on over my underwear. I tugged on a clean t-shirt and was about to ring the buzzer when Czari opened the door to my suite and bustled in.

"Is something wrong?" I asked. My heart raced and sweat sprang up on my hands. Where did I put my knives before I fell asleep last night?

The servant's expression gave away nothing. "Come on, I'll show you." We headed across the corridor a trot, as a handful of women and children appeared from their own doors, most were as sleep-tousled as me.

Bain, back rigid as ever, but rested, stood beside the door to the women's sanctuary. Another guard stood on the other side, his back just as straight. Bain's eyes flicked toward us, but he seemed indifferent to see me.

I met his disinterest with a bland look of my own, even though the sight of him made me want to recreate the statue of the gods. He could be Hades. Dex could be the other guy.

"Viva." Bain gave me a nod, "Czari."

I tried to ignore Bain's familiar scent and spoke lightly. "Good morning."

For some reason I couldn't fathom, he seemed amused at this. Not enough to smile, but lines around his eyes crinkled slightly and the corners of his mouth twitched.

"Whatever you say," he replied.

I raised my chin. "Are you here to stop me from leaving?" I gestured toward the door.

The other guard chuckled.

"No," Bain replied easily, "The door is guarded against outsiders who wish harm to the women and children who seek sanctuary here."

"Ah," I nodded. "So what were the horns for? Are we under attack?" The shifters seemed far too relaxed for that.

His companion laughed. Bain almost smiled again. He seemed surprised at himself and the look was gone so quickly, I wasn't sure I hadn't imagined it.

Before he could reply, the door opened and two more guards stepped inside. The pair wore the same sulky expression. They both saluted Bain, but undisguised resentment was etched on their features. If he noticed, Bain gave no indication, but his companion grinned.

"Here's our replacement, just in time." Bain stepped toward the door and spoke to me over his shoulder. "It's a sand dragon. Maybe I'll save you a scale." He headed away at a trot and left me to stand and shake my head in confusion.

"Well, that explains it," I muttered sarcastically. Sand dragon? Were we closer to a beach than I realised?

"You'll see, come, come." Czari grabbed my hand and pulled me toward a set of stairs. A parade of women, children and a handful of men bustled up, smiling and talking in excited voices, even as they jostled to be first.

The stairs curved around at the landing on the second level. Puffing lightly, I patted my hair down with my spare hand and let the servant pull me up a second flight, steeper and narrower than the first.

They looked as though they were designed to keep intruders from entering the residence from above. They didn't deter the throng, they only slowed them down somewhat.

Czari released my hand and we walked single file out a door which led to the roof.

The simple but expansive terrace afforded a stunning view of the Vault and the desert beyond.

Wait. That's not possible.

"How is there a desert there?" I shook my head. The nearest desert was… I don't know, but a lot further than virtually outside the door.

"The bubble," Czari said, as though that explained everything.

I suppose it did. Everything I saw so far suggested the Vault was outside the normal world, like we'd stepped through a portal into somewhere else entirely. At this point, I couldn't rule out anything.

"We are definitely not in Kansas anymore," I said under my breath. I'd never been there to begin with, but this sure as hell wasn't it.

The expanse of sand was to the east. The Vault hugged the coast for kilometres both north and to the south. To the west, the harbour jutted like a nose into the ocean. Beyond that, I imagined I could see Narnia or Wonderland on the far horizon of the glittering sea.

Weird. As. Fuck.

I walked to the edge of the terrace, placed my hands on the iron railing and peered down.

Only a wide yard and a few streets stood between the residence and the desert.

I glanced up, but saw only early morning sky, blue with a tinge of pink where the sun still rose. No planes, no smog, no high rise buildings.

"They're going," Czari called out.

At least three dozen figures were down on the ground. They moved through the yard at a trot. Bain and Dex jogged side by side near the front. The crowd on the roof let out a cheer. Dex and several others turned to wave.

Servants carried up chairs, which they placed near the back of the terrace. Others carried bottles, cups and plates of food.

Two men and three women dressed in bright blues and greens sat in the chairs. Around their wrists they wore bands embroidered with musical notes. Each had an instrument; a flute, a drum, a guitar, and two wind instruments I didn't recognise. They started to play an upbeat tune while the crowd clapped and handed around food and wine.

"So, we get to come up here to watch them leave?" I asked dryly. Unless I was mistaken, I could have sat up in bed and seen them pass by below.

Czari laughed. "Oh no. So much more. The warriors hunt the sand dragon, while we celebrate the hunt."

"Wouldn't it be more fun to *join* the hunt?" I asked. I couldn't keep a hint of wistfulness from my voice.

Czari waved a hand. "The hunt is dangerous. We ask Hades to return the men safety to us with wine, bread and cheese." She reached for two glasses and pressed one into my hand. "It's bad luck not to drink." She took a gulp. "A lot."

I took a sip of the soft, fruity wine. "Thank you. Any chance of a bourbon and cola?"

Czari gave me a funny look.

"Never mind," I muttered. How backwards were these people?

Czari gave me a nod and turned to someone beside her. They spoke in excited tones about this man and that, but none were any I knew, so I tuned out the chatter and looked back toward the yard.

A wide gate at the other end swung open and the men filed out two by two. They wound though the street and were lost from sight until they trotted out across the desert.

They quickly became specks, but I was sure I could tell which was Bain and which was Dex.

"I heard the sand dragon was near the oasis," a man remarked. He held a telescope to his eye and looked out, his other eye shut, his mouth pulled up to one side.

"Who told you that, Quentin?" a woman asked.

Quentin shrugged but didn't look away. "I just heard it. They're heading that way, anyway."

The men became dots before they disappeared out of sight.

Quentin let out a grunt of disappointment, which I totally got. I loved a good festivity as much as anyone, but I wanted to see this sand dragon.

Around me, people drank, ate, sang and talked.

I listened, but either they kept to day to day topics around me, or they had little to say but small talk. Either way, I soon tuned that out as well.

Gradually, couples slipped back down the stairs and I thought again of Izzy. I half expected to see her amongst the crowds on the terrace, but she was nowhere to be seen.

For some reason, I found her absence unsettling. I had no specific reason to think Dex harmed her, but I had none to assume he hadn't. In the end, we were both at his mercy.

I leaned against the rail of the terrace and surreptitiously watched other people while the music swirled around in a series of tunes I didn't know. I tapped my fingers against my glass, even after I emptied it. Bottles sat on a table to one side, but I decided against drinking more.

I should at least have been here a few days before I made a fool of myself.

I sensed someone staring at me. That was to be expected, especially as the crowds thinned. Anyone new tended to draw attention, and they probably knew a witch was in the midst. For a long moment, I ignored it.

Eventually, curious in spite of myself, I scanned those gathered. A woman looked openly at me, bare hostility on her otherwise pretty features.

She looked familiar. I frowned and tried to place her.

The woman scowled and looked away.

I decided I had never seen her before, it was just her expression which was familiar. Hate, for no apparent reason, or because she knew what I was. Or maybe because I rocked bed hair better than she did.

I sighed. I was far from home, and alone. That put me in a vulnerable position with no one to watch my back.

I would have to do that for myself. I had no choice.

5

BAIN

"I SHOULD HAVE YOU EXECUTED," Dex said lightly. "Or exiled."

The Keeper made that threat so often I didn't pay it much attention anymore.

"Okay," I replied lightly. "For what this time?" I picked my way across the sand with deliberate, cautious steps.

Dex gave me a dry look.

I responded with a raised eyebrow.

"For letting a witch come into my residence armed with a blade," the Keeper replied lightly.

He almost never shouted, or outwardly appeared to be angry. It made him that much more dangerous. People never saw him coming when he acted pleasant.

"Ah." I nodded. I wondered when Dex would bring that up.

Dexter Joseph Breakwater knew how to make people sweat and squirm. He knew the right amount of time to bide, to let them think they had gotten away unscathed with some offence or other. When they least expected it, he would pull the rug out from under them.

More than one person had found themselves in a cell after they thought they were in the clear. It was all part of the game, to be unpredictable, to out-manoeuvre friends and rivals.

I suspected he found it amusing. It used to work on me once, but not for a long time. As much as he tried, and he did, Dex rarely surprised me. Once in a while, I decide to humour him and play along.

I took a moment to reply. That was a part of the game. I would hesitate so it seemed I scrambled to think up the best response to save my ass. Truthfully, I preferred to choose my words carefully. It avoided a lot of bullshit later.

"I didn't sense malice on her part," I said finally. "No intention to assassinate you. If I had, there would now be no witch."

"You only sensed good intentions?" Now it was Dex's turn to raise an eyebrow. "No desire to manipulate the situation?"

I stepped around a pile of stones, which probably marked someone's grave.

I couldn't say I *hadn't* sensed that in her. Most people had their own agenda. That didn't necessarily mean they were a threat. It didn't mean they weren't either, but I trusted my instincts.

"She kept most of her thoughts to herself," I said, my tone neutral. "She was anxious, but determined to appear calm. Her suitcase was searched and nothing hazardous was found. Unless you consider dried flowers hazardous." My eyes flicked toward the Keeper. "She gave me no reason to presume she posed a risk to you."

"Apart from the Covener and his games," Dex pointed out. He seemed to refer to something in particular, but his emotions were closely in check.

"Apart from him." I averted my gaze. I could have delved deeper, to seek out Dex's true thoughts. That always felt like a violation, a line I wouldn't step across unless ordered by Dex or the Alpha himself.

"You didn't search her," Dex stated.

If I didn't know him well, I would think he was amused, as though we talked about nothing important. However, I noted the tightness around his mouth, the shrewd look in his eyes, the snap of anger held tightly in check. He was pissed.

Again, I hesitated. "For that, I should probably be fed to the sand dragon." Perhaps I had trusted my instincts too much, or failed to see past a pretty face. And a body I would enjoy writhing underneath me. I bet she was loud when she moaned.

I mentally cleared my throat and focused.

"However, the blade was ceremonial. Her only goal was to keep from becoming your bed slave." I was teasing now, but no one but Dex would know it.

"She could do worse," Dex said dryly.

"I believe that was also what she was trying to avoid," I said. "Being sent back to face worse."

From what I knew of witches, it was unusual, even for them, to give away one of their own. What was it about her that made them try? She had a smart mouth, but that wasn't unusual for witches or shifters.

"We're getting close." My inner wolf paced inside me, eager to be let loose.

The wind shifted. It blew a fine mist of sand into the air. There, in the breeze, was something else. Part earthy smell, part prickling of instincts.

My blood raced. I held up a hand. The entire party fell into two lines behind us.

I didn't need to look back to see. I sensed each individual presence, coiled tight, nerves jangling, ready.

I felt Dex's excitement, a thrill of both fear and exhilaration. I had to force it aside to keep it from swamping my own emotions. I breathed a hot, dry breath through my nose and calmed my mind and racing heart.

No one moved. No one spoke. The only sound was the wind and squeak of boots on the dune.

As one, we waited.

Finally, I turned my face toward Dex and nodded. One eye was on the Keeper, but the other remained on the sand.

"I see where to go."

Dex nodded. "Very well." Without hesitation, he gestured to the men behind him.

In near silence, the hunting party trudged toward the top of the dune. Each walked in the footprints of the man in front, although some stepped closer to my tracks. Dex was the Keeper, but no one questioned me while hunting. My instincts had kept us alive more times than anyone cared to count.

The trek up the sand was slow going. With each step, I sank almost to my ankles before I pulled myself free and took the next.

"Why do they have to live out here?" Dex grumbled good naturedly.

"What, sand dragons?" I asked. The side of my mouth drew back. "Hades only knows. Would you prefer garden dragons?" I slid back half a step. Perhaps Dex had a point, but the terrain was a part of the challenge.

Dex chuckled and threw his arms out to steady himself when he too slid. "Actually yes, depending on their size."

I smirked. "Hunting those would be no fun." I pictured myself pulling back vines in search of snapping teeth and talons the colour of bark.

"No, but they'd smell pretty." Dex grinned.

I shook my head and fought to cover the last few metres to the top of the dune.

There, spread out below us was one of the many oases which dotted the desert. Under the sand, we'd likely find the remains of horses and travellers; those fallen prey to the creature and the elements. Even this close to the Vault, death was queen.

"Any sign?" Dex panted and came to stand beside me. He sounded eager. His eyes shone with excitement.

I didn't respond immediately. I watched the dunes, eyes intent, ears open, nostrils flared slightly. I reached out with my wolf sense and delved, looking for a sign of life, intelligence.

Finally I pointed. "There." It lay in wait, cunning, but hungry.

"Are you sure?" Dex frowned, eyes squinting. No matter how hard he looked, he wouldn't feel what I did. Fortunately for me, my skill was invaluable to the Keeper, or I might have been executed by now. Or exiled to Melbourne.

"Have I ever been wrong before?" I asked.

"Not *yet*." Dex grinned.

I ignored the insinuation. "I'm not wrong this time either." I nodded for everyone to undress and leave their clothes in piles on the top of the dune.

I did the same, then closed my eyes and let my inner wolf out. Slowly, and with only the discomfort of twitching muscles and shifting organs, I shifted into a large wolf with dark fur and dark eyes. I tossed my head, happy to be free of my human form. My senses were heightened a hundredfold. I smelled the wind, the sand, my brothers and our prey.

It was close, so close.

It moved under the sand, fearful of the new creatures it felt nearby. Humans were easy quarry. Wolves... We were not.

I wanted to howl to the sky. Instead, on silent paws, I started down the dune. No need for my senses; Dex and the others would follow.

Halfway down the dune, I stopped. I gave a short bark-growl for the others to do the same.

Careful.

The sand shifted, writhed, then exploded upward.

I turned my face to shield my eyes. Sand stung like a thousand tiny pins under my thick fur. The dune moved under me, threatening to throw me off my feet.

A metre or two away, a wolf yelped in alarm.

The dune shifted again and sand started to slide down toward the oasis. Several wolves lost their footing and rolled toward the base of the dune.

I put myself between Dex and the incline, and held him in place with my body, while trying to keep my own balance.

I growled. My human self would have sworn.

Dex grunted in my ear. His dark grey muzzle whipped around, alarmed.

The sand fell still.

I stepped away from Dex and shook sand off my body.

The wolves at the base of the dune rose on unsteady feet. One raised a front leg bent at an awkward angle.

Dex gave me a look and I imagined the words he would say if he wasn't in wolf form.

"I spoke too soon about you being wrong," he'd remark.

I shot him a wry look that said, 'I found the dragon.'

Or the dragon found us.

The dragon lay on the sand, still half submerged, metres from the wolf with the broken leg. Scales almost the colour of the sand showed a tinge of green. A female then, the more aggressive of the species.

She tossed her head and bared two rows of teeth, the outer sharp, the back blunt and yellowing. Loose scales around her maw suggested she was close to shedding her skin. Her discomfort would make her all the more aggressive and dangerous.

Short legs with long claws slid out from under her torso. She dug into the sand and dragged the rest of her body free. She had no wings, but her tail bore a piece of bone which could kill a man—or wolf—with one blow if he got close enough.

I bobbed my head and the rest of the pack descended to the bottom of the dune.

Dex gave a short bark to the shifter with the broken leg and tossed his head back toward the top of the dune.

The wolf gave him a mournful look and whimpered, but with his leg, he would be a liability.

You live to hunt another day, I thought, even though he couldn't hear me.

The wolf, a shifter named Felix, sighed and began the trudge back up on three paws.

Lucky for him it wasn't his head he'd broken. Small consolation for missing the glory of taking on the dragon.

I barked for everyone to be quiet and stepped to the side, my eyes on the dragon's mouth.

A pointed red tongue flicked out past both rows of teeth and tasted the air. She had no eyes that I could see. Sand dragons hunted their prey by sensing vibrations and odours. She would have felt the us approach long before we got there.

For good measure, I asked Hades to watch over us all.

I nodded to a pale grey wolf several metres away. Most of Trevor's head was covered in scars, which left lines of white in his fur. He never said how he got the scars. In human form, he covered them with a beard. In this form, he had nowhere to hide them. To my eyes, at least, he looked badass.

Trevor threw back his head and howled, loud and shrill.

He bared his teeth and took off at a run parallel to the dragon.

Her head whipped around, tongue flicked toward him.

He ducked and rolled. The appendage missed him by a hair. Eyes wide, he lay still.

She whipped her head in confusion and anger, and let out a grunt of rage.

Another wolf approached her from the other side.

Pete was younger than me, but more solid. His white wolf moved lighter and slower than his size suggested. His gait was loose and fluid, but his eyes were half closed in concentration.

He moved closer, each step deliberate. He stopped a few metres from her, then charged. He swept his claws toward the dragon, deep enough to score her scales but not enough to draw blood.

A diagonal slash split her skin.

She swung her head toward him and lunged, teeth snapping. They narrowly passed over his head, so close she might have ripped free a strand of fur or two.

He threw himself sideways into the sand where he lay for a moment before he tried to scramble to his feet.

The dragon dragged herself forward, faster than I would have thought possible. One talon hooked into Pete's torso. Hard keratin ground against bone. Blood splattered, painted her foot red. Sand immediately coated it, stuck to wet scales.

The talon all but tore Pete down the middle. He barely managed a last whimper before he flopped like a doll.

I let out a howl of frustration. The death of any wolf always sucked. I tried not to take it personally. I would anyway. I led; I would always feel responsible.

I caught Dex's eye, his own look of anguish, and shook my head.

Mourning would have to wait.

The dragon trudged a few more steps. Pete dangled from her talon.

A sick feeling rose in my throat, along with the desire to dart forward and free the man's body.

I pressed my ears back flat, but suppressed the urge. Pete wouldn't feel anything now. Getting myself killed wouldn't bring him back.

The dragon turned to sniff at the body and licked at it like she would a wound on her own flesh. She shook her foot several times in irritation before Pete's body worked free and slid off her talon.

His blood stained the sand red. Not much was left that looked like a man or a wolf, except shreds of fur and skin.

The dragon moved away from the body. Breath huffed out of her nostrils.

Dex and I exchanged a glance.

I nodded.

I paused for no longer than a heartbeat before I rushed at the dragon. I slashed where Pete had scored her. The carefully placed blows opened the upper layer of scales, widening the slit. Fresh scales underneath flashed wet in the morning sun.

The sand dragon's tail whipped.

I ducked, but the knob of bone glanced off my shoulder. I gritted my teeth against the pain and kept low. My shoulder throbbed, but another few centimetres and she would have connected with my head. Dex would probably joke that my head was so hard, she'd do no damage. I didn't want to find out.

The dragon turned, neck stretched as far as it could go. She bared her teeth. Her whole body stiffened. She shook herself like a dog after a bath. Her head and tail swished back and forth so violently we had to throw ourselves to the sand to avoid being hit by one or the other.

The breach in her scales widened until the top layer hung like ripped fabric. It swung with each movement and slapped against her body. This made her angrier than ever.

Dex darted forward and grabbed hold of the edge of her skin with his teeth. He gripped hard and tugged before he let his muzzle slip free. He threw himself away as her tail swung around at him. It missed his face by a couple of centimetres, and he bared his teeth so it looked like he was grinning.

Irritated, the dragon growled, then flopped down, rolled onto her back and rubbed herself against the sand. Piece by piece, her old skin peeled away to reveal shining, fresh scales with only a minute hint of green.

She rolled back over and shook again. Most of her skin had slid away, but some remained tangled around her back foot. She grabbed on with her teeth and tugged until her foot popped free.

With a grunt, she stepped away from her shedded skin, burrowed under the sand and was gone.

Dex let out a howl of triumph, and shifted back to human form. His expression sobered when he looked toward the dead wolf, but he glanced away as others moved to gather the body.

I took a moment to ask Hades to look after the fallen man's soul, then bounded up the dune to shift back and dress.

From inside my jacket, I pulled out a knife and started back down the dune. I was the first one back down while others still shifted, or stayed as wolves. I understood their reluctance to go back to human form. My inner wolf was more natural, free. It would also die out here if we stayed for too long, especially covered in thick fur.

I crouched beside the skin and began to cut. One by one, I worked each double-hand sized scale free and handed them to the other hunters. Highly valued by paranormals, they were worth a couple of thousand bucks each. Some were damaged by scores and others by teeth marks, but many were still in perfect condition.

Dex waved me away when I offered one to him. The Keeper didn't need the money.

The rest of the hunters happily accepted theirs. Oliver took several for Pete's widow. She wouldn't go without the scales, and Dex would make sure of that. The pack looked after its own.

I pocketed my own scale and dug a hole in the sand for the rest of the skin. Left out here, it would draw predators.

"A good-sized dragon," Dex commented when I stood.

"She was," I replied. I didn't sense her now, but I looked in the direction she'd gone; toward the feeding grounds where she'd feast on her usual prey—desert worms, sand dogs and the like.

"Thank Hades we didn't have to kill her."

Dex nodded his agreement before we headed back up the dune.

AT THE SIGHT of our triumphant return, hundreds of people flooded the narrow streets on the edge of the desert to welcome us. Those on the terrace cheered and waved. The sound of music and revelry suggested the celebration which always preceded the hunt, was well underway.

I was sure it had been for several hours already.

We stepped through the gates and clattered into the city, boots ringing on paved roads.

Dex raised a hand to wave at the throng.

The crowd cheered.

I dropped back behind Dex to let the Keeper bask in the glory of our success.

As the night wore on, the stories about the hunt would spread and be exaggerated, until no one would be able to tell the truth from the bullshit. They'd probably have me breathing fire and flying over the dragon by midnight.

For now my face was just another amongst the hunters. I was okay with that. I preferred to keep a low profile.

A small boy, no more than four, stopped with his fist halfway and gaped at us, eyes wide. When Dex waved at him, he drew himself up as tall as he could and pressed his hand to his chest so hard it must have hurt.

Dex smiled.

I gave him a nod before we passed him by.

Someone started to chant, "Keeper. Keeper!" More voices took it up until it was all I could hear.

As they chanted, the people saluted, fist to chest, some in unison, many not.

Dex's expression changed from a smile to a frown before his good humour reasserted.

I didn't need to delve far to understand Dex's response.

In theory, the people should praise the Alpha, or even Hades, not just the Keeper.

For many, the Alpha was unapproachable, rarely seen.

Few people laid eyes on him in their lifetimes, although I had done so several times. Still, if the Alpha, Hades keep his soul, should hear of it and assume Dex encouraged loyalty toward himself instead, it might be his head, heir or no heir.

Thank all the gods the people didn't chant Dex's name.

I raised my gaze to scan the crowds on the terrace.

A dark haired figure stood apart from everyone else. Viva. I knew her, even at a distance, almost as clearly as I sensed her discomfort. While those near her were relaxed and jovial, she held herself stiffly, both body and mind.

Those who celebrated around her were open books, but

she held secrets tight like a phone with a forgotten passcode. Or a box with a lost key.

Secrets, I sensed, she was desperate to keep and aching to share.

It was none of my business, but I wanted to know anyway. I wanted to know everything about her. I doubted she would confide in me. At least, not unless I opened up to her. That was a risk I wasn't willing to take. Not yet.

Fortunately I had other methods for breaking open locked boxes.

I lost sight of the terrace as we drew closer to the residence, and my attention moved from Viva to the organisation of my men.

I sent Felix to the healer to have his broken arm fixed. He'd be back to work in a few weeks. Sometimes I wished shifters and witches didn't hate each other. A witch would fix him in a matter of moments. I thought about asking Viva, but Felix would probably refuse anyway. Prejudice ran deeper than it should.

Certain Felix was in reasonably good hands, I sought out the Keeper.

Dex had already changed into more comfortable shoes and a casual shirt, and was speaking to Jaq, his driver. Dex's hands moved as he illustrated his point, and his smile was wide. The driver listened, and nodded every few moments.

"She was one of the biggest, most aggressive sand dragons I've ever seen. One of her talons was the length of my arm." Dex held out his arm to its full length to demonstrate.

I smirked. By the end of the day, the dragon's talons would be bigger than Dex.

"Ah, there's Bain. Come over here." Dex gestured. "Jaq is suggesting the dragon wasn't as big as I made out."

The driver stuttered. "I didn't... I would never—"

"Of course not." Dex clapped him on his back so hard Jaq's jerked forward. "I was merely teasing."

"Oh." Jaq's face was red, but he gave a half smile.

"Dex's joking never gets boring, does it Jaq?" I asked, my expression deadpan except for a hint of humour I let creep into my eyes.

Jaq nodded. His long grey hair, tied back in a ponytail, bobbed. "Not. I've known the Keeper since he was young enough to toddle underfoot, and I can never get enough of his humour."

"*Now* who is teasing?" Dex asked, his eyebrows raised.

"That would be us," I replied lightly. "With the utmost respect, of course."

"I'm sure." Dex snorted. "But I think the word you're after is irony, not respect."

"If you say so, sir," I said.

My response was met with a chuckle from Jaq. "I should get back to work before I get fired." The driver gave the Keeper a bow and a lopsided smile.

"Yes you should. Shame you work for such an asshole." Dex waved him away with a grin.

Jaq walked away chuckling.

Still smiling, Dex turned to me. "He's a good man, we're lucky to have him."

"He is," I agreed. "For an asshole, you seem to inspire loyalty in some people." The sides of my mouth threatened to tug upward.

"Only because I have the best wine and beer," Dex replied. "Speaking of which—" He nodded toward the arched doorway which led into his residence. "Why don't you go and enjoy yourself?"

"You have a duty to perform first," I replied. "That duty is mine as well."

Dex sighed. "Very well, but I don't expect you to." He held

up a hand before I could speak. "I know. We have this conversation every time."

I nodded. "The men should have told her by now."

"Thank Hades it was only one."

"None would be better."

Dex murmured his agreement.

ALTHOUGH SMALL IN comparison to others scattered around the Vault, the residence's own temple to Hades was usually busy. Few people would stop by tonight while the festivities continued.

Tomorrow they would come to ask for an end to their sore heads, or for babies to have been conceived during the festivities. According to some, Hades bestowed the best of his blessings on those children.

Beside it, the temple of Eleos would receive visits from those begging forgiveness for whatever they did while drunk. The goddess was well known for bestowing mishaps on adulterers, liars and those who cheated at card games. The latter was especially frowned upon.

I ducked my head to step inside the temple.

Built at least a hundred years ago, people must have been shorter then than now. Or perhaps Hades wanted worshippers to bow upon entering his sacred space. Either way, most who entered had to bend to get through the door.

The temple flickered with candlelight, which bounced off the carvings on the walls. In some places, hands had all but rubbed them smooth. In others, they looked as if a master carver had worked them into the walls only days ago. A depiction of Hades and some long dead king with an exaggerated cock was especially untouched.

Before Dex became Keeper, it was covered, hidden for

reasons no one knew anymore. Dex ordered it uncovered and left that way.

I once asked Dex if he'd have a carving of himself made in the same style. He laughed, but did not say no. If anyone would do such a thing, if only to outrage some of the older folk in the residence, it would be Dex. No doubt his cock would be even bigger.

I bowed toward the image of Hades on the far wall. He stood with arms outstretched in welcome, a smile on his face. Two naked women sat at his feet. I guessed that was why he smiled.

Dex bowed too and muttered something about a dragon. Probably words of thanks for the day's hunt and our survival. Or perhaps he asked for a garden dragon next time. He should be careful what he asked for. Hades might just deliver.

Several people knelt in front of the simple stone altar in the centre of the circular room, upon which Pete's body lay. Wrapped in the same linens he'd been bundled in after his death, no one could see his wounds.

I remembered them all too well; it was not a sight for his widow or family.

I exhaled softly through pursed lips. That was enough to make the candles dance and throw distorted shadows. A winged dragon on the wall nearby looked ready to take flight, until the flame settled again.

Pete's widow knelt with her forehead on the altar, a long-fingered hand atop her husband's body. A simple silver ring adorned her middle finger to signify their marriage. Long hair obscured most of her face, but once in a while she would twitch with silent sobs. Deep grief rolled from her in waves strong enough to force me to take a step back.

Dex gave me a knowing look, but said nothing. He couldn't have felt what I did, but he understood grief and loss. The Keeper turned toward the widow.

"I offer my condolences—" Dex began.

The widow didn't move, but the man beside her twisted, rose and leapt at Dex. A blade in his hand flashed in the candlelight.

"You let Pete die!"

The man staggered as I shoved him back and threw myself between the Keeper and the blade.

The grieving man managed to keep his footing and stood with a heaving chest, teeth bared slightly

I held up my hand, eyes on the knife. My other hand rested on the hilt of my own knife. When I spoke, my tone was even. I didn't want to provoke the man further.

"Pete knew the risks, just as you know the penalty for attacking the Keeper."

"He's distraught," Dex's voice was tight. He stepped out from behind me, a slight smile on his face. His stance was loose, relaxed, as if he was in no danger at all. "He didn't know what he was doing."

I moved to put myself back between Dex and his would-be attacker. "Keeper—"

"Stand down, Bain," Dex said lightly. "And you. Aydin, is it not? You work in the kitchens. Pete was your son-in-law?"

"That's right," Aydin replied, his voice rough. His cheeks were wet with tears, but his mouth was set in fury. His knuckles were white around the blade.

"Hasn't your daughter lost enough today?" Dex sounded reasonable, but each word would have been chosen with care. When I learnt to be a soldier, Dex had learnt to be a statesman. An unconventional one at times, but a good one when it mattered, when his life was at risk.

From the corner of my eye, I saw the woman rise. Like her father, her face was also tear-streaked, but fearful.

"Papa?" Her voice was deep, sensual under other circumstances.

"I should not have…" Aydin sagged.

"No, Papa." The widow sobbed, a hand over her mouth. "Please. Please!"

"The penalty—" I started.

"Thank Hades he missed," Dex said firmly. "Bain would be grumpy if he'd had to add both of our bodies to the pyre. Mercifully, Hades will only get one new soul tonight."

Grumpy? I raised an eyebrow but nodded. Although, the soul of anyone who murdered a Keeper in a fit of grief would likely go to the goddess of fools. I stepped toward Aydin, hand outstretched for the knife.

Aydin turned it and handed the knife to me, hilt first, head down in shame.

I accepted it and tucked it away at my hip. Unlike Viva's, this was not ceremonial. It looked like nothing more than a kitchen knife, used to carve poultry or some such. Dex would likely joke later that he was almost assassinated by a man with a chicken knife. For now, however, it was safely out of anyone's hands.

"I'm sorry for your loss," I said. "Pete was a good man. His sacrifice saved the lives of many travellers." Platitudes such as these weren't my thing, but I owed it to the man and his family.

Pete would have laughed at the flowery words.

The widow wiped her cheeks and offered a wan smile. In one hand she clutched the dragon scales. When she spoke, she addressed both the Keeper and me in barely controlled words, hoarse with emotion.

"Thank you. We won't forget his sacrifice. Keeper, Pete would have been honoured if you both helped us to place him on the pyre."

"We would be honoured." Dex offered her a bow.

A family could take time with their deceased while they lay on the altar, but moving the body to the pyre—really a large oven kept alight for such a purpose—was a sacred duty. Family members had fought, and occasionally died, for the right to send their loved one's souls to Hades.

I glanced toward Aydin, who seemed resigned. The others who mourned with the widow and Aydin had stayed on their knees. Now they rose, but only to step aside to give them access to the altar.

I moved to one end, while Dex and Aydin went to the other. The widow placed her hands lightly on the cloth which shrouded the body. She may not bear any of the weight, but she still played her part in the ritual.

I lifted my end, the majority of Pete's form in my broad arms. Dex and Aydin kept Pete's legs from touching the ground. If even a foot touched, however briefly, it would mean bad luck, and another death soon after.

Gingerly, respectfully, we carried Pete to the oven. Intense heat forced me to turn my face. Carefully, I manoeuvred the body onto the stone lip that jutted out far enough for the purpose.

The flickering flames made the white shroud appear orange and red.

I stepped aside and stood next to Dex as the widow and her father bowed their heads over the body.

A priestess, in the wide black pants and blouse of those in the service of Hades, sprinkled water onto the shroud. In a moment, it turned to steam and wound like ethereal fingers toward the ceiling.

"Hades guard him," the priestess said.

The widow echoed the words in a whisper just loud enough to be heard.

"Hades guard him," the men repeated the words.

With a grunt and a moan, the widow and Aydin pushed the body off the lip and into the fire. When it landed, the flames died back for a moment, then the shroud began to blacken and crinkle.

Smoke wound its way up the chimney and out toward the settling evening light. I imagined I saw a face, twisting and ghostly, but it was gone before I could blink.

"He's gone to Hades," the widow declared, her voice soft. "Thank you."

"If you need anything, you have only to ask," Dex replied. He gave her a bow and gestured for me to precede him out of the temple.

6

Viva

A LIGHT BREEZE caressed the side of my face.

Twilight bathed the city in gold. The fading sun set the ocean on fire. In a few hours, it would be cold, but right now it was still warm.

Like everyone else in the residence, I slept through the worst of it. I awoke just in time to eat and watch seven hunters return.

The man they lost was one I hadn't met. Still, I asked Hades to take care of his soul and hoped he hadn't died horribly. If the shrouded body was an indication, he had. Hunting any kind of dragon was dangerous, even the kind that shifted into people. They tended to be much smaller, and slightly easier to reason with.

From below the terrace, the nightroses opened out their petals. At twilight they were at their most potent, their most irresistible.

The scent tickled my nose. I drew in the slightest hint of

power, just enough to make my fingers tingle. Even that would be enough to—

"There you are."

"Shit." I jumped and turned at the sound of Dex's voice. Accustomed to my own, worn out clothes, I felt self conscious in the fitted, pale green t-shirt and dark skinny jeans the tailor gave me. I never had jeans that made my ass look so good, but they must have cost a small fortune.

"You scared the crap out of me," I said, hand to my chest.

He looked apologetic before slipping back into his usual easy smile. "I thought maybe you'd hidden in the sanctuary." He raised an eyebrow. "Or run away across the ocean." From the top of the stairs, he walked across the terrace toward me. He moved like a man who was self assured. One who got what he wanted, one way or another.

"I thought I might rest for a day or two before I dive in," I said lightly. To my surprise, only a few other people were on the terrace.

They sat in corners in small groups and talked and laughed in low voices. None paid me or the Keeper any attention. The musicians had probably left hours ago, but I couldn't recall hearing the music stop.

My thoughts must have tangled me so tightly I forgot the rest of the world existed.

Dex laughed and lounged against the railing beside me. "Unless you're a sea serpent, you might need more time than that."

I smiled. "Perhaps I am." If I was part shifter, then it might as well be sea serpent. I might enjoy the taste of seamen.

He chuckled. "Is that the secret you keep?"

I barely contained a flinch. "My…secret?"

He eyed me speculatively. "Of course. Everyone has them, is that yours?"

I realised he was teasing, or at least fishing for information. He gave no indication he asked about anything specific.

I gave him the side-eye. "I hope not, I'm a terrible swimmer and hate having pruned skin." I wrinkled my nose.

"Perhaps you're better suited to being a garden dragon then." He smiled as though he remembered something. A past joke maybe? As far as I knew, there was no such thing as garden dragons. Although, until this morning I thought the Vault was in the middle of Sydney, so what did I know?

"I like trees and flowers better than water," I agreed. Uncomfortable with this line of conversation, I changed it. "You were looking for me? Was I supposed to be somewhere?" Czari hadn't said anything, but I hadn't seen her for hours. If she let me miss something important, I'd be pissed.

Before Dex could reply, Bain trotted to the top of the stairs. He nodded toward me. His eyes lingered for a moment before he looked away.

"Keeper, you got a moment?" he asked. His face was as unreadable as ever, but he seemed uncomfortable.

"Excuse me." Dex flashed me a smile, but his brow was creased.

"Of course." I stepped aside so they could speak without me overhearing. That didn't stop me from trying.

Bain whispered something in an urgent tone and slipped something into Dex's palm.

The Keeper said something back, but nodded and shrugged.

"Go and enjoy yourself," Dex told him. "I'll be fine."

Bain gave me a look, his dark eyes unreadable.

I regarded both men and my heart skipped a beat. I remembered the statue of Hades, Persephone and the other god and wished we were all alone.

Silence hung between the two men like a mist, before Bain disappeared back down the stairs.

Dex moved to stand beside me, but his body was stiffer than it had been. He seemed…tense.

He cleared his throat. "Most people are in the great hall celebrating the hunt, but you don't have to be there if you don't want to."

I didn't know where the great hall was. The sound and smells of 'most people' would probably guide me if I bothered to look.

"I don't have a map," I reminded him. "Shouldn't you be there? People will notice if you're not." The smell of spices, smoke and blood washed off his skin. They were heady, if a bit overwhelming.

"They'll be too busy drinking to notice," he said with a shrug. "Besides, I have something for you." He held out his hand and opened his fingers.

I looked down onto his palm and my eyes widened. "Is that—"

"A dragon scale," he finished for me.

The size of his palm, it was almost perfectly round, and nearly the exact green of my t-shirt. No way in Hades that was a coincidence. I would bet every cent in the Vault Dex told the tailor what colour to put me in. Uneasy was an understatement. His control was more benign than the Covener, but for how long? No, I totally didn't have trust issues, much,

"Was that his?" I asked, confused. "Bain's?" Why the fuck was Dex giving it to me?

"No." Dex shook his head, his eyes intent on mine. "He always insists I claim one." He looked amused for some reason. "He knows I will only give it to someone else, so he suggested you. I think he thought you'd be impressed."

"Oh, I am," I said. Weirded out, but impressed. I reached out a finger to touch the edge of the scale. A jolt of something like lightning passed through me. I jerked back my finger.

What the shit?

"Viva? Are you all right?" Dex glanced at me, then down at the scale and frowned. "It can't bite, the rest of the dragon is gone."

I gave a short, too-high pitched laugh. "I know, it just ..." I must have imagined it. The scent of him must have triggered…something.

I touched the scale again. It was firm, but slightly yielding, like a fingernail. The natural kind, without a diamond topcoat.

It felt strangely warm, as though it buzzed with some kind of power. Whatever power the scale held, it was nothing I could use. It was more like—power recognising power.

Had Bain known what might happen?

I glanced toward the stairs. If he was anywhere nearby, I couldn't see or smell him. Presumably, he couldn't see me here either, but that didn't mean he and Dex wouldn't talk about me later.

Certain the scale wouldn't harm me, I took it and held it up in the last of the sunlight. It gave a glow, like a pulse, then went dark and cold. What power it may have contained, I guessed it was gone now.

I looked over it, to Dex, who looked expectant. If he saw anything weird, I couldn't tell. He looked curious, maybe a bit hopeful that I would appreciate the gesture.

"Thank you. It's cool." I watched the scale with half an eye, in case it flared back to life. If 'life' was the word for it. Nothing happened.

"You're welcome." He propped an elbow on the railing and pressed his cheek to his fist. "You can sell it if you need anything," he said. "Or don't want it."

"I want it," I said firmly. "It really is cool. Almost as cool as if I'd hunted the dragon myself." If the scale was an object of power, I would keep it, if only to experiment on it. Hades only knew what use it could have, that no one knew about. I could discover a new artefact. Maybe one that made chocolate out of sand. No one could say that wouldn't be useful.

"You didn't kill the dragon, did you?" I asked.

"No." He waved me over to a chair and sat beside me. By the time he finished telling me the details of the hunt, probably embellished, it was dark, and we were the only people left on the terrace.

My stomach rumbled. "Have you eaten since you got back?" I asked. "You must be starving." I knew I was. And I should probably not be monopolising his time, with a party going on. Sooner or later, people would notice.

He gave me a wolfish smile. "I am ravenous."

I hesitated, sure there was double meaning to his words. "I meant for food," I said dryly.

"Oh, I need some of that too," he agreed. His eyes shone in the light of the moon that hung over the city.

"Then maybe we should eat," I suggested. Not that I'd mind being nibbled on, but I needed my strength, and so would he. More than he might imagine.

"You haven't eaten?" His head jerked up. "In that case, let's go down to the festivities."

"Can I ask you something?" I asked as we walked down the stairs.

"Of course," he replied. "Well, within reason. I mean, I can't divulge the Vault's secrets."

I snorted. "I wouldn't be so rude as to ask." Or dumb enough to think he'd answer. "I wanted to know if anyone in particular objects to me being here?" I thought back to the woman who had scowled at me.

"Ah," he replied in a way which made me think he knew

exactly what I was talking about. "There are women in the residence who I have been with. They may see you as a rival. Or they may have sons you'd compete with in an archery competition." A smile flashed on his face.

I gave a short laugh. "And how would they know about that?"

"I have no idea, I'm sure," he replied lightly. "It is more likely they think you've come here to undermine me, or the Alpha."

I presumed that much. I could deal with catty women, but politics between shifters and witches sometimes got ugly. I could easily find myself in the middle of that.

"Is that all?" I asked.

"Some of the women want me to marry them," he said. "They won't like it when I choose one over the others."

Was he implying what I thought he was implying? Naw, that was just my imagination running away with me again. Probably.

"Sounds messy," I said.

"No one said being this hot was easy," he said with a grin.

"I know, right?" I agreed, mostly joking. "It's hard being the shit."

"It really is." He sighed loudly. "Harder when they expect an heir. If the Alpha doesn't, then someone has to."

"You don't have one?" I asked. I eyed his groin speculatively. Men had fertility problems as often as women. Sucked if you wanted, or needed kids.

"Not for lack of him trying," he said wryly.

"I bet." He didn't seem like the kind of man to spend too many nights alone. "So there are some jealous women in the sanctuary, and you're afraid they'll start a war with each other unless a woman has a son to elevate her above the rest," I concluded. "Or unless you give up trying and settle down."

"Something like that," he agreed. "There are one or two... feistier women, but most of them are harmless. For now."

I grimaced. "Women can be horrid to each other." So could men, but they generally ended things quickly, with a claw, a sharp blade or an army. Or by sending people away to live with the enemy.

"You're thinking about home?" he asked.

"A little bit," I admitted. "Men sometimes did some dumbass things to each other for the sake of rivalry. I'm surprised they didn't go after each other with swords or knives. Although there was that one time . . ." I shook my head.

He chuckled. "I'm sure your family is an interesting one. It sure sounds like it."

"Yours too," I said. "Calista certainly is. How many women has she scared away from you?" I bet if she didn't like any of them, they'd be gone, no matter how much he liked them. There was a fine line between overprotective and controlling.

Dex stopped and turned to face me. "If we had a competition to see whose family was the most interesting, I'm sure we would have a tie. That includes some of the women, and men, here at the residence who I'm not related to by blood."

I suspected he meant Bain.

"But please," he continued, "don't worry about the jealous ones. I won't allow any harm to come to you, or any other women here. All right?"

"I know you won't," I said. I could smell several kinds of poison in a bowl of food in front of me. That was the most likely method anyone would use to kill me. Failing that, my power could knock an attacker flat, if I had enough warning. I would keep my guard up, at least until I was sure no one was coming after me. Even after that, I would be careful.

As far as I could tell, Dex had no power beyond the ability

to shift. Maybe I should swear to keep *him* safe. Although, if I ever lost control, who would keep him safe from me?

I asked Hades to make sure that day would never come. If it did, I might destroy us all. Even now the scent of him threatened to let power course through me. It pressed at the tips of my fingers, itching to be used for something. Anything. To soothe, to heal. To create. To destroy.

I forced it back.

"We should go and eat." The smell of food wafted up the corridor and for once it only made me hungry.

THE SCALE LAY on a table beside the bed. It was the first thing I saw when I awoke.

I eyed it for a moment. Nothing happened. Perhaps I only imagined I saw or felt any power in it yesterday. Whatever it was, whatever it had been, I suspected it was gone for good.

"What about the other scales?" I wondered out loud. I got no answer. That reminded me, I still hadn't seen Izzy. I was so absorbed in myself, I hadn't asked Dex about her.

I felt a stab of guilt. I would ask him or Bain about Izzy the first chance I got.

I considered marching up to Dex's room, or the audience room where I first met him, but I would get hopelessly lost. Better to wait a few more days before I made a fool of myself.

Instead, I had a long shower in the bathroom attached to my suite, and dressed in another outfit the tailor left, this time black jeans and a grey blouse.

"I can do your hair," Czari offered. She picked up a brush from the table and started to run it through my damp tangles.

"I assume my hairstyles are out of fashion?" I asked Czari's reflection in the mirror.

"I didn't want to be rude…" Czari replied carefully.

I snorted. "Would you prefer I walk around embarrassing myself with an out of date style?" I asked. As if I cared about that shit.

From the look on Czari's face, the servant didn't realise I was joking. Or she didn't think I was funny. Naw, it couldn't be that. I'm hilarious.

"Certainly not," the servant replied. "The very idea—" She stopped and blinked a few times before she smiled. "Is that witch humour?"

I smiled wryly. "You might call it that, I suppose."

Czari nodded. "Sorry. Sometimes it can be hard to tell." She looked over her shoulder as though we weren't alone and lowered her voice. "Some of the women here get offended if a servant laughs when they say things they don't intend to be funny."

"Maybe witches and shifters aren't so different," I said. "Plenty of witches would throw the nearest chair if someone did that to them." To say witches were touchy was an understatement. At least, the ones I knew were. After the coming of age ceremony anyway. The whole lot lost their sense of humour around me the moment I knelt. Fucking Hades and his fucking sense of humour. I shouldn't provoke a god, but he could be such an asshole.

Czari looked miffed, but I wasn't sure if it was a response to the comparison, or the idea someone would throw furniture for trivial reasons. It was rather extreme, but witches were proud, to a fault and beyond. Fortunately I rarely took offence to anyone who laughed at me. Life was way too short for that.

Czari braided my hair in a style that didn't look all that different to how I wore it, but then slid two clips into the sides of my hair. Shaped like long, sinuous dragons, they looked made of real gold. Rubies and sapphires covered their bodies and emeralds made a pair of glittering eyes. They must have been worth a Keeper's ransom. For all I knew, they were really made of glass and stainless steel. I would prefer it if they were. I would feel less guilty if I lost them then.

"A gift from the Keeper," Czari said, patting them into place gently.

Who else?

"Thank you, Czari." I touched a clip lightly with the tips of my fingers. Unlike the dragon scale, I felt no power in the clips. That was fortunate, but not surprising. Outside of actual artefacts, I'd never felt power in inanimate objects like these. I had no reason to think I would now. It wasn't as though Dex would give me artefacts to wear around in my hair. Unless of course, he had something to gain from doing so. I guess I couldn't rule anything out.

"You're welcome." Czari put down the brush and stepped aside to let me stand. What would it take for them to believe I didn't need a nursemaid? Although, was that all she was? Her job might also include spying on me and reporting back to Dex or whoever else. The Alpha maybe.

I heard voices coming from outside my room, not loud enough for me to understand what they were saying. From the unhurried tones, they were just having a chat. Perhaps about nothing more important than the weather.

I glanced at Czari, who nodded and smiled.

"I'm sure they won't bite," she said. Apparently she forgot I might.

I recalled the woman on the terrace yesterday. I wasn't absolutely certain they wouldn't bite. Or at least try to.

Lucky for me, I could take care of myself.

On bare feet, I stepped out into the courtyard.

The sun was barely up. Why in Hades name was I up this early? I woke up an hour ago, at least. Something about this place threw off my internal clock. I was a night witch, usually, and slept most of the day. I didn't plan on changing that. I'd have to work on resetting myself somehow.

A group of children ran past, kicking a ball back and forth between them. They ranged in age from four or five to around eight. Several were girls dressed in the same style of loose pants and blouses Calista wore.

I all but heard my mother click her tongue at the idea of girls dressed like little adults. At least they weren't wearing short skirts and shirts with plunging necklines, like some of the clothes I saw for sale in human shops. Growing up was hard enough without doing it when you're nine. Still, the clothes did look hard to run around in. Maybe if they saw enough of me, they'd all start wearing jeans.

Viva Taylor, fashion icon. That had a ring to it.

The children ran on by, pausing only to glance at me with open curiosity before the game drew their attention back. One of the girls kicked the ball into the space between two sticks embedded in the ground. She squealed with excitement and ran after it, the others close behind.

"Wherever I go in the world, someone is always playing soccer." A woman stood a few metres away, a slow smile to match the way she spoke. "Or football, if you want to call it that."

"It is?" I asked. I was more interested in making a friend here than I was in sport, but it didn't hurt to be polite.

"Oh yes." The woman closed the distance between us. "It was invented after a bitter battle between witches and shifters, around three thousand years ago. They started kicking the severed heads of their enemies back and forth between swords they thrust blade-down in the dirt or sand. Terrible for the blade." She grimaced and brushed black hair back from her face.

"Ah. That's…nice." I wrinkled my nose. "Who won?"

"The game or the battle?" She shrugged. "I don't know the answer to either. I'm Zophia." She pronounced it 'zoe-fy-uh'. "And you are?"

"Viva." Zophia was blunt, so I decided to be the same way. "I'm sure they used their enemy's swords."

Zophia gave a tinkling laugh. "You know, you're right. I hadn't thought about that. Why waste a perfectly good blade when you can ruin the blade of a dead enemy? Men can be so bloodthirsty."

She sniffed. "Thank Hades we don't have to listen to them too often." She paused for a breath. "You're new here, aren't you?" She was enveloped by the subtle scent of roses. The perfume was like a warm balm on my jangled nerves.

"Yes, I am." I told her briefly about my arrival. Every few moments I stopped to inhale. The smell was better than wine.

"Ah, you're the witch." Zophia didn't seem bothered by the fact. "I went to the Council once, as a child. Well, in a manner of speaking. My father had business with them. He stopped the car just out the front, but he wouldn't let me step foot outside." She laughed. "He was terrified I'd be stolen and sold into slavery."

"I'm sure that wouldn't have happened," I said. I wasn't sure at all. If it happened to me, it could have happened a hundred times before. The Council wouldn't take in a shifter child. The shifters would probably go to war with them to get her back. The Council would more likely have killed her quietly and made it look like the work of humans.

"At any rate, I was only allowed to watch out the window." Zophia gave a dismissive wave of her hand. "I thought about running away, just for the excitement, but shifters are notoriously good at tracking. When they want to. Usually if people leave the Vault, it's not by their choice. Dex does the best he can, but people have to disappear from time to time."

I frowned. "There was a shifter. She accompanied me here. I think she was punished for not watching me closely enough. She wouldn't have been—"

"Possibly," Zophia replied. "Here, come and sit with me. Standing is so tiring." Now I looked, I noticed lines around her eyes. Was she sick? She didn't seem like she had anything contagious.

She waved me over to a stone bench beside a small pond. Trees drooped low to form a green veil over the bench.

"It's likely she was sent away," Zophia said. "To prevent her from spying on Dex. Well, the Vault as a whole, really. You said she slept with some guy on the train. That probably wasn't random."

"Izzy must know she'd be found out . . ." I stopped. Of course she had. She'd all but flaunted what she did for me and Bain to see. "I suppose she did. Why not just leave the Vault if she wanted out?"

Zophia shrugged one shoulder. "She wanted the Keeper to know she's working for another Alpha? Or with some other faction of paranormals. She was probably sent here as a message to the Keeper, as well as a spy."

"Is that normal?" I was aware of other pockets of shifters, and other paranormals out there, but I didn't know they shared the same animosity as the witches. The information was interesting. I filed it in the back of my mind, in case I could use it in some way later.

"Only for the last few thousand years," Zophia said with a short laugh. "Dex does the best he can to keep the peace for the Alpha, but he's stepping on hot, treacherous stones at times. Take your being here for example. Before he became Keeper, no one would have dreamed of a witch stepping foot in the Vault, much less living here. He's changed a lot of things. He's a little vague at times. He's sweet, but sometimes he pushes things a little further than some shifters are ready for. Of course, he wouldn't listen if anyone suggested that. I think it's something to do with being a Keeper."

I laughed softly. "That sounds like every leader I know." I thought for a moment and added, "Every man I know."

Zophia threw back her head and laughed. "You're right!" She chuckled for a while, then wiped tears of mirth from her cheek with a swipe of her finger. "Is it true that your Covener tried to sell you into slavery because he was worried you'd overthrow him?"

It was my turn to laugh, but only after I stared at the other woman for a good half a minute.

"Me? Overthrow *him?*" The idea was hilarious, and absolutely what I would have stuck around for if it wouldn't get me killed. "Fuck no."

Zophia giggled. "I know I shouldn't listen to gossip, but that's what they're saying. Some contingent had a plan to replace him. Isn't that why you asked for asylum?"

"No." Strangely, it made a certain amount of sense. The Covener wasn't the most popular man, but to replace him with me? "I suppose that's the way of gossip," I said slowly, "there's just enough truth in it to make it plausible." If anyone would fight back against the asshole and his asshole son, it would be me.

"Yeah, that's true." Zophia leaned back and stretched out long legs in front of her. "So how do you like it here?"

"I don't know yet. It doesn't seem like there's much to do," I admitted. "Back home I had a lot of siblings, or other witches I either spent time with, or spent time trying to avoid." I had an equal amount of both.

"Some of them had children. Were those the only ones in here?" I nodded toward where the young ones had been playing. There was no sign of them now.

"One or two of the women have babies," Zophia replied. "The sanctuary didn't have any in here for a long time. The last Keeper was Dex's uncle. He and Calista only had one child and he died when he was barely old enough to walk. Anyone of his age is grown now. Dex likes children, so he's encouraged the women here to have them. He'd prefer to have a few of his own, but of course the next Keeper will be the Alpha's child anyway. It's nice to have the young ones running about, even though they can get noisy at times." She made a face.

"You've been here for a while then?" I asked.

"About a year." Zophia waved a vague hand in the air. "Have you seen the library?"

I got the impression she didn't want to talk about herself, and I wasn't going to press it. If the woman wanted to tell me anything, she would.

"There's a library?" I asked instead. That certainly got my interest.

"Of course there is." Zophia smiled. "Do you want to see it?"

"Am I allowed to?"

The question drew a frown from Zophia. "Were there many places at your home that you weren't allowed to go?"

"A few," I replied. "I was allowed to use the Council library, although it was frowned upon." Reading wasn't high on the list of things my mother thought I should spend time doing. It took time away from practicing magic, and helping her clean the house. Practical shit like that.

"So you're a bit of a rebel?" Zophia's smile was back. "That's good. Some of the people here can be so stuffy and uptight."

I thought of Bain and nodded. "Yes, so I've noticed. So, you were going to show me the library?"

∾

THE LIBRARY in the Council was smaller and duller than this one. While it contained shelves upon shelves of dusty documents, and classic literature, the library in the Vault contained books I actually wanted to read. Wooden shelves ran from the floor to the ceiling and held paperback, hardbacks, and leather-bound books in every genre I could think of. And a few I had never heard of before.

"I don't even know where to start," I said in awe.

"How about here?" Zophia handed me a book and laughed when I opened it to see the pictures inside.

I gaped. If the statues and friezes in the Vault were explicit, they were nothing to this.

"Can people really bend themselves like that?" I asked. I turned the page sideways and peered at it. I tried to imagine myself like that, with Bain or Dex crouched beside me, but couldn't. Although maybe if we—

I realised Zophia was watching me and closed the book. "Shifters aren't shy about sex."

Zophia laughed. "No, we're not. It's perfectly natural. I've never understood why humans are so embarrassed by it."

"I don't know," I said. "Witches are just as bad." I handed her back the book. "Maybe something with a plot?" I looked around, eyes wide. "We're really allowed to take books from here?"

"Of course. Calista collects novels from all over the world and they end up here after she reads them. As long as we don't damage them, we can help ourselves."

"She's read all of these?" I was impressed. "Well damn. I have some catching up to do."

Zophia grinned. "That's nothing, you should see the pile of books she *hasn't* read yet."

I shook my head. "She has some catching up to do then," I joked. I pulled out a book and opened it at the first page. It seemed to be about dragons of some kind. That was as good a place to start as any. I tucked it under my arm.

"Is that the only one you're getting?" Zophia picked up two, then added a third to the pile.

"If I get one at a time, I have an excuse to come back." I wandered over to a window set in the far wall. Two plush armchairs sat in front of it. Even sitting, I had a view of the bay from here. I scanned the water, but couldn't figure out where the Vault ended. Did it end? Were we even on the same continent? Hades, we might be in an alternate universe for all I knew. One I couldn't leave and see my mother again.

A stab of homesickness left me breathless for a moment. I looked to the horizon and imagined for a moment I saw a doorway. I pictured myself stepping in and being welcomed home. Even the Covener was there, smiling and happy to have me back.

No, that wasn't how I wanted my homecoming. I wanted him and Max on their knees, grovelling for forgiveness. Chains around their wrists and ankles were optional, but preferred. Then I would exile both their asses so fast their heads would spin.

Honestly, the idea left me cold. I hadn't realised until now, but the Covener always wanted me gone. If Zophia was right about a potential coup, he had good reason to send me away. If there was no coup, then all he had was stone cold hate and bigotry. And no one lifted a finger to stop him.

Fuckers.

I sighed and turned from the window.

Zophia still stood beside the novels and watched me with open curiosity. I had the sense I could trust her somehow.

"I'm hungry, would you care to join me for breakfast?" Zophia asked.

It was probably closer to lunchtime, but I nodded. "Yeah, I'd like that. Thanks."

Zophia offered her arm. With only a moment of hesitation, I looped mine through.

To my surprise, rather than taking me to a dining room, Zophia led me to the kitchens where we helped ourselves to food before we stepped out a small door into a garden full of herbs and vegetables.

A patch of grass occupied the space under some fruit trees. Seemingly unconcerned about grass-stains, Zophia sat into the shade and waved for me to join her.

"This is my favourite place in the residence," Zophia said. "Few people come here, and they don't usually stick around too long. They pick what they need and go."

I gave a half smile and tried not to inhale too deeply. The herbs warred with each other, vying to overwhelm my senses. Even the fruit trees made my skin tingle and my stomach growl.

"It's nice." I blocked out the trickle of power which threatened to become a flood. If Zophia noticed, she gave no sign.

I crossed my legs and began to eat. "Thank Hades this is milder than what Calista and Dex like," I remarked. Warm chicken with cold vegetables wrapped in a thin bread was plain but tasty.

Zophia nodded around her food. She took a moment to swallow before she replied. "Calista isn't happy unless her mouth is burning. The rest of us prefer to leave the heat to the sun. Sometimes I think she forgets other people don't have the same preference as she does. And other times…"

"Yes?" I prompted.

Zophia made a face. "The rest of the time I think she knows, but she likes to have a laugh."

I snorted. "I'm not sure if I should take that as an insult. Most witches would."

"No sense of humour?" Zophia guessed.

"Not much of one, and what many do find funny is usually at the expense of someone else." I sighed. "Sometimes I wondered where in Hades I came from." I hesitated before adding, "I still do, to be honest." I wanted to tell her about the shifter bit of me, but I didn't. Not yet. Sooner or later I would have to. Maybe then I could get some answers about who or what I really was.

Zophia chuckled. "I think that's people, paranormal or otherwise. You stayed for the whole meal, didn't you?" she asked. "I've seen women leave in tears. If Calista doesn't like someone, she'll tell them about it. At length. She must like you."

"Me?" I frowned. I suspected she did, but I had no idea why. I guessed she shared the same open philosophy about witches as Dex did. "I'm nothing special."

Zophia shrugged. "That's a matter of opinion." She paused. "We're a long way from the Witches' Council, or any other paranormal factions, but even here, there are those who might choose to infiltrate the Vault. To—undermine Dex. If I was him, or Calista, I would be very careful who I trust. I would surround myself with only the strongest and most loyal. Calista is a good judge of character. If she approves of you, then she must see something in you." She gave me a look under her lashes.

I shifted uncomfortably on the grass. "Um." Heat crept up my cheeks. "I suppose so." I wanted to believe it. I was an outcast for so long I wasn't sure I would ever be anything else. I wanted to belong. Who didn't? But I suspected it wouldn't be that simple.

Zophia laughed softly. "Believe me. If she didn't like you, you'd know. I could say the same about myself. In fact, I would."

"Me too," I said softly. I have never been good at hiding my dislike for people, especially when they deserved it. "So, your father deals with the Council?" I asked to change the subject.

"He did." Zophia's smile faded and she let out a soft sigh, her generous lips parted slightly. "He was killed several years ago. My mother had her own business, making and selling clothing. Without him to distribute her wares, she struggled. She brought me here to petition Dex to help her."

Her eyes glazed like she was thinking back to those days. "Calista saw her work and convinced Dex to invest in her."

I frowned. "She swapped you for their help?"

Zophia snorted. "Hardly. I oversee the Vault's arm of her thriving little empire. Calista lets me stay here in return for the best new designs."

"You're not one of Dex's women?" I asked without thinking.

"Oh Hades, no." Zophia laughed. "The Sanctuary really is just that. It's not about housing women for his pleasure. Oh, most of the women dally with him because having a child and marriage offers stability they couldn't achieve otherwise, but they come and go as they please, and *with* who they please. Dex would never force any woman to do anything they didn't want to."

I nodded. I couldn't imagine him trying. Not with physical force anyway. "But you've never... I'm sorry, it's none of my business."

Zophia placed her food on her plate and put a hand on mine. "I don't mind. I'm open about most things. It's refreshing to meet someone else who feels the same way." She gave my hand a squeeze before she drew back. "I prefer women to men. I've never been with a man and I probably never will."

"Oh." They did explain the vibe I got from her.

"Is that a problem?" For the first time, Zophia's expression was guarded.

"No, " I replied firmly. "Not even a little bit."

"Really?"

"I swear to Hades." I put my food down and placed the tips of two fingers of each hand against my forehead. In witch society, the gesture meant my words were sincere. I'd be held accountable by Hades himself if they weren't. I wouldn't use it lightly.

I just hope it didn't translate to 'fuck you six ways from Sunday' in shifter.

I lowered my hands as Zophia relaxed.

"Thank you. Some people have strange ideas about women like me."

"One of my brothers preferred men," I said softly. "Some of the other witches had some ideas about beating it out of him, or marrying it out of him, as if that would help." I averted my eyes. "He was the least shit of my brothers."

"Was?"

My throat tightened. "He gave himself to Hades rather than face any more bullying."

"You don't mean he became a priest, do you?" Zophia asked gently.

"No. He threw himself from the top of the Council when I was twelve years old. He was only fifteen." I met her eyes. "He was just a kid. He did nothing wrong." A tear trickled down my cheek.

I wondered if the Covener hoped I'd do the same.

I swiped the tear with the back of my hand.

"Of course he didn't," Zophia said firmly. "I'm sorry that happened to you both. My mother was disappointed in me, but she accepts me now, and here no one cares. I'm not the only one in the Sanctuary who dabbles with other women. Gia and Kim have been lovers for years. I'll have to introduce you, they're adorable. You'll love them."

"I'm sure I will." My breath hitched. "I…"

"It's all right, you don't have to tell me you're not like me. I didn't tell you to make you feel uncomfortable, I just like to be open and honest with people. Sometimes the consequences of that aren't . . . Why are you staring at me like that? Do I have food on my face?"

While Zophia wiped at her cheek with her hand, I smiled. "No, it's not that. I—" I grimaced. "Dex said I might be seen as a rival for some of the women who want to marry him."

"You're relieved I will never look at you that way?" Zophia asked.

"Well...yeah." I replied, "But instead you suggested I might be the Covener's rival. It seems I can create trouble without doing a thing." What can I say? I have skills.

Zophia grinned. "I suspect most of us have that ability, especially around here. If you say anything, someone will assume you mean something else." She gave an exaggerated roll of her eyes and smirked. "As you said, sometimes there isn't much to do around here except to gossip. Before long, they'll have us as lovers, while you share Dex's bed. Or someone else's."

"I don't want them to think—"

Zophia interrupted. "They'll think all sorts of things and gossip about them as well. It never does anyone any real harm. Sooner or later they'll move on to talk about someone else."

I sat back. There were worse things they could say about me than whose bed I was or wasn't sharing, but I always tried to stay away from gossip, especially being the subject of it.

I supposed it was natural they would talk about someone new, especially a witch, but it made me uncomfortable.

"I hope so. There must be many more interesting people in the residence to talk about."

Zophia snorted. "More interesting than a witch who

talked Dex out of making her a slave? That may be difficult to top."

I grimaced. "I'm dull as shit, really."

"I beg to differ," Zophia said firmly. "You like books; that immediately makes you interesting. Much more interesting than who you have or do not have as a lover." She barely stopped for breath before she added, "Did you know that several old scrolls said Hades had many lovers, both male and female, and was actually part witch?"

I blinked. "He was?" I hadn't given it much thought. I assumed he was just a regular old god, if there was such a thing.

Zophia grimaced. "My father traded old scrolls, amongst other things. They were extremely valuable and he only got his hands on a couple of them. The priests of Hades would all but go to war with scholars over them. My father said the priests would destroy them, so no one could question them."

"And the scholars wanted them so they could question them?" I guessed. Shifters really were as bad as witches. Witches would go to war to hide the truth too, which made no sense to me. Who cared if a god was part toad, for Hades' sake?

"Precisely," Zophia said. "My father had me transcribe them, because history shouldn't be lost, or some such. He'd sell the scrolls to the priests, then the transcriptions to the scholars, mostly to the university here in the Vault. The priests didn't care much for that."

I blinked. "They killed him because of that?"

Zophia looked regretful. "I can't prove anything, but that's my suspicion. That's another reason I'm here. If anyone knew I had done the transcribing, they might assume I remember what I wrote."

"Do you?" I asked, suddenly compelled to glance over my shoulder.

"Most of it. So do Calista and Dex, and a dozen other people here, but the priests won't act against the residence. As long as Dex doesn't talk about it, they keep their peace."

"I don't understand why it's such a big deal." I picked up the rest of my food and went on eating.

"That's because you don't know what else the scrolls contained." Zophia smiled secretively.

"There's more?" I was curious in spite of myself.

"One of the scrolls suggested he was screwing his own sister." Zophia made a face. "Although the other said she wasn't her sister, but something else entirely."

"What sort of something else?"

"Anything from a demon, to the darker part of Hades. It's not clear. It even hinted that Hades was the darker half. I suppose I can understand why they wouldn't want people thinking *that*."

"It is a little sacrilegious," I agreed. I learnt long ago that just because someone said a thing, it didn't mean it was true. My curiosity or mistrust in the Council's motives for sending me here made me seek out ways to keep myself safe, and avoid becoming a commodity. That did beg one question.

"What does Dex do with slaves?"

My question clearly took Zophia by surprise. "That depends on the slave. Most work to buy their freedom, and then stay on afterward. Dex and Calista are good to their people. However," she added, "most aren't women."

"What do you think he would have done with me?" I frowned.

"I don't know, it's never happened before. Perhaps he'd have sold you off to someone else. You'd be worth enough to buy an army."

I opened my mouth to retort, until I realised Zophia was teasing. I closed my mouth and huffed instead, throwing a side-on look for good measure.

"Oh, I'm sorry," Zophia looked as though she was trying to hold back a laugh. "I didn't mean to offend you. Slavery is all but dead amongst paranormals. People would have come from all over to stare."

I grimaced. "Thank Hades it didn't come to that."

"You know, your knowledge of the Council would be invaluable to the Covener's enemies, slave or no slave."

I couldn't argue with that. I would have to watch my back.

7

BAIN

I SENSED Viva before she approached the sanctuary door. She gave me a surprised glance and reached for the handle.

Like always, parts of her thoughts were closed off to me. What I could read suggested she was worried about something.

Back rod straight, I started to turn away.

"Bain."

I didn't need to delve into her thoughts, they were written on her face. If I brushed her off now, she would find me again later. She already proved her persistence by finding a way to get asylum. If she had something to say, I would have to listen, sooner or later. She was determined it would be now.

"Viva." I gave her a nod and tried to keep my expression disinterested. It was difficult with the way her clothes hugged every centimetre of her. They left enough to the imagination for mine to go wild. I wanted to tie her wrists to the nearest railing and pull the fabric from her body with my teeth. Then—

I caught the eye of Cowan, the other guard on the door. The man moved away a few metres under the pretence of speaking to a passing servant.

"Did you want something?" I asked.

Her eyes lingered on mine for a moment. I would almost swear she was thinking the same thing I had a moment ago.

"Good morning to you too," she said sarcastically.

I raised an eyebrow at her. When she didn't respond, I gave her a bow and a smirk. "Good morning then."

It was her turn to raise an eyebrow at me.

"Viva," I said again. "Did you need something?" I delved, but couldn't tell what was on her mind. Her emotions were a tight web. I never sensed anyone like her before. She both intrigued me and made me nervous.

"As a matter of fact, I do." She crossed her arms over her chest. "Two things in fact."

I sighed. "All right." I gestured for her to step into the sanctuary courtyard and closed the door behind us. "The first?"

She fixed me with a firm look. "I was going to ask Dex, but since you're here—was Izzy sent away?"

"Yes," I said simply. My direct answer seemed to take her aback, but I didn't flinch. "I took her back to the train myself. In the company of the guy she screwed. Both seemed happy with the arrangement." Not precisely happy, more like pissed, but she'd had no choice in the matter. She could go to her lover's faction, or live amongst humans. Remaining in the Vault was not an option.

"Oh. I see." Viva looked disconcerted for a moment and gave a subtle shake of her head.

"You were expecting some other answer?" Maybe she thought we had Izzy killed and ate her for lunch. Witches seemed to think shifters were savages. We felt the same about them. The only difference was, we were probably right.

"No, I just . . ." Her brow creased. "Thank you for telling me."

"You're welcome. Now what was the other thing?"

She blinked. Apparently she'd forgotten there was something else. If she had, she remembered quickly.

"The scale," she blurted. "Why did you give it to Dex to give to me?"

"The dragon scale?" he asked.

"No, a fish scale," she replied sarcastically. "Yes, I mean the dragon scale."

I bit back a snort. I had certainly walked myself into that one. "I gave it to him because he never takes one," I replied. "I didn't know what he'd do with it afterward." I averted my eyes. I knew full well. In fact, I'd hoped that was what Dex would do. What had the scale done to her?

She lightly put a hand on my arm. Her touch felt like fire in my blood. It was all I could do not to shove her against a wall and fuck her silly.

"You're a crappy liar," she said. "Tell me why you really did it."

I found myself responding with words I had no intention of saying.

"Dragon scales contain residual power and someone with power—" I forced my mouth shut and grimaced. What had she done to me? And how?

I shook off her hand and stepped away, eyes on her, hand instinctively near my knife. "It's not nice to use power to make people speak."

She jerked her hand back. "What makes you think I did?"

I hesitated. I hadn't intended to catch her out, but now I had, I would have to deal with it.

"Those words weren't mine." I frowned. "I mean, they were, but that was something I would never speak of to—" I glanced around and rubbed my forehead with my fingertips.

"To a witch?" she suggested.

"Yeah." There was no point in sugarcoating it. She might be as lickable as fuck, but she was still a witch. The enemy, more or less. "The scale did something to you?"

She shrugged. "It glowed. That was all. Why? Was it supposed to kill me or something?"

That was a fair question.

"No," I said firmly. "Dragon scales are harmless if they aren't attached to a dragon. I wasn't sure if it would respond to you at all."

"Why?" she asked.

Another good question. One I took a moment to respond to.

"I wasn't sure if it would react to a witch. There's something about shifters." I shrugged. "I thought maybe it was just us. I guess it wasn't. Unless you're part shifter." I chuckled at the idea.

Her eyes widened slightly and she swallowed. "Right. Haha."

I frowned. Her mind was almost as guarded as a shifter. Could she be— That would explain a lot. Like why the witches wanted her out so badly. And why Dex let her in here. Did he know? He must have suspected something. The man all but dragged his tongue across the floor every time her name came up.

"What?" she asked.

I regarded her for a long moment. "The dried flowers in your bag."

She stiffened. "What about them?"

"You draw power from them," I guessed. "You don't need incantations or objects."

For a while I thought she might deny it. Then she exhaled through pursed lips.

"Yes, that's it," she said. "From the scent of things and people around me."

My whole face twitched. "From me?" That would explain how she took my exhaustion away the other night. At the time, I assumed she had some small artefact, maybe her earrings. Now I knew that wasn't the case.

She looked uncomfortable. "Only once. Or twice."

"The Covener knew?"

She gave me a flat stare. "Of course he does, but he wants it kept a secret."

"Too bad for him," I said dryly. No wonder he wanted her gone. The ability to use power without effort would be dangerous. If other witches knew, they'd want the ability too. I ran a hand over my forehead. So would the shifters. Lucky for us, she was here, not with the Council.

"My mother came from a poor family. My father married her for her power. He had no idea her bloodline was so different." Viva looked bitter.

I nodded. Clearly she expected to be used or mocked. I would do neither. But it would satisfy my curiosity.

"Why, are you?" I was more direct than I intended, but once the words were out, they were out.

"I…" She glanced around. "I think you know why."

I thought, then nodded slowly. "Because you have shifter blood."

"The witches call it tainted," she said. "What would you call it?" She lifted her chin and gave me a challenging look.

Damn, the woman was hot enough to set my soul on fire.

"Well, not tainted," I replied. "Shifter blood is the best thing going."

She looked surprised for a moment, then smiled. "You would think that."

"Damn right I would," I agreed.

"What about the witch blood?" she asked.

I hesitated. I could very easily say the wrong thing here. I doubted she'd hesitate to put a knee in my groin if I did.

"Can you shift?" I asked.

"I have no idea," she replied. "If I can, I haven't yet."

I nodded slowly. "Even if you can't, I say your shifter blood means you belong here. Your mind feels more shifter than witch anyway." I sensed that for a long time, but I hadn't realised until now.

Her eyes studied mine for a long while. I held my ground. We both had our secrets, she had to know she could trust me with hers.

Finally, she nodded. "You're going to tell him, aren't you?"

"Dex? He should know, yes, if only to keep you safe."

She looked doubtful. "If you guessed, then others might, including him." She cocked her head. "What do you mean, my mind? Can you—"

"I sense thoughts," I said. "Sometimes I can read them, but only if I try, which I usually don't. With you, I can sense your intentions, but not the reason behind them. Perhaps you don't know yourself."

I was baiting her a little, but not knowing what she was thinking annoyed me for some reason. I liked to be in control and with her, I wasn't.

"Can anyone else do that?" she asked. "Dex? Calista?"

I grunted. "Dex has no power beyond the ability to shift. Calista either, but there might be others. All the more reason he should know."

"Why can you sense minds?" she asked. "Are you part witch? Can you do what I do?"

"No." Her question might have bothered a shifter with smaller balls. "It's just an instinct thing."

"Like animal instincts?" she asked.

She was on the verge of earning herself a spanking. Comparing shifters to animals was the most witch remark I heard her say so far. I'd happily dish out the punishment, but the idea was making me harder than I could afford to be right now. A knee in the groin might snap my dick right off.

I glanced around us. "It's something we shouldn't talk about here."

"What about the others you mentioned?" she pressed again. "Can anyone else use scent? Can they do other things? Can they—"

I held up a hand to cut her off. "We *really* shouldn't talk about this here. Have you heard the expression *the walls have ears?* Well here especially. It's part sanctuary, part nest of serpents."

She looked around. "Who are you referring to as a—"

I interrupted her again, "I'll talk to you later. You can tell Dex or I will. Either way, the sooner he knows, the better for you."

"All right." She held her hands up in surrender. "Maybe you should. You know him better than I do." She looked vulnerable, scared, then pissed at herself for showing me that side of her.

I understood. There were those who, if they knew what I could do, would try to use me for their own gain. For her, it would be the same, or worse. Showing weakness gave those others a chance to exploit it. She was still a badass, but seeing a flash of her softer side made me wonder what else there was to see.

"Bain?" Her voice snapped me out of my thoughts.

"I'll speak to Dex," I said, my stone mask back in place. "Good day." I gave her a hasty nod and hurried away.

~

"WHAT IS SHE?" Dex asked. He looked back at me over the desk. He seemed composed but for a slight twitch of his chin. Barely noticeable, I knew to look for it after so many years. It was a sure sign Dex was more agitated than he let on. The greater the twitch, the higher the agitation. At the moment it was only subtle.

"She's a witch with shifter blood. How much blood, I have no idea. She doesn't know if she can shift."

"I see," Dex said. "Is she dangerous?" His twitch increased.

"I don't think," I replied. "She seems controlled well enough." I should have guessed what she was when I saw her dried petals.

Witches with shifter blood were rare enough. I put my self-blame aside before it took hold. That line of thought wasn't helpful or productive.

"She seems grateful to be here," I added. "I believe her gratitude is genuine."

"I agree," Dex replied. The twitch eased somewhat.

My eyes flicked away, but I forced my gaze back. Thinking about a woman was a bad excuse for not focusing on my job. Worse still if it created problems between Dex and me.

Of course, Dex was astute enough to notice my discomfort. He looked amused.

"She has that effect on people, doesn't she?" He laced his fingers and rested his elbows on his desk.

"Keeper—" I started.

"It must be serious if you're resorting to formality." Dex sat back. "I have no claim on her. Not yet."

"But you want to?" I asked.

Dex shrugged with one shoulder, but I saw the look in his eyes. He wanted her as badly as I did. "Possibly. But for now, she can do what she wants. So can you."

My face heated. I couldn't remember that happening since I was a kid. "There are some lines ..."

"There is no line," Dex assured me. "There is no commitment, no competition."

"A child of hers would be powerful," I said, my voice rough. My throat was dry. I coughed to clear it. "She might not appreciate being talked about like this."

Dex gave a short laugh. "I suspect she wouldn't." He stopped and looked thoughtful. "Do paranormals usually breed others with their power?" He cocked his head. "Is that where yours comes from?"

"If my parents had powers, I have no knowledge of it." Both were long dead, so I couldn't ask. "Viva mentioned her mother. I don't think she shares her daughter's power."

I watched Dex carefully, but stayed out of his thoughts. An heir with power might prove a threat to the Alpha, or an asset. A choice like that wouldn't—couldn't be made lightly.

"You know about Zophia?" I asked, if only to change the subject.

"I heard from Calista that rumour has them spending time together." Dex shrugged, apparently unconcerned. "I could no more restrict either of them than cage a sand dragon."

"A sand dragon is less powerful, and potentially less dangerous than Viva. Trying to restrain her might be difficult," I said. Unless she consented.

"Perhaps she's the garden dragon I asked Hades for," Dex remarked. He looked away, toward the window.

I shrugged one shoulder. "Maybe."

Dex turned back, his expression unchanged. "Guard her, Bain, keep her safe. Something tells me we may need her in the days to come."

I gave him a questioning look, to which he responded by pushing a sheet of paper across his desk.

"Bad shit, if that is to be believed."

"The source is—" I picked up the sheet and scanned it.

"Reliable, but second-hand," Dex replied. "If even half of that is true, we may have to plan for trouble."

"Rumours like this arise every year or two," I pointed out.

"Not like this. Read to the bottom."

I frowned and read more carefully this time. "If the Alpha gets wind of this—"

"All the more reason we need to put it down as soon as possible." Dex rose and moved to look out the window. His thoughts were tumultuous, troubled. "What do you think of all of this?" he asked over his shoulder. "Some might suggest the Alpha doesn't have the strength, or following to hold the Vault."

"Talk like that is treason," I replied warily.

Dex turned back, a wry smile on his face. "If I was going to execute you, I would have done it by now."

"Perhaps, but there's still the Alpha. He might have us both executed."

Dex spread his hands wide to take in the room, empty except for us. "I won't tell him if you don't."

Backed into a corner, I sighed. "Would the Vault in your hands mean a great deal of change? Your leadership is as much law here as that of the Alpha. Assuming anyone who staged a coup let you live."

Dex perched on the corner of the desk and supported his chin with his finger and thumb. "A big assumption," he agreed.

"However," I continued, "if you became Alpha, you would still need an heir."

"Yes, I would," Dex agreed. "And quickly. I could name you."

I jerked. "Me?"

"You think that would be a bad thing?" Dex asked.

"Someone not related to a very long line of shifters?" I asked. "It would set a dangerous precedent. It might even cause the kind of unrest the witches and other factions have been waiting for. The Covener would rub his hand together at the idea."

"You're assuming he too would be allowed to live," Dex remarked.

"It sounds as though you've given this a lot of thought." As soon as I spoke the words, I realised. Of course Dex had. He would have thought about every move and countermove that might come about. Hades only knew how many moves ahead he was of everyone else.

"That's why this bothers you." I tapped the paper in front of me. "You didn't foresee this."

"The priests of Hades speaking out against the Alpha?" Dex frowned. "No. They usually stay in their temples and carry out their rituals. Hades has kept his nose out of the affairs of the Vault for who knows how long."

"First treason, now sacrilege," I said. I crossed my arms over my chest. "Perhaps I should send word to the Alpha after all."

Dex chuckled. "I suspect the priests are aware their influence is waning. Fewer young people are choosing to join the temple. In a generation, the Vault might have forgotten Hades altogether."

"That makes them dangerous," I concluded.

"It does indeed," Dex agreed. He rose from the desk and moved to sit in his seat. He rested his elbows on the desk and pressed steepled fingers to his lips. "The question is, what do we do about it?"

I sat back and considered before answering slowly, "We either shut them up by force—"

"Which would upset the believers," Dex interjected.

"We let them continue to spread dissent—"

"Which would anger the Alpha and potentially cause civil war."

"Or you become a priest and show the Alpha your undying dedication to Hades," my words and expression were deadpan.

Dex looked surprised for a moment, before he burst out laughing. "Nothing so extreme," he said after his gales died down to chuckles. "Perhaps a generous donation. I'll speak to my advisors and settle on an amount. Eye-watering, no doubt. I'll need you to escort the donation to the temple."

I nodded. "Okay. Although, can I make a suggestion?"

Dex nodded.

8

Viva

I waited for either Dex or Bain to come and find me. My nerves grew. By the third hour, I considered trying to run before they had me killed. Or worse, sent back to the Council.

I touched my throat lightly. I liked it uncut and unbroken.

"Hades." I paced across my room. "Should I pack my shit and run?"

Where would I go? Fleeing across the desert alone would be a death sentence, a slow one. I joked about swimming away, but I had no idea which direction to go. I might travel along the coast for a while, but what would I do if I hit a wall? I'd be trapped there until they came and found me, and they would. I could kill a few before they killed me, but I didn't like that idea much. Way too messy and I still wound up dead.

I forced in several slow breaths and sat down at my solid

but simple dresser. Eyes anywhere but on my reflection in the wide mirror, I opened a drawer.

Inside lay a dozen tiny bags, each tied tightly shut. I reached for the pale purple cotton one. After a moment of wrestling with the knot, I eased the bag open and inhaled the scent of the lavender. Floral and fragrant, it was one of my favourites.

The warmth of power spread through me. Another breath or two and I could throw back anyone who came to harm me.

Images came to my mind: Dex flying through the air, Bain lying slumped on the other side of the courtyard, guards with necks snapped, eyes staring, accusing me.

I grimaced. I could do all of that and more, but the idea made my stomach turn.

I wanted to throw all of my dried petals off the terrace. Let them scatter harmlessly to the wind. Better yet, toss myself, before I could kill.

I shook my head. I chose lavender for a reason. After years of practice, trial and error, I knew the smell of the flower was harmless. Even if I inhaled until my body was full to overflowing with power, I could only use it to relax myself and anyone I touched.

I breathed in more lavender scent. It was just what I needed. I let my stress wash away, bit by bit, let my head clear, then closed the bag and placed it back in the drawer. The effect of lavender only lasted an hour or two. It had to be enough. Now was not the time to do something stupid because I was agitated and impatient.

I steeled myself to do what I had to. If they weren't going to come to me, I would go to them.

I rose and now looked at my reflection. The calm rested on me, soothed my face into a mask. The soft blue of my blouse complimented my hair and made my eyes appear even more blue. Even my hair seemed to respond to the lavender; it lay in neat waves over my shoulders.

Part witch, part shifter. If that was what I was, I might as well embrace it.

Bain said we would talk later about my power. I intended to live long enough to hold him to that.

My mother wouldn't discuss my abilities, even after lots of wine. Instead, she gave me a dark look, as though she regretted my existence. Fortunately, Persephone was responsible for the souls of those who murdered, especially those who killed children. A lifetime of disgust at her offspring was better than an eternity of torture.

Still, it left me without much understanding of myself. In my younger days, I might have easily caused deaths without meaning to. Some instruction might have saved a lot of anguish, and the need to sneak away to experiment.

"What are you?" I asked my reflection. "Blessed or cursed?" My reflection had no answers.

"I think of mine as a gift from Hades," Bain said softly.

I jumped as his reflection appeared beside mine. I turned, hand at my hip, to see an apologetic look on his face.

His expression was gone before I could register that I wasn't armed.

Only the influence of the lavender kept my heart from racing. I didn't want to kill anyone, but I hated to feel vulnerable.

"I didn't hear you," I said, accusingly. I dropped my guard. That was a stupid mistake. He could have walked up behind me and slid a blade between my ribs before I knew he was there.

Why hadn't he?

"So I noticed." He seemed on the verge of amusement, but stepped back from it. "I spoke to the Keeper."

"Congratulations." The word slipped out before I was able to bite my tongue.

Bain snorted.

I ignored him. "Am I going to be executed? Or exiled?"

"Which would you prefer?" he asked.

I blinked. "Neither. Am I allowed a choice?"

He regarded me for a long, silent moment. "As much as I am intrigued as to which you might pick, I've come to take you out of the residence."

My heart leapt. "Where am I going?"

"To the temple of Hades, on the other side of the Vault."

"Oh." I hadn't considered that. A life of devotion might be better than no life at all. "Do I have time to pack, or will my things be sent later?"

My question took him by surprise, but he recovered as quickly as ever. "You're not going to stay. Unless you want to. I merely need your presence for a transaction."

"If you think I'm going to kill for you—"

He held up a hand. "No, not at all. The priests are stirring up dissent; there's talk of overthrowing the Alpha. You're coming as an indication the Council and the Vault are solid allies, with the Alpha's knowledge and blessing. It's been a hundred years since we all got along so well." He smirked slightly at the irony.

"I see." That was not what I expected. "I don't have to do anything?"

"Just look pret—loyal," he said. "And for the record, I can kill for myself. I don't need a woman to do it for me."

"I'm sure you can," I said. I was surprised he hadn't said witch. "Does this mean you're not going to kill me?"

"Not today," he replied easily. "Not if you can be of use to Dex. And not before any talk of rebellion is suppressed."

I nodded slowly. "People would use my execution as a

reason to assume the Vault is in upheaval. And if it is, why not hold a coup?"

"I see you've come to some conclusion, but I can't tell what." Bain sounded uneasy.

"I was wondering if the Covener hoped you would execute me. In a fit of outrage, he might strike back. Tear up the artefact. Declare war on shifterkind." I cocked my head at Bain. "I guess you should keep me alive then."

His mouth turned up slightly. "It would seem so. You're a pawn after all."

I bristled at the words, although he wasn't wrong. What-ever game the Council was playing, I was in the middle of it. Bride, lover, excuse for war, where had they intended me to fit? Maybe any of those would satisfy their plans.

"All the more reason my loyalty should be to the Vault," I said. At least to Dex. Anywhere but the Council. It occurred to me I was being used by Dex at least as much as I was being used by the Council.

Who the fuck did I dare to trust?

"CAN YOU RIDE?" Bain led me through the maze of corridors, down to the garage.

"Ride what?" I asked. I gave him a sly smile when he raised an eyebrow at me. "Motorbikes? Horses?" *You?*

"Dragons," he replied.

For a split second, I thought he was serious.

What? Dragon shifters were a thing. For all I knew, they gave rides all over the Vault.

"Cool," I said, as though he hadn't caught me off guard. "I hope they come with a saddle."

Bain snorted. "A dragon would sooner eat you than let you ride it."

I suspected he meant the shifter kind as well.

"Ouch," I said. "You know how to hurt a girl."

He gave me a long look. "You have no idea."

Ohhhh, shit. Now I wanted to find out.

I eyed him sideways. "Promises, promises."

"I don't make promises I can't keep," he said, slightly too fast.

"I'm sure," I said. "Neither do I."

"Unlike the average, full-blooded witch," Bain muttered.

"Yeah, they can be like that," I agreed. "Especially with those they consider beneath him."

"If I were to guess, I would think that's everyone." Bain didn't even try to contain his disdain. He opened the garage door and leaned his arm against it while he regarded me.

"That's probably true, but some might say the same about Dex." I ducked under his arm and stepped into the garage.

"Would you?" Bain followed me inside.

I turned and cocked my head, one hand on my hip. "No. He seems as though he genuinely cares about his people."

"He does," Bain said firmly.

"What is he going to do afterward?" I lowered my hand to my side and followed him toward a handful of motorcycles which stood off to the side.

"When there's an heir?"

When I nodded, he continued. "There has to be one first. The Alpha and his wife have been married a long time, but it's not too late to happen. Then the heir has to be old enough to lead. Of course, they also have to reach adulthood."

"As inheritances go, your system seems overly complicated," I remarked. "Why not just leave Dex and his heirs to rule? Or vote on it."

"Because the Alpha leads, and no one wants to admit he can't get his wife pregnant. Men can be..."

"Stubborn?" I finished. "You'd think people were questioning the size of his dick."

"They probably are." Bain shrugged. "People will gossip. If no child comes, eventually he'll have to hand over the leadership.

"Would that be a bad thing?" I almost missed catching the helmet Bain tossed to me. I grabbed it at the last moment and ignored the amusement on his face.

"It would be bad if others thought they should lead instead of Dex. That would end in war."

"I'm starting to think that might be inevitable anyway." I threw my hand up when he frowned at me. "I'm not going to support the witches if the Covener tries to take advantage of the situation, but it has to be difficult for Dex to keep control when the Alpha is never seen. Are you sure he's real?"

"He's real," Bain grunted. "He shows himself a few times a year, to remind everyone he exists and to ensure their loyalty."

"I assume you're not suggesting Dex's loyalty is in question?"

"Certainly not," Bain agreed evenly. "You shouldn't either." He led me toward a bike, pulled off the cover and tossed it toward a nearby shelf.

"What happens if he has no kids?" I asked. "Or Dex for that matter?"

He turned to regard me, brows lowered heavily. "Then the Vault is doomed. Best not ask Hades for that."

I shivered.

"Exactly," he said upon seeing my reaction. "Ask Hades for heirs for the Alpha, and lots of them." Before I could respond to that, he turned and wheeled the bike he'd chosen toward the door.

"Something to remember," Bain said over his shoulder. "Wherever the walls may be, they always have ears." He glanced toward a young mechanic, who was busily folding the cover Bain had pulled off the bike, making it neater than it probably needed to be.

I pursed my lips at the guy's back. I was sure he wasn't close enough to overhear our conversation, but I would watch myself in future.

"So, I don't get my own bike?" I asked.

"I figured it would be easier this way," Bain said. "You might get lost on one of your own. Or damage it."

"My sense of direction isn't that bad," I argued. I'd never ridden a motorbike before, so damaging one wasn't out of the question. I also might hurt myself, which wasn't on my to-do list for the day.

"Do you need help to get on?" Bain asked. He moved toward me, but I shook my head.

"I think I can manage." I stepped to the bike and tried to figure out where to grab on.

"This is quicker." Bain grabbed my waist and picked me up. His hands brushed over my hips and sent a jolt through my whole body. If he wasn't careful, I would slide right off the seat.

I swallowed at his touch and scent and forced myself to focus. If my power let me fly, I would take off from the smell of him, even though it was negated somewhat by the stink of oil and fuel.

He lowered me onto the back of the bike at such an angle I almost slid off the other side. At the last moment, I drew on my power and wound it like a shield to stop myself. I bounced against it lightly and came to rest with my hands on the leather of the seat.

"Interesting." Bain stepped back.

"You did that on purpose?"

His eyebrows twitched upward. "Not at all." He looked

like he might say more, but his gaze flicked toward the door and he gave a faint nod.

He mounted the bike in front of me. "Put your arms around me and relax. You don't need to do anything but stay on."

"I'm surprised you don't ride horses around the Vault," I remarked.

"Who said we don't?" he replied.

At the same moment, two more bikes and riders stopped outside the garage.

"Here's the rest of the entourage." Bain started the bike and we moved slowly toward the door.

"The rest?" For some reason, I felt a knot of disappointment. I shoved it back down. We were on the Keeper's business. It stood to reason it wouldn't only be the two of us.

Idiot, I told myself. What was with the disappointment anyway? It wasn't as if he was interested in me. He might laugh at the idea, or be pissed. Part shifter still meant a whole lot of witch. He probably went home at night and didn't give me a second thought. Where did he live anyway? Somewhere in the residence, I guessed, but I could be wrong.

No, I told myself, *he might not be interested, but alone, he might give me answers he wouldn't give with others around.*

I didn't know any of the four shifters who sat on bikes outside. They fell in behind us when we roared out into the heat of the morning. They nodded to Bain, then almost as one, we pressed helmets onto our heads and fastened them in place.

Engines rang in my ears as we rode toward the gates which opened slowly as we drew closer.

The Vault looked different from the back of a bike. Without the worry of slavery or death, I could drink in the sights and smells.

The Vault, I decided after a short time, wasn't that

different to any other part of Sydney. Except for the whole desert thing. The smells were the same: plants, people, bustle and crap.

The house and buildings near the Keeper's residence, each with terraces and balconies to catch the sea view, were pressed closely together. The smells were slightly masked with row upon row of roses, freesias, jasmine and a dozen other flowering plants I didn't recognise.

Frangipani trees towered over most streets. Their twisted trunks looked like sculptures of tortured souls frozen in time. Was that what shifters did with their criminals? I was only half joking. They certainly looked like people trying to escape.

We rode past several small parks, each with a fountain in the middle and statues dotted here and there, seemingly at random. None were as explicit as the ones in the Keeper's residence, but most were of some naked god or other.

The further down we went, the statues began to crumble, or be missing limbs or even a head or cock. One looked to be dotted with paint, or was it bird shit? Either way, it didn't look like it was cared for.

Was Dex aware the lower city was so grimy? Chances were, he was, but the Vault's coffers didn't extend this far. In my experience, they rarely did. Human, witch or shifter, if the rich couldn't see it, then it could be ignored in favour of more important stuff. Like war, or hunting sand dragons.

Near the base of the hill, closer to the harbour, the crowds became thicker and more diverse.

A pale faced woman with a high collar and sleeves which hung halfway over her hands skirted around a darker skinned man in a brown leather jacket.

Several children wearing tall, conical hats stepped carefully under a sign for electronic devices, and ducked under another outside a bar. They looked like stereotypical witches. Bizarre for inside the shifters' Vault.

How did they keep them on their heads? And why? This place was weirder than I suspected.

Everyone, regardless of strange hats or clothes, moved out of the way to let the bikes through. Some paused to look, others hurried to the side, without so much as a glance.

A young girl tugged her dog out of the way by its collar and stood wide-eyed while we passed.

On the back of one of the bikes, a box was fastened tightly with rope.

I gave Bain a questioning look when I first noticed it. If he knew what was inside, he gave no sign.

At a glance, it was an ordinary wooden box, free of carving, with a lock on the front.

I remembered Bain's mention of a transaction. Presumably a gift of some kind lay inside. It was too small for a person, unless a child was stashed in there.

When I sniffed the air, I smelled Bain, our escort, motorbikes, leather, oil and the timber of the box itself. The faint hint of flowers came from somewhere, but I couldn't tell where.

Whatever was inside the box either had no scent, or was masked very well. No hint of decomposing anything, or of terror.

I looked at the back of Bain's head and told myself I was being paranoid. A lot of things had only a subtle scent, at least to me. As far as I could tell, I was able to smell better than the average witch; a shifter gift, or curse, presumably.

However, I didn't have the senses of a dog, or a dragon. Thank Hades for that, or I might be overwhelmed by the smallest stink.

I frowned toward Bain. According to one of my brothers, animals could smell fear. I could. Could the big guy do the same? Maybe we weren't that different. Was that why he said he would tell me more later?

I cursed myself for not having pinned him down sooner to get answers. Now, surrounded by people, I could only sit on the roaring bike and guess what—

We stopped at a red light. Even here in the Vault we had to wait, in spite of there being no traffic coming the other way.

A rush of air passed my ear.

Instinctively, I ducked. A moment later, Bain slammed the bike to a stop, leapt off, grabbed my shoulders and pulled me off onto the road. He turned us both and pushed me into a crouch.

"What the—"

"Shhh!" He pressed my head down lower and shielded me with his body. "We're too exposed here, we need to move."

"How do we—"

He cut me off again. "Shhh. This way." He hauled me to my feet, grabbed my hand and tugged me toward a nearby shoemaker's shop. He shoved me inside and pushed me down behind the front window.

"Stay there," he ordered before he hurried back onto the street.

Outside sounded as though chaos had broken out. People shouted. At least one child cried loudly.

"I'm not helpless, you know," I muttered.

"Of course you're not," a voice said behind me.

Keeping low, I whipped around to see a small woman behind the work desk. At first, I assumed she was older, skin darkened with age and sun. Then she wiped her brow and whatever she was working with came off in a streak.

"Uh, sorry, I didn't mean to intrude." Like I had a choice. What was Bain's problem anyway?

The shoemaker shrugged, but flashed a smile. She

grabbed up a cloth and wiped her face. Under the grime, she wasn't much older than me.

"It's not every day we get such excitement around here."

"Thank fuck for that," I said wryly.

"Who tried to kill you?" The shoemaker kept an eye on the door and picked up a piece of leather. She began to work it around a chunk of wood the shape of a foot.

"I don't know. They probably weren't trying to get at me." I rose enough to peer through the window.

The guards stood near the bikes, knives in hand. They'd already shed helmets and jackets, ready to shift if they needed to.

The box seemed intact. If thieves tried to attack, they failed. So far, at least.

"Maybe. Most folk who go around throwing knives at the Keeper's men don't miss," the shoemaker said. "I'm Urla Hassir. You?"

"Viva Taylor," I said over my shoulder.

"Ohhh," Urla said in a tone which made me glance back. "You're the talk of the Vault at the moment."

"Just what I need," I said under my breath. "Don't believe what you hear." I looked back toward the street. Bain appeared from somewhere to the left, a knife held in his hand like he hardly dared to touch it. He pulled a handkerchief from a pocket and wrapped the blade in it.

"You weren't granted asylum by the Keeper?" Urla asked.

"That part is true." I started to stand, but Bain glanced toward the window and I ducked back down.

"They say with the Covener and his family dead, you'll be the heir to his seat on the Council," Urla added, matter of factly.

I whirled around to face her. "I beg your pardon? The Covener and his family are *what?*"

Urla's eyes widened. "You didn't know? Word is doing the rounds this morning. I guess it didn't reach you yet."

I gaped. "I guess not." My ears rang with the sound of blood pounding through me. Could it be possible? Did Dex or Bain know and not tell me? I felt faint. Was that why someone threw a knife at me? I tried to draw a bit of power, to defend myself if nothing else, but the small room was overpowered by unpleasant odours; the smell of leather and whatever substances Urla used to make her boots.

"Such a shame, that." Urla put down her tools, wiped her hands on the cloth she used for her face and stepped around the work table. "What would happen if no one from the Council was left alive?"

"I—" Now I rose, my hands to either side. "I suppose the witches would appoint a whole new Council."

"Or a king," Urla said. "Or maybe a queen." She picked up a long, sharp-looking awl up from the table and took another step closer.

"Possibly." I didn't think the witches would accept a woman as their leader, but if this was part of a coup, they might not get a choice.

I shook my head slightly. Gossip, that was all this was, surely. The Covener and his asshole son, along with the rest of the witches who turned their backs on me, couldn't be dead. They certainly wouldn't be thinking of replacing any of them with me. I was nothing. My mother, my siblings... Surely one of my brothers would be better suited. They were full witches and none would go down without a fight.

"Why do you care?" I took a step back, toward the door, but found only a wall behind me. I felt around for the door-frame. It must be further than I thought.

"Oh I don't," Urla replied. "I only care that I get paid for the work I do. A handsome sum, you're worth."

"Am I really?" I asked. Where the fuck was the frame? I took a tiny sidestep as Urla drew closer.

"Dead or alive, they said." Urla nodded. She cocked her head. "I suspect you won't come alive, will you?"

"I *might* be convinced to go along quietly," I replied. "I'd prefer not to die today."

Urla smiled. "I'm sure you wouldn't, but I suspect you might put up a fight later."

"I have to ask again, why do you care?" I turned my face slightly in an attempt to inhale some useful scent. Again, all I found was leather, oils and wax. I searched for beeswax, but if there was any here, it was covered with other odours.

As though someone knew I was coming.

"You won't be around when whoever wants me deals with me."

"Maybe not, but if you escape, I don't get paid." Urla stalked closer.

"Right. Well, before I die, can you at least tell me how you knew to cover any natural scents with ones made by human hands?" Just a small bundle of dried petals would do, but everything here was cooked, the power boiled away, or suppressed.

Urla hesitated. "I was told to. That's all I know."

"I suspect you're lying," Bain said from behind me. He must be just outside the door. That was close enough.

I inhaled the scent of musk and sandalwood and drew in as much power as his scent would give me. It was too much, but I didn't care.

I wound it around Urla and picked her up. The woman's eyes widened and she windmilled her arms while she hung in the air.

"Don't kill her," Bain said. "We need to know who hired her."

I bared my teeth, and hurled Urla gentler than I wanted

to. The shoemaker flew backward through the air and struck the far wall with a thud. She slid down and lay still, unconscious but alive.

"She wouldn't have spared me," I growled.

"Probably not." Bain put a hand on my shoulder.

I still held a lot of power I had drawn from him, but I could take more. In the back of my mind, it tingled, itched at me to draw in every drop and blast the city to ruins. I could draw and destroy until only I remained, standing in a pile of ashes.

I gritted my teeth, stepped away and used the excess to calm myself and pick up the awl which lay near Urla. She must have dropped it as she fell. I placed it on a shelf, far from the shoemaker. I didn't want anything to do with it, any more than I wanted to be stabbed with it.

"Are you all right?" Bain asked.

I glanced over to him, unsure if he was referring to the attack, the power or both.

I sniffed. "I'm done throwing people around, if that's what you mean."

"But?" He must have known there was one before I did.

"But if what she said about the Covener and his family is true and you and Dex knew but didn't tell me—"

Bain cut me off. "If it's true, I'm unaware. I'd bet a chest of dragon scales Dex didn't know either." He held up a hand. "*If* it's true. She might have been goading you."

"Why would…" I caught my lip between my teeth. "To see what I could do?"

"Maybe. I'll… talk to her later and see if I can find out her motive."

"Can I be there?" I asked immediately.

Bain didn't answer right away. "That will be up to Dex." He gestured to his men who stood outside the door. "Take the shoemaker to the residence and put her in a cell." To me, he said, "We have a job to finish."

I gaped. "We're still going?"

The side of his mouth jerked upward. "Why wouldn't we? You're not going to let a little ambush scare you, are you?"

I mouthed, "Little ambush?" to his back, but followed him to the bike. He helped me remount, but I kept my head down, gaze this way and that. Whether or not the person who threw the knife had tried to kill me, they were still out there somewhere.

They might easily try again.

I snorted to myself. If they had any sense, they would be far away by now, not going after me while I was in the middle of a group of shifters who would now be even more vigilant. Safer to chase a dragon into the mountains and try to pin it down in a cave. Unless they also had some kind of power. If they were anything like me, they could choke me while I—

I dismissed that line of thought. If they had, and wanted me dead, they would have done that first. No, they created a ruse for a reason.

I glanced back to the shoemaker's as two guards carried a tightly bound form between them. They hefted her over the front of one of their bikes and rode back back the way we came.

With any luck, they would get some answers from Urla.

I turned back around and tried to let the thrumming engine of the bike between my legs soothe me.

The only thing which really settled my nerves was the feeling of the power I still held, laced with sandalwood and musk.

9

Viva

THE TEMPLE of Hades in the lower part of the Vault was huge. I could barely stop myself from gaping as we stepped inside.

The walls were lined in stone reliefs of Hades, and others, in almost every pose imaginable.

Here, he danced with a man with a conical crown. There he sat, listening to a group of bare-headed children. Beside that, he lay horizontal above a man with a giant dick.

I caught Bain's raised eyebrows at the last relief, but he wouldn't look at me when I tried to catch his eye. After a moment, I gave up and turned to look at the multitude of statues scattered around the temple.

Most were simple; Hades with his hand outstretched, either to offer help or, I thought cynically, to ask for payment. Someone had placed coins in his palm, which no doubt the priests and priestesses would collect at the end of the day.

I toyed with the idea of pulling a condom out of my

wallet and placing that on the god's hand. Any bastard who thought I should be mated to Max Crane obviously had a sense of humour.

"Careful with that." Bain's words drew my attention away, to the guards who carried the box into the temple.

"Brothers...and sister." A priest with a completely bald head, including eyebrows and lashes approached, palms pressed together. His face was round, as was his belly and his lips were full.

Apparently the temple took good care of its own.

Bain bowed. "Brother—"

"Harold," the priest said down his nose.

"Ah," Bain said as if he knew that already. "Brother Harold. The Keeper has sent a gift to the temple—"

"Gifts don't go to the temple, good sir," Harold interrupted with a sniff. "They go to Hades. We are merely the ones who keep it safe."

A flicker of annoyance crossed Bain's face, but it was gone in a heartbeat, replaced with his usual indifferent demeanour.

"Of course, my apologies. I am just the humble head of the Keeper's bodyguard, sent to deliver this gift on the Keeper's behalf."

I bit back a laugh at the look on the priest's face. He clearly didn't miss that Bain had left out the respectful title of 'brother'. On top of that, the head of the Keeper's bodyguard was no small matter. Unless I missed my guess, Bain's reputation preceded him, regardless of any title.

Harold cleared his throat. "Bring it this way." Shoulders back and with another sniff, he turned and stalked toward a doorway with enormous columns to either side.

"Should you be antagonising him?" I whispered. "If they're plotting to—"

Bain cut me off with the faintest shake of his head. In the

same moment he nodded toward a couple of priestesses who stood to one side, pretending as though they weren't watching.

When I looked directly at them, they looked away, but not before they exchanged frowns.

Even here, they obviously knew what I was. I suspected they'd throw me out on my ass if they could. If we weren't facing the other direction, I would flip them both the finger. Maybe two fingers. One each.

"Brother Harold," Bain said loudly. "I have a personal donation to make."

I glanced over at him and gave him a confused look. What the fuck?

I was halfway to assuming I was the gift, when Bain drew out the cloth-wrapped knife and offered it to the priest.

Harold accepted it and drew the cloth aside. Either he was an exceptional actor, or he had never seen the knife before.

"Hades thanks you, brother," the priest said and closed the cloth over the knife. He tucked it into a pocket and waved the men holding the box into a large room.

Bain and I followed, but not before I looked back for the two priestesses. I saw no sign of them. I wasn't sure if that was a good omen or a bad one. Hades knew what they might be planning.

I stayed near the door, my back to the wall, while the guards lowered the box onto a wide table and stepped back.

The room we stood in was simple in comparison to the rest of the temple. It had no windows, but two doors. The one we entered through and one on the opposite side which was fitted with a huge lock. The kind you see in movies about bank heists. The Vault's vault. Or one of them at least. Presumably the Keeper and the Alpha had their own.

The Council had one too, although I was forbidden to

step foot inside. Me and everyone else not authorised, which were only the councillors themselves. That hadn't stopped me from peeking in once or twice, before the door was shut in my face.

Max Crane found that hilarious, before I tripped him and he fell on his ass. I was lucky no one else saw. Max's pride kept his mouth shut, or I would have suffered a few blows of his father's cane. He wouldn't have held back anything if he got the chance to belt the shit out of me. I made sure I didn't give him a chance. No way he was getting that kind of satisfaction.

I considered the implications if they were really dead. I wouldn't shed a tear, but I suspected I couldn't hide out here and avoid the fallout. For once, I actually hoped they were alive. I wished for giant boils on their asses, but I didn't want them dead if I got caught up in their shit. Life was too damn short for that.

"Please do the honours," Harold said. He gave a nod of his large head, which doubled the number of his chins for a moment. His gaze was fixed on a tall, slender priest who looked half his age.

Dispensable was the word which came to my mind. If the box was fitted in some way with a trap, the young brother would set it off first. Harold was a real hero. Not.

The brother's mouth twitched with obvious nerves, but he stepped forward and lay his hands on the top of the box.

Dex's guards moved back to stand beside Bain. If there was a trap, they would all be caught in it as well. So would I. I kept an eye on the door, feet ready to bolt if I needed to. At the same time, I got ready to draw a shit load of power to shield myself.

Hands trembling, the brother undid the latch on the left side of the box, then the right. He paused, during which nothing happened. He took a noisy, wheezing breath through his nose and opened the box slowly.

I craned my neck to look around Bain. Nothing nasty jumped out, as far as I could see. No baby dragons ready to make their first meal of those gathered in the treasury. No angry cats seeking vengeance on those who would dare to stuff them in a box. Not even a stray scent of anything but gold and a hint of…

I squinted. At least half a dozen dragon scales sat on top of a pile of gold and silver coins.

I was tempted to poke at them and see if any held remaining power. I swallowed and stuffed the urge down. If anyone here was trying to test me, they would be disappointed.

From the look on Harold's face, he was anything but disappointed. He touched a scale with reverent fingers, eyes wide with unbridled greed.

Gifts go to Hades, my ass, I thought. If the temple wasn't lucky, Harold would snatch up a fistful of scales and gold and run from the Vault on the next train. Of course then his fate would be decided by Hades. That alone would keep him here. Well, that and the fact he could spend the gold just as easily from here on whatever projects the temple saw fit.

"The Keeper is very generous," Harold declared. "And you as well." He pulled the knife back out and laid it across the pile of gold. "Very generous indeed. We will ask Hades for his continued good health."

"And that of the Alpha," Bain reminded him.

Harold blinked. "But of course. We ask Hades for that with each breath we take."

I bit back a snort and Bain even looked amused for a fraction of a moment.

"Good brother," Bain went on, "myself and the Keeper's

guest would like to attend the altar and give our own thanks to Hades."

When Bain jerked his head toward me slightly, Harold looked surprised. He recovered quickly and favoured us with a greasy smile.

"Certainly. Knox will escort you."

The slender brother looked as anxious as he had before opening the box. Perhaps that hadn't been the cause of it after all. With his still trembling hand, he waved toward the door.

"Y…yes. I'd be hap…happy to," Knox stammered. With a watery smile, he stepped outside and started back toward the main section of the temple.

I fell in beside Bain and left the rest of the guards to return to the horses while priests and priestesses buzzed around the box, muttering in admiration.

"Wouldn't a bank transfer have been easier?" I asked. "I mean, why the coins?"

Bain gave me a look, but didn't respond.

I shrugged and turned to Knox. "Have you been here long?" I asked. If Bain wouldn't talk, maybe he would.

"N…not long, sis…sister," he replied.

"It's just Viva, please," I said.

"Vee…Vee…" He blinked rapidly, then frowned.

"It doesn't matter," I said quickly. "Vee is fine."

He gave me a grateful smile and led us around a corner. There, he stopped and looked back.

He drew himself up taller and any sign of trembling was gone.

My heart skipped and I reached for Bain's scent. I drew in power and let it tingle through me. If he moved a hair toward us…

"You shouldn't be here," Knox hissed, his voice free from stutter. "They will kill you, given a chance."

"They?" Bain echoed. "The temple?"

Knox shook his head. "No. They have infiltrated the temple. They seek to influence…events."

"You seem to have infiltrated it yourself," Bain said dryly.

Knox flinched, barely enough to be noticeable. "I'm the Alpha's man. I'm watching—" He slumped back down again as a couple of priests rounded the corner. "Th…this relief wa…was carved a hu…hundred years ago."

The priests passed without a glance in our direction.

Knox's tongue darted over his lips. "They believe a man who cannot speak clearly also cannot think or hear. They pity me, while they let me go almost anywhere."

"I assume they would kill you too, if they knew?" I brushed my fingers lightly over the relief as though that was all we were talking about.

"Basically, yes."

I shuddered. Whatever was going on must be bad, for him to take a chance like that.

"What more can you tell us?" Bain asked.

"The…the relief is…is said to be Hec…Hec…"

"Hecate?" I suggested. I sensed more people passing behind us, but didn't turn to look. Instead, I played along with the game. Whatever was going on here, Knox might be our only way to find out.

"Yes, that's right," Knox agreed. "Perhaps we can meet later and I can tell you more." He spoke low, furtive.

"I would like that," I replied. I turned slowly now, my interest in the relief worn out already, in spite of the fact it showed the Goddess of Magic, and therefore witches. That was a strange thing to find here, but not the strangest thing I had seen recently.

As surreptitiously as I could, I glanced around. "Can you tell me anything about the Covener's family?"

Knox responded with a surprised double-take and barely

imperceptible shake of his head. "If there is anything to know, I haven't heard."

I exhaled softly and let out the power I held. Bain must be right, the shoemaker had goaded me into a reaction and I fell for it, scale, tail and talons.

"We should worship now, before someone thinks it odd that we're standing here talking," Bain said.

"Y…yes." In spite of us still being more or less alone, Knox fell back into his persona. It was probably safer that way. If walls had ears, then temple walls likely had a metric shit ton of them.

"I'll show you wh…where." He slumped and walked with an uneven gait toward a wide archway. Beyond that lay the familiar shape of a stone altar. Stone benches, each worn down from years of asses, sat in lines, facing the altar. Many of the benches were occupied, as was the small section in front of the altar for worshippers to kneel.

Knox led us to the last row, where our backs would face the wall.

Bain nodded his approval at the choice and sat. He bent his head and closed his eyes.

I was certain all his other senses were on high alert. Mine recoiled at the smell of human sweat, anxiety and fear. The latter might have come from me.

I placed my hands in my lap and curled them tight, as though that might help.

Honestly, the sandalwood scent of Bain and a hint of bergamot from Knox steeled my nerves better than anything else could have done. I clung to a finger-full of power and held it close. Hades knew I might need it at a moment's notice.

"Hades, forgive the souls of those who gather here." A priestess spoke in a bored monotone from beside the altar.

If I were a god, I'd probably yawn and find something

more interesting to do. As it was, I struggled to pay attention. That, I knew, was dangerous. My mind could wander in a dozen different directions and distract me while someone approached us.

I forced myself to focus, not just on the words, but on the room itself.

No one moved or made a sound until an older man at the front of the room leaned on the woman beside him and began to snore.

I bit back a laugh and glanced sidelong at Bain. A faint smile graced his lips.

So that was what it took to make him show some emotion. What would it take to make him laugh? Why in the name of any gods did I care?

I told myself I didn't. I just saw him as a challenge, like learning to use a bow. Truthfully, I should be more worried about looking out for myself, rather than worrying about what amused anyone else.

"Go in peace," the priestess said in conclusion. She looked relieved to be done with what she apparently found a boring part of her day.

The worshippers rose. Several didn't bother to hide a yawn.

"Having to sit still is hard," Knox muttered sarcastically.

I rubbed my nose to hide a smile. When he spoke without pretending to stutter, he was certainly more eloquent. He had a pleasant speaking voice, and confidence when it wasn't masked by caution. If he wasn't really a priest, then what was he? Or who?

I itched to ask, but held my tongue. Time would come for that, if Hades allowed. If he didn't, I would have to make it come, but not right now. This place felt like a nest of spiders. Silent, but creepy as fuck.

"Ah, Brother Knox," the priestess approached before they

could step out the door. "Have you come to learn how to speak to the worshippers?"

"Sis...ter D...Dolores." Knox gave her a shallow bow. "I wouldn't pre...pres...pres..."

"Presume?" She looked down her nose at him. "Of course you wouldn't. I'm surprised you're entrusted with such important guests." She ignored me, but turned an ingratiating smile to Bain. "Perhaps I could show you around the rest of the temple, *brother?*"

Bain's eyes quirked slightly. "Thank you, ah, sister." Had he forgotten her name already, or was he pretending? "We have important business we should get to. Thank you for your...hospitality."

Dolores' eyes flashed and she glared daggers at me. She clearly placed the blame for the rejection firmly at my door.

I gave her a dry look in return. At another time, I might have told the other woman to fuck off.

The Vault was nothing if not an exercise in biting my tongue. And making enemies without doing anything, apparently. I almost suggested he stay and humour the priestess while Knox and I talked, but thought better of it.

Dolores seemed like the type to push straight through the door if it was open, even a crack. Not to mention the idea of Bain screwing anyone but me annoyed me for some reason. He was free to do whoever he wanted. And yet...

"Yes," I said finally. "We shouldn't keep the Keeper waiting any longer." I stuck out my chin, faked a haughty look, and swept past the priestess without another glance.

Dolores stepped back and muttered, but I ignored her. This behaviour was probably what they expected of a witch, so I might as well give it to them.

"S...sorry sister." Knox didn't sound sorry at all. If Dolores had a response, I didn't hear it.

"Please excuse us, Brother Knox," Bain said. "I'm sure we'll see you again, Hades willing, but we must get back. It's time for Viva's nap. You know how witches get when they're tired."

I shot him a look. Maybe I should tell him to fuck off instead.

His expression was completely deadpan. I was almost certain he was teasing, but he let nothing show.

"Yes, we're likely to destroy a building or two, just for shits and giggles," I said. I tossed my head and strode toward the front door leading out of the temple. There, let Bain stew on that for a while.

"I hadn't realised you had a sense of humour," Bain remarked as we neared the bikes.

"Who said I was joking?" I accepted help from one of the guards to get into Bain's bike and pushed my helmet onto my head.

"I could toss you in the ocean right now if you like," Bain said. If he was serious at all, I couldn't tell. As usual, his face was as blank as a stone wall.

"I'm sure you would if you could," I retorted.

"Who says I can't?" he asked. "You just threatened the safety of the Vault. For all I know, you meant it. You might do it if you get as bored as you obviously were during the services. Witches aren't known for their patience."

He was right, I was bored, but I wasn't as out of control as he seemed to think. In fact, I was both in control and being controlled. I had no say over much of anything here, apart from my own actions. Even that was limited.

"You're judgmental for someone who agreed I'm part shifter," I said bitterly. "I told you whose side I'm on."

"That could change," he pointed out.

"Not while shithead and shithead junior are still in charge." I couldn't be loyal to them after everything they did to me.

"And if they're not?" Bain asked evenly.

I shrugged. "Then we cross that bridge if it comes. I'm part of both worlds, remember?"

Bain nodded. "And Dex seems to like you."

"I'm likeable," I said modestly.

"Possibly," Bain agreed. "Or maybe Dex is being rash. He's been known to do that once in a while."

Probably more often than that. "Isn't that treason?" I asked.

Bain shrugged. "Perhaps, but he would agree with it."

"I don't understand you," I said without thinking. *Speaking of acting rashly.*

Bain looked surprised. "What is there to understand?"

"I have no idea," I replied. "Sometimes I think you wouldn't step a toe out of line."

"And other times?"

"Other times I think you're unaware there even *is* a line."

"My relationship with the Keeper is complicated." Bain climbed onto the bike and waited until I wound my arms around him. "He's like a brother."

Being so close to Bain made my head spin a little. Maybe we could ride off somewhere and be alone for an hour or three.

I cleared my throat. "A brother with power, who could have you executed if he felt like it?" I suggested.

"Much like your whole Council, I would think," Bain said.

His words hit close to home. In spite of myself, I flinched. "They don't just go around killing people," I said, more defensive than I intended. "If they did, I would be dead." Long since, probably. And forgotten by everyone but my family.

I fixed my eyes on the back of Bain's helmet. "Dex would never actually have you executed, would he?"

"That depends on how obnoxious I am." Bain looked at me over his shoulder, and seemed on the verge of a smile.

"Well, as far as I can tell, you're pretty fucking obnoxious," I replied smartly. "He must be extremely tolerant." I hoped so, because I had my obnoxious moments once in a while. Not often, of course, but occasionally.

Bain snorted. "You might be right there." His eyes snapped forward, toward the street in front of them.

Every nerve in my body was immediately on alert. "What is it?"

He shook his head slowly. "I don't know. Something feels…wrong."

I sniffed the air as surreptitiously as I dared, but all I found was the usual smells of the city.

Except—

I inhaled again. Bain was right, something was off. Something weird. Whatever it was, it was familiar, but not enough for me to put my finger on it.

"Try to act naturally," Bain said.

I frowned at him. "I thought I was," I whispered.

He glanced back at me.

I sat up straight and fastened my helmet. "Perhaps we could get going. I find myself tiring."

"Yeah, good idea," Bain replied. He started the bike and headed down the road slowly. The other bike followed a moment later.

I bounced uncomfortably over a pothole, but managed to hang on to Bain and stay on the seat.

The street twisted to the right, then headed upward. People hurried to move out of our way. More than one glared or cursed even after they saw the uniforms of the Keeper's bodyguard.

The higher we went, the stronger the strange smell became.

Something in the back of my mind clicked and I gasped.

"Bain, I know what the smell is—"

A shadow passed over our heads.

"Let me guess," Bain said dryly. "Is it a dragon?"

I watched, mouth an O, as the huge beast wheeled around. Scales of green and brown glittered in the morning sun. Wings which ended in wicked-looking spikes rose and fell slowly. Narrow eyes sat in an elongated reptilian face, like a massive snake, with needles for teeth.

"It just so happens it is," I said, much more calmly than I felt.

Bain drew the motorbike to a stop. "Get off and get into the doorway of the building beside us," Bain said, his voice loud enough to address all of his men and me.

I tore my eyes off the dragon, who had tucked back its wings and fell into a slow glide toward us. "What are you going to do?"

"Keep you safe," Bain snapped. "Do as I say." He slipped down from the bike and stepped away from it.

I inhaled as much power as I could hold, but slid down from the bike. I followed the other guards into the relative safety of the doorway, but kept my eyes on Bain.

Gradually, I became aware of the sound of screaming. Had the dragon attacked people in the city? Perhaps the fact that the dragon—I wasn't sure if the creature was male or female—was headed straight for us was nothing more than a coincidence.

"I've never heard of a dragon behaving like that," I said to the guard beside me.

"They usually don't," he replied. He ushered me further into the doorway and placed himself between me and the dragon. "They stay away from people, unless they're alone and easy to grab."

Like Bain?

I peered around the man, my heart in my throat.

Bain stood in the middle of the now empty street, knife in hand, eyes on the dragon as it drew closer.

"He looks hungry," said the other guard, a man with a large nose.

"Yeah, it looks like the dragon could eat too," a third guard, this one with greying hair which hung in a braid down his back, agreed.

The first guard snorted at the attempt at humour.

I shook my head. They all seemed happy to stand back, make jokes at Bain's expense, and watch. Would they let their leader be killed and do nothing, just to keep me, and themselves, safe?

I glanced around the tense faces. In spite of the joke, the guard with the braid looked hard-faced, like a cliff watching the tide pound a rocky beach. Beside him, the guard with the large nose looked terrified, and younger than me. No battle hardened old man then.

"He can handle himself," the guard closest to me said softly. "Bain," he added when I gave him a sharp look.

"Alone?" I snapped.

"Yeah." But he didn't look as confident as he sounded.

"We can't leave him out there," I insisted.

"Orders are orders," he said simply.

That made me pause. He was right, but Bain didn't command me, not exactly. He might yell at me later, or Dex might. They may send me back to the Council, but I couldn't stand by and do nothing.

I slipped past the guard and back toward the street.

"Hsst, don't be stupid," the guard hissed.

I ignored him.

"I told you to stay put," Bain said when I got closer.

"Fuck that," I replied.

He hadn't taken his eyes off the dragon for a moment. He must have sensed me coming.

Two could play at that game.

I inhaled the scent of his fear, but that was all but overwhelmed by firm resolve and duty. Stupid man. He should run and hide with the rest of them.

I tore my eyes from him and looked to where the dragon flew in a lazy circle overhead.

"Like an animal circling its prey," I whispered.

"Exactly. He's biding his time. Would you get back behind the guards?" Bain spoke as if we were having a friendly conversation, but his tone held an edge of tightness.

"Only if you do," I replied. "You know I can take care of myself."

"I do, you do," he agreed. "Does the whole of the Vault need to?"

"If it means keeping the city safe," I said, but now I was unsure. People had already gone to some effort to see what I could do. What would happen if everyone knew? I might become as big a target as the dragon.

"You have no idea what's at stake, do you?" he asked.

"Why don't you explain it to me?" I said reasonably.

"I can't do that if you're dead," he said.

"You can't if *you're* dead," I pointed out.

"Touché," he said dryly.

"Then let's—"

I was interrupted by a terrified squeal and a shout of frustration. The urgent clatter and thud of hooves and feet was followed by the sight of a horse bolting down the street, its rider in pursuit.

The dragon's wings snapped back and he fell into a steep dive.

"Look out!" For the second time in a few hours, Bain shoved me down onto the road and threw himself over me.

My shoulder hit the tar hard enough to send a jolt of pain right through me. I cried out.

The dragon soared over us, so close I could have reached out a hand to touch his scales.

I drew magic from the scent of him. For a moment, his scales glowed like sand dragon's had in my hand.

The dragon grabbed the horse in his powerful talons. The terrified animal squealed, legs pawing to find the ground.

I lost every drop of power when the dragon shook his enormous head, shaking the horse so hard its neck broke.

The sound echoed like a crack of thunder.

"Oh shit." I bit back a sob and lifted my head to watch the dragon fly off, the poor horse hanging like a sack of potatoes, saddle and all. "Poor thing."

"Are you all right?" Bain rolled off me and pulled me to my feet in one smooth motion. "You're bleeding."

I touched my cheek lightly. I must have hit a rock or something sharp when Bain pushed me down. "It's nothing," I said absently. "I guess the dragon was hungry." My stomach turned at the idea of the horse being a snack.

"Better the horse than us," Bain said. He didn't look as though he believed it. "We're going to need to find out why he came here at all. Dragons usually avoid cities and people."

"He must be desperate if he did then," I concluded.

"Very desperate," Bain agreed. "I should get you back to the residence before you do something rash."

"Funny," I gave him a wan smile, "I was going to say the same to you."

He smiled faintly. "If you ever risk yourself like that again…"

"You'll what?" I asked.

He shook his head. "I don't know, but I don't think you'll like it." He turned on his heel and headed toward his men.

"Promises, promises," I muttered and followed along.

10

"A DRAGON?" Calista looked astonished. "This far north?"

"Yeah. A hungry one too apparently," I said. I winced as Zophia touched my cheek lightly with a warm, damp cloth. "He took a horse for a snack."

"It was probably an entire meal or two," Calista said distractedly.

"Well that makes me feel better," I muttered. At least it hadn't snatched me or Bain. What was he planning to do with a knife anyway? Surely his shifter form would be a better weapon. Unless he shifted into a cute female dragon. I had no idea what his animal form was, but my money was on a lion or tiger. Something big and fierce, but graceful and beautiful.

Zophia grinned.

When I looked questioningly at her, she said, "I'm sorry, but it does mean the dragon won't be back for a day or two."

"I guess that's a good thing," I said. The horse wouldn't be feeling any pain either, so there was that.

"Yes it is, now keep still while I clean this up." Zophia dabbed at me again. "Bain should learn to be gentler."

"I'm sure the next time he has to push me out of harm's way, he'll keep that in mind," I remarked. His protectiveness was nice and all, but one day he had to learn I really could take care of myself. And him as well if need be.

"You certainly have had an eventful day," Calista remarked. "Knife attack, temple visit, dragon attack."

"I hope to have a more boring life in the future," I said. "That was more than enough excitement for one day."

"You'll turn Bain's hair grey," Dex remarked. He stepped into view and leaned against the doorframe, arms across his chest.

"I'm reasonably certain that's your job, nephew," Calista said affectionately.

Dex chuckled. "I think you might be right there." He looked toward me and cocked his head. "Are you all right?"

"I'm fine," I replied. I assumed Bain filled him in. Had he told the Keeper every detail? Judging by Dex's expression, he had. Then he knew about Urla and what she said about the Council.

I waited, but Dex said nothing. Nor did he seem especially worried. Concerned about me, yes, but not rattled by the day's events. Not a man troubled by the death of his newest allies and the potential for unrest so close to home.

He nodded and gave me a lopsided smile. "You won't try to take on any dragons in the future, will you?"

I fixed him with a firm gaze before I replied. "Actually, I was going to get myself a bow and go out hunting." For a moment I thought my response might have made him angry, but then he laughed.

"It's true what they say about witches."

I bristled. "And what is that?" I mean really, what *didn't* they say, but I wanted specifics here.

He lowered his face and looked at me from under his brows. "That they're brave."

"Ah." I didn't believe for a second that he intended to say that. I decided not to call him out in front of the other two women. That could wait until later.

"I would bet Bain had some other words." Zophia tossed the cloth into a bowl and handed it to Czari, who hovered nearby. The servant insisted it was her job to clean up my injury, but Zophia wouldn't let her. She'd taken the bowl right from the woman's hands and shooed her away.

I wanted to tell them I could heal it myself, with a little power, but I kinda liked them fussing over me. I wasn't used to having friends who cared. Not since the mating ceremony.

"Perhaps one or two," Dex agreed. "You know what Bain is like."

"Indeed we do," Calista said. Did she sound disapproving? "He was always the honest one. To a fault, some may say."

"Better honesty to my face than a knife in my back," Dex said. He turned to me and smiled. "I thought you might like to listen while we talk to the shoemaker."

I was so surprised I almost fell out of my chair. "Of course! Um, I mean, yes please."

"So polite." Dex looked amused. "Come on then." He gestured toward the door, but his gaze flicked toward Zophia and Calista. "I'd appreciate your discretion, as always."

"Our lips are sealed." Zophia stretched languidly in her chair like a cat and yawned. If I had to guess, I would think she shifted into a black cat.

"Naturally," Calista agreed. I had no idea what she might become, but I bet it was awesome.

He nodded and closed the door to the woman's sanctuary behind us.

"What was that about?" I asked, my voice low so the bodyguards who fell in behind us couldn't hear. At least in theory. They probably had wolf hearing, or something.

"What do you mean?" Dex asked. He opened another door and ushered me through. Another door or two and I was lost already.

"I'm sure everyone's heard about the dragon already," I replied. "What else is there for them to share?"

"You didn't tell them about the—" He looked at me meaningfully. He didn't seem to fully trust the guards who watched his back. Or the walls and their ears.

I assumed he was referring to Urla, and her suggestion that the Covener was dead. They knew about the attack on me, but that was all.

"I didn't get a chance to," I replied. "No doubt the whole place will know before too long."

How many people saw the shoemaker brought to the residence? Gossip and speculation would spread faster than fire in the sugarcane fields of Queensland.

"They'll know what they *think* they know," Dex said mildly. "Or what they're told."

"You want me to leave the telling to you?" I guessed.

"If you think that would be best."

I rolled my eyes. "At the moment all I know is what everyone else knows, which isn't much."

I glanced back toward a window, meaning to admire the garden outside. In the corner of my eye, I saw one of the guards jerk back as if caught out listening.

The temptation to turn around fully and glare was strong, but I resisted. Instead, I turned back ahead and looked sidelong at Dex. If he noticed anything, I couldn't tell, but I had a feeling he hadn't missed it.

"With any luck, we'll know more soon." Dex opened a smaller door and led me down a flight of steps.

The idea of having a potential enemy at my back while making the descent was disconcerting to say the least. Instinctively, I drew a few drops of magic from the warm scent of cinnamon from Dex and prepared to defend myself or break my fall.

Hades, I was becoming paranoid. Or vigilant. The two things weren't so different.

We reached the bottom of the stairs without incident and Dex waved at the guards to walk ahead of us instead.

"I wouldn't want anyone to jump out at us," he said lightly. He grinned as though amused, but his eyes suggested he knew exactly what he was doing. If he hadn't seen the guard's inadvertent movement, he was aware of something amiss.

I recognised the slight curl of the fingers on one hand. He expected trouble and was ready.

His other hand, he pressed lightly to my back. His thumb stroked my spine once, twice, and my mouth went dry. Apparently trouble wasn't the only thing he was ready for.

"I've had enough surprises for one day," I agreed. I smiled brightly, but knew it didn't reach my eyes. No, those were wide while I tried to suppress the sudden spike in desire which coursed through me. So much for vigilance.

"Keeper," Bain stepped out of a side room and nodded. His face was damp and slightly red, as if he'd recently washed it, but he still wore the same clothes he'd had on all day. Anxiety showed in the slight lines around his face, but that was all the emotion he showed.

Was he anticipating some kind of punishment for letting me get in harm's way twice? Three times if the potential for trouble at the temple was added to the list.

"Everyone is being formal today." Dex clapped Bain on the shoulder. "Is the prisoner ready?"

"Yes, sir," Bain replied. "She's restrained. For her protection as well as ours."

I assumed that meant they wanted to keep Urla from harming herself before we got any answers from her.

"Very good, Bain. Remind me to give you a promotion." Dex clapped him on the shoulder.

"To what, Keeper?" Bain asked.

Was that an attempt at humour? I cocked my head at him.

Dex scratched his forehead. "Good question. I'll think about it. Maybe a new title."

"Dragonbane?" I bit back a smile.

"Wasn't that the title you were after?" Bain asked. He blinked at me slowly.

Dex chuckled.

"How about Vault comedian?" I asked. I wasn't sure if I wanted to stick my tongue out at Bain or glare at him. Or kneel in front of him and suck his—

Dex laughed more loudly. "You could share both titles."

"Jester Dragonbane," Bain mused. "A name to strike terror into the hearts of young children for a century to come."

I snorted. "It's all yours."

"You're too gracious, milady." Bain's mouth twisted slightly with sarcasm.

"So I'm told." I smiled sweetly.

Bain opened the door to a cell near the end of the row.

Most of the other cells we walked past were empty. Dust was the occupant more often than a person. Several contained boxes, all closed so I could only guess at the contents.

The one or two people I saw seemed to be asleep. Maybe recovering from the hunt celebrations in a place they wouldn't cause havoc. It wouldn't be the first time cells were used to house the intoxicated while they sobered, it would probably not be the last.

"Gordon, Lewis, you should go in first," Dex said lightly. He nodded toward the two guards and stepped aside with a flourish.

They might have missed the look which passed between the Keeper and Bain, but I didn't.

They clearly expected trouble.

I barely finished that thought when Gordon shifted with a tearing of fabric and blur of fur, and lunged at Urla.

The shoemaker let out a squeak and rolled to the side.

The guard brought up a large, pure white paw, claws extended and aimed for her throat.

Bain shifted into a snarling wolf, shook off a boot that stayed on his paw for too long, and threw himself at Gordon. He hit the white fox with a thud and they both flew into the wall.

Gordon let out a grunt and slashed at Bain's face.

Urla dropped herself off the narrow bed and rolled underneath, just as Lewis shifted into the same kind of white fox.

"Choose your side carefully," Dex warned. He stood between me and Lewis, knife in hand.

I heard booted feet running, but I acted before I stopped to think. I drew power from Dex and reached around him. With a shove, I knocked Lewis off his feet and pressed him hard against the wall.

Bain, muzzle flicking back and forth, was barely managing to fend off Gordon. Apparently the man decided he had nothing to lose. His teeth bared, he nipped at Bain like a rabid beast.

With more space, Bain could tear him to bits, but in close quarters, and with Gordon so frantic, he was forced to duck and weave until his tail was to the wall.

Bain growled and looked in my direction.

"Shit, sorry." I drew from Gordon, although his foxy scent wasn't appealing. I slammed power into him and pushed him aside before his teeth connected with Bain's cheek.

Gordon's jaw went slack with surprise, but it was enough to give Bain time to clamp his teeth on the fox's throat. The fox whined, eyes wide. His legs kicked frantically, but he couldn't break free of Bain's powerful jaws. After a minute, maybe two, he slumped. Bain dropped him, lifeless, to the floor.

I grimaced at the puddle of blood which stained the white fur red.

A contingent of guards trotted toward the cell.

I whirled to face them.

"Keeper!" The guard in front didn't even seem to notice me, her eyes were on Dex.

"I'm fine, thank you, Kerina." Dex raised a hand. He slid his knife back into the sheath at his hip and grimaced at the dead fox at Bain's feet. "It appears we had some dissenters here. Where did they come from?"

Bain shifted back into human form, knelt and pressed his finger to Lewis' neck.

"Both have been here for at least a year. They came together, if I recall." Bain looked toward Kerina, who responded with a curt nod.

"Arctic fox shifters from the northern part of the Vault," she said, as though the two men's presence was an old argument. She lifted her chin so her long red braid nearly touched her behind.

"Ah yes." Bain nodded and rose. "Well they're not a problem now." He looked toward me.

"He's dead too?" I swallowed. "Fuck. I didn't mean to…"

"Of course you didn't." Dex put a hand on my trembling arm. "He would have killed an…unarmed woman."

I was sure he had been about to say 'innocent' but thought better of it.

Urla looked the part, lying under the bed, eyes wide, but she was anything but innocent.

"But I could have—" I caught a look from Bain and closed my mouth.

"Do you want to sit out this interview?" Dex asked. "I'm sure Kerina could escort you back to the sanctuary."

Kerina looked as though it was the last thing she wanted to do, but gave me a questioning gesture with one hand.

"No. Thank you," I replied. "I want to hear what Urla has to say." Besides, Bain was butt naked and I didn't want to miss the opportunity to admire his chiseled body and impressive dick.

Apparently that was the right answer, Kerina gave me an approving nod and stepped back from the door. "I'll have someone remove the traitors." She waved to two of her companions, who hurried forward to drag Lewis and Gordon's bodies out of the cell.

Another guard handed Bain a shirt, which he shrugged into. It fell half way down his thighs. Damn, there went my ogling. At least I won the bet I made with myself. He was a wolf shifter. I made myself a side bet that Dex and Calista were too. Judging by her hair and response to the bodies, Kerina was a fox.

Bain knelt beside the bed and pulled Urla out before he deposited her on what looked like a lumpy mattress.

"Why would those two want you dead?" Dex asked.

Urla shrugged with one shoulder. "To keep me from talking. They shouldn't have bothered, I have nothing to say." She turned her face toward the wall.

"That's unfortunate," Dex said. "Bain here loves to encourage prisoners to open up to him. Isn't that right, Bain?"

"It is amongst my favourite pastimes, yes," Bain said, his expression deadpan. "I also have no qualms about throwing uncooperative prisoners to the sand dragons."

Urla's eyes widened, but she seemed disbelieving.

"He really enjoys that," Kerina said, a hand on her hip. "So do I. There's nothing I love more than hearing people scream as they get torn apart."

Urla paled

I glanced at Kerina. Was she really like that or was she putting on a show for Urla's benefit?

"He collects the scales from the sand dragons," Dex remarked.

They were all enjoying this far too much.

"I'm sure they would prefer you don't die," I said, not sure at all. "What you said about the Covener and his family, is it true?"

Urla curled her lip at me. "What do you think?"

I regarded her for a long moment. "I think you're sure the Keeper will have you killed if you say nothing, and that you'll take your secrets with you. I also think they'll keep you alive for longer than you'd like them to."

"Yes, we will," Dex agreed. "No one else will be allowed in here." He stepped closer to her and spoke in a surprisingly menacing voice. "No one is coming to save you. However, if you tell us everything, we might even let you go."

"If I tell you everything, you'll kill me, because you'll have no need of me," Urla said. She moved her shoulders in a way that suggested her restraints were tight and becoming uncomfortable. "And if you don't, they will." Her gaze flicked toward the blood on the stone floor.

"We could protect you," Dex said.

Urla gave him a flat look of absolute disbelief. "Why would you?"

Dex tilted his head. "You make good shoes."

Urla blinked in surprise. "I make the best, but…"

"Well then." Dex stood up straight and smiled. "Answer Viva's question."

"Loosen my restraints," Urla said, soft but insistent.

Bain glanced toward Dex, who nodded.

"I assume you know by now what Viva can do," Dex said with a quirk of his lips.

Urla gave me a sullen look but nodded.

For her part, Kerina seemed unsurprised. Perhaps Bain told her about me, and perhaps she understood Lewis' death had something to do with power. At any rate, she leaned against the door looking almost bored.

"Remove them," Dex said.

Bain nodded once and held out his hand to Kerina.

From her hip, she pulled a small knife. The blade on it was only long enough to cut small things like food. She handed it to Bain and gave him a sardonic smile.

He waved for Urla to turn around, and sliced through the rope around her ankles, then wrists.

She shook out both and sat with her legs crossed at her knees, arms folded over her breasts."I don't know anything about the witch's family," she said. "I was told to goad her, nothing more. I was going to get a bag of money for it."

"Is that all?" Dex asked. "That sounds harmless enough."

A flash of relief crossed Urla's features. "Yes, that was everything."

"Horseshit," Kerina snapped. "I can tell a lie when I see one. You're laced in it."

I looked at her in confusion. Did she mean that literally? I could smell emotions and Bain could sense them. Was it possible the woman could *see* them?"

Urla dropped her arms and sat up. "I swear to Hades, that's all I know."

Kerina sauntered forward. "Why bother to try to kill you then, if that's all you know?"

Urla squirmed. "Because I saw the person who offered me the job," she suggested. "I could point them out if I saw them again."

"Can you describe them?" Bain asked.

"They—" Urla started.

"Without lying," Kerina said.

"Yes, preferably without that," Dex agreed.

Urla looked toward the ground. "It was a woman. She had long dark hair and was dressed all in black."

"That only describes half the city." Kerina turned and stalked a few steps away before she turned back. "What else?"

"She… She had a mole on the side of her nose," Urla said after a moment.

"And?" Kerina prompted.

"A northerner accent," Urla added.

"That figures," Kerina said, "since those guards came from there too."

Dex sighed. "If the north of the Vault is trying to start a war, I'm going to be annoyed."

Bain snorted softly. "Just annoyed?"

"No," Dex said. "*Very* annoyed."

"Ah." Bain nodded.

"Why would they?" I asked.

"They're a long way from here," Dex explained. "Some think that means they don't fall under the Alpha's rule. They have their own Keeper and a city smaller than this. More like a large town. It's landlocked, for the most part. What coast they do have is only accessible over the Onyx Mountains. Every now and again, they try to expand their Keeper's influence to include an accessible seaport."

"And every century or so, the Alpha has to put down a rebellion," Kerina said. She was back in her spot against the doorframe and was cleaning her nails with the tip of her blade.

"Let me guess, the last time was a hundred years ago?" I asked.

"One hundred and fifty, give or take," Dex said. "The south was busy with dragons, and drinking beer, and never got around to it."

"So this might be preemptive?" I suggested.

Dex shrugged. "Possibly."

"Would you know if they planned anything?"

The Keeper hesitated. "I hope so. I'd hate to be caught with my pants down. So to speak." He glanced at Bain and grinned.

"So you think," Kerina pointed her blade toward me, "they either assume she's the Alpha's weapon, or they want her for theirs."

My heart skipped a beat. "Fuck that. I won't be anyone's weapon," I said firmly. No way. Killing Lewis was an accident. Helping Bain kill Gordon was to save his cute little ass. I wasn't going to make a habit of it.

"I'm sure it won't come to that." Dex put a hand on my arm and led me toward the door.

I stopped and looked back at Urla.

"Which is it?" My voice was almost drowned out by the pounding in my own ears.

Urla stared back at me, unblinking.

I jerked my arm out of Dex's grip and stepped deliberately toward Urla. "Which is it?" Fury rose inside me, white hot and raw.

Urla flinched. "I don't know. I only know what I was told. They wanted to know what you could do. That was all."

"How did they know?" Without thinking, I had drawn power from Bain and Dex, maybe from the vanilla scent of Kerina, and picked Urla up by her shoulders.

The shoemaker's legs kicked as I pressed her hard against the wall of the cell.

"I don't know, I swear." Urla's eyes were wide with cold terror. "I swear to Hades, in the name of my ancestors and descendants."

"Descendants?" I echoed. "You don't deserve—"

"Viva!" Bain snapped. "Let her down."

His words hit me like a blow across the face. I let go of every ounce of power and let Urla drop in a heap on the cell floor.

"Oh shit!" I rubbed my forehead. "I didn't mean to…"

"Of course you didn't." Dex put a firm arm around my shoulders and drew me back. He guided me out of the cell, past Kerina, who watched me with undisguised curiosity. "This was very difficult for us all. It got the better of you."

"I shouldn't have let it," I said. I could have killed Urla with a flick of my power, or pounded her body to a pulp against the stone. And for what? Because I was scared of what was nothing more than a guess? An educated guess, but still…

"You raised a good question," Kerina asked. "How did they know?"

"I'd like the answer to that myself," Bain agreed. He closed the cell door, locked it and ordered two of the guards to stand watch outside. "I searched Urla's thoughts, but found nothing she didn't already say."

I looked at him sharply, but said nothing. I understood he wanted to keep his—whatever it was—from scrutiny as much as I did with my abilities. I had fucked that up. If the guards talked, the whole place would know by morning.

Dex ushered the four of us toward the guardroom. He helped me into a chair before he sat in one opposite. He took my hand in both of his and ran his thumb over my fingers as he spoke.

"Who can you think of that knows what you can do?" he asked gently. He gave me a moment to think and reply.

"My mother," I said slowly. "My siblings. My stepfather. A couple of my childhood friends. And you guys." I glanced toward Bain.

"Yes, and us," Dex agreed.

"And anyone you might have told," I said, my tone more accusing than I intended.

"Just the Alpha," Dex said. "And anyone he told. What about the Council?"

I shrugged. "Possibly."

Bain frowned. "If the Council knew, they'd find a way to exploit it."

"So no," Kerina said. "No witch is dumb enough to put someone like her into shifter hands."

Bain's frown deepened, either at her blatant bigotry, or because she was right.

"I agree with Kerina," I said. If the Covener thought I could be used as a weapon, why send me here? Unless he wanted me to help kill a few shifters. Mission accomplished if so.

"Not about witches being dumb," I added. "If they could use me, they would."

"They did," Dex said. "They couldn't have realised what they had." He gave me a hungry look that suggested he did. And now he did, he wasn't going to let me go without a fight. I wouldn't kill for him, no matter what he thought. No way. I wasn't a killer, I was just an ordinary, okay, more than ordinary, woman with powers. The fury rose again.

I wanted to pick up Dex and hurl him against a wall. At the same time, I wanted him to fuck me and tell me he wouldn't let anyone exploit me, even him. I wanted to—

I sucked in a breath and suppressed the overwhelming, conflicting emotions. Killing Dex would result in death and considerable regret. I don't know what might come of screwing him. Or Bain for that matter."

"We need to make sure they don't find out," Bain said evenly. "Witches or northerners."

Dex nodded. "You're right," he said. "We should have anticipated the attack on Urla and kept Viva away from it."

Kerina propped her booted foot on a spare chair. "They've been here for a year, and most of us would vouch for them. We couldn't have anticipated. Slade, the Watcher, is more than capable of biding his time."

"Apart from Izzy, you didn't hear anything about any trouble brewing?" Dex asked, the question aimed at both guards.

Bain shook his head slowly. "No, they acted quietly. Izzy should have given us a clue, but people like her pop up from time to time. We couldn't have known they planned anything more, just based on her presence."

"Is it possible this Slade is working with the Council?" I asked. "Or doesn't like that you are?"

"She makes a good point," Kerina said. "I wouldn't put it past the Council to work both sides. I also wouldn't rule out the possibility Lewis and Gordon were loyal until recently. If you offer someone enough money, they'll do just about anything."

"Including you?" Dex asked, an eyebrow raised.

"Great Hades no," Kerina replied. "I like my job. What would I do with a pile of money anyway?"

"Buy a small kingdom?" Dex suggested.

Kerina snorted. "I'm no queen."

Bain's mouth quirked upward slightly. "That's true."

She flipped him the finger and grinned. "Is your pubic unicorn getting cold yet?"

Pubic unicorn? I snorted.

Bain glanced down at his bare legs. "I should probably put on some pants."

Personally, I think he should have taken off the shirt and paraded around naked for a while longer. Maybe long enough to bend me over a chair and—

"Yes, get some pants," Dex agreed. "After that, you and Kerina go out to the city and ask around. See if you can find a suspicious looking woman dressed all in black."

11

BAIN

"How does she do it?" Kerina took a bite of her apple and tossed the core into the water beside the dock. A dozen brightly coloured fish darted forward to fight over it.

"How does who do what?" I squinted at a larger fish who took off in pursuit of the smaller ones. It caught up with the ones which lagged behind and swallowed them. The others darted away, apparently oblivious. Or maybe relieved they weren't lunch themselves.

"Viva," Kerina said, as though I was deliberately being obtuse. "She's powerful, beautiful..." She clearly fished for something as hungrily as the predator in the water.

"Stubborn, difficult," I added for her. "Much like you."

"The best women are," she said tartly. She looked as though all of her attention was focused on our conversation, but I knew her better than that. Her senses would be as alert as mine were.

"You might be right," I conceded.

"Of course I am." Her body stiffened slightly and her hand curled near her knife. "I'm always right."

"Except when you're not." I followed her gaze, but saw nothing more than dockworkers going about their business. I reached out to the minds of those around us, but sensed nothing out of place.

Wait—

There, on the edge of my perception, something was off.

"Someone is watching us?" I asked nonchalantly.

"They're trying to pretend they aren't, but I can see strands of duplicity around them."

I didn't fully understand what it was she did, but I believed she saw what she said she saw.

She had never been wrong yet, any more than I had. Her skill was similar to mine, in a way. Like me, she would have known Gordon intended something, if not what.

Unlike her, I didn't need to see the person.

Neither of us could see past carefully guarded thoughts. I only gleaned Gordon's intentions a moment before he shifted. Too late to stop him, but late enough to leave no question as to what the man planned. To act too soon might have revealed my abilities to those I preferred to keep it from.

Gordon, Lewis, Urla and the guards in Kerina's company; none needed to know.

While I was sure it was nothing more than enhanced shifter abilities, some might think them witch-given. That would create complications Dex and I didn't need.

I reached out with my senses and touched the mind of a man on the other side of the docks. He stood looking into a crate of fish as though interested in purchasing some.

Nearby, the fishmonger served a woman who handed

him a coin in return for a calico bag of the same fish as the predator in the water.

The man shifted from foot to foot when he came under the fishmonger's scrutiny. He mouthed something which looked like, 'I haven't decided yet,' and took a step away.

As far as I could tell, the man didn't know why he watched. Like Urla, he'd probably been paid.

"Are you sure?" I asked. "He seems confused. He doesn't know why he's supposed to keep an eye on us."

"I see what I see," Kerina replied. "Maybe he's committing adultery. Or planning to steal a fish."

I nodded. "That's possible," I conceded. "Although I don't sense any concern Hades might be watching."

"Sometimes people think with their nether regions, not their afterlives." Kerina sauntered toward the man, a smile on her lips.

I opened my mouth to stop her, but she was already out of reach. Calling out to her back would only draw attention to us. I had a feeling that was her intention anyway.

That was confirmed a moment later when she walked right up to the fishmonger and spoke loudly.

"Why are you staring at me?"

The fishmonger looked startled. "I beg your pardon, miss?"

I groaned to myself. I would appreciate it if women would stop trying to get me killed. Had I forgotten to pray to Hades today?

I'll try to do better if you let me live through this.

I strode up behind Kerina and offered the flustered man a nod.

The other man sidled away as if to run. At his hip he wore a knife, the sheath of which was worn enough to suggest he knew how to use it.

"Is there a problem here?" I asked, as though attempting to rescue the fishmonger from being accosted by the angry redhead. Perhaps I was. Kerina was pretty feisty.

"I…was just standing here and she—" He raised a thick finger and pointed at Kerina.

"He was staring at me," Kerina said. She sniffed.

The fishmonger spluttered. "I swear on my mother's life, I was not!"

The watcher stepped beside a truck which stopped on the street beside the dock.

"You were and you know it!" Kerina insisted. She pulled a knife from her hip and, before the sun could glint off the blade, she threw it. It struck the truck beside the watcher's head, missing his nose by a hair. The watcher froze.

"Sorry," Kerina said sweetly, "I meant *him*."

The fishmonger shook his head and made a hasty retreat behind his boxes, eyes wide, muttering something about crazy women.

The watcher raised his hands. "Please don't kill me. I needed the money. My family…"

He wore worn clothes and, now I could see properly, bare feet. He had the hungry look of the homeless people I saw in the human world.

Dex would be pissed. He liked to think his people were well taken care of. If not by him, then by the temples. Doubtless leaders all over the globe preferred to make the same assumption. Or pretend to care if anyone was looking, but do nothing.

It wasn't up to me to tell the Keeper how to do his job, Dex had advisors for that. Or Kerina, if she was feeling especially feisty. But this—this was something I would have to tell him myself.

Kerina's hips swung until she was almost nose to nose

with the man. She leaned against the truck with one hand, and yanked the knife out with the other.

"What's your name?" she asked.

The man's eyes, more white than iris, glanced toward me. I nodded.

"Answer her questions," I said, my tone perfectly even.

"Mason," the man replied, a quaver in his voice. "Aden Mason."

"All right then, Aden." Kerina straightened away from him. "Who paid you?"

He averted his eyes. "A man."

"Well that narrows it down," Kerina said with a snort. "What kind of man? Short, tall, pale skin, dark skin?"

"Neither short nor tall," Aden replied. "Medium skin. Like him." He nodded toward me. "A bit darker, perhaps. Brown eyes. Dressed all in black."

Kerina turned a perplexed expression toward me.

I nodded. Another person dressed in black. It may mean something, it may not, but I sensed Aden told the truth.

"How much did he pay you?" I asked.

Aden swallowed. "Five hundred dollars and the scale of a sand dragon."

I did a double take. "Sand dragon scale?"

Aden nodded fervently. "Yes, sir. A whole one."

"Show me." I held out my hand while Aden dug around in his pocket. The man pulled out a scale identical to the one I gave Dex to give to Viva, but with no hint of power left in it. It could have come from the creature hunted only days before, but I couldn't be sure.

Had someone from the residence given this directly to Aden, or had they sold it? The man in black could have bought it from any number of traders in the Vault, but I suspected otherwise.

I handed the scale back to Aden, who tucked it back into his pocket quickly and with obvious relief.

"Let him go," I said.

"Are you sure?" Kerina was one of the few who got away with questioning my orders. She did it more than she probably should, but I wouldn't call her out in the middle of the docks.

"I'm certain." I nodded.

She stepped back and put her blade away.

"Thank you, sir." Aden bobbed his head repeatedly in a series of awkward bows.

"Stay out of trouble," I advised. "Get out of the city and buy a farm somewhere." Anywhere the man in black wouldn't find him if he wanted to rid himself of a witness. We should probably throw him in a cell for his own safety, but we couldn't keep him and his family there indefinitely. Not to mention anyone else who might have been paid to watch or ambush us.

"Yes, sir. I will sir." Aden bobbed again and hurried away.

"Has it occurred to you," Kerina said slowly, "that maybe this is about you?"

I frowned at her. "What do you mean?"

"I mean," she counted the points off on her fingers, "the attack on Viva happened while you were there. Then there was the dragon and now this. Who have you irritated?" She smiled and added, "Recently."

I shook my head and almost let myself smile. "Plenty of folk, I'm sure, but none I can think of specifically. Apart from you." I gave her a speculative look.

She laughed. "If you did anything to upset me, I would just tell you. No need for subterfuge. Unless, of course, I was up to something and needed a distraction so you wouldn't notice."

"Do you?" I asked.

She tapped the side of her nose. "That's for me to know."

I sighed softly. "There's room in the cell beside Urla."

Kerina pouted. "You wouldn't."

"I would if I thought you were up to something. Fortunately, I don't. No more than usual anyway." I scanned the crowds, which had thinned since we arrived. That wasn't surprising, people often found other places to be when knives started to fly. Wise of them, especially after the dragon's appearance earlier.

"Thanks," she said dryly.

I responded with a distracted, "You're welcome. You don't really think the dragon has anything to do with this, do you?"

She toyed with the end of her plait. "Not unless someone has learned to control them. People have tried since the gods created people and dragons, but as far as I know, no one has succeeded. Yet."

"That's true, they have. I wonder if Viva…"

"You wonder what?" she prompted.

"I wonder if she could move a dragon."

"What would that achieve?" Kerina frowned.

"I don't know," I admitted. "But such a power would be formidable. An army of dragons."

"A person could conquer kingdoms with it. Or empires."

"Or a continent," I said softly.

"Only if they get really greedy," she said dryly. "That sounds like far too much work."

"Indeed it does, but when people get a hunger for power…" I ran a hand over my head. I didn't think whatever was going on was as big as that. At least not yet. This was the start of something which might get ugly if it got out of hand. It was my job to ensure that didn't happen.

"Who, though?" she asked as though thinking out loud. "Does the temple want more power? Is it Slade? The witches? Some other group or paranormals?"

"Maybe Slade wants to expand," I said. He always was ambitious. I preferred to think it was that, or even the witches, than some other group who hated shifters.

"Maybe none of these things are related and we're jumping at illusions and shadows."

She snapped her fingers. "Or that's what they want us to think."

"What do you mean?"

"Who has something to gain from us running around looking into all of these things?"

"Dex. He's getting his money's worth out of us today."

She looked at me in surprise. "Bain, did you just make a joke?"

The side of my mouth tugged upward. "I might have. What are you getting at anyway?"

"What I'm getting at," she walked beside me as we made our way toward the marketplace, "is that while we're doing this, we're distracted from other things."

"That's true," I agreed. "If they want us to look in a different direction, then which way *should* we be looking?" The question was rhetorical. I didn't expect an answer and I didn't get one.

We stepped to the edge of the marketplace and began a slow walk around the perimeter.

Within was a cacophony of noise and bustle. Sellers called out about their wares, buyers haggled and jostled for the best fruit, vegetables, leather, cloth, cheap electronics, and car parts; just about everything imaginable.

Men and women wove through the crowds dressed in the deep purple of the Intimacy Guild. The oldest organisation with the Vault. Older even than the roles of Keeper and Alpha. Each and every one of the Intimates was impossibly beautiful, apart from the knowing look in the eyes of the older ones. Men and women alike wore their hair long and loose, to hang down their backs in waves, or pin straight. Each wore a smile, which broadened each time they spotted a potential customer.

I eyed a woman who stood behind a table full of what she claimed were dragon eggs. A dubious claim at best, they looked more like painted wood. She smiled at me as I passed, but the look was a nervous one. She clearly expected me to take the 'eggs' and shut down her little business.

I wouldn't bother. If people wanted to let themselves be taken by such an obvious scheme, then so be it. She was unlikely to be the worst in the market.

"I hate this place." Kerina wrinkled her nose. "I can't look without seeing strings and cloth of lies and deceit. Only the Intimates seem to be honest."

I murmured agreement. If I let my senses wander across the crowd, I might be overwhelmed by the emotions of sellers and buyers alike.

Kerina probably exaggerated the level of deceit; many would be minor lies, such as suggesting a pair of trousers fit better than they did. That was a normal part of business anywhere.

Kerina went on. "It makes it hard to tell who might be watching us or planning something."

"This is the perfect place for them then." I said. "If they know what we do. Where better to confuse us?"

She stopped and turned in a slow circle. "I can't think of a better place."

"Nothing says 'trying to blend in' like doing that," I pointed out.

"Is that what we're doing?" Kerina gave me a lopsided smile.

"Apparently not," I said under my breath. "You could try shouting for anyone who might be up to something."

Kerina cupped her hands around her mouth, but grinned

at me through them. "Don't worry, I wouldn't do that. I can do subtle, you know."

"I never would have guessed." Over her guard uniform, she wore leather pants and jacket, which clung to her every curve. Her hair, the colour of flame, was rare for the Vault. She had a good dose of fox shifter blood inside her. Her boots ended halfway up her thighs and sported a blade on either calf. She undoubtedly wore a few which weren't so obvious.

Subtle was *not* the word I would use for her. I wouldn't have brought her here if it was. No, I wanted whoever watched us to know I knew. I wanted them to show their hand, the sooner the better. I would leave subterfuge to others. Of course, no one would approach us directly. That would be far too—

"Uh, Bain?" Kerina gestured behind me.

I turned to see a man dressed in black trousers, a loose black shirt, black boots and a black scarf over his head. His brown eyes bore into mine with the intensity of the dogmatic.

"You're looking for me?" The man's voice was gravelly, his accent difficult to place. He might have come from the south, or around the corner.

"Am I?" I asked. "Should I be?"

"How are you not sweating to death in all that black?" Kerina asked.

The man ignored her question and kept his attention on me. "You believe we mean to cause trouble in the Vault."

That was precisely what I assumed. "I've never met a mindreader before," I stated.

The man's expression became derogatory. "I do not need to read your mind. Your Keeper harbours a witch. Such an arrangement is an offence to Comus."

"Who?" I asked.

"Some think there's a god with that name" Kerina said dismissively. "That's he's somehow the son of Hades, Proteus or both."

My eyebrows jerked upward. Who was I to question the methods of deities? Brothers raising the same child was not unheard of after all.

"Comus is the one, true god," the man declared. "Born of man and Hades."

"Let me guess," I said slowly. "Someone declared themselves a messiah and you think a witch is a threat to him?"

"Ugh, religious zealots are the worst," Kerina muttered. "Tell him to crawl back into his hole and stay there."

I glanced at her and urged her to silence. "Where does one find this Comus?"

"One does not," the man replied. "He will show himself to those who are worthy. Obtain the witch for him and he will give you eternal life."

I frowned. "What does he want with her?"

The man made a slicing gesture through the air with his hands. "That is not for me to know or for you to speculate."

"If I was to 'obtain' her for him, what then?" I asked.

Kerina made a sound of disgust in the back of her throat. I didn't need to look or sense her emotions to know she was angry. With me and with the zealot.

"He will contact you," the man said easily. "He has eyes in every corner."

And ears in every wall, no doubt. Although if he had a sizable following, I would have heard of him before now. That I hadn't made him uneasy.

"What if we don't do as you ask?" Kerina asked.

The zealot fixed her with a look which would have made most people step back. Typically of Kerina, she was unfazed and simply raised her chin to stare him down.

"We have people close to the Keeper," the zealot said finally. "Obtain the witch and the Keeper may live."

Apparently that was too much for Kerina. She pulled a knife and had it at the man's throat before I could register she moved at all.

"Give me one good reason why I shouldn't kill you right now," she growled.

The zealot didn't even blink. "I do not fear death. Eternal life awaits me. However, you will suffer eternal damnation if you murder an unarmed man."

"I'll take my chances." Kerina pressed the knife enough to break the skin, but not to make him bleed.

The zealot swallowed. It seemed he had a survival instinct after all.

"Let him go," I said wearily. Twilight started to descend on the Vault. The day had been long and according to the old legends, to kill a person during the golden hours was bad luck. It was certainly bad for the deceased. I suspected it wouldn't end well for Kerina either. The zealot was unlikely to be alone and I risked the lives of others in the marketplace if I provoked a fight now.

Kerina exhaled loudly through her nose to show her annoyance, then stepped back. "A word of advice, if you threaten the Keeper, or any member of his family, you'll wish for eternal death. Instead, you'll get a nice, long, long life in a hot, damp cell."

"I do not fear any punishment you may impose upon my mortal body," the zealot replied. In spite of his words, he looked unnerved. He might believe everything he said about his god, but he wasn't ready to die for him. Not yet at least.

"I wish you good evening. Another will make contact when the time is right." He gave a hasty nod and disappeared into the thinning crowds.

"I don't know if I should follow him and kill him when

the sun sets, or kill you and bad luck be damned," Kerina grumbled.

I raised an eyebrow at her. "I didn't realise you were so attached to Viva."

"I'm not, but—" She jerked her head to the side and we walked roughly in the direction of the residence. "You're not seriously considering this, are you?"

"Consider what? Giving up a virtual stranger to save the life of the Keeper? What is the question here? Our job is to keep him safe." Yeah, like it was that simple. Dex had become attached to Viva. If I was honest with myself, so had I.

"And members of his family," Kerina said.

"Which Viva is not." Yet.

"She's a guest. What would Dex choose?"

I scowled. "He doesn't always make choices which are the best for him." He wouldn't be the first man to think with his dick, he wouldn't be the last. It wasn't just that, though. Viva was powerful and Dex liked nothing more than to surround himself with powerful people.

"It's not up to you to decide this for him," Kerina said.

I had never seen her look so disappointed in me. We had our differences, but when it came to matters such as this, she would have my back, just as I would have hers.

"If it is not, then who is it up to?" I said softly. "You know Dex would laugh off all of this and continue as though there's no risk at all."

"Probably because he expects his guards to do their job," she said sharply.

"And that is exactly what we will do," I said firmly. "Our job. You will continue to follow orders, whether you like them or not. If you fail to do that, you will be removed from your post."

She looked stung at his words, but nodded. "If you say so, sir."

"I do say so." I had probably damaged our working relationship beyond repair, but I would do what I had to, like I always did. I didn't like to be the one who had to think with my head and not my heart. I knew other people thought I was stone cold. So be it. I owed my life and livelihood to Dex, I would let no harm come to him, no matter what it took.

"We should return to the residence. We've been away for long enough." I turned on a booted heel and headed back.

12

BAIN

"ARE YOU CERTAIN ABOUT THIS?" I asked.

"Aren't I always?" Dex replied. He straightened his sword belt and gave himself a nod in the mirror.

Usually," I agreed. "But hunting airborne dragons is dangerous." Not to mention leaving the residence for perhaps days.

Dex turned and grinned. "That's half the fun. The thrill of the chase."

"The potential to be eaten," I pointed out. "Or clawed to death."

"Would you prefer I curl up on a chaise in the shade and read a book?" Dex chuckled.

"Yes, I would prefer that," I agreed. "I can find you a good adventure book. Maybe one with pirates."

Dex laughed harder and shook his head. "You've missed your calling, my friend. You should have been a nursemaid."

He snapped his fingers. "It's not too late to change jobs, but I'd have a Hades of a time replacing you. Maybe Kerina—"

"I don't want to be a nursemaid," I said firmly. "I also don't want to scrape your remains off a dragon's talon." Nor did I want to do anything which might put the Keeper at risk. That included leaving the residence. Staying might be dangerous as well, but here I was more confident I could ward off any threats until I decided what to do with Viva.

I glanced around at the servants who bustled around the Keeper's quarters. I had known all of them since I was a kid. Many I used to play with in the residence gardens, or the streets of the Vault. I liked to think I could trust all of them, but right now I could barely trust myself.

Kerina hadn't spoken to me the whole way back to the residence or when I saw her in the dining room off the kitchen that morning.

She made it clear she couldn't trust me either.

I sighed softly.

"All right, out with it." Dex planted his fists on his hips and looked at me with concern. "You've been stomping around like a headless elephant all morning."

"I'm reasonably certain elephants without heads don't stomp," I said dryly. "Or do much of anything."

"Possibly not, but you do. You're usually excited at the idea of a hunt." Dex cocked his head. "It's usually your idea."

"That's true," I conceded. "But after all the strange happenings and talk of unrest, do you really think it's a good idea to go?"

"Wise?" Dex rubbed his chin. He looked as though he hadn't shaved for a few days. "We need to know why a dragon attacked the city and flew off with a perfectly good horse. Thank Hades that was all he did." At least, we had received no reports of injuries, death or anything other than folks seeing the dragon pass overhead. Of those reports, there were plenty. The creature caused quite the spectacle.

"You could send Trevor and a contingent of soldiers out to look for it," I said. "A company of archers, maybe a cannon. There's no need for you to go yourself."

"I'm starting to wonder if it's you who doesn't want to go," Dex said lightly. "Would you prefer to stay here? I'm sure Kerina would welcome the chance to lead. You could sit in the shade with a good book." He smiled, but a flash of annoyance crossed his eyes.

"That won't be necessary," I replied, my voice tight. "My place is by your side, no matter where you go. Unless you order me to do otherwise," I added quickly. I couldn't protect the Keeper if the man removed me from my post.

Dex nodded. "I could order you to tell me what's bothering you."

I opened my mouth to protest, but closed it at a gesture from Dex.

"I won't order that. You're entitled to keep your thoughts to yourself in certain matters, as long as it doesn't impact your job. However, I will ask you one thing."

"What's that?" I asked carefully.

"Is it about a woman?" Dex grinned.

I snorted. "In a manner of speaking, yes." Not in the way Dex thought, but let him believe whatever he wanted.

"I thought so." Dex clapped me on the shoulder. "There's nothing quite like a complicated romance to drive a man to distraction. Or woman, for that matter."

"Yes, absolutely," I agreed. "I'll try not to let it get in the way of my work."

"I know you won't let that happen." Dex nodded. "You're aware Kerina and Viva are coming with us?"

I stiffened. "I'm aware."

Dex gave me a speculative look, which I interpreted as

curiosity over which woman, if either, might be the cause for the complication. "I assume that's not a problem."

"Not at all," I said. Having all three together would make it easier for me to keep an eye on them. With any luck, Kerina would keep her mouth shut. I would have to find a moment to speak to her alone and order her to silence. I couldn't afford anyone getting wind of the conversation we had with the zealot, especially Viva and the Keeper.

"Good." Dex turned away. "With Viva's abilities, I think we'd all be safer with her coming along. With Kerina's, too. The fewer of us go, the fewer can see if she has to use her power. I wouldn't trust that with Trevor. He's a good man, but I trust you with my life, and with Viva's."

I was glad the Keeper had his back to me, so he couldn't see the uncomfortable expression on my face. "Thank you," I said, with a certain amount of irony. "I won't let you down." Shit, I hoped I wouldn't. If I did, I deserved an eternity of whatever Hades might dish out to me.

"Of course you won't." Dex turned back and moved aside to let me grab his pack.

"Are you taking the residence?" I asked, relieved to be able to lighten the topic of conversation somewhat.

Dex chuckled. "Not the *whole* residence, no. Just the most important parts."

I cocked my head. "Oh? The roof? The walls?" *And their ears?*

"Clothes, boots, a book or two. A box for scales. A scale to measure the scales." Dex grinned at his own pun.

I groaned. "Couldn't you put the scales on the scales if we come back with scales? We may not. Personally, I think you should—" I paused.

"Were you about to suggest I scale back the amount I've packed?"

"I might have been," I agreed. "I prefer to leave the puns to you."

"I don't mind if you claim a pun or two once in a while." Dex led the way to the door. "Sometimes I think I'm…dragon the conversation down."

I groaned again. "Did you plan that one?"

"No, I just winged it." Dex grinned. "Puns are so much better on the fly."

"Can I claw myself out of this conversation?" I asked.

Dex threw back his head and laughed. "See, you're just as bad as I am."

"Unlikely," I muttered. If the zealots didn't kill me, Dex's humour might. I opened the door and handed Dex's pack to a waiting servant. "See that tied to the Keeper's horse." That was another bone of contention. I would prefer an armoured car or two, but he Keeper wanted to travel the old fashioned way.

The servant made a face, but nodded and hurried away with it. Hurried as much as one could whilst carrying his own body weight.

"Maybe I did overpack," Dex mused.

"Just a bit," I agreed.

"I presume you under-packed?"

I hesitated. "I never under-pack. I pack sparingly, knowing you'll make up for it. We don't want to kill the horses for a few spare shirts."

"I like to look good." Dex led the way down the corridor toward the stables.

"You could do that better if you stay here."

"Are you going to let up on that at some point?"

"No, probably not." I nodded to Czari as she passed in the opposite direction. "At least until we get back in one piece."

"It's your job to make sure I do," Dex said.

"Hence the reminders that staying here is safer."

Dex stopped and squinted at me. "Perhaps I should leave you here and take my chances alone with Kerina and Viva." His mouth was upturned, but his eyes flashed with annoyance.

I squared my shoulders. "That won't be necessary. My opinion has been made clear enough. I'll shut up about it." Truthfully, from the look on Dex's face, he might actually follow through on his threat.

"Good." Dex resumed walking. "I would suggest that woman trouble has made you uptight, but it's no more than usual. Maybe you need to spend some time with an Intimate or two."

"I'm just concerned," I replied. "I don't mind admitting the dragon scared me. I've dealt with a dozen sand dragons, but I cannot predict what *they* will do. A winged one…" I shuddered slightly. "Its mind was more—" I searched for the right word. "Chaotic. I don't think it knew what it might do until it did it. An unpredictable human or shifter on the ground, I can deal with. A great creature with talons and an appetite is another matter."

"You really were scared," Dex said, a hint of wonder in his voice. "I didn't think anything frightened you."

"Turns out I'm only mortal after all." I smiled slightly.

"I suspected you might be, but I didn't have proof until now." Dex clapped me on the back. "I feel better knowing you're as fallible as the rest of us."

"I didn't say I was fallible."

"You're quite the comedian this morning. Is it possible you've found your true calling, after all these years?"

"I wouldn't want to take that honour from you." The banter was a relief from the tense conversation of a few minutes earlier. I would have to step lightly to keep Dex from asking too many questions.

"Good call," Dex said. "I'm quite jealous of my reputation. It usually means I don't need to pay an Intimate."

"Are you bragging, your highness? Intimates need to eat too."

"Of course— Ah, here's Kerina and the lovely Viva."

"Hey," Viva greeted. Her cheeks were red as if she'd rushed to arrive at the stables ahead of us. She looked even more beautiful.

From the look on Kerina's face, she had pushed Viva every step of the way.

Viva gave me a nod, which in no way suggested Kerina told her anything.

Kerina, on the other hand, cast daggers in my direction with every glance.

Dex looked from them both to me and back again, but said nothing. Let him assume he knew what was going on. It wouldn't do him any harm. At least not yet.

I asked Hades to help Dex understand when he found out. He was going to be furious. I would be lucky to avoid the executioner, for real this time.

Dex shook his head and disappeared into the stables, presumably to choose his mount for the excursion.

A stableboy hovered toward him. "Wind is ready, sir," he said, a quaver in his voice as though he was scared of me for some reason.

"Thank you." I gave the boy a nod. He couldn't have been more than twelve. Young enough to still be in awe of his elders. He would learn, soon enough. We were all only mortal.

"Can you lead her out here, please?" I asked.

The lad straightened up, eyes wide as though he'd had a great honour bestowed on him. "Yes, sir!" He turned and trotted off.

"It looks like you have an admirer," Viva remarked. Her

hair was tied back off her face and tucked behind her ears. Her blouse was the usual loose style of the women of the residence, but she wore trousers like Kerina's. They clung to her in a way I would have found appealing if I didn't wish she wore nothing at all.

I tried not to imagine her naked, lying on my bed in front of me, hair spread across my pillow, mouth—

I shrugged. "He should look up to the Keeper, not a lowly bodyguard like me."

"Probably, but there's no accounting for taste," she teased.

I grimaced. "I see Dex's humour is contagious."

"You say that like jokes are a bad thing."

"They're not, it's just—"

"Bain is a grumpy old man with no sense of humour," Kerina said.

"Hardly old," Viva said graciously.

Kerina gave a twist of her lips. "You're right, he just acts like an old man who long ago lost the ability to bend."

I narrowed my eyes at her. "Perhaps this conversation can wait for a more suitable time."

Before I could say more, the stable boy led out Wind. The mare danced on the end of her reins.

"She's beautiful, sir," the lad breathed.

I favoured him with a smile. "Indeed she is. You're a good judge of horseflesh."

The lad beamed, then ducked out of the way as an older boy led out a midnight black gelding with snapping teeth.

Dex walked a few steps behind. "Isn't he magnificent?"

Viva moved back behind Wind, and even I took half a step away from the creature's hooves.

"That's one word for him," I replied. "Wouldn't a quieter mount be easier to manage?"

"Afraid of a challenge?" Kerina asked.

I snapped my fingers in her direction. "I knew the horse's temperament reminded me of someone."

Dex chuckled.

Viva looked unsure as to whether or not I was joking.

"I'd rather have a cranky temperament than be a horse's ass," Kerina retorted. She stalked off toward her own horse, a chestnut mare the same colour as her hair, but without the fire in her eyes.

"Are you two going to be like this the entire time?" Dex asked. "Maybe it's not an Intimate you need."

Past his shoulder, Viva looked uneasy. Was it the mention of Intimates, or something else? Not everyone was comfortable with the idea of people who made a living from selling their bodies.

I didn't think it was that though. She seemed—

I shook my head to myself and checked Wind's saddle and girth. It would be better for everyone if I didn't speculate about the woman's thoughts. Truthfully, I wanted to distance himself from her, in every way possible. What was to come would be easy if I didn't think of her as... didn't think of her at all.

"Only if he wants to get stabbed in the groin," Kerina muttered, loud enough for them all to hear.

Dex gave her a funny look, but shrugged and swung himself up onto the gelding. The horse danced beneath him, but settled when the Keeper leaned forward to pat his neck.

"See, nothing to it."

I left Wind where she stood and made a stirrup for Viva to climb onto her horse. Her mount was a brown gelding, unremarkable to look at, but with a calm eye. Evidently she thought so too, because she let out a soft sigh as she settled into the saddle.

"This one won't end up like the one on the street," I assured her.

She turned a soft smile on me. "I hope not. That was…"

"Yes, it was," he agreed. "We'll make sure the dragon can't do it again. Or take a person."

She drew up the reigns and held them as though she'd ridden all her life. "It could have been you."

"He would have dropped me," I assured her. "Once he tried to bite into me. I probably taste like old leather." Hades, why was I trying to make her feel better? Shit, now I was thinking about her tasting me.

She laughed, deep and low. "I'm sure you're not that bad." She glanced toward my groin.

Shit, if I stood here any longer, talking and thinking like this, I wouldn't be able to sit on my horse without an uncomfortable, raging erection.

"Hopefully the dragon won't try to find out," I murmured. I felt like a kid with my first crush. *Idiot,* I told myself.

"We won't let you come to any harm," Dex said in a way which suggested he'd heard most, if not all, of the conversation.

I glanced toward Dex, then snorted when I realised the Keeper had addressed me.

"Thank you, your Keeperness." I offered an ironic bow. "I feel much safer knowing you and your mount will protect me. That's certainly preferable to a company of trained, experienced archers."

Dex grinned. "Finally, you've come around to my way of thinking."

"Archers can come in useful," Viva said.

Dex held up a finger. "I've organised a bow and quiver for you. You might get to use them yet."

Viva looked surprised, but pleased. "Shit yeah. Thank you, Keeper."

"Just Dex," the Keeper said. "It's just us, we don't need to be fancy."

"Says the man who packed enough so he could look good," I reminded him.

Dex looked thoughtful. "You're right. You three don't need to be fancy. Leave that to me."

"Consider it left." Kerina flicked her braid over her shoulder and kneed her mount toward the door. "I wouldn't know how to be fancy if my life depended on it." She shot me a look through narrowed eyes and turned away.

"I wasn't going to say a thing," I said to the air in front of me. I swung onto Wind's back and leaned down to tighten the girth.

"Of course you weren't." Dex shrugged at Kerina's back and let his horse follow hers out into the warm, humid morning. "This is going to be a long journey if you're at each other's throats the entire time." Before I could speak, he added, "I am still going, even if I have to order you to stop snapping at each other." He looked away to smile past me.

"Viva, why don't you ride beside me, you can tell me all about your visit to the temple yesterday." Dex manoeuvred his horse beside hers and they chatted amicably.

A small contingent of guards, each chosen by me, fell in around us.

I rode at the back, eyes on the streets and every person we passed.

Many in this part of the Vault knew the Keeper on sight. They stopped to wave, and gawk at Viva.

Few paid any attention to me or Kerina. To them, I was just another guard, another servant working for the Keeper. No one to take notice of, in case it inflated my unworthy ego. That gave me the chance to watch their faces, empty smiles and insincere waves.

I wouldn't swap places with them for all the money in the Vault.

Dex drank in the attention and Viva didn't seem to mind

it. Kerina's lip curled slightly at the sight, but she quickly resumed her indifferent, bodyguard expression.

The road sloped down and we headed into the poorer parts of the Vault. The waving became less, but the bustle increased.

To the left, someone shouted. I caught a blur of motion in the corner of my eye.

I tensed, but it was nothing more than a child throwing a ball to another.

I glanced ahead and caught a smirk on Kerina's face. She must have seen me react. I responded with a knit of my brows and a gesture to keep her eyes ahead instead.

She rolled them, but turned back around anyway.

The further south we went, the more tense I became. The streets became narrower and increasingly flatter. Houses gave way to shops, the condition of which decreased as we rode.

We went from freshly painted signs for tailors, and cutlers who displayed their wares outside their shops, to peeling paint and grimy windows.

Dex's back stiffened, but he said nothing. Even he knew he couldn't solve all the Vault's problems. That must have pissed him off. For all his humour, he was a proud man, who hated even the suggestion of failure.

The horses' hooves clattered as we reached the city's southern canals. Sewerage from the upper city flowed in the canals before it washed out to sea. The smell which lingered was overpowering on a hot afternoon.

Even in the relative cool of the morning, the stink forced me to take shallow breaths.

Viva pulled out a scarf from somewhere and wound it around her head and over her nose. If she was as sensitive to smells as I thought, she must feel sick here.

"Keeper!" a man shouted. He looked over a pile of boxes and gave Dex a wave.

Dex's returning wave must have encouraged him. He climbed up onto the pile of boxes and began to chant.

"Keeper. Keeper. Keeper."

Others took up the chant, tentative at first, but then becoming louder.

My hand rested on my knife, but the gathering throng of people seemed content to stand and watch the Keeper pass, or walk along the street a few metres from the horses.

At least for now.

"Down with the Alpha!" a woman shouted. That was all it took for the chant to change and the mood with it.

"We don't need him here!"

"The Alpha doesn't care about us!"

"Alpha Dex!"

That last had the Keeper turning around in his saddle to stare in surprise.

I took the opportunity to catch his eye. "We should return; go back to the residence, Keeper." A scene like this could turn ugly in a moment. It would only take one—

"Long live the Alpha! Long live the Vault!"

"Your highness," I urged.

Kerina glanced back, her brow creased. She too had her hand near her knife.

Viva gave her a wide-eyed look and pulled down the front of her scarf. Her nostrils flared once before she grimaced and tugged it back into place.

Dex pulled his horse to a stop, raised a hand and waved at the crowd. "Peace, folk!" he called out, but his words were lost in the noise. He tried again, "Peace, please!"

The crowd settled enough to hear his words, but they jostled and several muttered in complaint.

"The Alpha has not forgotten the Vault!" Dex declared. "I would never let him forget. He is working hard to make an heir for his favourite part of the Vault."

A few people muttered in disbelief, but others cheered.

"Have faith that Hades is watching over us all," Dex continued. "Keep the faith, in case a lesser god would try to hold their power over us instead."

Almost as one, the crowd shuddered.

"Praise Hades," an older woman said loudly. "Praise the Keeper and praise the Alpha."

Dex grinned. "Yes, praise all three. They are intertwined, now and forever, for the good of us all."

More than a few faces in the crowd looked sceptical, but they just muttered and shook their heads.

In the middle of them, but slightly apart from those around him, stood a man whose face was covered in a scarf, not unlike Viva's. That wasn't all that unusual in this part of the city, but that wasn't what caught my attention. The man's eyes were firmly fixed on Viva. They narrowed as Dex kicked his horse and the four of us continued down the street. He barely turned his face as Viva rode past, but his gaze was completely unwavering. He didn't even blink.

Then in one moment from the next, he turned and melted into the throng.

For a moment, I thought of going after him, but I wouldn't leave Dex's back unguarded. I would mention the man to the city watch on the way out, although the description would be vague at best.

"See, nothing to worry about," Dex said once we were past the throng.

"I'm not sure I'd call that nothing," Kerina remarked.

I silently agreed and looked back. The crowds had largely dispersed, but a few lingered. If this could happen once, it could happen again. Next time we might not be so lucky. Had Dex not been there, it might have escalated.

Of course, it might not have happened at all, but I suspected it happened more often than I was comfortable with. Between the zealots and the priests, the Vault sat on the tip of a knife, ready to be sliced down the middle.

Did the Alpha know about the growing sentiment amongst the citizens of the Vault? Surely Dex had told him? Although, the Alpha might view the unrest as incompetence on Dex's part and seek to replace him.

With who, I didn't know. That was the Alpha's business, not that of a lowly bodyguard, even if I had known the Keeper for most of his life.

I had met the Alpha, but he'd always been distant. Handsome, but cold like a good sword. He had to be, to hold on to power.

I exhaled softly and regretted the deeper breath I took in. The sooner we were away from the smell, the better.

13

I UNWOUND the scarf from my face and breathed in the fresh air. The stink of the city lingered, but it was all but overpowered by the sweet scent of the ocean.

The sea was flat to the horizon. If there was any land to the west, I couldn't see it. No bruise of islands, no long bridge or tunnel for car or horse travel. No wall to mark the edge of the Vault

Nothing but waves which lapped against the sand in a gentle rhythm. It might lull me, if I wasn't still on edge.

The crowd back in the city had unnerved me. Well, not so much them as the timing. At some point in the past, I dabbed a bit of perfume on the scarf, but too long ago to be effective. In a pinch, I couldn't do more than flatten a crease in my blouse. Even that would be difficult.

The stink of shit and Hades knows what else, overpowered my senses and made me sick to my stomach. If we came under attack, I would have to bury my face in my horse's mane and hope to find a pleasant scent in there.

Failing that, I hoped Bain would throw himself over me again, so I could take it from him.

Too much could go wrong with both of those scenarios. To my relief, Dex settled the crowd and we moved out of the city, into areas with small, coastal farms.

Rows of small grains and alfalfa were interspersed with grapes and orchards of stone fruit.

Here and there, sections of field lay open in rows, with regular looking PVC pipes lying beside them.

"They bury the pipes just under the surface," Dex explained. "Water from under the ground is then funnelled through the pipes. The water drips slowly, but keeps the roots of the plants wet so they grow. Or so that was explained to me." He grinned.

I nodded. "I was wondering how they managed to grow anything this close to the desert." Not to mention why there was a desert in the first place.

"People grow crops *inside* the desert, but those are few and the danger from sand dragons is great." He seemed to be remembering something, but he didn't elaborate.

"That sounds very isolating." I toyed with my scarf, but left it in place. The sun wouldn't be forgiving as the day wore on. I wished I brought a hat. "Peaceful though, I suppose."

"It is," Dex replied. "I've been to one of the villages a few times, when they've had problems with sand dragons, or other predators. There's nothing out there but silence and their tents beside the rows of grains. They are the most warm and welcoming people though. At least, at first. After a few hours, they want their silence back."

"I don't blame them," I replied. I didn't think I'd like to be so isolated, with no restaurants or bars, and only the occasional stranger to break the monotony. You would have to *really* like the people around you.

"Where are we going?" I asked after a moment.

"Along the coast. In two days we'll reach cliffs where they're known to roost. The closer we get, the more dangerous it will become. They're highly territorial and often have young hidden in caves amongst the rocks."

"Don't tell me, you've climbed and found some?" I guessed.

He grinned. "When I was much younger and wasn't the Keeper, yes. Bain and I scaled a cliff and went into one of the caves. It was empty, but the dragons found us anyway. We had to sit there for two days until they moved away and let us escape. As it was, we barely made it down before they came after us again."

"I bet you got into trouble for that," I said. I could imagine two young, reckless boys getting into all sorts of trouble. I wished I'd known them then. I would have followed them into the trouble, and had fun doing it.

"We would have, if anyone had found out." He wiggled his brows.

"Does Calista know?"

His smile faded slightly. "I'd prefer she not know, but she probably suspects anyway. We were always up to something in those days."

"Did he ever pull you into anything?" I asked. "Bain, I mean."

Dex looked thoughtful. "Once or twice, but he was usually the one pulling me out of trouble, or trying to convince me something was a bad idea." His smile returned. "Sometimes I listened, sometimes not." He fixed me with a knowing look. "I bet you were almost as wild."

I shrugged slightly. "I might have gotten into a little bit of trouble once in a while. What kid doesn't?"

"Like what?" He seemed genuinely curious.

I looked toward my horse's mane for a moment. I didn't even know his name. Maybe that was for the best, I didn't want to get attached, in case it ended up as dragon lunch. It occurred to me that might be why we rode, instead of travelling by car. The animals could be a meal while we made a run for it.

I realised Dex was watching and waiting for an answer.

"Just the usual things," I said. "Swapping salt for sugar. Putting pepper in the bed of one of the Counsellors."

"Learning to use weapons," he added for me.

"That too," I agreed. "I tried with practice swords, but I wasn't very good with those. I wanted to learn to use my stepfather's gun, but he won't let anyone touch it. Most witches hate guns." Honestly, most witches didn't need anything but their own power, but my stepfather liked antique things, including his old pistol.

"That's good to know," Dex said thoughtfully.

I made a face. "I suppose I shouldn't tell you things like that, in case the witches go to war with the shifters."

"I won't tell anyone." He had a teasing sparkle in his eyes, but I knew he would if victory depended on it. "Any more witch secrets I should know?"

I cringed inwardly, but lifted my chin and said, "We're fierce fighters and never give up."

"I guessed that about you," he said. "I'm surprised the shifters ever dared to piss the witches off."

"I suspect that's the other way around," I said. "Most witches also don't know when to keep our mouths shut."

His gaze fixed on my mouth and his eyebrows twitched. "Nothing wrong with an open mouth," he said.

My eyes went to his groin, but I managed to keep most of my mind on the conversation. "It depends what comes out of the mouth."

"Or what goes in," he said with a smile.

"What would the other shifters think?" I asked.

His smile faded. "They would want proof you're part shifter."

"And if you can't give them that?" I asked.

The look he gave me was a very clear, 'I don't give a fuck what they think.' His desire to have me and my power was unwavering.

"I'm also a fierce fighter who never gives up," he said firmly.

"At the risk of being replaced by the Alpha?" I asked.

"One does what one must," he agreed.

"What would your aunt do if that happened?" I didn't think Calista would be too impressed.

"She would stand by me, no matter what." He seemed very certain of that. "I also have my witch allies." He seemed amused.

"The Covener might help," I replied. "But only if he could get something out of it for himself."

"I would expect nothing less from Denis Crane," Dex said with a chuckle. "Will of iron, mind of cash. Or jewels, or trade deals."

I cocked my head slightly. "That sounds accurate." He'd work both sides against the other if it was to his advantage in some way.

My tongue darted over my lips before I asked, "Why were those people calling for an end to the Alpha's leadership?"

Dex looked surprised before his expression became guarded. "People often call for odd things in the heat of the moment."

That was true, but there was more to this. "They seemed pretty adamant. Maybe the priests have been talking to them. Offering them…guidance."

"Stoking the fires of rebellion?" he suggested.

"Something like that," I agreed.

"It is possible," he said slowly. "That donation might have helped. With Hades's blessing, the grumbles will die back down."

"And if they don't?" I sensed I was walking on territory I should avoid, but I couldn't seem to stop myself. Story of my life.

"Then I'll deal with it," he assured me.

"Do you really think Slade is behind it all?" I asked. I caught the jerk of Kerina's head, as if she wanted to hear our conversation better.

"I don't know," he admitted. "I have people looking into it. Whatever is going on, we'll get to the bottom of it. At least we know to be careful for a while. I became complacent and that could have cost you your life. I'm sorry about that." His regret seemed genuine.

"Shit happens," I said. "I don't think they would have been deterred, regardless of anything you or Bain might have done."

"Possibly," he said. "I would prefer if an esteemed guest wasn't killed while under my protection. If nothing else, it's terrible hospitality."

I smiled and glanced toward the hard packed road ahead. "I would prefer not to be killed while I'm here either. Or anytime soon. I feel like..."

"Like what?"

I turned back to face him. "I feel more at home here than I did with the Council. People reply when I speak. And most people don't look at me like I'm a piece of cat shit on the bottom of their foot."

Dex grinned. "You're definitely not cat shit. Cat shifter, maybe?"

He was fishing, but I had no answer for him. If I could shift, I didn't know what it would be. If I had to guess, I think maybe some kind of dog. A chihuahua, knowing my luck.

"That's for Hades to know," I said finally. "He might share that information someday. At any rate, thank you. It's nice to feel like I have some control over my life." A little bit, at least. I could have stayed back at the residence, for example, but I wouldn't miss seeing dragons up close any more than Dex or Bain would.

Dex smiled warmly. "That's excellent. I'm pleased to hear it. One thing surprises me though."

"Oh, what's that?" I asked.

"Most newcomers want to know more about the Vault. You jumped on a train in the middle of Sydney and ended up here. You must have a million questions."

"I am curious," I admitted. "It feels like another world. Is it?"

"Not as such," he replied. "Back when shifters and witches hated each other a little less, the witches created a bubble of power. It took dozens of them and almost killed a few. It created a..." He searched for the words. "A compressed version of the world outside. Distorted too, obviously. Hence the desert. The witches declared it a failure and abandoned it. The shifters moved in and we've been here ever since. Every hundred or so years, the bubble needs to be reinforced."

"If it's not?" I asked.

"It collapses," he said. "Fortunately, it takes less power to reinforce it than it did to make it. Also fortunately, we don't have to kidnap any witches and force them to help, like last time." He frowned. "Or was it the time before?" He waved a hand. "It doesn't matter. It's history now."

"That might explain why witches don't like shifters," I said dryly.

"It really might," he agreed, as though he hadn't thought about that before. "It might also explain your existence."

I did a double take. "What?"

"Those witches were kept in the Vault," he said simply. "In case they were needed."

"So," I said slowly, "one might have met a hot shifter, fallen in love and had a fully consensual relationship."

"That might have happened," he agreed, obviously humouring me.

No one wanted to think they were the product of sexual assault no matter how many generations back it went.

"And then one left one day and rejoined the witches." Or got given away, like the Covener tried to do to me.

"I'm only guessing," he said.

"Yeah. I suppose the how doesn't matter now. Unless you have records on the kind of shifters witches fell for in those days?"

"Maybe in the back of the library," he said. "Otherwise, I don't know. There might be a way to find out. If there is, we'll track it down. Bain and me."

"Thank you, Keeper… Dex," I said. "I appreciate that. You and Bain have been…nice." More than nice, but I wasn't good at this kind of thing. I was better at telling people to fuck off.

Did I hear a snort from Kerina? I frowned at the back of the woman's head, but nothing in her posture or scent suggested she was paying much attention.

"Dragon!" A shout came from one of the guards behind us.

I twisted around in my saddle and cupped a hand over my eyes.

The dragon skimmed the horizon, just above the surf. It tucked its wings back to either side of its body and dove into the water. If it caught a fish, or any other sea creature, I couldn't tell from this distance.

"It's closer than we thought," one of the guards said.

Dex frowned and nodded. "Yes, but if it's eating fish, it might not come after us."

"It might when it sees us," Kerina pointed out. She too had twisted in her saddle to look.

"We can't help that." Dex offered me a smile, but his eyes looked troubled.

"Could that be the one we saw yesterday?" I turned further, but Bain was behind a handful of guards. Too far to have a proper conversation.

"It's possible. Does it look the same?" Dex asked.

I squinted, but shook my head. "I can't tell. It's too far away."

"I hope it is," Kerina said. When Dex gave her a funny look, she added, "If it's not, then there's two in the area. They might even plan to nest here."

Dex grimaced. "If that's the case, we'll have to encourage them not to."

"Will you ask them to leave?" Kerina gave him a sly smile.

The Keeper chuckled. "I could try diplomacy, but I think weaponry might be better." He glanced at me for a moment before he looked away.

My blood boiled. All of the niceties of the last few moments melted away. Was that all he saw me as? I was more than just a tool to be used whenever people felt like it.

When this was over, I might leave the city and travel south. I could meet the Slade guy they keep talking about, even though it sounded like he wasn't any better.

Still, if the Vault was big enough, I could hide somewhere, start over where no one knew me.

Kerina might know a place. I would ask her if I got the chance. *When* I got the chance, I corrected myself. I would make sure that happened.

Under my thighs, my horse moved restlessly, the first sign of uneasiness since we left the residence.

I leaned down to pat his neck. Did he feel my discomfort or was he aware of the dragon?

Maybe both. Animals were more aware of dangers than people. Although, like some people, they didn't have the sense to run away, and ran toward it instead.

I choked down a laugh at myself. I had walked out onto that street. I wasn't as powerless as a horse was under the talons of a dragon, but I was stupid for even thinking I could take on the creature. I asked myself why. Bain could more than look after himself.

Against a dragon though—

If it wasn't for the horse, the gods only knew if either of us would have survived. I grimaced at the idea of being torn apart by those enormous teeth.

"Keeper, it's seen us!" That was Bain, who had kicked Wind to catch up.

His words jerked me out of my thoughts.

"What—" Dex's eyes widened. He swore and all but threw himself out of his saddle. "Everyone down."

Bain echoed the order.

I slid down before Dex tossed me a bow and quiver. "Form up with the others."

I didn't hesitate. This was my chance to prove myself, and not just with my innate power. I would show them I was a badass in other ways as well.

I swung the quiver onto my shoulder and trotted over to the other archers. I ignored the funny looks they gave me. Instead, I focused on tightening the string on my bow and pulling out an arrow.

At Bain's order, we arrayed ourselves in front of a wiry coastal shrub and pressed ourselves as far back as we could. Skinny branches scratched at my skin, but I inhaled the scent of a handful of half-dried flowers and drew power as I drew my bow.

Was that cheating? Probably. Did I care? Not right now.

"It's getting closer," someone shouted. No one bothered to laugh at how obvious that was.

As one, the archers raised our bows and waited.

On the edge of my awareness, I caught the scent of vanilla, cinnamon and sandalwood, mixed with fear from the guards who grabbed the reins of the horses and led them to the relative shelter of the trees.

"Hold," Kerina said softly, when someone shifted and cursed.

Everything went still except a whisper of warm wind, the faint sound of waves breaking on sand and the beat of dragon wings. I hadn't noticed them the first time, but now they sounded loud.

The closer it came, the louder the wing beats. Did they move in unison with the rhythm of my heart, or did I imagine that?

"Sweet Hades," someone breathed.

"Hold." That was Bain this time. He must be close, but I didn't look. I kept my eyes on the dragon. It was almost close enough to dominate my vision.

The dragon grunted as though in anticipation of a fine meal. Perhaps the chance to take abundant meat back to his mate and young.

"Not today, Hades," Dex said, his voice clear and confident.

I suspected the point was to lift morale. From a subtle shift in the scent of those around me, it worked. At least for the moment.

The dragon spread its wings and fell into a glide toward us.

"Now!" Bain shouted.

As one, the archers loosed their arrows.

I was maybe a hair behind. Not enough to feel any shame or disappointment. That came a moment later when my arrow missed the dragon's wing by a fingertip.

"Fuck," I muttered. That wouldn't add any points to my badass card.

Several others' arrows found their mark in the dragon's wings and one grazed his chest.

The dragon flicked its head back and screamed, but it was more a sound of annoyance than pain. It shook off all but one arrow, which lodged in a wing sail, and banked.

For a moment, I thought he might come back around again, but he soared off in a southerly direction and disappeared from sight.

I exhaled through pursed lips and lowered my bow.

"Stand down," Bain said.

Around me, the other archers lowered their bows. They mumbled in obvious dissatisfaction at not having brought down the beast.

"It's injured, it's going to be angry," Bain said.

The way his eyes glazed, he was feeling for the creature, empathising with its discomfort.

It wouldn't have shown us any mercy, but it raised my opinion of Bain. For all of his manly manliness, he didn't enjoy the dragon's suffering.

That was kinda hot.

I shook my head and slung my bow over my shoulder. I shouldn't think that way about him. About anyone, if I planned to leave the city.

I reclaimed my horse and caught Dex's amused look. For a moment, I wondered why, but then realised I hadn't handed back the bow.

Fuck that. I had no intention of it, unless he insisted.

Besides, the dragon may return and I wanted to be ready if he did.

I climbed back on my horse, without help or much grace, but I managed to haul myself into the saddle and pull up the reins.

"I thought a dragon would be tougher than that," said one of the guards, a man named Tallis. He gave a short laugh.

"I thought we were lunch," another agreed. "What a way to go. I just got married too."

"Being a dragon's lunch might be better," Tallis said. He laughed longer this time.

I turned and arched my eyebrows at him, but he gave me an unapologetic look in return.

"Watch your tongue or you'll lose it," Kerina snapped.

That made Tallis blink and stand up a little taller. "Sorry." He didn't seem all that sorry, but he fell silent.

Kerina glanced toward me and rolled her eyes before she winked conspiratorially.

I grimaced in response. If nothing else, Tallis' attitude might make him complacent and that could end badly for us all, especially him.

He was right about one thing though, scaring the dragon off was too easy. I didn't think the next time would be. The injury wasn't fatal, unless the creature couldn't fly and eventually starved. I wouldn't wish that on him. He was just doing what creatures do; trying to survive.

"Are you all right?" Dex's question broke through my thoughts.

"Hmmm? Yes. Just reflecting on the nature of dragons."

He smiled. "That was a nice shot you got off."

I made a face. "It was crap. I'm out of practice."

"I'm sure you'll make up for that before too long," he assured me. "You handle a bow well."

I shrugged slightly. "Thank you. I'll do better next time."

"Keeper." Bain rode up on the other side of Dex. He gave me a nod and Dex a meaningful look.

Dex nodded. "Excuse me, please." He gave me a brief smile and let his mount fall back behind me. He and Bain spoke in low tones so I couldn't hear, but Bain's tone was insistent.

I only caught a word or two, not enough to make sense of it, so I gave up trying and turned my attention to my surroundings instead.

The road turned inland and meandered through a series of low hills and sparse thickets of some kind of tree I didn't recognise. The further we went, the higher the hills became. The grass which formed a sparse covering became thicker and taller.

I nudged my horse beside Kerina's and said, "I thought the Vault was nothing but desert."

Kerina looked at me in surprise and laughed. "Because the city was built on the edge of one? No, the Vault is vast. The interior is dry for a hundred kilometres, but the east coast is virtually rainforest. The plains of the south are lush farmland."

"Why have a city here then?" I asked.

"Because it's easy to defend," Kerina replied. "And because the port is on one of the best bays in the Vault. It's easier to deliver goods there and take it overland to some of the southern towns, than it would be to take it there directly. The dragons in the area make that prohibitively difficult, as well as the lack of a sheltered port."

I nodded. "Has anyone tried to…"

"Hunt the dragons to extinction?" Kerina suggested. "I imagine so. Dex and the Alpha wouldn't allow it. If their ancestors tried, they obviously failed. In a group, it would be difficult to take down more than one or two. Their mate would make you a snack before you readied another arrow."

"I see," I replied. I noted a look of worry on Kerina's face.

"You think they tried? That's why that dragon has come so close to the city?"

Kerina shrugged. "That's my theory. Someone has chased them here, or given them no reason to remain in their caves." She sighed softly.

"You don't agree with hunting them either?" I guessed.

"I don't approve of killing for the sake of killing," Kerina replied. "And I don't believe in provoking creatures with sharp teeth and talons. Self preservation—that's another matter. Then, I'll do what has to be done."

Did I imagine the dark look Kerina gave Bain?

"Why would anyone chase them here?" I asked. "Is that a part of whatever Slade might be up to?"

"Possibly," Kerina agreed. "If that's the case, they must be desperate. Otherwise, why tangle with dragons?"

"Yeah." I nodded and glanced around and up a slope. Had I not done that, I would have missed the glint of sun on steel. I squinted.

"I think someone is up—"

The ground rumbled. A couple of dozen large rocks tumbled down the incline toward the horses. Several struck the legs of the lead beasts, causing them to shy and whinny in fear and pain. They backed into the animals behind them.

My mount tossed his head and bared his teeth at Kerina's, which snapped in return.

A dozen men surged to their feet and started down the hill, swords bare in their hands.

"Hold!" Bain shouted.

I didn't mistake the thunderous look Kerina gave him this time. I was as confused at that as I was by his order. Did he mean for us to do nothing? To be killed between these hills, our bones left to bleach in the sun?

Fuck that. It wasn't going to happen. I inhaled deeply from the scent of vanilla and drew on my power.

Nothing happened.

I inhaled again and tried frantically to draw.

Nothing. It was as though I was cut off from my own power.

"And so you learn how little you know." The voice wasn't loud, but it seemed to boom down from the top of the hill.

I turned my face to lock eyes with a woman dressed from head to toe in black. Even without knowing, I understood this was the woman who paid Urla. The woman who wanted to know what I could do.

Another shifter, witch hybrid. How I knew that, I don't know, but I did.

Armed men surrounded the horses.

"They will come to no harm if you come with me," the woman said.

Kerina growled. "Let me go!" She shook her head and snarled. Her hand twitched near her knife, but she didn't pull it.

Couldn't pull it, I realised. I swivelled in my saddle.

Dex sat with wide eyes and his mouth set in a line.

Bain's face was pink, but he too seemed frozen in place. The look he gave me seemed apologetic. For what? Not acting sooner? No doubt he'd hoped to avoid bloodshed, in spite of the bare blades.

I turned back toward the woman. "Let them go." I tried to force the power to come to me.

I failed.

Shit.

"When you agree to accompany me, they will be freed."

"Viva," Dex ground out. "You're mine."

I nodded. "I know." He looked pissed, like a kid whose favourite toy was snatched out of his hand.

"She will be safe with me." The woman held out a hand, palm up to signal her assurance. "No one needs to die today."

Kerina growled again.

I hesitated for only a moment longer before I nodded and slid down from my horse.

"It would seem I have no choice," I said, to myself as much as to anyone.

Double shit. If I didn't go, this wouldn't end well for anyone from the city. Frozen as they were, they couldn't fight back.

I hated feeling powerless more than anything, but I wouldn't have blood on my hands just to save my own ass.

I placed my bow and quiver on the ground, untied my bag from the back of my saddle and swung it over my shoulder.

With a last nod at Dex, I started up the hill.

14

"Who are you?" the woman asked.

"Like you don't know," I replied. I glanced back down the hill.

Dex rolled his shoulders and raised his hands as one of the brigands moved toward him.

Bain stood nearby, back stiff as stone, face toward Keeper except for a long look in my direction.

"You said they wouldn't be hurt." If they were, all bets were off. I couldn't use my power, but I could use my fists.

"They won't," she said, as though she was talking about a bug. "My people will keep them there until we're safely away. Now, who are you?"

"I'm nobody," I gave Dex and Bain a last look, turned away and walked beside the woman, across the crest of the hill. It stretched out longer than I thought.

"Hardly," the woman snapped. "I am Helene Karman. I am hemitheos. What is your name?"

"Viva Taylor." I frowned as the woman waited. "My Latin is rusty." Okay, nonexistent. "I'm a witch too." For some reason, I sensed using the term might irritate Helene.

I was rewarded with a twitch of the woman's mouth, but that was all.

"You have spent your life denying what you are," Helene stated.

"Denying? No. Being made to feel ashamed, sure. I guess I know why now." I looked directly at Helene, unblinking, unflinching.

To my surprise, Helene laughed, a tinkling sound, but bordering on derisive. "You think you know, but in truth you'll learn soon enough. You'll learn a lot, including the full extent of our power."

"Why would you teach me that?" The hill narrowed and I had to step carefully to avoid falling.

"Because we need you."

I frowned. *Yeah, you and everyone else, lady. Get in line.* "All right, so why not just ask if I want to learn? Why the bullshit? Why kidnap me?"

Helene swept the black scarf from her head. Her hair was almost the same shade as mine, but touched with grey. She must be at least twice my age, if not three times. "Because you might have said no. And you might have suspected the witches were behind this."

"Are they?"

Helene snorted. "Hardly. They prefer to pretend we don't exist."

"You seem to know a lot about me and where I come from," I observed.

"We've been watching you for some time. When you boarded the train, we got ready."

Yeah, that wasn't creepy *at all.* "Ready for what?"

"To take you from wherever the Keeper sent you. You

managed to prevent him from doing that yourself." Helene seemed almost impressed.

I shrugged. "Maybe if I'd known you were out there, I wouldn't have bothered." That was crap. I would have done everything I could, regardless. I wasn't sure if this wasn't some kind of slavery anyway.

"Letting you know we existed would have risked exposing us. We couldn't take that chance in the human world. We had to bide our time and wait. And...be sure you were what the whispers said you were."

"You talk a lot about 'we'," I pointed out. "Who else is there?"

"You'll discover that in due time," Helene said. Her tone assured me I would get no more than that from her.

I changed tack. "Are you working with Izzy?"

Helene looked surprised at the question. "The shifter on the train? No. To my knowledge she was working with Slade."

"So, you're not working with Slade?" This tangled web was getting more knotted by the moment.

"No," Helene said simply.

"Okay." I nodded.

"Do you have something to do with the dragon attacking the city, and us, an hour or so ago?"

"No," Helene said again. "We saw the dragon and kept it at bay with the power. It may have drawn the creature to you, but I did no more than that."

I inhaled sharply. "I'm not sure why I shouldn't push you off this hill."

Helene snorted. "Because you couldn't. You lack the skill for that. In a year, perhaps." She took in my disbelieving expression and stopped to spread her arms. "You can try."

To my surprise, I was able to pull in power from the subtle lavender scent Helene wore.

Without hesitation, I threw all of my power at Helene.

It hit what felt like a solid wall of stone and bounced back hard enough to knock me off my feet.

"Shit!" I tumbled down the hill, and only stopped when I slammed hard into a rock. My arm cracked audibly. Pain shot through my arm and into my shoulder.

Stinging tears poured down my cheeks, part agony, part humiliation.

I closed my eyes and didn't open them when the swish of grass told me Helene approached.

"There now, child, it's just a broken bone."

Warmth washed up my arm and pain receded, then disappeared altogether.

"What the fuck—" I blinked my eyes open and dashed away tears.

Helene sighed patiently. "As I have said, you know very little. Have you never tried to heal anyone?"

"No." I pushed myself up until I was sitting in thigh high grass.

"Just as well. Neither the priests, nor the witches, would have been able to ignore it if you had. We can heal some things, but not our own deaths."

"Why would the priests care?" I asked. "Surely it's Hades's work?"

Helene grimaced. "Or Proteus. Some see the power as dark work, destined to bring bad luck to the hemitheos, or the injured person. Some would prefer to die rather than risk their afterlives."

"You don't really believe in the gods, do you?" I asked.

Helene laughed softly and helped me to my feet. "Not really. Most things can be attributed to the actions of people."

"Including having the power in the first place?" I tried to draw in power, but found myself blocked again. I shouldn't be surprised. Whatever this woman wanted with me, I suspected it came with a shorter leash than Dex's.

"I prefer to give credit for my power to my mother, not to a deity I can't see."

"Right." I glanced over my shoulder. "You know they'll come for me."

"No, they won't. Their leader, Bain, helped us."

I blinked. "I beg your pardon. He helped you to do this?" I must be hearing things.

"Why do you think he told his men to hold?" she asked.

"Does he know what you want with me?" The idea he might have helped plan this made my skin itch. The motherfucker.

"No. He was told nothing other than to take you to a place we could retrieve you. He did that quite nicely, don't you think? Kerina knew as well." Helene turned and resumed walking.

Power must have tied me to Helene in some way, because I was forced to stumble after her until I was close enough to walk more comfortably.

"Kerina knew?" That might explain the dark looks she gave Bain, but she had done nothing to help, no warning, no indication I shouldn't accompany them on this hunt. That stung almost as hard as Bain's betrayal. The pair of motherfuckers.

When Helene didn't answer, I asked, "What if I don't help you with whatever you think you need me for?"

Helene barely turned her face. "You will obey, or you'll be *made* to obey. I don't want to break you, but this is too important to let a kid screw it up."

Her words were like an icy wind over snow. She left me in no doubt she would shatter me if she thought she had to.

"If you could just tell me, maybe I *want* to help."

"You'll be told what you need to know in due time."

The hill dipped downward, toward a dozen hobbled horses. A man stood with them, no older than me, but with dark skin and hair. Like the others in his band, he was dressed in black, but wore a bright gold ring in one side of his nose and another in his ear. A chain hung from one to the other, across his cheek.

"Luther, ready the horses and take her bond. I'm weary." Helene wound the scarf back over her head.

Luther nodded. "Sure, Hemathea." He leapt to unhobble three of the horses and drew the reigns over their necks.

At the same time, I felt a shift in the air around me. I tried to draw and still couldn't, but now I felt compelled to follow Luther. If I could get close enough, I could punch Helene, but the damned bond kept me from stepping any closer to the woman.

That might be just as well. I didn't think hurting her would go unpunished. Helene could break my bones into pieces and leave them unhealed.

Would she go that far? I decided she might, but it was best to not try to find out. I would bide my time and wait for an opportunity.

"Do you need help?" Luther asked, his voice smooth like honey. He smelled almost as sweet, but I couldn't place the scent itself.

"Why did you call her that?" I asked. "Hemathea. Did she pay you to do this?"

"She is a powerful hemitheos, and leads us," Luther explained. He made his hands into stirrups. "She can't be queen or empress, so she is Hemathea."

I stepped onto his hands. "What if she wasn't a woman?"

"Then a Hematheo would lead." Luther pushed me up onto a tall, pale coloured horse.

"Why do you all wear black?" I settled into my saddle while he flashed me a smile.

"It makes us look mysterious."

I arched an eyebrow at him.

He chuckled. "We don't dress like this normally, just when we have an important mission. It's too hot this far south to wear it too much."

"We're not here for a social visit, Luther," Helene said dryly.

"Sorry, Hemathea." Luther gave me a wink and hurried onto his own mount.

Helene turned her horse south and kicked it forward.

Luther followed her example and my mount plodded after his.

I wondered what would happen if the horse went in a different direction, but the answer was obvious. The power would pull me off into the dirt.

Still, I was tempted to try, but Luther slowed to let my animal walk beside his.

I glanced back, but saw no one following. If there was anyone, it would only be Helene's armed men anyway. Dex and the others were probably on their way back to the city, or continuing on to the dragon caves, without so much as a second thought about me.

The idea made me fume, but I forced the anger aside. It wouldn't help me now.

"We're heading inland, in case you're worried about dragons. They shouldn't bother us there." Luther smiled as if we were old friends and not captor and captive.

"It sounds as though you're capable of managing if they attack us," I remarked. I focused on the space between my horse's ears. I didn't want to like him, but his smile was infectious. If I looked away, it was easy to remind myself he was the enemy.

"We are, but they can be daunting," he replied lightly. "And that was one. If several came after us, we may find ourselves in Hades's hands. Literally."

"You believe in Hades? She doesn't." I jerked my head toward Helene, who seemed to be ignoring us.

"The Hemathea is a heathen," Luther whispered loudly.

"I believe in gods older than Hades," Helene said without turning her head. "With age comes wisdom."

"Helene is very wise." Luther chuckled.

She turned in her seat to give him a look which made him fall silent. Apparently she didn't have a sense of humour.

Luther wasn't silent for long. He launched into a monologue about dragons and our journey south.

I only half listened, although I was curious about our destination.

"Where are we going?" I asked, while Luther stopped to take a breath. When he didn't respond, I guessed. "Slade's place? A hole in the wall that leads out of the Vault?" Helene said they weren't working with Slade, but I was trying to provoke a response, any response which might give me some answers.

"He won't tell you," Helene said.

"Because you won't let him," I presumed.

"Because I don't know," Luther said. He didn't appear to be bothered by that.

I frowned. "What happens if something happens to her?" I waved a hand toward Helene's back.

"If that's the case, then we would already be dead," Luther said lightly. "She's more powerful than two of me. You might be her equal someday..." He trailed off when Helene gave him a dark look.

I returned my attention to my horse's ears and considered what he'd said. If I had the potential to be as strong in my power as Helene, then someday I might knock the woman on her rear. The idea was juvenile, but I didn't give a shit right now. That led to another thought. One I didn't expect an answer for, but asked anyway.

"How do you get your power?"

Helene surprised me by answering. "The same means as you, through scent."

Luther nodded.

"Is there another way?" I asked carefully. I owed Bain and Kerina no loyalty, not now, but if Helene didn't know about their abilities, then I wouldn't tell her. I owed her nothing either.

"There are other forms of power," Helene agreed. "Lesser forms." She made no attempt to hide her disdain. "They are insignificant."

I might disagree. Bain's skill kept him and others alive, so far as I was able to tell. Kerina's too, if she could see lies. Neither could throw people down a hill or bind them, but they could do those without the kind of power I had.

"I see," I said finally. The land to either side began to flatten out. Green became twisted brown, stunted trees. Wiry coastal grass gave way to dry dirt. "We're going through the desert?"

"We'll skirt the edge of it." Apparently Luther knew that much.

"Shame, I was hoping to see a sand dragon," I said. I was hoping one might rear up out of the sand and make a snack out of my captives.

"We saw one on the way down," Luther enthused. He launched into a story which involved shifting dunes in the distance and one of their party guessing about the cause.

I lost myself in thought while he chattered on and on. I glanced skyward and realised we had turned slightly to the west. If we kept going in this direction, we would skim the desert and make straight for the Onyx Range.

That made sense. We could get lost in the mountains and

no one would find us, even if they were looking. Perhaps when the Alpha got word of my abduction, he would insist Dex send people to search.

The idea was so ridiculous, I almost laughed out loud at myself. Idiot, he'd probably be as happy to see me gone as the asshole Covener and his asshole son. Or use my disappearance as an excuse to make war with the witches.

I suspected Helene wouldn't bat an eye if that occurred. Whatever agenda she had likely didn't rely on the stability of the Alpha's leadership. The opposite, perhaps, if she wanted to make use of the unrest to carry out some sort of plot.

Here I am, I thought, *a pawn yet again. This time, I have no idea what game I'm being used for.*

The clattering of hooves behind us jolted me out of my thoughts. For a fraction of a heartbeat, I thought it was Dex.

That hope was dashed when I turned my head.

It was Helene's armed men, catching up with us at last.

The leader, I assumed, waved the men to a trot and then a walk as they fell into a loose formation around the three hemitheos. Did they have power too, or were they hired blades?

I couldn't tell by looking, but it was safer to assume they all had power.

"Elgar, there you are. We thought you got lost."

Elgar gave Luther an unreadable look and kicked his horse to catch up with Helene. With one hand on his cantle, he leaned toward her and addressed the Hemathea in a voice too low for me to make out.

Luther grinned and leaned back in his saddle as if he was on a pleasure ride.

I sighed. I would like to feel as carefree, but I wasn't sure I wasn't going the long way to my execution.

I sensed someone watching and turned my face enough to catch the faint shake of a head.

Only by sheer will did I keep from glancing back again.

What was Knox doing here? The apparently bumbling brother had indicated he was involved in something, but I wouldn't have guessed it was this.

Whatever *this* was.

The only thing I knew for sure was he didn't want me to acknowledge his presence. He must be here as a part of some ruse, like his time in the temple. Hades, was that only yesterday? It seemed like a lifetime ago already.

My tongue darted over my lips and I forced myself to look straight ahead until Elgar called a stop for the night.

The place he chose was a small copse, beside a thin trickle that could barely be called a stream. By the state of the ground, they had camped here before, maybe as recently as last night.

Had they sat and planned their attack in minute detail; talked about me until everyone understood their role in the ambush?

Had they laughed at Bain's intention to betray me? If I saw him again, I was going to kick him in the nuts. Before I killed him.

I slid down from my horse and forced myself not to grind my teeth. Better I focus on biding my time and waiting for a chance to escape.

"Set up a tent for the child," Helene ordered. She waved a hand in my direction and lowered herself into the shade of a small tree. She closed her eyes and let her head fall to the side.

To a casual observer, she might look as if she was asleep, but I doubted she was. She would likely have all of her other senses on alert against anyone or anything.

The soldiers and Luther would also watch me closely. The surrounding land offered little in the way of a place to hide. If anyone attacked, they would be spotted long before they reached the camp.

That also meant I couldn't run and hide, even if Luther did remove the bond.

"Don't worry, I'll stay nearby," Luther said in a tone that was clearly meant to make me feel better.

He may be a greater threat than any of the swordsmen, so I forced back a snort. My mother once told me to always look past a smile, or pretty words. The intention behind them could be more poisonous than a glare. I didn't always take my mother's advice, but when it came to Luther, I would step lightly and carefully.

I led my horse to a patch of grass on the edge of my bond, and let it nibble at the meagre blades.

"I know how you feel." I patted his smooth neck and spoke in a whisper. "I don't want to be here either." Where did I want to be then? The witches didn't want me, nor did the shifters apparently. Dex might have called me 'mine', but I belonged to him like the knife at his hip. Or a table fork. Useful until broken.

"Are you all right?" A swordsman, with a saddle in his arms, stopped to peer at me.

"Yeah, just fabulous," I said sarcastically. I drew myself up and gave him a scowl worthy of Helene. I regretted it when he took a step back and hurried away. I hadn't meant to snarl, but he was as complicit in all of this as Helene.

"You learn fast." Luther appeared from around my horse and leaned against the animal's belly, arms crossed over his chest.

"I beg your pardon?" I narrowed my eyes at him.

"You almost have Helene's manner down to perfection. You'll be commanding us all before long."

"Would that work?" I asked.

He considered for a moment, then smiled. "No. She

would have my hide for a belt if I followed your orders instead of hers. Perhaps some day, that will change. When you can be trusted."

I wanted to laugh in his face. "I wasn't the one doing the kidnapping. I'm not the one holding anyone prisoner. I was just—"

"Going to kill some dragons?"

I frowned. "No, we were just going to see why they attacked the city."

Luther chuckled. "No offence, but you're naive."

"Offence taken," I said dryly, even though he was right. "What are you trying to say?"

"The Alphas," he said the word as though it was an insult, "have been trying to rid themselves of the dragons since before there was ever a Vault. They saw you as a way to do that at last."

A pawn, yet again, assuming I believed him. His words rang with a certain amount of truth, but all good lies did.

"Then they're dumbasses," I said, my chin raised. "I wouldn't have killed any dragons with my power."

"Did you loose an arrow?" he asked. "You would have used whatever you have, if the dragon was coming for you, and they all would have called it self-defence. That's how they operate, they manoeuvre people into the place they want, until they get what they want from them. Then they toss them away like scraps to a dog."

"If that was true, then they're coming after me, to help with the dragon," I reasoned.

He shrugged, but his expression was unwavering. "This scenario might better suit their agenda."

Too many seeds of uncertainty were sown in my mind for me to dismiss the idea out of hand. I wouldn't admit that yet though.

"Should you be hobbling my horse?" I asked.

He grinned. "There's that manner again. Maybe it's a woman thing. You all act as though you own the world."

"Being a smug, sexist jerk must be a man thing," I retorted.

His eyes flashed with something like anger and for a moment I thought he might hit me.

I held my ground. If he lost control, he might also lose the bond. That might be my best and only chance to escape this close to the coast.

"I am not sexist," he said through clenched teeth. He moved to take the reins from my hand and caught a set of hobbles he was thrown by a swordsman.

I crossed my arms and watched. I might need to learn to take the hobbles off at some point and I may need to do it quickly.

Luther straightened and removed the saddle from my horse. "Your tent is ready. I suggest you get out of the sun before it burns you."

I interpreted his words and expression as 'get out of my sight before you make me even angrier' but I was unapologetic and undeterred. I would provoke him until he slipped, if that was what it took to free myself.

15

Viva

"Psst."

The hushed whisper woke me from a doze.

I wasn't sure if I felt the bond or just imagined it, but it pulled on me each time I rolled over to get comfortable. That was often. The ground under my thin bedroll was almost as hard as a sheet of rock, and just as lumpy.

In spite of that, I slept, and dreamed I was laid out on the altar as a sacrifice to Hades. In my dreams, I was tied with silken rope that held me hard like iron. I writhed and fought to free myself from the bindings, to get up and run. The more I fought, the tighter they became, until they gripped my wrists and ankles like a vice. They pressed in, tighter and tighter, until blood trickled down my skin. The trickle became a flood. Blood poured down my arms, down my legs and over my feet. Off the altar and onto the floor. It started to rise like the tide, washing back and forth.

I opened my mouth to scream.

Before I could, I awoke with a gasp. My eyes snapped open.

After a moment, I remembered where I was and really wanted to scream.

"Viva?"

I recognised Knox's voice. He sounded strong, assured, but soft. A puff of wind might be louder.

"Brother Knox?"

A flash of teeth showed near the tent flap. "Just Knox."

"Right. What are you doing here? Were these the people who infiltrated the temple?" What had he said? He was the Alpha's man. If one thing was clear it was that these people were anything but.

"I suspect so. I'm not sure of their agenda, but when I heard their intentions, I had to insert myself into their band."

"Why? Who are you working for?"

"I am the Alpha's man, heart and soul," he whispered. "It's my job to search out his enemies."

"You think they're plotting against him?" I frowned. They certainly had no love for the city, but there was more to this, I was certain of it.

"I'm not sure. Until I find out, we need to pretend we're strangers."

That would be easy enough, I hardly knew him, but his presence was strangely comforting. "Do you know where we're going?"

"Elgar mentioned something about a mountain hideout."

I guessed that from the direction we headed. "I've never met a spy before."

His teeth flashed again. "You probably have, but they didn't let you know it."

"I suppose so," I conceded. They'd be a pretty crappy spy if they went around telling everyone.

"I should go. Remember what I said and know I'll be watching. Where I can keep you safe, I will."

I almost asked if he could cut Helene and Luther's throats so we could both escape.

I bit back the words. Whatever they were up to, it was bigger than little ol' me. Knox would refuse, and rightly so. Besides, I wasn't bloodthirsty enough to murder in cold blood, or ask someone else to do it.

"Why should I trust you?" I asked.

He hesitated. "You don't have a choice?" he suggested. "But you can. I swear that on my life."

Considering he was spying in the heart of the enemy, according to him, then his life might not be worth much. It was better than nothing. At the moment, it was all I had.

"Right," I whispered. "Thank you."

The flap closed with a soft whoosh of canvas.

The darkness closed in on me. It pressed down hard, like it might cut off my air.

I forced slow breaths in and out. My power was still out of reach.

I curled my hands into fists and went back to sleep.

When I woke an hour or two later, I found half moons in my palms from my nails. A trail of blood trickled down to my wrist. I wiped it off onto my bedroll and stared.

It glowed for a moment. Barely, but enough for me to be sure I saw it.

Had that happened before and I hadn't noticed? I didn't pay much attention to my blood unless I was badly injured. Even then, I wrapped it and left it alone to heal.

"Maybe I'm part dragon," I muttered to myself. That was ridiculous, of course, I had no scales or wings. Some days I had the temper of one, such as now, when I remembered the bond and yesterday's events.

Dragon shifter maybe?

That begged the question—could anyone tell the difference when the shifter was in dragon form? Maybe the dragons weren't dragons at all.

"Time to get up." A hand tapped the top of my tent. Luther, I presumed from the voice.

"What if I don't want to?" I asked wearily.

"You can be made to get up." That was Helene. "And tonight you'll sleep in the open, with no tent."

"Near a swamp, with biting insects," Luther added.

Sadists.

I grimaced and crawled out through the flap.

I stood as quickly as I could. The last place I wanted to be was on my knees in front of them, like I was begging. I remembered the last time and wished I had a knife with me now, even the ceremonial one. I might enjoy stabbing Helene in the eye and twisting the blade while she screamed.

Of course, that would be the last thing I did.

Surreptitiously, I wiped my hands on the front of my jeans and accepted the bowl of oats, dried fruit and honey Luther handed me. It even had a spoon. For a minute I indulged in thoughts of what I might do with that in place of a knife.

Instead, I just picked it up and started to eat.

"Thanks," I muttered around my mouthful. "Are you going to watch me eat?"

Luther smiled with one side of his mouth and started to dismantle my tent with the help of one of the swordsmen.

I felt a difference in the bond and realised Helene must have taken it back.

"What do you call yourselves?" I asked. "As a group, I mean."

"We have no need for such a thing," Helene said curtly.

"All right, what do others call you then? The Marauding Band in Black? Hade's Squadron?" My vote was Band of the Travelling Assholes.

"We operate in secret. Few are aware we exist," she replied. She waved impatiently for me to finish eating.

"I see," I said slowly. "I'll think of something then." In my head, I began to call them Helene's Band of Motherfuckers, if only to give myself petty amusement and take my mind off the situation.

"Save your energy, we have a long ride yet," Helene said. "And save your words, or I'll be forced to silence you." She gave me a cold look, which left no doubt she would do as she threatened.

I responded with a nod, but threw in a one shouldered shrug. I wouldn't be cowed so easily. If Helene needed me as much as she said she did, then she would only go so far.

Or so I hoped.

I ignored Luther's hands and climbed up onto my horse without help.

The animal was probably influenced by the bond, he stepped in behind Helene's horse and followed almost nose to tail.

I decided not to spend the day glaring at the woman's back, or trying to escape straightaway.

Instead, I watched the landscape around me and committed as much of it to memory as I could. Truthfully, that wasn't difficult. To the west was sand and dirt. To the east was dirt and sand. In front was more of the same. The only thing which broke up the monotonous view was the road which trudged wearily through the nothingness.

After an hour or two, I gave up and let my mind wander to other things, like why my blood glowed. I considered drawing out a few drops to see if I imagined it, but I wouldn't do that where the other hemitheos could see.

That raised another question though; did their blood glow? If it did, what did that mean? Would Knox know? I would have to find a way to talk to him without being overheard or raising suspicion. If they found out who he was, his bones would lie lost in the sand until the end of time.

I knew without question they'd kill him. Helene probably wouldn't bat an eye.

I shook my head and sighed to myself.

"Ten bucks for your thoughts." Luther had ridden beside me for the last while, but I hadn't noticed him until he spoke.

"I'm not sure they're worth it," I replied.

"Why don't you let me decide that?" he suggested.

I gave him a steady look, but he was unruffled. "I was just wondering how many hemitheos there are," I lied. I hadn't wondered that until the words came out of my mouth. Now they had, it was an interesting question. One I'd very much like the answer to.

Luther regarded me with a tilt of his head. "I know of only a handful. Some from the south." He waved a finger toward Helene, then pointed at me. "Some from the city, or outside the Vault. My mother was one."

"Was?" I asked without thinking.

"She went to Hades when I was a kid," Luther said with no inflection in his tone. "Too long ago to recall more than flashes of her face. I will always remember her scent." He half closed his eyes and inhaled through his nose slowly, as if he could breathe it in now. "Lilacs and lavender, with a hint of roses and a scent all her own." He let the breath out slowly.

"I'm sorry." I hadn't missed the smell of my own mother until now. Hers was similar to the one he described, while my stepfather smelled of musk and bravado. I scrunched up my nose and pressed my tongue to the back of my teeth to keep my emotions in check.

"It doesn't matter now," Luther said. "Helene and the

others are my family." He gave me a look which suggested they could be mine as well, if I let them.

I ignored it. Helene was my captor, nothing more. Part of me was curious as to what the woman might be able to teach me, but I wouldn't be used. Now I had more idea of what I could do with my powers, I would teach myself if I had to.

"So, there are probably others out there you don't know about," I stated.

Luther shrugged. "Potentially, yes. If it's Hades's will, they'll find their way to us."

"And if not, you'll kidnap them as well?"

Luther chuckled. "Is that what you think this is?"

I frowned, surprised at his response. "What would you call it? I'm restrained against my will, cut off from my power, forced to follow like a dog on a leash." I didn't bother to keep the accusation from my voice.

"We saved you from the Keeper," Luther declared.

"Strange," I said slowly, my temper just this close to boiling over, "I didn't feel as though I needed to be saved. I certainly didn't ask. Is it customary in the Vault to save people against their will and force them to bend to yours?"

If I expected him to become angry, I was mistaken.

He laughed again. "In time, you will come to understand," he said.

"Or you could explain it to me now."

I barely finished that sentence when what felt like a fist of air slammed into my face.

I jerked back, but it slid across my mouth and clamped down hard. I tried to gasp though it, but nothing would come.

I sucked in several frantic breaths through my nose and raised a hand to my face. My fingers found a mass of warmth a centimetre from my mouth. I curled my fingers around it and tried frantically to pull it away.

"That will stay there until I remove it." Helene barely turned around in her saddle to speak. "Until then, you will remain silent."

As if I have a choice. I tugged again, but the gag of air was firm on my face. Tears of frustration spilled down my cheeks. My hatred of Helene cemented even harder.

I would learn from the woman, then I would beat her until she cried. More than that, I wanted the woman to scream.

"Apologies, Hemathea," Luther said meekly. "I shouldn't have engaged her in conversation. I was merely trying to be friendly. She's…not the enemy."

If that was the case, I shuddered to think how they treated people who were.

"Precisely," Helene said smoothly. "She must learn obedience, or she will endanger herself and the rest of us. You, of all people, know the dangers of the power."

I shot him a glance, but his face was turned away. What did he know? Had he injured someone while he learnt to use the power?

I shook my head. It didn't matter. I had no intention of sticking around long enough to find out. I shot Helene a look, but the woman rode with her back firmly to me.

Calm, I told myself. I had managed to bide my time before I came to the Vault. I had found a way to avoid slavery. I had entered the presence of the Keeper with a blade. I had argued for, and won, my freedom. I could and would do so again, no matter how long it took.

Helene would not break me.

I focused on breathing through my nose, slow and steady. I needed to calm my mind to stay in control.

It didn't work. My heart raced. The pressure from the binding over my mouth threatened to drive me to the edge of panic. I wanted to throw myself off the back of the horse and wrap my hands around Helene's throat. She would see how it felt to be cut off from air.

I let my vision blur and counted my breaths in and out.

One.

Two.

Three.

The gag fell away so suddenly I jolted and took a gasping breath through my mouth.

"You need to work on clearing your mind," Helene said without so much as a backward glance. "That can be your task for the rest of the journey."

Luther leaned over and whispered loudly, "The appropriate response is, 'Yes, Hemathea.'"

I gave him a look just short of rolling my eyes and said nothing until I felt the press of air on my cheek again.

"Yes, Hemathea," I said more quickly than I intended.

I caught an approving look from Luther in the corner of my eye and grimaced inwardly.

Evidently he saw that as a point won by him and Helene. No doubt, Helene would agree.

I was determined they wouldn't win any more of them.

I caught a glance from Knox, who rode to the side of me, and a little toward the front. He clearly heard some of the exchange, although he wouldn't have seen it all. He couldn't have seen the gag, but he must have watched me clutch at something over my mouth.

He looked disapproving before he, too, turned away.

I glanced to the other side of me, but if Luther caught Knox's expression, he didn't let on.

Helene was right about one thing, now was a good time to concentrate on clearing my mind. Frustration and anger would get me nowhere.

I set my gaze on my horse's ears and half my attention on the landscape. The other half I used to watch and listen. The swordsmen said little, but once in a while Elgar would shout an order, or listen to a scout who returned from ahead or behind the group.

From what I could tell, no one followed us. Elgar seemed more concerned with the way ahead. As the day wore on, his face seemed grimmer and grimmer. He shared words with Helene here and there, but for the most part he just scowled.

Between Helene and Luther, it seemed to me not much could pose a real threat. Why, then, was Elgar so concerned?

I tried to listen, but the man only let a stray word escape here and there. Not enough for me to make sense of it. I sought out his scent—the bond hadn't suppressed that ability—but all I found was sweat and irritability. That was common to all of us right now.

Even with a scarf over my head and most of my face, the sun was merciless. Why didn't we travel at night? Maybe the risk from sand dragons was higher than the risk of sunburn or heatstroke.

Neither held a great deal of appeal. I missed the ocean breezes from the residence in the city. Hades, I'd kill for some AC right now. Why the fuck weren't we travelling by a comfortable bus, or a plane? Surely the Vault had those?

The further we rode, the fewer breezes of any kind blew. Those which did, were hot and dry, like a blast of the sand itself, and laced with the subtle scent of dried bones.

I could have imagined that last. Stories about deserts often mentioned hallucinations to drive a traveler to distraction. Or worse.

I pushed away the idea, but the scent remained in my nostrils. I'll probably remember it for the rest of my life, after the other details of this journey were long forgotten.

Some smells lingered.

I didn't say a word until we made camp that night. Even

then, I slid down from my horse in silence, took his saddle off and set it aside beside my tent.

Knox walked past on some task or another, but I didn't glance at him twice. I kept my eyes down after I was handed a plate of food. I didn't acknowledge anyone else until Luther flopped down on the ground beside me.

"You want to know what happened," he stated.

"Do I?" I replied. I regarded him over a chunk of bread before I put it in my mouth.

"I killed a man," Luther said, as though he'd entirely missed the irony in my tone and expression.

"It happens," I replied nonchalantly, but my curiosity was piqued. I could tell he saw that in my eyes and continued speaking.

"He was a friend, of sorts." Luther leaned back and rested his weight on the palm of his hand. "When I was younger, I was small for my age." In spite of the regretful reminiscence in his eyes, he grinned. "I grew, eventually."

I nodded. He was taller than I was, so clearly he had caught up to his peers. I didn't want to appear interested, but I waved for him to go on.

"Anyway, Gallen teased me about my height. I came to his chest, more or less. He was unusually tall for our age, so the difference was…somewhat obvious." Luther shifted to his other palm. "At first I took his teasing with good humour. Then I began to tire of it. I tried to ignore him, but he knew how to say just the thing to piss me off."

He sighed softly. His eyes glazed at the memory. "I got tired of his shit. One day, I got angry. I picked him up and threw him into the river. He couldn't swim."

My mouth formed an O. "You fought back against a bully," I said. My eyes flicked toward Helene, but the woman wasn't looking in our direction. "I'm sure you tried to save him once you knew he couldn't save himself." I didn't know that at all, but I guessed it. Luther didn't seem the type to stand by and watch a man drown.

His tongue traced his lips. "I shouted for the city watch. I also can't swim. They arrived too late. I...told them he fell. No one else saw. I went home to my father and my father's wife and didn't say a single word until I met Helene."

I wanted to ask if the woman had bullied the story out of him. The words were on my lips, but I sucked them away. "And now you're telling me."

"I felt it important for me to tell you."

"Ah." He seemed so awkward, it was hard not to like him, in spite of everything. "Why?"

"So you understand you're not alone."

I frowned. "I've never killed anyone."

Yet.

"You have lost control." There he was again, stating the words as if he read my mind.

"In the past, yes," I spoke slowly.

"And it scared you."

"At the time."

"We all need to learn control. That is Helene's first and most important lesson."

"Even if she breaks me to teach it?" I asked bitterly.

"Don't let her break you," Luther said in a low, conspiratorial tone.

I gave him a surprised look, which faded a heartbeat later. "You mean do as she says so she doesn't have to punish me. Did she tell you to say that?"

"No, but it was another thing I learnt from her. She's not a bad person, she just..."

"Likes to get everything her way?"

"To achieve what must be done," Luther argued. "Because this is too important."

"What is *this?*" I asked. For a moment it seemed I caught him by surprise and he might give me some answers.

Instead, he pressed his lips together to hold back the wrong words. "I told you, I don't know."

I shook my head. "I don't believe you."

"That much is clear." A smile graced the corners of his mouth. "You'll have to trust me a while longer."

I barked a laugh. "I don't trust you now."

He pressed a hand to his chest, over his heart. "You cut me to my very soul."

"You have a soul?" I countered.

"Do I—" He shook his head and chuckled. "Helene would have us believe they don't exist. I believe they do. I *must* believe, or what are we fighting for?"

"I have no idea," I replied dryly.

"Ah, I don't mean now, I mean all our lives. The struggle to be born, to grow, to live from one day to the next. What is it for if we have no life in the embrace of Hades after we die?"

I set aside my empty plate and rubbed my forehead with my fingertips. "It's too late in the day for deep and meaningful conversation." He did have a point though. Why work so hard to live, only to die someday?

He chuckled again. "I apologise. It has been a long day and this kind of talk is better done over several glasses of wine, and in more comfortable surroundings."

"Yes." That would be anywhere but here, on the hard ground, with the sun beating its last merciless rays down on the camp.

As the night before, we stopped beside water; this time a small oasis. Little more than a pond, it barely held enough water for the horses and a few sips for us, but it was the best place I saw since we left last night's camp. Or perhaps the least worst.

"We'll pass into the mountains in a few more days," Luther

said. "It will be cooler there and have a lot more streams and rivers. We might even get to wash." He sighed at that.

"I thought you couldn't swim," I pointed out.

"I learnt," Luther said with a half smile.

"Let me guess, Helene taught you."

"Sweet Hades no," he replied. "Another of the hemitheos did. I didn't want what happened to Gallen to happen to me."

"I suppose not," I agreed. It wasn't until later I wondered if he meant drowning, or being killed by another witch.

16

Dex rubbed his chin for the umpteenth time and regarded me over his desk. His eyes looked weary. "You're telling me this now?"

I stiffened my back and fought the desire to glance away. "Keeper, I—"

Kerina interrupted. "Had to tell you or I would have."

She wasn't spared from Dex's cool gaze. He looked at us both as though he hardly recognised us. "You didn't tell me any sooner either. Viva was taken weeks ago. Neither of you thought to come and explain. Or better yet, inform me *at the time*." He punched a fist into his palm with each word.

"Keeper." My eyes followed Dex as he rose and moved to the window. "We had to deal with the dragons, for the good of—"

I jumped as Dex turned and slammed a hand down on his desk.

"*I* decide what is best for the Vault," Dex snapped. "Not you." He huffed out a furious breath. "Perhaps I am to blame. I have let you overstep time after time. I should have reined you in sooner."

"Yes, Keeper." I wasn't good at being meek. Dex would no more put me on a leash than he would put himself on one. I couldn't do my job efficiently if he did. Now, however, was not the time to point that out.

Dex grimaced, obviously not fooled for a moment. He perched on the side of his desk and crossed his arms. "All right, tell me again what happened."

I spoke with considered words, not wasting a single one. "When Kerina and I arrived back at the residence after the man in black spoke to us in the marketplace, I was approached by a woman. She confirmed that she and one other operative were in the residence. One was a man who cleaned your rooms. She insisted Viva travel with us to hunt the dragons."

"That was already planned," Dex said.

"Yes," I agreed. "I let her think I was reluctant to include Viva in the party. She was adamant. I'm certain she would have had the would-be assassin carry out his job if I hadn't given in." Or pretended to.

"So you sacrificed Viva for me?" Dex asked.

I met his gaze unwaveringly. "Not precisely, no. I chose each of those who accompanied us." I nodded toward Kerina. "They were told to watch for anything unusual." Before she could argue, I added, "Kerina already knew."

She scowled, but I ignored her.

"I also informed an operative who works for the Alpha. He was working in the Temple for some months. I gave him time to leave the city, in the hope he might infiltrate the attackers. I presume he was successful, he was one who held a sword while the others left with Viva."

Kerina stared at me. "You planned all of this?"

I shrugged with one shoulder. "We should have been able to stop them from taking her. I misjudged the power the witches hold." I had kicked myself a dozen times for making such a dumbass mistake. I thought I understood Viva's power, but I was wrong.

"And why not tell us when the witches left?" Kerina asked.

Dex gestured for me to answer the question.

"I hoped to hear from Knox. This goes beyond Viva. I hoped he would find out what they wanted. If this is a threat to the Alpha, or the Vault, he might learn what and report back."

Dex's lips twitched and I knew he was holding back another comment about me overstepping.

"And?" Dex prompted.

I drew a scrap of paper from my pocket and handed it to Dex while Kerina stared at me in disbelief.

"You were going to tell him anyway?" Her eyes flashed with anger and confusion. Perhaps a little hurt. She had hardly said two words to me in the last couple of weeks, and then only when she had to. I was surprised she hadn't left the residence, either to follow Viva's captors or just in disgust.

"I hoped to tell the Keeper sooner," I replied, "but there was nothing to act on, until now."

I nodded toward the paper. "After reading that, I believe the choice I made was the right one. The woman who took Viva is powerful and dangerous. Knox doesn't know what she wants, but he gave some idea of the direction they were headed." Knox had slipped the note to another traveller along with a gold coin. He risked both of their lives in doing that. Hades willing, the man hadn't been caught. If he was, chances are we'd never find him.

Dex's eyes shifted back and forth while he read. He

nodded and tossed the note onto the desktop. "What do you propose?"

I tapped a hand on my thigh. "I don't think we should send an army after her."

"An army wouldn't be stealthy," Dex agreed. "And if this—Helene—is as dangerous as Knox suggests, we should learn what she's up to." He sighed. "I hate to admit it, but you're right. This is much bigger than Viva. So much so that..." He looked regretful.

"You'd let her die if necessary?" Kerina asked. Her expression was guarded, but clearly unhappy.

"If it comes to that," Dex said. "I cannot sacrifice the good of the Vault. That has to be my priority. However, we need to find out who these people are and why they took Viva. For that, we need—"

"Stealth?" I suggested.

"Yes, lots of that." Dex walked away a few steps, then turned back and rubbed his chin yet again. "I don't want to trust this to anyone else. The fewer people who know about this, the better."

I nodded. "Understood."

Kerina frowned. "Wait. You presume we can work together on this?"

"If anyone can keep Bain in hand, it's you," Dex said.

Kerina snorted.

My eyebrows rose. I would have to keep Kerina from running straight into trouble, but she was no idiot. Between us, we may not get each other killed. As long as she didn't aim for my back, that was.

"We have worked together for quite some time," I said evenly. "We can do it again." As long as she followed orders.

"I'm certain," Dex said, his expression distracted. "There's one more thing. If this Helene is a threat to the Vault, I expect you to take care of her. And *anyone* in her company."

I did my best to hide my surprise. "I understand."

Shit.

Ever since she was taken, I'd thought of little else. Duty was one thing. Having to stand back and watch Viva be taken was another. I'd come to care about her more than I should. More than once I wished I could go back and make her stay in the city. Or hide her somewhere safe. Somewhere I could hold her close until the storm broke over us both and blew out to sea.

If I had to choose between duty and her again, I wasn't sure which I would pick. I sent a plea to Hades, to beg that it not come to that.

"You expect us to be able to kill someone with that kind of power?" Kerina asked.

"That's where your stealth will come into it," Dex said with a curt nod and no hint of his usual humour. "Do whatever you have to do."

He frowned over my shoulder and shook his head a fraction.

I glanced back, but saw nothing there. "Dex? Are you all right?"

Dex blinked at me. "Hmmm? Oh, yes of course. I just thought..." He waved a hand and grinned. "Trick of the light."

Kerina cocked her head and looked bemused, but said nothing.

"We'll leave within the hour," I said. "It will be faster to sail south to Cape Massin and travel overland to Onyx. From there, we'll head into the mountains."

Dex nodded. "Good. I'll tell everyone you were sent to the Alpha as an envoy. No one will question that."

"Are you suggesting people might question you?" Kerina asked, a lopsided smile on her face.

"It's hard to believe, isn't it?" Dex replied, a smile on his own lips. "The Keeper of the Vault himself, under scrutiny." He clicked his tongue.

I held back a smile. "I doesn't bear thinking about."

"It really doesn't, perhaps I should hang a few people now and again."

"That might be somewhat extreme." A flicker of movement outside the window caught my eye. When I turned my head, the sill and sky beyond it were empty. A passing bird, more than likely. Perhaps a blossom blown on the wind. I should stop jumping at shadows.

"It might," Dex agreed. If he noticed my distraction, he gave no sign. "I'll have to live with people's questions."

"I'm sure Calista will keep you in line," I said with the hint of a smile.

Dex sighed dramatically. "She's going to love that. She can tell me what to do and I'll have no one to stand up to her for me." He seemed on the verge of laughter.

"I'm quite sure you can take care of yourself," I said dryly. "If it'll make you feel better, I'll leave Trevor in charge."

Dex grimaced. "He has even less sense of humour than you do."

"Yeah, but that's a sacrifice you'll have to make for the sake of the Vault." The side of my mouth tugged up slightly.

"Wait a moment," Kerina said, as if she had something urgent to say. When we both turned to her, she said, "Someone here has less sense of humour than Bain?" She grinned and her eyes shone with the point she scored at my expense.

I was undeterred. "It's difficult to believe, but it's true." I raised an eyebrow.

"I don't need to use my power," Kerina said drolly. "Trevor is duller than a sandworm, but good at his job. We can rest assured the Vault will be safe while we're away."

"Speaking of leaving," I said. "If we stand here chatting, the hour will end and we'll still be here, talking, or making jokes." I offered Dex a salute, hand to my chest.

Dex nodded in response. "Go with Hades and return with haste. Oh, and this." He opened a drawer in his desk, reached in and pulled out a bag.

He tossed it to me.

I caught it and noted the clink and the weight. There must be enough coins inside to buy a nice estate on the green plains north of the city.

"That will supply you with whatever you need. Horses, mercenaries, bribes, an Intimate or two."

I shook my head and tucked the bag into my pocket. "Thank you. We'll send word when we can." I gestured for Kerina to precede me out the door.

Calista bustled in as we exited, but she hardly gave us more than a glance before she closed the door behind her. That was unlike her, but I took no time to wonder or ask questions. Doubtless she had her reasons for everything she did.

"I hope you realise I get seasick," Kerina remarked.

We started down the corridor toward the guard's quarters.

I nodded. "That's exactly why I decided on a sea voyage."

She glanced at me for a moment, then socked me on the arm. "I see and hear your lie, asshole."

I rubbed my arm where she likely left a bruise. "We need to travel as quickly as possible. If we didn't, I'd ride over the desert, rather than take a ship. In this case, speed is more important than comfort. Even yours." I made a mental note to suggest Dex invest in a helicopter or two. Surely one would fit on the train?

She frowned at me. "Don't try to flatter me. I'm still angry with you. More so now I knew I was angry at you for no reason. You knew they would take her and you planned for it."

"Yes," I agreed simply.

"You should have told me."

I hesitated. "Yeah, maybe, but it's done now. We should focus on the job."

"Do you really mean to kill Viva if she's a danger to the Vault?" Kerina eyed me carefully.

I hesitated before letting out a long sigh. "Only if it's absolutely necessary. It's something you need to be ready for too. I don't like the idea, but we will do whatever we have to. If you can't, I will have to find someone to take your place." I fixed her with a firm look. I half wished someone could take mine.

She set her chin with equal firmness before she too sighed and sagged. "I will do what I have to, but only as a last resort."

I nodded. "Agreed." Cold blooded killing was not my thing, nor did I want it to be.

I headed toward the stairs leading down into the lower levels of the residence.

A child stood near the balustrade and waved, then disappeared.

I almost missed my step. I blinked and shook my head to clear it. "What in the name of Hades?"

"Bain?" Kerina stopped with her hand on the railing, centimetres from where the child had stood.

I squinted. "You didn't..." I straightened and shook my head. "A trick of the light." Or I was losing my mind.

Or—

There was a third option, but I didn't want to consider it. Not yet. I sought around with my senses and found only

Kerina and a servant or two who walked past without a glance.

"I didn't see anything," Kerina said. "It's dark in this part of the residence."

I glanced in her direction and pursed my lips. She was right, it was dark, but I was sure a child stood there, a girl, with dark hair wound in a long plait, and a dress in bright colours. One moment she stood in front of me, the next she was simply gone. I would have seen her walk or run away, maybe heard her giggle as she played whatever the latest game the residence children played.

I would have sensed her there.

Instead, I sensed nothing.

A chill passed through me, but I steeled myself and started down the stairs. I had to put the incident out of my mind. Even if I saw a real child, surely she was harmless?

Part of me wanted to explain to Kerina what I saw, but I didn't. She might think I was crazy and insist Dex make me stay behind. I couldn't, wouldn't do that, unless he ordered it. I needed to find Viva and her abductors. Before her smart tongue got her killed. The idea of her lying dead made my heart twist in my chest. I was almost certain Dex felt the same way. If he could come with us, he would. His place was here. I would find her and bring her home. I swore that in the name of every god I knew, and all the ones I didn't. If she was alive, I would get her back.

"You seem bothered by something," Kerina said. "Don't say it's nothing, I'll know if you lie."

"It's nothing we need to worry about," I replied. That was the truth. Odd occurrences happened once in a while, it meant nothing. "I'll arrange our belongings. Send word to the harbourmaster that we need a ship to Cape Massin. I want to be gone before night falls."

"Scared of the dark?" she teased.

I snorted. "No, but if we wait until morning, we'll be wasting time. We have none to spare, not if Knox is to be believed."

"You think he is?"

"Yes." The time it took for his message to arrive concerned me. Hades only knew what might have changed since then. Viva might be dead already. Helene too. In the back of my mind, I knew that wasn't the case. I had nothing to base that assumption on, but I was as certain as I was that Kerina stood in front of me, a smirk on her face.

"I hope you're right," she said slowly. "I'm not a fan of wild dragon chases." She frowned. "That's not true, I like chasing real dragons, not shadows. Especially broken shadows."

I nodded. That's exactly what we would be chasing if I was wrong. Still, I knew I wasn't, so I waved for her to do as I asked, and strode into the guard's barracks.

Wide and cool, the barracks held room for nearly three hundred men. The women were housed in a smaller dormitory across a narrow courtyard. In the days before the Alpha's father, men occupied both. The women's barracks were used for officers, or for storage.

These days, it only ever held a handful of women at a time. Few of them wanted to be guards and fewer still had the skills necessary to fight off an attacker. For the most part that was because of the lack of training for girls. Many of the older trainers wouldn't let them train alongside the boys, unless, like Kerina, they refused to be told no.

Like Viva too, I mused. If they wanted it enough, they found a way. I made a note to mention it to Dex. If women wanted to defend the Vault, why shouldn't they be allowed to? Encouraged to.

I found a servant and ordered him to find two saddlebags and fill them with water bottles and food for the journey. I found two more bags myself and started to pack as lightly as

I could. Hades knew how long this might take, but what I didn't pack now, I could buy later.

The servant returned with the saddlebags and Kerina followed virtually on his heels, arms piled with clothes and other items.

"The *Shade* leaves in two hours." She picked up her own bag and began to stuff her belongings into it. "The captain wanted a grand for the journey. Transferred electronically."

When I responded with a twist of my lips for the price, she added, "Each."

I swore softly. "Thief." Not to mention the time it would take to have the funds sent from Dex's bank. Plenty of people in the Vault preferred to trade the old way. More and more were turning to methods used by the outside world. That was inevitable I supposed.

Kerina shrugged her bag onto her back and picked up her saddlebag. "I think he sensed the importance, or it would have been half the price. And you're sleeping on the deck."

"Of course I am." It didn't matter to me where I slept, as long as I slept, but I would let Kerina score another point. If that was what it took to have her speak to me again, I would put up with her ribbing. If nothing else, we needed to have each other's backs. If not…

I wouldn't think about that. I swung my bag onto my back and followed Kerina out to the stable yard.

A car greeted us outside. Specifically a Second World War era Volkswagen. Tiny and worn, I'd be lucky to squeeze inside next to the driver.

Kerina caught my glance and returned it with one of her own. "What? it was all I could find at such short notice."

"It will do," I said with a grunt. I would have preferred one of the limos, but nothing about them said stealth. At least we didn't have to walk.

I swung my bag into the boot and climbed in beside the driver.

Kerina gave me a stony look through narrowed eyes and I smiled back. Neither of us would sit comfortably in the back, but she was smaller than me. She could sit in there or stay behind.

The driver, a man named Harold, nodded to me and turned over the engine. Contrary to the way the car looked, she purred like a proverbial kitten. It hummed past through the residence gates and out onto the street.

I wound down the window and watched the scenery pass by.

An unusual stillness hung over the city, heavy with the heat of the afternoon. Ever since the attack by the dragon, the Vault had fallen into an uneasy watchfulness. People only went out and about to do important business, such as work or to buy food. No one lingered for a conversation and an eye was always on the sky, or the citizens around them. As if they might turn into a dragon without warning, or incite a riot.

There was something more, something I couldn't put my finger on.

"That music is weird," Kerina remarked as she climbed down out of the carriage at the docks. She tossed a coin to the driver, who nodded and only waited long enough for me to grab our bags before he drove away.

"What music?" I asked, my eyes already on the *Shade*. She was a small ship, but would be quick, if not comfortable.

"Are you losing your hearing in your old age?" Kerina teased. She gave me a hard poke in the ribs and headed toward the ship.

"Don't make me demote you," I growled. I listened, but heard no music at all. I shook my head and shrugged.

She stopped and waved a hand in the air. "I can hear it, as

clear as anything. It's… violins and something I don't know." She shook her head. "It sounds mournful. You must hear that?"

I strained, but I couldn't hear any kind of music at all. I turned in a slow circle. Just the usual dock sounds. People talking, laughing, moving crates, the barking of dogs and bleating of a large box filled with sheep. Perhaps a drumbeat now and again, but no music. Certainly no violins.

"I don't hear it. Perhaps my hearing is failing."

Kerina frowned. "It's stopped now anyway. That's strange. No crescendo, no fade away, it just stopped."

"They might have been practicing," I suggested.

"I suppose so," Kerina replied, but she seemed unconvinced. "It doesn't matter anyway, we should hurry. The captain said he wouldn't wait. After you, sir." She waved and grinned.

"Thank you, but be careful how you address me."

"Of course. you wouldn't want anyone to think you're in charge of me." She laughed at the last word.

I snorted. "Right." I drew out the word. "That and from now on, we have to pretend to be other than who we are."

"Naturally," Kerina agreed. "I told the captain we were brother and sister."

My eyebrows twitched. We had no family resemblance, and spoke with slightly different accents. Thank Hades most people didn't bother to ask questions as long as they were paid. They would probably assume we were lovers escaping disapproving parents, or unhappy marriages.

"You can be the younger sibling this time," I said. I made a face at her that drew a laugh.

"But it's such fun when you're the baby brother," she teased.

"I don't have the temperament."

"I suppose you do suit grumpy older brother better," she mused.

"Precisely. The crew will ask fewer questions if I toss you overboard."

She chuckled. "If I go, you're going with me."

"I don't want to be food for the sea serpents." I nodded to the crewman who waved us aboard and started to draw up the gangway from the dock.

"You wouldn't be more than a snack, brother dear," Kerina said, obviously for the benefit of the crew. If we said nothing important, we wouldn't draw any attention. They'd forget us the moment we reached the Cape.

"A chewy, hard snack, sister dear," I agreed.

I caught the eye roll of a barefooted woman who wound a length of rope around her arm. She evidently assumed we were a pair of spoilt brats, off on some sort of adventure which would get us killed, or visiting estates in Cape Massin. No one, certainly, worth paying any attention to.

I shot her a smile which I hoped was ingratiating, greasy even, and she looked away.

Kerina snorted softly. "You've still got it, dear brother."

"Thank Hades for that," I muttered. I didn't need anyone trying to attach themselves to me.

Except maybe Viva.

Guilt made my heart hurt. She was in danger because of me. I let her go into it, without at least some idea of what she might face. And I had done fuck all to stop it. I wouldn't be surprised if she hated my guts after all of this. That hurt even worse.

On top of that, I was worried Knox's presence might endanger her even more. I sent him to keep her safe, but knowing her, she wouldn't be able to keep from talking to him, or trying to get answers.

Although, I reminded myself, she wasn't stupid. A woman

smart and determined enough to survive the Council, discarded by the mate Hades chose for her, who made a place for herself in the Vault, would be smart enough not to take stupid risks, regardless of her curiosity.

At any rate, nothing in Knox's message suggested she was other than alive and well. At least, at the time it was sent. I had to hold onto that and beg Hades to give me a chance to explain.

I forced the woman to the back of my mind and set my bag down on the bed of the cabin I was shown to. Not, as Kerina suggested, a corner of the deck. It was nothing special, I could touch the opposite walls without raising my arms, but it would do.

I closed the door behind me and headed back up on deck. I claimed an empty spot by the rails and watched the city slip further and further away. I scanned the sky for dragons, and the waves for sea serpents, but saw neither. The eerie feeling of a city waiting extended far behind the docks. Even the sailors seemed to be waiting for something. They went about their jobs, moving around on deck as though it didn't rock, but every last one seemed tense, tied tighter than one of their knots.

It was my imagination, I decided. That was all.

I turned and caught a glimpse of a small figure hurrying down belowdecks.

I blinked.

What was the child from the residence doing here, on the same ship? The one who disappeared when I looked at her.

I crossed the distance between the rail and the steps. I looked down, but there was no sign of anyone, adult or child. A frown creasing my brow, I descended slowly.

Wherever the kid went, I couldn't see her now. She could have gone into a cabin. Or disappeared into thin air again.

Kerina stepped out the door to the cabin opposite mine and stopped to cock her head at me.

"What?"

"Did you see a kid come down here?" I described what I saw at the residence and waited for Kerina to laugh.

Instead, she looked thoughtful. "If you were anyone else, I would tell you you're crazy. But you don't jump at shadows. Well, not usually."

I snorted softly. "Thanks. I'm not this time either. I saw someone… Something." My brow creased more deeply. "My mother used to tell stories about naughty sprites, who like to play games with people."

"Sprites? What did they do with those people?"

"They'd grow bored and then lure them to their deaths," I replied more lightly than I felt.

"Ah. Well, let's hope that's not the case here." Her eyes sparkled before she added, "You'd bore them faster than most."

The corners of my mouth turned upward. "That's likely," I agreed. "At least I wouldn't drive them crazy with my jokes."

"At least they're funny," she said modestly.

Her eyes glazed and she seemed to be thinking back to a memory. "My father used to talk about the 'pale ones', as he called them. The souls of the newly dead, who hadn't gone to Hades. They wander the world until they can find rest. They envy the living, so they follow them, in the hope of taking their body for their own."

"You think a ghost wants my body?" That wasn't the strangest thing I ever heard. It sent chills down my spine.

"If they're not discerning," she replied with half a smile. "They might be looking for me."

"Possibly," I agreed. "We'll need to keep our eyes open either way." I hesitated before I asked, "Did your father mention some way to help them move on, or to encourage Hades to take them?"

Kerina propped her elbow against the wall and placed her hand on her chin. "Not as I recall, no. I'd imagine we'd have to sacrifice a chicken to a sea serpent, or some such."

I raised my eyebrows. "That would be weird. Maybe we can light a candle and ask Hades for help. Although…"

"Although, what?" she prompted.

"Candles infuriate sprites. If we light one, they might attack us."

Kerina rubbed the side of her nose. "So one of us lights the candle, while the other stands nearby with a knife, or claws out."

"Uh…."

"No knives or claws?" she guessed.

"No," I echoed. "We have to throw peas at them."

She laughed. "You're joking. Peas?"

I gave an 'I don't get it either' gesture with both hands. "Apparently they hate them."

Kerina wrinkled her nose. "I don't blame them, so do I."

"They're good for you."

"Not if you're a sprite," she retorted.

"Are you one?"

"Not that I know of, how could I tell?" She seemed sincere in her question.

"You'd be mischievous," I said evenly. I tilted my head. "Energetic. Devious and smart." I knitted my brows. "I'll get some peas."

She socked me on the arm. "Keep those things away from me. Besides, I'm sure there are none on board. Next time I arrange a ship, I'll make sure there aren't."

I shook my head. I knew she wouldn't bother. Still, I enjoyed our banter. She still looked at me with accusation in her eyes, but she wouldn't let it get in the way of our mission. That was the only thing that truly mattered right now.

That and getting Viva back. After that, I would do everything to make her understand, if it was the last thing I did.

"When we reach Cape Massin, I'll find a candle and some peas." In the back of my mind, I had the growing feeling neither would help and that the kid was important in some way. I had no idea how though and that bothered me more than anything. I didn't like unexplained things.

"Get some rest. You'll need it."

"Of course, brother dear. You too."

I gave her a nod and headed back up on deck.

17

Bain

Cape Massin grew up on the side of a cliff. The port itself was nestled against it. Long docks wound around a spit of land high enough to avoid all but the highest tides.

Here, it looked like people lived a couple of hundred years ago. Most of the ships and boats tied to the docks were made of wood. Many had sails, now lashed out of the breeze. A wide vessel bobbed beside a narrow one with twin hulls. A large ship with a sea serpent figurehead sat low and heavy beside a sleek seventeenth century-style warship.

Most of them would have an engine, and the power of any modern navy, or billionaire's super-yacht. Why didn't Dex have one? I would have to ask him if I saw him again.

"We could have traveled in that," Kerina remarked. She nodded toward the pseudo warship.

I eyed her. "That wouldn't be very stealthy. Besides, it was on the wrong side of the straight."

"A minor detail or two," Kerina said with a grin. She

looked as though she'd slept well, in spite of having bedded down in a bed as narrow as mine.

I, on the other hand, had lain awake. When I had slept, people passing in the passage outside my cabin woke me. Some stomped by like a herd of elephants. The quiet ones sounded like cattle.

"Perhaps we can sail home on her," I said, distractedly. My mind was on other things.

"Or we could fly home on the back of a dragon," Kerina suggested.

"What?" I frowned before her words and sarcasm sank in. I snorted. "I suspect they would sooner eat us than let us ride them."

"Same here," Kerina said. She grinned and swung her bag onto her back.

I rolled my eyes, threw my own bag over my shoulder before I followed her down the gangway. I glanced back to see a sailor watching with half-lidded eyes. The man scowled before he turned away. I shrugged to myself and trotted to catch up to Kerina.

"We'll need to wait for the lift." She gestured up toward it.

Suspended by enormous cables, the lift was a wide platform, capable of holding a few dozen people at a time. Drawn up by a large wheel at the top of the cliff, the lift stopped at each of the two levels of buildings built into the cliff face, and moved slowly toward the very top. Right now, it hung beside the second level and seemed in no hurry to finish the journey up or start the journey back down.

"In times past, they had a ladder as well," I remarked. I don't know why they burrowed into the cliff to put a modern elevator in there. I supposed the old ways die hard the further from the city we went.

"Yes, it was burnt when some tiger shifters tried to take

the town over a hundred years ago. Would you really want to climb all the way up there?" She pointed.

"If it got us there faster, yes," I replied. Thank Hades I didn't have to follow through with that claim. I was fit, but the cliff was a long way up. It would suck if I almost made it, then slipped on the top rung. If the fall didn't kill me, the landing would. If I survived that, I would have to endure a lifetime of Kerina reminding me about it.

"You're a terrible liar," she said. She paused, then frowned. "Shit."

I followed her gaze and exhaled through my nose in frustration. The lift was rising. So slowly the movement was barely discernible, but it was continuing its journey to the top.

"We'll have at least an hour or two to wait for it to come back down." Kerina didn't bother to keep the frustration out of her tone.

I grunted my agreement. If there was another way up, I would take it, but since there wasn't, we would have to suck it up for a while longer.

"Let's find a tavern and have a meal while we wait. We might find some jellied eels for you." I suppressed a smile and stepped aside before she could sock me again.

"I could do with a beer and some fresh bread," she said, eyeing me as if I might say more.

I nodded. "There are a few places at the base of the lift." I led the way through the crowd of people who either just arrived on other ships, or were about to depart. Some pushed small trolleys covered with items for sale. Their trolleys were narrow enough to navigate in a tight space, but wide enough to display knives, belts, hats and the occasional colourful bird or small monkey.

"A gold coin, sir," one said when I glanced at a bright red parrot with yellow tail feathers.

"We're not idiots," Kerina snapped. "The moment we hand over a coin, you'll open the cage and the bird will fly back to wherever you've trained it to go."

The man pretended to be offended, but bustled on through the crowds, muttering to himself.

"The oldest scam there is," Kerina said darkly. "He's probably sold the poor thing a dozen times before. The city watch should stop him."

"I'll be sure to let them know, if I see any," I said. I wouldn't though. I knew some of the watch; I had trained several. For now, I wanted to stay out of their sight. They would either insist on knowing why we were in Cape Massin, or they'd want to help. I didn't want the hassle of either right now.

We passed the first tavern with only a glance. The taproom was empty except for a man who swept the floor which looked clean already.

I stopped at the second tavern, which held only a handful of patrons, but a clear view of the lift as it neared the top.

"I'm always suspicious of an empty tavern," Kerina remarked, as though the choice had been all hers. "The beer must be terrible."

"And the customers haven't heard any good gossip," I added.

"That as well," she agreed. "If there's no good gossip, is it even really a tavern?"

I snorted softly in amusement. "Not a good one."

The Lioness' Favour was a two story building, with rooms above the taproom. Presumably travellers who arrived after the last lift for the day spent the night in places like this. I wondered if the taverns ever paid the lift crew to finish early, so they could take advantage of people like that.

If they did, I was determined I wouldn't be one. If I had

to, I would pay more than the taverns combined to get out of Cape Massin before nightfall.

"Beer and lunch, please." Kerina flipped a coin to a server and chose a seat near the wide windows.

Like the others in the Cape, they sported heavy shutters which could be closed quickly if the weather turned particularly bad. Right now, they were wide open onto the street, letting in sunlight and sound.

I sat opposite Kerina and nodded to the woman who sat a bowl of stew and a mug of beer in front of me. I would have loved a burger, but apparently the old ways included avoiding modern food. Or at least fast food, since the woman at the table beside ours had spaghetti bolognese.

"Any peculiar music?" I asked when the woman had moved away.

Kerina looked surprised, then glanced around. "You think what I heard yesterday was a..." She mouthed the word "sprite."

"I don't know," I admitted. "But if only you could hear it and only I saw the kid, if there was one, it stands to reason the two things are related. Odd shit tends to be."

"None of this occurred before Viva arrived at the Vault," Kerina mused.

"I'm surprised you would be the one to point that out," I said. "I thought you liked her."

"I find her power incredible and I hate the idea of allowing anyone to be taken like that." Kerina's voice was even, but her eyes flashed with the anger she'd put aside for the past day.

"I'm sure her arrival and this—whatever this is, is a coincidence. I arrived back on the same train as she did." So did Izzy.

"So it might be your fault." Kerina's smile was back, but guarded this time.

"Potentially," I agreed. "You haven't answered the question."

A frown flitted across her brow. "No, I don't hear any strange music. No music at all. Just chatter." She gestured around the room. "That man over there is annoyed at the amount of tax he had to pay on cows. The man at the table beside him is telling his wife he doesn't have a lover. He's lying, of course."

"You overheard all of that while we were talking?" I was impressed.

"I keep my ears open," she said with a modest shrug. "There's a surprising number of people here who are lying to the people they're with." She paused for a moment before she added, "All right, it's not that surprising. Most people lie about something a dozen times a day, but it's different here. More…duplicitous. Everyone has an agenda."

"To get to the top of the cliff?" I suggested. "Or is there more to it than that?"

She shook her head. "I don't know."

"Is it possible you're seeing something that isn't there?" I asked.

"Normally I would say no and challenge you to a duel to keep my honour." She smiled faintly. "But this feels so off to me. Can you sense anything strange?"

I hadn't until she said that, but once she had, I realised my senses picked up something weird since we walked in.

"Yes. Everyone is uneasy. I don't think anything has happened, but they're expecting it to. They don't know if it's good or bad, but it's…something."

"They anticipated our arrival?" Kerina joked.

"Possibly," I said with a hint of humour. "We might be perceived as ominous by some."

"If they knew why we're here, especially." She turned and

propped a boot on the chair beside her. "Or they have weather sense and something bad is coming."

"I hope to Hades that isn't the case." I grimaced. "The lift will stay town-side all night and so will we." No amount of gold would make them take the risk of pulling the contraption up in high winds or heavy rain. If it was damaged, parts of the town would be cut off from the others for days. We would have to board a ship back to the city, or head south. Either way, it would mean wasted time we couldn't afford.

"As do I," she agreed. "I don't think there are enough rooms in the lower town to accomodate us all until a storm passes."

I nodded. We'd likely end up sleeping on the taproom floor.

I glanced around and caught the eye of a man who sat at the other side of the taproom. Tall and slender, he reminded me of a stick insect if stick insects dressed in blue from head to toe. It wasn't a startling blue, like the sky, but a deep shade that might disappear on a dark street.

The man raised his glass and gave me a nod.

I nodded in return and looked away, but my gaze returned a moment later. The man's eyes were still on me, and he didn't disappear. Not a trick of the light then. If he was a trick of Hades, he was more solid than the kid, but I suspected he was an actual person.

The man rose like a cat uncurling and approached the table, wineglass in one hand, worn travel bag in the other. He moved with slow, deliberate steps, like a dancer making an entrance onto a stage.

"May I join you?" He spoke in the same slow, deliberate way he moved. His accent suggested he'd spent a lot of time away from the Vault. In Scotland, unless I was mistaken.

I regarded the man for a moment before I waved toward the spare chair. "Help yourself."

The man didn't so much as sit and he seemed to flow into the seat. He tucked his long legs under him and placed his glass on the table.

"You're not from here," he stated. The quirk of his brow suggested he hoped we had an interesting story for him.

He would be disappointed. "Neither are you," I stated.

The man gave no sign of annoyance. Rather, he smiled and offered me his hand.

"My name is Wesley, I'm a musician."

"Bain. Kerina." I nodded toward her.

Kerina lowered her boot from the chair beside her, turned to face the table and sat forward eagerly. "A musician? So you sing? Do you play as well?"

"Indeed I do." Wesley spoke in a deep, melodic voice that had undoubtedly soothed even the most rowdy bars. It would probably put me to sleep.

The man leaned down and pulled a small stringed instrument from his bag. He plucked at a couple of strings. The instrument made a soft, pleasant sound, like a harp. Wesley's long fingers strummed a short, but jaunty tune before he lay the instrument on his lap and sipped his wine.

"What is that?" Kerina asked, "I've never seen the like before."

"It's a lyaer," Wesley replied. "Peculiar to the northern parts of the Vault. It's similar to a lyre, but smaller, and more pure of tone." He talked about the instrument like it was a lover.

Kerina nodded with interest and asked several questions I didn't hear.

I listened to their conversation with only half an ear until I found myself interrupting.

"Have you seen anything odd around here?"

Wesley stopped mid-sentence, his mouth open, but his

eyes showed no hint of surprise. For some reason, he expected the question.

I would bet a gold coin he had come to our table in the hope we would ask. Now I had, he didn't seem in a hurry to respond.

Wesley steepled his fingers and pressed them against his lips. "Odd," he drawled. "I have seen a few strange happenings in my day." He spoke like he was an old man, but he wasn't much older than me. Perhaps mid-thirties at the most.

"What about here?" Kerina asked. Her curiosity about the lyaer had apparently been forgotten, her eyes focused instead on the bard.

"At this particular tavern," Wesley nodded, "and in the lower town in general, I have. Strange comings and goings. Talk of people seeing a collection of things which are there in one moment and gone in the next."

"What kind of things?" I struggled to keep my impatience from showing, but the bard's manner started to irritate me.

Wesley looked thoughtful. "People, animals."

"Children?" Kerina asked, without a glance toward me. "Strange music?"

Wesley smiled and plucked a chord or two. "Perhaps. Most folk who talk of these things find themselves the object of ridicule. They talk of peculiar sightings, but then they're laughed out the door."

"What did you see?" I stated.

"You are a very direct man," Wesley said in approval. "Yes, I saw something. A woman. Tall and slender, with dark hair that fell down her back. She stared at me with eyes of vivid blue. I went to say something. I must confess she had me quite tongue-tied, but then she was gone before I got out more than a murmur." His pale skin turned slightly pink.

I shared a glance with Kerina, who furrowed her brow. I

did the same. The woman Wesley described sounded a lot like Viva, but so did a metric butt ton of other women.

If it was her, what did it mean? Was she dead? She might be a pale one, lost between worlds, searching for peace.

My stomach clenched at the idea, but I dismissed it. I shot Kerina a glance and she nodded. Wesley told the truth, at least as he saw it.

I could have figured that out myself; I sensed no deceit in the man's thoughts or feelings. At least where the sighting was involved. In fact, he seemed more than a little scared.

"You were worried you would be ridiculed?" I guessed.

Wesley looked down into his glass, and nodded. "Perhaps not ridiculed so much as not believed. Travelling musicians, bards if you will, tell tales of fancy as a matter of course. If I told this tale, they would expect it was just that."

"Why tell us then?" I asked.

"Perhaps he could tell, just by looking, that you're the kind of man who doesn't laugh," Kerina suggested, a twinkle of humour in her eyes.

"I knew you for honest folk," Wesley said. "Folk who would listen. Folk, perhaps, who have seen odd things yourselves."

I hesitated before I told the bard about seeing the kid. I didn't say anything about Kerina hearing music. I wasn't sure why, but I felt we should keep that to ourselves, for now.

"I thought so." Wesley nodded. "A child, you say. I've not heard tell of one of those. It's usually men and women. Perhaps it's a portent for the future." He looked from me to Kerina and quirked a brow.

Kerina snorted. "Not with me it's not." She propped an elbow on the table. "You may have a point though, maybe it's Hades showing us glimpses of our future."

"In parts of the Vault, Janus is considered the god of the future and the past," Wesley said.

I shrugged. I wasn't going to engage in a conversation about religion. "If it is our future we're seeing, we should keep our eyes out, in case it comes to be. Hades, or Janus, might show us minutes ahead." A kid was certainly not in my immediate future. At least, not that I was aware of.

"Are you sure what you saw wasn't the past?" Kerina asked.

"If I'd met a woman like that, I would remember," Wesley said. He took a gulp of wine as though the idea rattled his nerves and he needed to soothe them.

I nodded. "I don't remember ever seeing a kid like that. Although, just because it's not *my* past, doesn't mean it isn't someone else's."

"That's true," Kerina replied. "I'm still not ruling out sprites or pale ones."

Wesley shuddered. "Don't wish the pale ones on us, dear girl. If they can't move on, they eat flesh." He took another gulp of wine.

"Eat flesh?" Kerina echoed. "I thought they just took bodies."

"Let's hope we don't meet either," I said. "Neither of those sound especially awesome."

Wesley vigorously nodded his agreement. "You're right, man, you're right. Sprites are wicked little buggers, but we can deal with them."

"Yes *we*," I emphasised the word, "can. Kerina and I. Once the lift descends, we'll be on our way."

"I'm coming with you," Wesley said immediately.

"No, you're not," I said firmly.

"Then I'll follow you," Wesley said, equally firm. "You have no authority to stop me from getting aboard that lift as well."

I did, but that would mean getting the city watch involved and likely slow us down by hours. We may miss the lift and the one after that.

I exhaled through my nose in frustration. "Fine, but if you get yourself into any shit, we won't stop to help you. Our business is urgent."

Wesley responded with another vigorous nod. "Indeed, I hope not to need any assistance. From you or anyone else. I have traveled the Vault, and the outside world, from top to bottom and side to side and I've never found trouble I couldn't talk or play my way out of."

"I don't doubt that for a moment." Bards were known for having all the right words to say, at just the right moment. That's why they were bards and I was not. That and I didn't have a musical bone in my body. I couldn't sing unless I was drunk, and that was bad, according to Dex. No, best to leave the barding to others.

"Excellent, where are we headed?" Wesley rubbed his hands together.

"I'm not telling you where we are going," I replied. At the first chance I got, I would leave the bard behind.

"Then I shall have to guess," Wesley declared. "Are we travelling to the south, to the Watcher? Gossip suggests something is going on there."

"What kind of something?" Kerina asked before I could respond.

Wesley opened his mouth, but closed it again with a click of his teeth. "I'm not sure if I should tell you, unless you're going to be forthcoming with me," he said finally.

"In other words, you don't know," I concluded.

Wesley sniffed. "Indeed I do know."

"We could always ask someone else." Kerina placed her palms on the table and began to stand.

"Wait," Wesley said quickly. "I'll tell you, but you should know it isn't much."

I waved for him to hurry up and speak.

"The word is there are whispers of war with the Keeper."

I cocked my head at the man. "War with Dex? Why?" We had heard that, but had no reason to believe it. Not yet. "There hasn't been trouble between the south and the city for a long time."

"Two hundred and twenty-three years, to be precise," Wesley said. "Whispers suggest Dex has an artefact Slade wants. Something about a stone dragon the witches had in their possession until recently."

"People have gone to war over less," Kerina said.

I nodded my agreement. Much less. An insult, real or imagined, had sparked many conflicts. A powerful artefact, that was something else completely. I hated to think what might happen if Slade got his hands on it.

"With any luck, it won't come to all out war," I said.

"That's not where we're going, is it?" Wesley asked.

Before I could confirm, deny or remind the bard I wouldn't tell him anything, Kerina spoke.

"The lift is almost to the ground. We should hurry if we're going to get a spot on board."

"Yes." I rose without hesitation and reclaimed my bags from the floor.

Wesley hastily pushed his lyaer back into his bag and followed, almost on my heels.

"Would Hades judge me too harshly if he accidentally fell out of the lift?" I grumbled low enough for only Kerina to hear.

"I would imagine so, yes." She gave me a smile without sympathy and hurried through the crowds who all headed in the same direction.

Someone stepped on my foot. With the closely pressed crowd, I couldn't tell if it was Wesley or a stranger. I glanced toward the bard, but the man's eyes were straight ahead.

I put the incident out of my mind and marvelled at how Kerina somehow stood at the front of the line for the lift.

Only three women stood in front of her. Who had she elbowed or bribed to get there so quickly?

"Excuse me." I had to push through a group of burly men and several small children to reach Kerina. Mutters followed me, but I ignored them. With any luck, there would be room enough for us all on the lift.

"A silver coin before you board," a woman called out as the massive platform gently made landfall and discharged a couple of dozen people. "A silver coin. Please stay in line. A silver coin. Please don't shove." The woman had obviously said the words a thousand times a day until she got bored of them.

"Anyone seen to push in will go to the back of the line and may miss this lift. A silver coin…"

Kerina handed the woman a coin for herself and me, Wesley eagerly reached around me to press his own coin into the woman's hand. I turned my face to avoid getting Wesley's nose in my eye and stepped aboard the lift.

We all shuffled to the far side to allow other travellers to board. I found myself pressed against a high, iron railing, similar to those on a ship. Hopefully it was just as sturdy, or more so. With all of the jostling, a lot of pressure would come to bear against them.

The woman shut a small gate from the outside and slid a bolt into place. A handful of people groaned and muttered about not being allowed onto the lift, but there was barely enough room as it was.

I sucked in a breath and held it as the lift gave a jolt and began to rise.

"A touch unnerving, is it not?" Wesley asked. The bard looked to be enjoying himself thoroughly, or perhaps he was enjoying the expression of discomfort on my face.

I schooled myself to my usual mask of calm and said, "Your elbow is in my ribs."

"Oh!" Wesley tucked his arms in closer to himself. "I'm terribly sorry. It is close quarters here."

"Yes," I replied simply. I leaned back against the railing. They didn't move, even a hair. Of course, the town couldn't risk having anyone fall, or the lift would have to be shut down. They might as well abandon the place now, it would die just as surely.

"Are you all right?" Kerina whispered in my other ear.

"I'm okay. I'm just resting for the journey ahead." Not sooner had I said those words than the first drops of rain hit my face.

What the fuck? I could have sworn the sky was clear a moment ago. Before I could open my eyes a crack, the rain began to fall in torrents. It poured down my face and drenched my clothes in a matter of moments.

Thunder rolled and lighting cracked.

The wind started to howl. It grabbed the lift with invisible hands and rocked it from side to side.

The surface under my feet became slick. The wind buffeted the lift again and I slid from the railing into the people who had stood in front of me.

I wiped the rain from my eyes and ventured to open them. The amount of people onboard seemed smaller now, with many huddled together, holding on to each other or sitting against the railing. Several held limbs in awkward angles. Broken against the railings, I presumed.

The lift had ground to a halt several metres below the first level on the cliffside.

The wind blew again, harder this time. Lighting flashed so close it seemed to skim the air just above our heads.

Someone screamed.

The lift bumped against the side of the cliff and ground against the stone with a desperate whine.

"Get us off here!" someone shouted, a woman with a long nose and eyes wide in terror.

"It's not too far to jump." A man dressed as a butcher peered over the side.

"You're crazy, Elmer," a woman told him, his wife perhaps. "It's a long way down already." She waved her arm at the top of the cliff and shouted, "Let us down!"

If anyone heard, no answer came. The lift stayed in place.

The wind grabbed it in the strongest fingers yet and blew it away from the cliff before it slammed it back in. The railing groaned and cracked along one side.

The lift rebounded and spun. A handful of people slid toward the now open edge.

I pushed through between two women, but could only watch as they slid over the edge and into the abyss. Screams followed them down, but ended abruptly after only a moment.

Silence fell until the lift rocked at an angle.

I glanced up, hand over my eyes. One of the cables which held the lift had begun to fray. Threads of steel unraveled like a poorly knitted scarf before the whole cable snapped.

One side of the lift dropped and spun on the last cable. Some were thrown against the remaining section of railing, but more plunged off the side.

I managed to grab a section of railing and hung with my feet dangling over the edge.

Don't look down, I told myself.

I looked down.

The ground beneath lit up by another flash of lightning. It was dotted with bodies

I swallowed and looked up. The only way off was up that last cable. If I could reach it.

I started to pull myself up the broken railing, which

somehow held my weight. Like a monkey, I swung hand over hand, even when my arms began to ache.

I worked my way up under the cable. I would have to swing myself onto the upper side of the lift and grab the cable.

I took a breath.

The cable groaned. The lift rocked and shuddered. Shards of something fell along with the rain and I realised it was pieces of the second cable. It too had begun to fray.

I worked my way to the side of the railing and—

"Bain? Bain?" The voice was persistent. Sound snapped in front of my face. Not a cable, something else.

I shook my head. "Kerina?" I blinked several times. She held her hand up in front of my face and waggled her fingers.

"It's time to get off, we're at the top."

The sun shone on my face.

A glance at the railing showed the lower town far below. The lift, and everyone on it, was intact.

A man unbolted the gate and I stepped onto solid ground.

18

Bain

"So you saw—what?" Kerina cocked her head at me.

I sighed and shifted on the hard seat. By the time we arrived at the top of the Cape, it was too late to secure horses, or get too far before dark. It chafed me, but after the weird experience on the lift, the chance to sit in another tavern, with a mug of beer and a plate of roasted meat and vegetables was welcome.

"I saw the lift destroyed in a storm." I kept my voice low. The taproom was packed and everyone seemed interested in their business. "I lived it. It seemed real."

"Could it have been a dream?" Kerina suggested. "Horses fall asleep standing up."

The side of my mouth twitched. "I am not a horse. I have never slept standing up." I sucked in a breath and spoke more evenly. "I have known guards to fall asleep at their post. This…" I searched for the words, "was vivid. I *felt* the rain. I *saw* those people fall." I couldn't contain a shudder. "I was *there*."

"Like the kid was there?" Kerina asked. For once, she sat with both boots on the ground, a sure sign of her agitation, even if outwardly she looked calm.

I chewed on the question for a moment. "I suppose so. She felt real, but I only saw her for a matter of seconds. With her… I felt as though I got a glimpse into her world. This time I was *in* that world." If Hades was trying to tell me something, I wished he'd stop. Or be more clear.

"It may be a warning," Kerina suggested. "A storm might really," she glanced to the side and back again, "do that."

"If it does, you weren't on it," I replied. "Neither was he." I nodded toward where Wesley strummed his lyaer and sang a cheerful song.

It sounded like 'The Maid Goes A-Courting', an old song, even by the standards of those who kept the old ways. In this version, the woman in the lyrics was no maid and it was much more than a *courting* she was after. The crowd in the taproom seemed to enjoy it, especially the more explicit verses.

I only half listened. I'd heard worse in the bars in the Vault and in the human world. At least the bard had a pleasant voice; the kind which could be tuned out if necessary.

"Well, that's good to know," Kerina said dryly. "All you need to do is stay off it for the rest of your days and everything will be fine."

I snorted into my beer. The feeling of impending trouble would be more difficult to shake. I had felt myself about to plunge to my death. The faces of those who fell in front of my eyes were starting to fade. I tried to picture them all, but couldn't. Like a dream, the details slipped away when I woke, but the chill sat heavy in my bones.

"Do you think," Kerina said after a few minutes of silence, " anyone else saw it?"

I blinked at her in surprise. I was so shaken by the…whatever it was, vision? Hallucination? Illusion? I hadn't thought about those who travelled on the lift with us.

"Why?" I asked slowly. "Did you see anyone who looked—"

"Scared? Horrified? Confused?" she suggested. She tapped her fingers on the tabletop. "Aside from the man who sat in the middle with his hands over his face. A few people looked as though they may leave their last meal behind."

"Nothing to suggest they'd witnessed their own death?"

"I was paying more attention to you than to them, but I—"

Kerina was interrupted by a shout of surprise. A woman leapt to her feet and all but threw herself backward, halfway across the room.

"Vermin. Vermin!" she said, lip curled in disgust. With a trembling hand, she pointed toward the table where she was sitting.

I shot to my feet and followed her gaze. Everyone cleared a space around the table, but the table itself was empty.

Empty.

Until I squinted. A rat the size of a large cat lay curled up, washing a paw with its tongue. It was there, but it wasn't. The creature was opaque, like a shadow. Through it, the rest of the room was clearly visible.

I stepped toward the rat.

I watched it, unblinking until I stood right in front of the table. I raised my hand slowly and reached out toward it. The rat sniffed at me, then went back to cleaning its paw. Right when my hand should touch fur, it went straight through.

"I see nothing," someone grumbled.

Lucky you, I thought. Although, the rat was a bit more harmless than a falling platform, high above the ground.

I pulled back my hand slowly and the rat disappeared, as if it had never been there at all.

The woman gasped. "Thank Hades."

I managed to stop myself from flinching as someone put a hand on my shoulder.

"What was it?" Kerina asked.

"A trick of the light, I suppose," I said, for the benefit of those around us, especially the woman. If I could convince her that was all it was, then she might forget all about this.

A few people around us muttered, but most simply nodded and returned to their tables. Later they would talk about a hysterical woman who imagined something, but they hadn't seen a thing.

I scanned the room on the way back to my own table. If anyone saw the rat, no one gave any sign. They seemed annoyed at having their meal interrupted, but nothing more.

I flopped down in my seat and reclaimed my beer.

"You saw nothing?" I asked.

Wesley went back to telling his audience a tale, as though he hadn't so much as paused.

"No, but the woman who shouted, she wasn't lying about seeing vermin of some kind." I described what I saw in as few words as possible.

"That does sound like a pale one," Kerina said thoughtfully. "No wonder she was frightened." She cocked her head. "You didn't seem too bothered by it."

I shrugged. "It was as real as the kid. Less so. I didn't feel as though it posed a threat to me or anyone here."

"Unless she died of fright." Kerina nodded in the woman's direction.

"Let's not hope for that," I said dryly.

Kerina looked embarrassed at having suggested it, but it was as fleeting as it usually was for her. She never took anything to heart for too long. Even her anger burnt out eventually.

"I wouldn't, but—"

Whatever she was about to say, I don't know because I rose so quickly I knocked my chair back almost into the man behind me. The man spluttered, but I ignored him. My eyes were on the woman who saw the rat, as she hurried toward the door.

"Excuse me," I said hastily to Kerina and pushed through to the street.

In the gloom, I couldn't see for a moment. When my eyes adjusted to the dimly lit street, illuminated only by light from windows and open doors, I spied a dark shape bustling away around a corner.

I trotted after her, my senses open, seeking her. Her emotions were fear, laced with something else. Humiliation maybe. Had the people she was with laughed, or ridiculed her? None seemed to have followed her into the night.

I rounded the corner and stopped. I still sensed her on the edge of my perception, but I saw no sight of her. No shadows in the doorways, no flash of movement in front of a window.

"Hello?" I called out softly.

"Hello, what are we looking for?" Wesley spoke loudly behind me.

I jumped.

Shit.

"Shhh!"

"Oh sorry, I—"

I cut him off again with a hiss. I reached out, but any sign of the woman was gone. I growled under my breath in frustration.

"I was trying to speak to the woman in the tavern," I said without turning around. "She might have seen other things as well." I glanced over my shoulder. "Did you see the rat?"

"I, er, no. I saw you touch, well, air." Wesley came around to stand beside me as the moon cast a dim ray over the upper town of Cape Massin. "I did wonder what you were about. A rat, you say? That is curious." He ran his hands up and down the sides of his long chin.

"It is?" I asked.

"Oh, most certainly. Do you think she was scared of rats before tonight?"

"That was why I wanted to speak to her." I barely contained my irritation.

"Ah, shall we look for her then? I think she went around the next corner." Wesley waved.

The moon rose a little higher. If the moon was fuller, we could spot her as clear as day, but that was several nights away.

"There you are." Kerina appeared out of the shadows, knife in hand. She slipped it away and crossed her arms. "Well? Which way are we going?"

"This way." Wesley headed off before I could stop him. The bard was going to get himself killed if he ran into trouble so fast. It was a wonder he hadn't already.

"Come on," I muttered to Kerina and moved carefully down the street after the bard's back.

I kept my senses open for signs of anything which might be out of place. In spite of that, I almost missed the presence of two—no three minds up ahead.

"Wesley," I whispered. "Wait."

"What is it?" Wesley said loudly. He almost got a knife in the chest for his trouble. It missed him by a whisker and clattered against the wall beside him. He let out a squeak of fright, but the knife hadn't been thrown hard enough to do more than graze.

Kerina grabbed it up before anyone else could move.

I held up my hands to either side. "I just want to talk."

"Who are you?"

I recognised the woman's voice. "I saw the vermin too. I just wanted to—"

"I imagined it," she snapped. "I must have." Her voice trailed off and her certainty with it.

"No, you didn't," I replied. "It was a huge rat. I've never seen one so big."

A figure stepped closer to me. I lowered my hands but kept one near my knife.

"You're the man who tried to touch it," she stated. "Your hand passed through it. It can't have been real."

"Can we go somewhere to talk?" I asked.

"Why?" she asked. "It wasn't real. We need to accept that. Forget about it. Pray to Hades to—to…"

"Keep rats away?" I suggested.

The shudder she gave in response was physical and mental. "Horrid things." I felt her disgust.

"Were you scared of them before tonight?" Kerina was cleaning her nails with the knife she'd picked up.

"Yes," the woman replied. "I always have been, ever since one bit me when I was small."

"That would do it," Kerina agreed."I'm not a big fan of them myself. They're still better than spiders."

"Yuck," Wesley muttered. "They're all horrid."

While they talked, I squinted at the other two figures. Young women, unless I was mistaken. The woman's daughters perhaps.

"You could use some practice in knife throwing," I said, guessing the closer one had been the thrower.

She sniffed. "I almost got him."

"You're fortunate you missed," I said. "The city watch would not have taken it well if you hadn't."

"You were chasing my mother. I was defending her." The

young woman had no hint of apology in her voice. I appreciated that, even though throwing knives at strangers in the dark usually did more harm than good to everyone concerned.

"We didn't mean to scare you," I said evenly. "We'll let you go about your business." I went to turn away, but the woman spoke before I could.

"My name is Latika. You're welcome to spend the night in my house. I have two spare rooms you can use. Two of you will have to share."

"We wouldn't want to impose," I said slowly.

"It's no imposition. It's the least we could do after Aisha almost killed one of you."

Aisha hadn't even come close, but I didn't bother to correct her.

"We would appreciate that, thank you. The taverns seem pretty full this evening."

"Yeah, they have been lately. There's been strange things going on in the countryside around the Cape. Folks have wandered into town on business and then stayed longer than they need to. Some are muttering about war. Others are talking of strange creatures coming out of the mountains to feed on paranormal flesh."

She shuddered again and I felt her fear like a cold glove on my chest.

"Perhaps we should get out of the dark," Wesley suggested.

"Yes. Please lead the way, Latika." I kept half an eye on her and her daughters and the rest of my senses on the street around and ahead of us.

If Kerina sensed any deceit on their part, she would have said so, but that didn't mean there weren't other folk around who meant us trouble. Or meant Latika trouble.

We reached a small cottage without seeing another

person, and Latika opened the door into a warm space lit by low lights and candles.

Kerina and I exchanged a glance. I almost saw her thinking and suppressed a smile. We would be safe from sprites, at least for tonight. Pale ones—we'd deal with them if they became a problem.

In the light, I now saw Latika was in her late forties. Aisha and her sister were no more than twelve or fourteen. Young to be throwing knives to defend their mother.

"I know what you are," Kerina said suddenly. "I should have seen it."

I gave her a sharp look. She looked furious, but when I delved I saw it was with herself.

"Kerina" I asked.

From the corner of my eye, I saw Latika and both daughters with their hands at their hips. They watched not my face but my shoulders.

"What are you?" I asked carefully.

"They're assassins, like I used to be," Kerina said.

Wesley gasped. "Assassins?"

"Well, not just assassins," Kerina replied. "They're trained from birth to kill. They're highly skilled and kill without mercy."

"I take what jobs I am paid for," Latika stated. "Aisha and Erin aren't old enough, or trained enough yet."

Aisha scowled, but said nothing. Of course, she would have been taught to obey before she learnt to walk.

"That knife," I said slowly, "you meant to miss."

"Certainly," Aisha replied. "If I wanted to kill you, and was allowed to, you would be dead now. All three of you." She seemed very certain.

Her confidence reminded me of Kerina. While she might not have been capable of killing me or Kerina as easily as she assumed, she would have done some damage. She might have died in the attempt, so thank Hades it hadn't come to that. I drew the line at killing children, but to defend myself, I'd do what I had to.

"So, a deadly assassin is afraid of vermin?" I stated.

Latika stared at me, unblinking. "No one is without fear." Her chin lowered slightly. "No one in the Cape can know what we are. I pretend I'm a scared village woman. No one looks twice at us."

"Except they will now, with you seeing giant rats," Kerina replied.

Latika sighed. "That is unfortunately correct. We will need to move on."

"But, Mother—" Aisha protested.

Latika held up a hand and Aisha fell silent immediately. "Tomorrow we'll leave. Tonight, we must rest. Erin, show them to the spare rooms. We all leave at dawn."

I frowned. "You're not coming with us."

"There is safety in numbers. Besides, Aisha and Erin would benefit from learning from another assassin."

"I'm sure they would, but another time. Where we're going is dangerous. We don't need children to come along."

Aisha's eyes flashed with anger, but Latika was unmoved.

"The decision is made. I suggest you rest as well." Latika gave me a curt nod.

My mouth turned down and I had to suppress a knot of anger. "You are not in charge—"

Erin touched my arm lightly. "Best do as she says," she said softly. "She always gets her way. It's easier to go along with her."

"I can see that," I said dryly.

"It will be a jolly company," Wesley remarked cheerfully. "I could teach the girls some songs."

I assumed Latika might object, on the grounds music was frivolous, or some such crap. To my surprise, she nodded.

"I have had to pretend to be a bard, but I know only a handful of songs and few are recent. I would like to add to my repertoire."

"Oh, wonderful. why don't we pretend to be a band of travelling musicians?" I said sarcastically.

Apparently only Kerina took note of my tone, because she snorted softly.

Wesley clapped his hands and grinned and even Latika seemed pleased at the idea.

"Hades help me," I muttered.

"You're going to need it," Kerina said.

I couldn't disagree with her. Dex would probably find the whole situation hilarious. That knowledge did nothing to assuage my fear that this could all end very badly.

"Rest is a good idea," I said. When the house was quiet, I'd rouse Kerina and sneak away without the others. Although, something told me that wouldn't be so easy.

Hades help me indeed.

19

"IT'S FOR YOUR OWN GOOD," Luther assured me. He slipped a length of black fabric over my eyes and tied it behind my head. "You'll have more freedom this way."

I strained to see from under the bottom of the blindfold, but he'd put it on too well.

"By not being able to see?" I asked.

Luther chuckled. "Only for the next hour or two. If you can't see the way in, you won't find the way out. Before you think to try, these mountains are unforgiving. Unless you know exactly where you're going, you'll get lost and die up here. Now, you'll need help to get back on your horse."

I bit back a comment about how much easier it would be to mount without a blindfold. I even thought of suggesting they trust me when I say I wouldn't run. In the end, I didn't bother to say a word. Neither Luther nor Helene would listen anyway.

Even if I wanted to, I didn't have time to speak before Luther picked me up with the power and plopped me onto the saddle a little too hard. My horse shifted under me in indignation. I grabbed for the cantle before he could toss me back to the ground.

"Sorry," Luther said. "We don't mean you any harm. The sooner you accept that, the better for you. I was hoping we could be friends. I still want that." Silence fell before the scent of him moved away.

I tried to exhale through my nose, but the fabric was so tight, I was forced to use my mouth instead. I grunted to myself in frustration. When I first met Luther, he'd seemed nice enough. Now... How could anyone expect me to make friends in this situation?

In spite of his warning, I would run the moment I got the chance. I would find my way to the nearest town. No matter what they thought, I wouldn't die on the mountain.

Thank Hades I still held on to the cantle, because my mount moved forward without warning. Luther, or someone else, must hold the reins. I wanted to grind my teeth at the indignity. Perhaps slavery wouldn't have been so bad. I might have ended up working in the kitchen of some wealthy merchant, or cleaning their toilets. It had to be better than this.

I shivered in the cooler, thinner air and drew in several slow breaths. If I couldn't see where I was going, at least I could smell it. The heavy scent of trees: the loquat flowers, the sap of the hevea, the leaves of some type of gum. If I wasn't bound, I could throw my captors and their escort off the side of the mountain.

Unless Helene threw me off first.

I gritted my teeth and focused on memorising the scents we passed. At least, I tried. Having my nose covered impeded me, and with so many strong smells, they soon became a mishmash.

I leaned forward instinctively as the horse strained up the increasing incline. None of this was the animal's fault, I wouldn't make it harder for him than necessary.

I gradually became aware of the sound of water trickling —no, gushing from somewhere nearby. A stream? Maybe a waterfall?

I breathed in a hint of the scent of water. There was no power in it, not even a hint, but it was sweet and helped clear my mind.

The further we went, the louder the sound of water became. The vegetation smell became that of plants which only lived beside a water source. Vines with some kind of pungent flower, twisted around more hevea.

At least, that was what I pictured. Perhaps fish darted through the water and small animals stopped on the bank to sip before they scurried off to hide. A tiger might lurk in the shadows and hunt us all.

I wasn't too worried about those. Luther and Helene would drive them away before they got close enough. Still, I would prefer to see for myself.

Shit.

I startled at the sound of a short cry from above, but quickly laughed at myself. It was a bird of some kind, or a monkey; too brief to make out for certain.

A moment later, Luther said, "We're almost there."

Not an animal, then, but a human watcher, signalling our presence?

My heart pounded and the blood ran colder in my veins. Whatever they needed me for, I should find out soon enough.

The call came again, closer this time. How could I have mistaken it for anything but a human?

Even with the blindfold blocking most of the light, the day turned darker. The air cooled even further. I shivered. What sounded like a gate clanged behind us and the tread of hooves on dirt turned to the clip clop on stone, or pavement.

Another clang sounded behind us, a door this time. The slide of a heavy bolt and my horse stopped.

"Do you need help to get down?" To my surprise, that was Knox's voice.

"Yes, please." My hands twitched to pull off the blindfold, but I would wait. If I seemed cooperative, they would drop their guard. At least, I hoped so.

"Here, take my hands." Knox slipped his hand into mine and held me steady while I swung my leg back over the horse's back. I paused and leaned my weight against the saddle before I slid down to the ground. When I landed, Knox was there to steady me. The warmth of his body felt better than I expected. I might have stood there for a few moments longer than necessary.

"Thank you," I said softly.

"Any time." He squeezed my hands gently, then moved away.

Another set of boots approached.

"We can take this off now," Luther undid the blindfold and tugged it down. He slipped it into his pocket, a smile gracing the corners of his mouth. For some reason, the look gave me chills.

I glanced around, partly to look for Knox and partly to take in my surroundings. I saw no sign of the spy now.

The escort, with the help of a handful of kids, led the horses into stables which looked like they'd been around since the birth of Hades. Worn down in places, the stone was covered in moss here or showed the path of water there. Most of the blocks were stained.

I touched the side of a stable doorway with my fingertips.

It was smooth as though hundreds of people had brushed past it over the last thousand years. They probably had, and horses too.

Another doorway, this one wide enough for four or five people to step through at the same time, led to an enormous room.

"Where the hells are we?" I kept my voice low, reverent. The place was ancient. Shouting here would be like sacrilege somehow, maybe to a deity older than Hades or his contemporaries.

"It's the Citadel of Comus, in the old city of Jintaro. When Jintaro was the capital of the Vault," Helene said, her tone brusque. "Now it's merely a relic of the past, and a beacon for the future." She bustled by me without a backward glance.

I took my bag from the boy who offered it and hurried after Helene.

"What the fuck do you mean by that?" I demanded. The bond tugged, but Luther's long strides caught up and eased the sensation. *Even here, I'm bound,* I thought bitterly.

"Don't tell me I'll find out soon enough. I want to know what's going on. *Now.*"

Helene stopped and turned so quickly I almost took a step back. At the last moment, I stood my ground.

"According to the tales, Comus is one of the younger gods," Helene said as though speaking to a kid. "Hecate gave birth to him, but later incarcerated him so she could gain his power."

I frowned. "So what? What the gods do is none of our business."

"Foolish girl, there are no gods," Helene snapped.

My frown deepened. "You say according to the tales... You mean they—" I shook my head. "Even if Comus was a man, he'd be long dead by now. Hades and Hecate too."

Silence fell.

Luther filled it. "Assuming they didn't find a way to cheat death."

Helene snorted. "That is just as foolish. The Great One was taken aside from death. Frozen, if you will. Come." She turned and bustled on, leaving me to catch up.

We passed through the huge room, which might once have been a greeting hall for the supplicants of a past ruler.

The ceiling had holes where the stone had crumbled. Trees and vines had climbed over the building and filled some of them, almost to the point that little rain would enter. It gave the place an eerie look and feel. The air in the chamber was cool and damp, a pleasant change to the climate of the city, or Sydney in summer. I would miss the sunshine if I was here too long though.

At the rear of the chamber, a jagged opening might once have been a small doorway. Parts had crumbled in and the stone removed, so it looked more like a gaping mouth, leading into a cavern.

The closer we came, the more I wondered if the doorway had once been closed in, and later forced to reopen. I eyed Helene and Luther, but neither of their expressions revealed anything.

Helene stepped through the opening and walked into the increasing darkness with deliberate pace.

"Are you sure this is—" I followed, only to find that gaps here and there in the stone walls gave enough light to penetrate the gloom. Enough, thank fuck, that I didn't trip when the floor became uneven.

"It's perfectly safe," Luther assured me. "Nothing can harm us here."

"Except me?" I asked. "Do I really need to be bound now? It's not as though I'm gonna hurt you." Yet. "You're both stronger and better trained than I am." I was guessing that about Luther, but it seemed a safe bet.

Luther glanced toward Helene, who looked thoughtful for a moment before she nodded.

"Very well. As you say, we are stronger and you cannot run."

I might have imagined feeling the bond slip off, but I was immediately able to touch the power again. I drew in a few drops to reassure myself I could.

If I thought I would pull it off, I would throw them both against the wall, hard enough to snap them. In spite of myself, I wanted to know more about this Comus and his apparent imprisonment. It sounded like a kid's story to me, but Helene seemed to believe it.

Helene's eyes narrowed, but she nodded, clearly satisfied I would behave. At least for now.

"Come along then, time is short."

We continued on down a tunnel, and stepped out into another chamber, this one circular and with a domed ceiling. At least, it must have looked that way once. Like everywhere else here, gaps showed through the roof. Muted sunlight slanted down to hit the approximate centre of the chamber, illuminating a puddle of old, green water. It was probably full of mosquito larvae. Just the thought made me want to scratch.

"I think you need better servants here," I remarked.

Luther chuckled. "That's what I keep saying."

"When the Great One is free, there will be no need," Helene said. "It's unlikely the citadel will remain standing."

"Perhaps we should leave now." I eyed the ceiling uneasily. "I'd hate to come this far and die when that collapses on us."

"We are safe enough," Helene said.

If that was supposed to reassure me, it failed.

"So you say," I said under my breath. I waited for Helene to gag me again, but she didn't. Luther didn't put the blindfold back on me either, thank Hades. Evidently, wherever they were taking me, I was allowed to see it.

At the end of the tunnel, we started up a series of stairs. Like everywhere else I had seen so far, they were worn, but these had been cared for. I expected the treads to be slick with moss or moisture, but they were firm and dry, if short and narrow. Whoever built them must have been shorter and with smaller feet.

Beside me, Luther seemed to have even greater difficulty. He slowed and took each stair with deliberate care.

"According to a book I read once, people are taller now than they were a few hundred years ago," I remarked.

"That, or these were built by children," Luther grumbled. His smile was forced.

"Possibly," I agreed. "They kept children as slaves back then too."

Luther's brow twitched, but he didn't reply apart from a slight grunt.

"There will be no slaves when the Great One is released," Helene declared. "Everyone in the Vault will be free."

Luther nodded, but his expression changed from pleasant to ardent. "And those outside the Vault."

I pursed my lips. Whoever or whatever this Comus was, it sounded like he might make trouble for the Witch's Council. On one hand, I couldn't give them too much sympathy. On the other, they weren't all bad.

"I see you don't believe us," Helene said, "but you will come to."

"Really? When?" I asked dryly.

Helene sniffed. "Luther did not believe, at first."

I blinked at him. "Did you have to be convinced the same way I'm being made to?" I asked.

"I needed less persuasion to come here," he replied. "The

moment I knew Helene was Hemathea, I was bound to the cause, by my own choice."

"At least you were given one," I remarked. "Not kidnapped, or handed over by someone you thought you could trust." If I ever saw Bain again...

"The subterfuge was necessary," Helene said. "The Keeper needed to see a display of our power. He would not have believed it otherwise."

I had to concede that point. Dex was not the sort of man to take words at face value. He would have wanted a full explanation of Helene's interest in me. Did Bain have one? I might never know the full extent of his involvement. I certainly wouldn't ask Helene. The woman would only tell me whatever she wanted me to hear, and no more. Luther too.

"Dex said I was free to go wherever I pleased, and do whatever I wanted," I said finally.

Helene stopped at the top of the stairs to regard me through heavy lidded eyes. She looked tired, as though the last few weeks had taken their toll on her. I couldn't bring myself to sympathise with her either.

"The Keeper is like anyone with power," Helene said slowly. "He likes to play at being benevolent, but he keeps his toys close to hand until he tires of them."

"You think he saw me as a toy?" I asked.

It was Luther who responded. "You're powerful and beautiful. He wouldn't be the first man to aspire to own a woman like you."

"And yet, you're the asshole who threatened to break me." I wiped a bead of sweat from my brow and puffed lightly from the exertion of climbing the stairs.

"Because this is bigger than you," Helene said curtly. "Breaking you is a last resort. We prefer to have you be one of us. Dex would discard you once he grew bored, just as the witches discarded you. Just as your Hades chosen mate did."

I wanted to deny that, but I couldn't. The Covener and his asshole son had done exactly that, with the blessing of the Council. Dex had probably forgotten all about me already, in spite of what he'd said when Helene forced me away from him.

If Comus truly wanted to free the world, in return for living out his days, then he might be the lesser evil.

I would consider it at least.

I looked past Helene. "Where to now?" The tunnels seemed to have reached a dead end.

"This way." Helene led us into the deepest shadows, her steps unwavering.

I followed, hands out in front of me, drops of power held instinctively against anything unexpected. Where I thought I would hit a wall, there was nothing. The darkness here was so absolute, it masked the way.

Something scurried across our path.

Shit. I jumped, my heart racing.

By the rapid sound of tiny feet, it ran from us, more scared than I was. A rat or mouse, most likely. I ventured a sniff and caught the musty smell of vermin.

After a few minutes, the dark gave way to gloom, which gradually became light, the same dappled green as down below, but the air here was cooler still and somehow thinner. It reeked of something I couldn't identify. Something unpleasant, but not disgusting like sewage. It was more like fruit which had hung too long on the vine. The vines covering the citadel might bear fruit, but I couldn't see any, just stalks and tiny leaves.

We stepped into yet another chamber, this one small and rectangular.

I hardly noticed. My eyes were drawn to a stone sarcophagus which dominated the centre of the room. The lid sat closed, carved with ornate symbols and images which tugged at my memory, but I couldn't quite place them.

"This is your Great One?" I asked. I winced as the echo in the room threw my words back to me.

"Merely where he rests right now," Helene replied. Her voice was soft, reverent.

"Ah." My tongue darted over my lips. "And how do you know what he wants, or plans? Or that he is even alive?"

"Quiet," Helene urged. "Listen. Feel." She gripped my wrist in a firm hold before I could move away from her. Luther moved to the other side of Helene. She grabbed onto his wrist as well.

I had the strangest sensation of power slipping from me and almost used it to shove Helene back. At the last moment, I realised the power lapped back into me like the ebb and flow of the tide. It didn't just come from Helene, but from Luther as well.

I was wrong about one thing. They weren't stronger than me. Their power was different, more refined, but I was their equal, if not their better, in strength. Did Helene realise she'd revealed that?

The woman stood with her eyes closed, mouth set in a firm line. I gave a slight tug on the power and drew some of it in.

Helene flinched. "Focus," she growled.

Torn between curiosity and the desire to push Helene against the wall and cut off the flow of air to her lungs, I gave in to curiosity.

I turned my gaze to the sarcophagus and half closed my eyes. I kept a portion of my attention on Helene, all too aware that if I could take their power, they could take mine.

I tucked a little bit away in the back of my mind, in the hope it might be enough to fight back if they tried anything.

I blurred my eyes and opened my thoughts to whatever I was supposed to open them to. At first, I felt nothing but the power, like the lap of a warm pool against my body. The sensation threatened to lull me, but I caught myself at the brink and held myself firmly there.

Gradually, I felt a fourth presence in the room. Faint at first, it grew until it was almost on par with Helene and Luther.

Comus? I thought.

The response was more a sense of agreement than a reply with words.

Helene says you're alive in there.

Again, the response came in the form of a sensation.

And you want to get out of there? I couldn't blame him, it must be boring as fuck inside there.

This time I heard a faint, "Yesss," drawn out like a hiss of wind. "We can all be free." The words came with such a rush of warmth, I almost stepped back. If it wasn't for Helene's grip, I would have.

You really want that, don't you? For everyone to be free of... Their burdens. Their chains.

"Yesss," Comus hissed. "Free."

How?

"The power. Only the power. You must learn. Then the world can...be free."

"Learn?" I said out loud.

"To use your power. My prison is strong." His voice became more faint. "You will need..."

"Need what?" But he was gone, along with any feeling of warmth.

I shivered. The room felt cold and damp. Helene no longer held my wrist, but had moved to look out through a small hole in the wall.

"Now you understand," she stated without looking over her shoulder.

I understood, but I wasn't sure it was what Helene wanted to hear. "You could have told me," I replied carefully.

"Would you have listened?" Helene turned slowly. Her eyes bore into me as if she tried to read my soul. "Would you have believed me?"

Not in a *million* lifetimes. Still, I chewed my bottom lip in contemplation for a moment. "I suppose not." I let my lip go and added, "But you couldn't be sure of that."

Helene's eyes flicked to Luther and back. "Most dare not take that leap of faith. We dare not take that risk. Time is running short. He gets weaker each time we speak to him." Her expression softened. She talked about him as though he were a lover, or something more.

I nodded. "I sensed that." That would explain why he trailed off mid-sentence. I would love to know what he tried to say. Had they heard the same words? I suspected not; they were directed at me.

Luther nodded, his brow creased with concern. His expression was no less awed than Helene's. "It's troubling, but we're confident we can work as quickly as we need to, now you're here."

"Yes, but we have no time to waste." Helene rubbed her hands together, then laced her fingers and held them in front of her. "We must begin as soon as we've rested."

I crossed my arms over my chest. My gaze went from one to the other and back. I saw the absolute certainty on their faces. They had worked, perhaps for years, and with me there, they were closer than ever. "Are you *sure* I can help you?" I asked slowly.

Helene's eyes opened in surprise, then narrowed. "There can be no doubt. Our power is almost enough. With three, we will succeed."

"Why me?" I asked. "Luther said there were others."

"They are not strong enough," Helene said curtly.

"Not strong enough or… You asked and they said fuck nope?" I said. That explained the whole abduction thing. I was just the unlucky one, not their first option.

Helene's face turned pink and for a moment I thought she'd lash out.

I drew as much power as I could, but the strange smell in the room made the power feel tainted, heavy.

"I do not need you to have a tongue," Helene snapped. "You will cooperate or we will break you. Nothing must stand in my way."

"I didn't say I wouldn't help," I said quickly. I could learn a lot from them. More than I could ever discover on my own.

"Viva—" Luther reached a hand toward me. "You heard him."

"Yes, I did," I said. I heard *something*. Or thought I did. It had been a long journey here and I was tired. Hallucinations were possible.

"Enough," Helene snapped. "We will all rest. Tomorrow, we begin work. Luther, see to her. If she's difficult, bind her."

"Yes, Hemathea." Luther shot me a warning look.

I pressed my lips together in response.

Helene gave him a curt nod and swept out of the room.

A small figure followed her. Dressed in red and gold, with long dark hair down her back, she looked like a kid.

I shook my head, closed my eyes and opened them again.

"Who is—" The kid was gone, as though she had never been at all.

"What?" Luther asked. his brow furrowed.

"I thought someone followed her."

"There's no one there." He sounded uncertain.

I was almost certain he had seen it too. I inhaled, but if anyone was there, they had no smell at all.

"I'll show you to your room," Luther said.

"Room, or cell?" I asked facetiously.

"Room, if you behave." He smiled as if he told a joke.

"Right. I'll be good." I gave the sarcophagus a long look, but nothing stirred. At least nothing jumped out at me. "Maybe you can tell me how you found this place."

"Of course, it's an interesting story."

20

Viva

"Again," Helene snapped.

I rubbed my forehead and inhaled the scent from the dried roses Helene had placed in a bowl on the table. I drew, but doing so became more difficult each time. I was tired and hungry and we had been at this for hours. Judging by the light which filtered through a gap in the wall, it was past noon. Helene had all but dragged me out of my narrow bed just after dawn.

"I'm hungry," I grumbled.

"When you can separate the grains, you may eat. This is a basic task. Any kid should be able to do it." Helene gave me an angry look down her nose. "Your mother should have taught you this before you could walk."

"Maybe." I shrugged. "But she didn't."

Helene sniffed. "Your stepfather's doing, I would imagine. She should have taught you anyway, for your own safety, if nothing else."

I bristled. I wished for the same thing, but the digs at my stepfather, my mother and pretty much everyone else I ever met were getting annoying.

"Perhaps you should have kidnapped me sooner," I said tartly.

"If I knew I'd have no choice, I would have," Helene snapped. "That may be a priority after the reconstruction. To obtain and train hemitheos children."

Obtain? I shook my head. "What do you mean by reconstruction?"

"There is much work to be done to bring Comus's vision to fruition," Helene explained patiently. Her tone didn't last. A moment later she snapped again, "The grains."

I sighed and focused on them. Some were long and white, others shorter. Still others were brown. It was on these brown grains I concentrated first. Mixed in with the white, I teased a few out and moved them to the side of the table.

"More than three at once," Helene said. "You should have no trouble dividing them all from the others at one time."

"Maybe if I could eat—"

I wasn't prepared for the strike of magic across my face. Helene struck me with such force, I fell off my stool and onto the cold, stone floor. Before I could catch my breath, or retaliate, I was hauled off the floor by invisible fingers and tugged to my feet.

"If you can't learn discipline, you will never learn this," Helene hissed.

She plopped me back on the stool so hard I yelped.

"Try again." Helene pushed the three grains back to the pile, crossed her arms over her chest and sat back.

Resisting the urge to rub my rear, I drew in more power and gave every drop of my attention to the brown grains. How many were there? Two dozen at least. I pinned as many as I could in place with minute amounts of power. When I couldn't hold any more threads, I slid the grains over to the side of the table. Sixteen, seventeen, eighteen, they shoved the white grains out of the way as they moved.

I exhaled and let go of the threads. Five or six grains remained in the original pile. I braced myself for more harsh words or another blow, but Helene nodded.

"Progress, finally. Go and eat. We'll return to this in the morning."

I glanced at her in surprise. I had expected to have a small break and then get back to it immediately afterward. I didn't bother to ask; Helene would not have explained anyway.

I rose and winced. I would have some nasty bruises. Thank Hades nothing was broken. Should I thank the god at all though? If Helene was to be believed, he was no god, just an ungrateful kid. A dangerous one at that.

"Wait," Helene said before I could take a step. I was enveloped in warmth and all the stiffness and pain evaporated. "We are all on the same side here. I don't want you to forget that."

"Thank you, Hemathea." I managed to speak normally and not through gritted teeth laced with sarcasm.

Helene gave me a gracious nod and waved me toward the door.

I hurried out before the woman changed her mind, and trotted down the few steps from the makeshift classroom, to the slightly less makeshift kitchen and dining area.

Someone, likely several someones, had hauled rocks the size of my head into place to make a large oven. A slab of stone served as a heating surface, while pots hung from the underside, directly over the fire. A tray half full of rolls sat on a table in the centre of the room, a plate of yellow cheese beside it. A bowl of butter and another of honey sat on the other side. Jugs of watered down wine, and goat's milk, both already half empty, occupied the other side of the table.

I grabbed a roll, dashed butter and honey on it and poured myself a cup of milk. I didn't like the bitter taste all that much, but it was too early in the day for wine, and apparently they had no coffee or tea. Heathens.

I slipped onto a stool beside a half boarded up window. It was far enough from the oven that even the heaviest rain and wind wouldn't put out the fire, but gave me a view across the mountains.

I hadn't realised how high we'd climbed until I looked outside. I half expected to see the ocean, but if it was visible from anywhere in the Citadel, it wasn't from here. I saw across from this peak to another even higher. Somewhere beyond there lay the city. Strange that the place didn't seem to have a name, just 'the city'. I would have to ask someone about that sometime.

"Coin for your thoughts."

I turned to frown at Luther, until I realised it was Knox who had slipped into the stool beside me.

"Is it safe to talk?" I whispered.

He shrugged and tore a chunk off his roll. "If we don't act like we're doing anything wrong."

I grimaced slightly. By whispering, I had done exactly that.

"Of course." I laughed as though he'd said something humorous. "I was just enjoying the view. Did you know this place was found eight years ago, while a hunter was following a big cat? They never found the cat, but this is quite the discovery."

Knox seemed impressed, but he glanced around with some measure of guardedness. "I wonder if we should be concerned that big cats lurk around the forest."

"I'm sure you're more than equipped to deal with one," I assured him.

"One, maybe," he agreed. "Several, however, might be a problem."

"That's true." I sipped my milk and winced at the taste. "They also found a sarcophagus." I kept my voice polite and conversational. No one had told me I couldn't talk about it. Presumably, most of the people here knew.

"Oh, that is interesting." Knox's eyes were intense now.

"Yes, it's… Something to behold." My tongue darted over my lips. I bit into my roll before my expression gave me away to anyone watching. Hiding my knife and intentions from Bain and Dex was easier than this. I hadn't known Bain could sense my thoughts. If I had, I might have betrayed myself. Here, I was certain Helene knew what I was doing before I did. She couldn't, of course, but the walls here would have ears too.

"I'd quite like to see it," he said casually. "Can you show me?" He smiled and I wondered how anyone ever bought the bumbling priest act. He was good at his job, that was undeniable, but he fit the role of soldier better than a stuttering priest.

I hesitated. "All right." No one had told me I couldn't do that either. If they asked, Knox and I would have to make up some excuse. He was probably faster at doing that than I was, and I was pretty good at bullshitting.

"Finish your milk first." He nodded toward the cup.

"Yes, mother," I replied tartly. I downed the last few drops and grimaced. Perhaps it wasn't too early for wine.

Knox smiled again. "I've been called many things, but never that."

""I'm certain you have," I agreed. "Especially from those who…" I stopped short of saying 'catch you'.

His smile widened. He clearly knew what I hadn't said. "If that ever happened, I would be dead now." He wasn't bragging, just stating a fact.

"True," I conceded. If Helene knew what he was, she would probably toss him out the window and down the side of the mountain without a second thought. She better not find out, especially since I was with him.

"Should you be seen with me?" I asked as we stepped into the dim corridor that led toward Comus's chamber.

"If I avoid you, they may wonder why." Knox nodded to another soldier who walked the other way.

"If it looks like you're singling me out, they may wonder at that too," I reasoned.

"Ah, no. I've sewn the seeds for that." He looked satisfied with himself. "I've talked to the other soldiers about you."

"Oh, you have?" I cocked my head at him and raised an eyebrow.

"Yes. I told them how beautiful you are and how I'd give my left arm to be alone with you." He winked.

My other eyebrow rose. "That's presumptuous," I said.

He chuckled. "It's not wrong, however. You are lovely and here we are, alone."

"Alone among dozens of people who might walk along this corridor at any moment."

"Who, if they see us, will make assumptions. Let them whisper. If nothing else, it will keep others from singling you out."

"Is that likely?" I wasn't sure if I liked that or not. I wasn't used to being noticed, and now it seemed I couldn't take a breath without someone watching.

"More than you might think," he replied. "But most are too intimidated by your power and the Hemathea and her protégé being in your company so often."

"Helene is…"

"Yes, she is," he agreed quickly. "Very much so."

We rounded a corner into yet another empty corridor.

"I'm glad you're here," I said softly.

"It's fortunate Bain was able to reach me in time."

I stopped. "He—what?"

Knox stopped and turned back. "He sent me to see what Helene was up to, and to keep an eye on you. He was worried."

"He handed—" I closed my mouth and started again, my voice low this time. "He handed me over to her."

Knox shook his head. He took my hand and drew me closer. "She gave him no choice, but he planted me here to keep you safe. I'm surprised he hasn't sent an army up here yet."

I didn't know what to think, but he seemed to believe what he said.

"Did Dex know?" The scent of Knox and the feel of his body so close to mine was a heady combination. He was one of the few people I was absolutely sure I could trust.

"I have no idea," he admitted. "I suspect by now he will." He let my hand go and reluctantly stepped away.

I almost spoke again, but then realised why he'd moved away from me. Two soldiers walked up the corridor, carrying a large box between them. All three men exchanged nods before the pair hurried on.

"Come on, we should see this sarcophagus before the day gets too late."

"Right. Helene will want me back soon," I agreed. I was thrown by what he told me, but I had to put it out of my mind. Bain wasn't here, nor was Dex. Whatever they thought of me, Knox and I were alone here. I would focus on learning and readying myself to help Helene and Luther. Where Knox fit into this, I didn't know, but I hadn't lied when I said I was glad he was there.

"It's just up ahead." I gestured toward the stairs and resumed walking.

"Dex might not approve of what we're doing here," I said

at a normal volume. "Comus might not allow the Vault to go on as it has."

Knox shrugged, but looked unworried. "The Alpha is strong. He has held the Vault together for this long, he will continue to do so."

"You admire him," I said.

He inclined his head. "Yes, I do. My sister and I all but grew up in his residence. My father trained his horses and my mother worked as his mother's seamstress. The Alpha is a few years older than my sister and me, but we occasionally played ball games together. He teased me like I was a younger brother." He looked wistful. "He still does, although I haven't seen him for the last two years or more."

"Because he sent you away," I said, not unkindly, merely curious.

"He gave me a task. I'm happy to do it." He raised his voice. "And then I met the Hemathea and was honoured to enter her service." He nodded to a serving woman who hurried by without a glance. "We should stick to safer topics."

"Yeah." But I found myself more interested in the one we were discussing. What was it about Dex and his family which evoked such a deep loyalty from those who knew them all their lives? I had experienced the opposite, where the witches were concerned. Friends were few. Most of those who gathered around the Council were there for what they could get for themselves.

"So I presume you're good with horses?" I asked. "Your father taught you?"

Knox responded with a lopsided grimace which suggested otherwise. "Horses and I have an awkward relationship at best. I will ride one if I have to, and they let me if *they* have to."

"Ah. Yes, I can relate to that." I wasn't the biggest fan of them myself. I preferred the back of the motorcycle like the one Bain rode. I sighed. For a while there, I considered him an ally. Now, I didn't know what to think. I believed Knox when he told me Bain sent him, but I wasn't convinced he knew the full story, or Bain's motives.

"Still safer than trying to ride a dragon," Knox remarked.

I laughed. "Slightly safer, yes. Much less chance of falling a long way and ending up in…"

"The arms of Hades?" he finished for me. "You're questioning your faith?"

I sucked my lip. "Helene says Hades and his sister locked Comus away out of jealousy."

"That would prove Hades's existence," he pointed out.

"Yes, but who was he really?" I frowned. "Or who is he? Surely locking an innocent man away for hundreds of years is an evil act."

"Certainly not a nice one," Knox agreed. "We may get answers when he's freed."

"Yes, we may." I puffed as we reached the top of the steps and moved toward the rear chamber. I led the way inside and waved toward the sarcophagus.

"There it is."

Knox cocked his head and stepped closer. "It appears harmless enough. Old, certainly. The Vault has several ancient ruins with similar carvings. According to the scholars, they date back almost a thousand years. Back to a kingdom which was dead long before the Alpha."

"The Jintano?" I suggested.

Knox looked surprised. "That's right. Their influence stretched this far, although this would have been a minor outpost in those days."

"Minor?" I looked bemused. "If this was minor—"

"The temples in the south were enormous. They believed the taller they were, the closer they were to the gods. They also used to push people off the side as a sacrifice."

"Charming," I said dryly.

He grinned. "History is seldom pretty." His eyes lingered on my face before he turned back to the sarcophagus. "Did you touch it?"

"No. I felt his presence just…in the air." Although now I was curious what would happen if I did touch it.

Before I could, Knox froze, his brow creased, head cocked.

"Do you hear that?"

I listened. "Hear what?" I made out nothing but the distant call of some kind of bird and the hum of insects in the forest. I drew a little power. As it had before, it was heavy and sat uncomfortably in my chest. Still, I probed about for other smells or signs of anything odd and found nothing.

"I hear music. Strange music." He shivered. "It's making my skin uncomfortable, like it wants to slide off my body and lie in a puddle at my feet."

I grimaced at that visual image and shook my head. "I feel nothing."

In the corner of my eye, I caught a flicker of movement. When I turned my face, I caught sight of a figure dressed the same as the kid who followed Helene out of the chamber the day before. Only this time she faced me.

No, I corrected myself. This was no child. She was short, but her face was mature.

Those who came before were shorter than people now.

She was the height a woman would have stood nearly one thousand years ago.

The woman's red dress covered her shoes and rose almost to her chin. The hem, cuff and collar were adorned with gold embroidery in swirls and flowers. Her hair was long and dark and her eyes serious, solemn.

She waved toward the sarcophagus and mouthed something, her expression earnest.

I shook my head. "I'm sorry, I can't hear you."

The woman looked frustrated and tried again. The same wave, a shake of her head, mouthed words.

Again, I shook my head. "I'm sorry—"

The woman threw her head back, her mouth open in a silent scream. Her face was twisted in a rictus of agony.

I took a step toward her, but she was gone.

"What—"

"It's gone," Knox said.

"Yes, she… I beg your pardon."

"The music," Knox said, "it's gone."

"Oh. Did you see a woman? She stood right there."

Knox looked confused, but said, "No, I saw no one but you. You said you couldn't hear me, but I wasn't talking."

"No." I told him what I saw. "She seemed anxious. She wanted to tell me something about the sarcophagus."

"What kind of something?"

"I'm not sure," I said slowly. "Maybe she wanted us to hurry in opening it. Perhaps she was warning against opening it."

"You said she screamed before she disappeared?"

"Yes."

He rubbed his chin. "She might be likewise locked away somewhere else."

"Not here," I replied. "If she was here, they would have found her."

"Would they have told you?"

I hesitated. "I don't know." I stepped closer to the sarcophagus and touched it lightly with the palm of one hand. It felt cool under my skin, just ordinary stone.

After a moment, I had a sense of the presence inside. Fainter than before, it felt like a heartbeat through layers of clothing.

"Do you know who she was?" I asked. "That woman. What was she trying to tell me?"

A sensation, like a jab of warning, hotter than a poker fresh from the flames, flashed through me. I wanted to jerk back, but my hand wouldn't move. I was fused to the stone. No, not exactly fused, but compelled to keep my touch on its surface.

Fuck.

I swallowed hard.

"I presume you think we should stay away from her, whoever she is?"

The warning pressed a little harder, then disappeared, along with the compulsion to keep my hand in place. I pulled it back and examined my fingers. If I expected to find them damaged, I didn't see anything.

"He didn't seem happy she was here," I remarked blandly.

"Are you all right?" Knox asked. "You looked scared for a moment there." He grabbed my hand and scrutinised my fingers. "No damage that I can see, but I don't think you should touch that again."

Anger flared inside me. I wasn't planning on it, but the choice was up to me.

"If it helps me understand, then I will," I said sharply. I was tempted to touch the stone again, just to spite him, but that would be silly. Childish. To risk myself solely to irritate him… I wouldn't do something so stupid.

I shook my head and moved away from the sarcophagus.

"Did you feel anything? A presence?"

He pursed his lips and shook his head slowly. "I just heard the music."

"At the same time the woman was here. That can't be a coincidence, surely?"

"It could be, but it seems unlikely." He rested his chin on

his thumb and forefinger and gazed thoughtfully at the front of Comus's prison.

"What power do you have?" I asked, the words out of my mouth before I was aware of having the thought.

His eyes swivelled toward me. "None that I'm aware of. Why?"

"I might have seen the woman because of my power, but that doesn't explain why you heard music. Have you heard it before?"

"As a matter of fact, I heard it yesterday, not long after we arrived here."

"About when I saw her the first time." But Luther didn't see anything. Helene had her back to me. It had nothing to do with the power then. At least, not entirely to do with it. I couldn't rule out power being the cause of these… Whatever they were. Imaginings? Illusions? Hallucinations?

"We should leave here before anyone comes," I said. "Or before they start to look for us."

Knox gave me a mischievous grin and pulled part of his shirt hem out of the top of his trousers. He leaned forward and messed up his hair.

"If you think I'm going to do that too—" I knitted my brows at him.

"You and I know the truth," he said evenly. "At least this way they won't ask too many questions."

I sighed and messed up my own hair, just a little.

"They'll gossip about us," I said. If they had nothing better to do than talk about us, that was.

"Nothing that I'd be ashamed of," he said firmly. "Who knows, someday—"

I gave him a lopsided smile. He really was presumptuous, but I wouldn't mind. Anywhere but here though, in this room. I might end up with more than a palm momentarily attached to the stone sarcophagus.

He smiled back. "Don't worry, I won't pressure you. I will, however, keep an eye on you, as ordered."

"*Because* you were ordered?" I cocked my head at him.

"No, not just because of that," he said softly.

I looked into his eyes and knew he meant every word. Right now, I should concentrate on my lessons and a dozen other things, like staying alive. Having him in my corner would make all of that a lot easier.

Bain and Dex both haunted my thoughts as well though, complicating everything even more.

"Should we hold hands?" he asked as we headed back toward the stairs.

I gave him the side eye, then slipped one hand into his, fingers laced together.

He grinned and strode beside me. If only the folk from the temple could see him now. Or me, for that matter.

21

Bain

A SMALL FIRE was all I let them have. I sat back from it, in the shadows.

Latika sat on the other side, eyes closed, back against a tree trunk. Wesley sat beside Erin, talking and singing softly while he plucked the occasional note on his lyaer. Kerina and Aisha talked about knives and seemed to be discussing the best technique for holding one.

"It depends if you plan to stab or throw," Kerina said.

I turned my attention to the dark forest around us. Something moved, leaves rustled, then fell silent. A small animal of some kind, more than likely. I saw several dozen birds and a monkey or two before the sun set.

Hooves shuffled as one of the horses settled closer to another.

"Where are we going?" Latika had one eye open and regarded me.

I should have known she wasn't asleep. A trained

assassin could operate on minimal sleep and still be highly efficient. I had long wondered if they possessed some kind of power, but knew better than to ask. Assassin secrets were held close, under penalty of expulsion from their guild at best and making themselves a target of their order at worst.

Although Kerina hadn't, as far as I knew, been a part of the order for some time, she still followed those rules.

"I have a direction," I replied. "Beyond that, I don't know."

"The Onyx Mountains are vast." She opened her other eye. "We could wander for months."

"You know otherwise," I said. "You've seen the signs as well as I have." A woman with her training wouldn't miss tracks, even covered as well as they were.

"They suggest we're outnumbered," she replied. "They'll position themselves in such a way they'll see us coming before we're aware of them."

"What do you suggest?" I asked. Even the most seasoned generals listened to their advisors. I was no general, but I was willing to listen. The other four had stopped to do the same.

"We should split up. Have the children and the bard take the horses back to the road and carry on south that way. The three of us," she nodded toward Kerina, "should continue with stealth."

Aisha opened her mouth to argue, but was silenced with a glance from her mother.

"I'll go with the horses," Erin said. "We will draw them away."

Wesley looked sulky, but nodded. "Better than listening to Bain sing in another tavern."

Kerina barked a muffled laugh. "They certainly were quick to tell him to shut up and let you sing again."

I grimaced ruefully. "I *did* say I couldn't sing. You all insisted I try."

"I didn't," Kerina pointed out. "I said better you than me. I also said the crowd was restless."

"Wesley needed a break," I said.

"My mother was ready to—" Aisha started.

"Quiet," Latika hissed.

The camp immediately fell silent but for the stamp of a hoof.

"I hear nothing," I said eventually.

My words were followed immediately by a snarl and the scream of a terrified horse. A shadow leapt out of the night and latched onto the neck of the closest animal.

The horse screamed again. A wet tearing sound was followed by silence, then a sickening thud.

At once, all of the horses panicked. They tore at the ropes which secured them to trees. Two or three snapped and the animals bolted into the night.

I swore under my breath. I picked up a stick, thrust it into the fire until it caught and stepped carefully toward the fallen horse.

The poor animal was missing a large chunk of its neck. Huge teeth marks raked across skin, leaving gaping holes bigger than anything I ever saw, except a sand dragon.

I remembered what Dex said about garden dragons. This might be a forest dragon, but I doubted it. No one had even proven they exist, but rumours of big cats in these mountains were rife. Once in a while a hunter would bring back a skin the size of two or three people. I would bet my last gold coin that was what killed the horse. And it was still out there and hungry.

The remaining horses danced on the ends of their ropes, eyes wide with terror of the cat at the fire.

"Black tiger," Latika breathed. "The second most dangerous creature in the forest."

"What is the most dangerous?" Kerina whispered.

Latika's teeth flashed and she had a blade in her hand she hadn't held a heartbeat before. "We are."

"You're suggesting we hunt this beast?" I wasn't scared, but to find a black cat at night was like chasing shadows. Except *most* shadows don't bite you.

Latika looked scornful. "Gods no. We need to move from here. The tiger won't be deterred for long. She will come back to eat her kill, and may bring her cubs."

"You seem to know a lot about them," I dropped the stick into the fire and picked up another one.

Latika put her knife away and picked her bag up from beside the tree she'd been leaning against.

"My father hunted them," she said simply. "He told me many stories. One day he left to hunt again and didn't return. I don't want to end the same way."

"Wise," I muttered. I swung my own bag onto my back and glanced up. Most of the stars were hidden by forest canopy, but I saw enough to figure out which way was south. Traveling at night was not my first choice, especially through mountains, but if we could put a few hundred metres between us and the dead horse, that would be good.

I untied the remaining three horses and handed their reins to Wesley and Kerina. I kept hold of one myself. The animals had instincts which would compliment mine. I would keep my senses open for the tiger and the other horses, and this animal would hopefully stop me from stepping off an unseen cliff. That seemed like a fair trade to me.

I reached out and found the tiger on the edge of my senses. She was hungry. The need to eat was slowly overcoming her fear of people and fire. The need to provide food for her young was greater still. I felt no cubs, they must be out of range. With Hades's blessing, we wouldn't trip over them in the dark. Even if they didn't bite, a big cat with a grudge would.

Aware the fire on the stick would burn down quickly, I stepped between the trees, each movement careful and deliberate. Behind me, the horse snuffled with unease, clearly not liking the fire held in my hand.

We walked for several minutes before the tiger moved. She made her way around us, toward the fallen horse. A moment later, several minds followed. Three, maybe four cubs, hunger uppermost in their thoughts.

A twig cracked under Wesley's boot and we all froze, including the tiger.

"Sorry," the bard whispered loudly.

I nodded and resumed walking. The tiger did the same, but her mind became more and more distant.

I exhaled, soft and long, as she passed out of range.

Latika let out a squeak of fear.

Shit. I jumped and tossed the stick aside as the fire flared, threatening to burn my hand. It hit the ground and went out, leaving us in darkness. It only lasted a moment before a soft glow lit the trees.

It was too early for dawn, and sunrise usually wasn't green.

Green?

Like the power in a dragon's scales. I reached out and found no dragon. No paranormals either, apart from Kerina.

Latika groaned. "Vermin."

At the same time, Kerina whispered, "That music is back."

In front of me, the child appeared, clearer than I ever saw her before.

I blinked. Not a child, a woman. How had I not seen that before? I shook my head, it didn't matter.

"Who are you?" I asked. "What do you want?"

She spoke, or at least her mouth moved. No sound came out.

I shook my head. "I'm sorry, I can't hear you."

The glow intensified.

Latika screamed, but the sound was short lived.

The small woman gestured toward the south. Pointed. Her finger turned toward me. She spoke again and this time I understood, even if I couldn't hear.

'You must hurry.'

The horse jerked back and the reins almost slipped free of my hand. I held them tightly.

"What about the others?" I jerked my head behind me.

The woman peered around. She gestured to Kerina and Latika and nodded vigorously. To the others, she frowned and gave an expansive shrug.

"Is this about Comus?" I asked.

She nodded vigorously and again pointed toward the south. She looked as though she might say something more, but her eyes widened and she was gone.

"Please, make them stop." Latika was wide eyed, pressed up against a tree trunk, her face pale in the glow of power which hung in the air in front of her.

"Mother, there's nothing there," Aisha insisted.

I squinted. "To her eyes, there is." In front of Latika stood at least a dozen rats. None were as large as the one in the tavern, or as visible, but they were there, nonetheless.

I tossed the reins to Aisha and closed the distance between us as the rats dropped to all fours and started toward Latika.

She let out a sob of fear.

"Latika, listen to me," I said, slow but firm. "They aren't really there. It's… I believe someone with power is playing with us. I'm not sure who, or why, but we need to find out. That includes you. And Kerina. Those aren't really rats you're seeing." What were they then? Manifestations of power might be much more dangerous than vermin.

"They are not really there," I finished finally. "If you took a step forward, you'd walk straight through them."

Latika whimpered and took a step back instead. "They look hungry." Her voice wavered. She seemed ready to bolt off into the night in the direction the horses had gone. Only her training, and possibly the presence of her daughters, kept her from moving too far.

"They're not," Kerina said, her voice as hard as I've ever heard from her. "They're trying to scare you. I heard music. Where could that have possibly come from out here, apart from the bard?"

"It wasn't from me," Wesley replied. His eyes were on the spot in front of Latika, but judging by his confused frown, he saw nothing there.

"Exactly," Kerina said. "Someone is playing with us."

"I saw a woman," I said softly. "She told me where to go. Me, Latika and Kerina. We need to hurry."

"Then the rats that aren't rats might be to slow us down," Kerina reasoned. "It's working."

"I'm sorry," Latika said, her voice high. "Go on without me."

"The woman was clear, you're needed too," I said. I kept one eye on Latika and stepped toward the rats. Where I should have stepped on one, I felt nothing. For several seconds, I stood there.

Then a jolt passed through me. Blood thundered through my ears so loudly it was all I could hear. Power wrapped around me like a blanket, picked me up and tossed me several metres into the wide trunk of a tree.

"Mother fuck—" I slammed into the bark so hard the wind was almost knocked out of me. I hit the ground with a thud and a short cry of pain.

"Bain!" Kerina shouted.

"I'm all right," I mumbled. I pushed myself to my feet and stood unsteadily until my vision cleared.

"There's something there," I remarked.

Kerina snorted. "Something that isn't rats."

"It's weakening," Latika said. "I can see through them."

"The glow of power is fading," Kerina said.

I blinked and shook my head to clear it. She was right. The night felt a little darker. Shadows reclaimed the spaces between trees.

"They're almost gone." Latika's voice was almost as faint as the glow.

I rubbed my back. I would have bruises later, but nothing was broken.

I was sure of one thing. The power was stronger here. In the tavern, it couldn't have thrown me. Didn't want to. The rats were meant for Latika, but I had overstepped this time.

What then, did it mean when I saw the lift falling? Another attempt to slow us down? If so, it hadn't worked.

"All right, we've delayed for long enough. Wesley, you and the children take the horses. Return to Cape Massin and wait for us."

Aisha looked outraged. "I don't follow your orders."

"You follow *mine*," Latika said. "Do as Bain says. If we're not there within the month, you know where to go to complete your training."

"Mother—" Erin turned pleading eyes to Latika, but she nodded. "We will do as you say. May Hades' blessings go with you."

"And with you," Latika said. Her expression was closed, businesslike. Leaving her children would be difficult, but she was an assassin. Nothing else would matter until the job was done, whatever it took.

I waited until the three of them mounted the horses. The sun had started to break, for real this time, so they would have the light they needed to make their way safely past the black tiger and her young.

It would help me and the two assassins as well, but it would also make us easier to see.

"We're going this way." I swung my bag onto my back yet again and moved through the trees.

"Are you sure about this?" Kerina asked. "The magic that threw you like a bag of oranges might have come from the woman you saw."

"Possibly," I agreed. "That's why only we are going. I'm not taking children and bards into a situation that might get them killed."

"Should we head back with them?" Kerina asked.

"Scared?" I asked, half teasing to lighten the mood.

She barked a laugh. "Hardly. If you think those who took Viva are this way, I'll follow you. For the good of the Vault."

"For the good of the Vault," I agreed. What would Dex make of all of this? Or Viva? Was she allied with her captors now, or resisting? As a witch, she had power like they did, but she was headstrong. She might bend, but she wouldn't break easily. If she joined them, that would make her more dangerous. Our knives, skills and amazing wits would do little against her and the others. I would have to make sure she didn't see me coming. Or smell me.

"I don't suppose the woman you saw said how far this place was?" Kerina's eyes were on the trees around us, but she glanced at me for a moment. "Or what we're looking for?"

"No, just the direction," I said regretfully. I reached out lightly, searching for any signs of life in the forest around us. No tigers, thank Hades, but smaller minds like birds and the occasional snake. I knew not to get complacent around forest reptiles, but as long as we didn't bother them, the reptiles would steer clear.

The sun rose higher, the trees became thicker. The slope

of the mountain steepened. Each step was more difficult and treacherous than the last.

My boots slid on loose rocks. My heart skipped, but I only slipped back a step or two before I grabbed hold of a slender tree and stopped myself from a hard tumble back down.

"I'm not sure we can go much further," Latika remarked.

I cupped a hand over my eyes and scanned ahead. The assassin was right. The mountain was steeper still in front of us.

"We'll have to skirt around," I said. "Try to find another way forward." If there was any kind of structure or even a cave up here, there must be an entrance.

I swallowed hard and carefully avoided looking down while I led them in a westerly direction. Only instinct told me we were headed the right way.

If you feel like appearing again, to offer some guidance, I'd appreciate it.

The woman didn't reappear.

Hades, a sign of some sort?

Nothing.

I sighed softly.

A large shelf of rock jutted out of the side of the mountain ahead. We could try to climb up and over the top, or down and look for a path underneath it. Before I made a decision, I sensed a mind up ahead. Their thoughts weren't clear, but their mood suggested boredom, bordering on sleepiness. A guard, who was certain no one would find them up here.

They were in for a nasty surprise.

I raised a hand and gestured downhill. As expected, the two women obeyed without a word or a sound. If I didn't know they were behind me, I would have thought I was alone.

I took note to have Kerina train more of the guard in the ways of the assassins. As much as she was allowed to share, at least. My subordinates were good, but some had all the stealth of a dragon in a fishpond. To be fair, that was why some of them were guards. Their presence was intended to act as a deterrent to would-be assassins, or anyone who might want to stir up trouble.

Still, a lighter step would do them good.

I gestured toward a spot below the lip of the rock. There, a lone figure leaned against the trunk of a tree. Dressed entirely in brown and green, they wouldn't be easily seen unless a person knew what to look for.

To me, they stood out like a cock on a bull.

"I'll go," Latika mouthed. She made a cutting gesture across her throat.

I frowned, but nodded. I didn't want to kill unless it was necessary, but I couldn't give the guard a chance to raise the alarm.

Latika slipped past me and flowed down the mountainside like water. No branches shifted in her wake, no twigs snapped. Even the dry leaves underfoot were silent. The only noise was the cool wind, which had picked up in the last few minutes.

I shivered. I preferred the coastal heat and breezes from the sea to lurking on mountains up this high.

A brief, wet cry broke the relative silence, followed by a loud gust of wind. It whistled through the trees like the guard's soul, pulled by Hades as penance for their lack of attention on the job.

I sent a short request to Hades to be gentle, if only to assuage my guilt at their death.

"It is done," Latika appeared at my elbow like a shadow in the night.

It was an effort to avoid jumping in fright, but I managed.

Then I told myself off for my own inattention. I caught a smirk on Kerina's face and shook my head ruefully.

"Good work." As far as I could tell, there were other minds somewhere past the guard's body, but hidden somehow. Shrouded.

Latika nodded. "I think they guarded a tunnel under the lip of rock. A pathway."

I nodded. That would explain why the minds felt muddy.

"Kerina, scout the way. We'll stand watch and make sure no one comes up behind you."

Her eyebrow quirked and the side of her mouth drew up, but she said nothing. She didn't need to. I knew if anyone took her by surprise, they would have to be exceptional.

I couldn't rule out the chance they might be.

She pulled the hood of her coat over her red hair and disappeared amongst the trees with the same care Latika had shown.

"We need to move into place to intercept anyone," I whispered.

Latika nodded and followed on my heels, so close I almost felt the warmth of her body, but far enough she didn't walk into me when I stopped suddenly.

"There's a track." I ducked down behind a few scrubby bushes.

"They tried to hide it." Latika dropped down beside him. "Except that." She nodded toward a series of broken bushes, too uniform to be random.

"I would bet my last coin that was Knox," I said.

Latika glanced at him. "From what you've said, I wouldn't take that bet. Whoever they are, they've taken too much care. Except the guard, but they're probably expecting a replacement soon."

I twitched. I should have thought of that. Kerina would,

and she'd be ready. I suppressed another sigh at the necessity of another death.

Latika shivered. "There is something wrong about this place."

I had been about to say the same thing. "Yes, there is. It's like— Like a jar of something rotten."

"Yes. Eel, or eggs. Not in smell, but in…"

"Taste," I finished for her. It was on the back of my tongue. "Not egg though. I smelled a rat once, which had been dead for days."

She grimaced. "Vermin, dog, person, they all smell the same when dead and rotting."

"Death and decay," I said softly. "That's what it tastes of. Death and decay."

Taste was a sense, so this must have something to do with power, unless we crouched above a fresh tomb.

"I hear some folk wear dried flowers in lockets around their necks," Latika said. "To counter the smell of their countrymen."

I chuckled softly. "I'd like one right now." If the taste was caused by power, I could lie in a garden and it wouldn't help. "Not to counter your smell," I said quickly.

A smile flashed across her face. "Of course not. Assassins are taught to minimise their own scent."

I considered that for a moment. I couldn't remember Kerina smelling bad since I'd known her. Or particularly good, now I thought about it. I hadn't realised it was something she did purposefully.

"That's a fine skill to have. If that's something you can share, I'd like to learn how someday."

I suspected Viva used my scent once or twice for her own power. If she had, other witches like her could as well.

"Possibly," was all the reply Latika gave before she fell quiet.

Just as well she did. A moment later I sensed people approaching from the direction Kerina had gone. Two of them, both dressed in black, swords at their hips.

I recognised them as men who held those blades toward my throat while the witches took Viva. Soldiers, probably mercenaries; they knew how to use those swords. It seemed unlikely they had the kind of power Viva did, but I couldn't rule out that they might have the same as me.

If they did, where was Kerina?

Neither of the soldiers seemed to be on high alert for intruders, but they were obviously less lax than the guard. One stopped near the bent bush and forced it back upright. The other swept a boot over something on the ground. A footprint, perhaps.

One spoke to the other in a low voice and they moved on. Any moment now, they'd find the dead guard.

"I pulled her under the bushes," Latika whispered in my ear. "It'll take them time—"

Her words were interrupted by a shout.

Not enough time, evidently.

"Fuck," I said under my breath and rose to my feet.

"Next time, throw the body off the side of the mountain," Kerina said as she stepped toward them, shining wet blade in hand.

"Where—" I shook his head. "Never mind. What did you find?"

"A tunnel. I suggest while they're distracted, we make our way inside." Kerina pushed her hood back, turned and disappeared back into the trees.

I nodded to no one and followed.

22

Bain

"ARE you certain this is the right place?"

I frowned at Kerina's question. "This was where the woman pointed."

"Can you sense Viva?" Kerina still held a knife in her hand, but her posture was loose, almost casual.

"No. There's no one here. Her or the others. It's—" I shook my head "Too empty."

"There must be *something* here," Kerina insisted. "Why send us here in the first place?"

"Misdirection?" Latika suggested.

"Or the tunnels lead somewhere else." I squinted ahead. Cracks offered dim light here or there, enough to see a few metres ahead where the tunnel widened.

"We can't rule out the possibility they were hunting tigers," Latika said.

"There's no tiger minds here," I said. I took a few steps

forward. "No cubs. No cat smell. Bat, maybe, but if they were here, they're gone now."

"There's not even a spider's web," Kerina pointed out.

"No vermin either." Latika sounded relieved at that, if surprised.

"Be careful," I warned. "I suspect there's power here. It may mask the presence of other paranormals." Or the gods knew what else.

Kerina nodded. Her posture stiffened just slightly, eyes shifted back and forth.

"What is it?" I asked, my voice low to avoid echoes.

We moved into a small cavern. The walls looked unnaturally smooth.

"I see lies," she replied softly.

"Yes." My brow wrinkled. I waited for her to continue.

"No, I mean I see them here. It's like—" She hesitated for so long I thought she stopped talking altogether. Finally, she said, "It's like a gauze curtain. I think… those soldiers were searching for something, but they didn't find it. It's hidden by power."

"Where?" I peered into the gloom.

She favoured me with a look through narrowed eyes. "If you could see it, it wouldn't be hidden. Besides, it's deeper in."

I waved at her impatiently. "Lead the way then, but be careful. Just because you can see through their veil, doesn't mean it won't kill you."

"I can't see through it," she explained patiently. "I just know it's there. Hades only knows what might be on the other side."

"Then like I said, be careful," I instructed. I almost wished I had an army with me. I could send in a dozen scouts, while another dozen guarded their backs.

"When am I not careful?" she asked.

"Do you really want an answer to that?" I asked.

"Later, over beer." She gave me a curt nod, turned her back and resumed the slow walk through the tunnels.

I waved Latika in front of me and took the rear. I kept my mind open, but felt nothing but the two women who walked ahead of me.

No, not precisely nothing, but the feeling we weren't alone might be straight from my imagination. Between my vision of the lift collapse and seeing the small woman and the rats, I wouldn't assume a thing.

"It just got colder," Latika said.

A step later, I felt the same thing. A sudden but significant drop in temperature.

"This is a cave," I said. They weren't known for being warm and cosy, especially up this high.

"Thank you, I had forgotten," Kerina said sarcastically.

"Anytime," I muttered.

Latika shot me a funny look over her shoulder, but stayed silent. She might think our banter was annoying, or badly timed. A deep, dark cave in the Onyx Mountains might be a strange place for humour, but it helped to ease the tension. For me it did anyway.

"Power," Kerina whispered. She drew to a stop, hand out in front of her. "The gauze is thicker here, like cotton."

I put out a hand and touched the air beside her. "It's even colder, but I don't see anything." I expected to be thrown off my feet, but nothing happened that I could tell.

"Can you see through it?" Latika asked. "Or push it aside?"

"It's not an actual curtain," Kerina said. "It's an illusion, like all the other things we've seen. Or heard."

"Can you hear any music?" I strained, but all I heard was silence so profound my ears rang.

"Just what's been playing since we entered the cave." Kerina paused. "You can't hear that, can you?"

"No." I shook my head. "Can we step through this curtain of yours?"

"It's not mine, but I think so." Kerina sheathed her knife and moved forward, both hands raised in front of her.

I followed carefully. There had to be a reason the soldiers left. It could be because they hadn't found anything. What had they hoped to find here?

"You know, it's not too late to return to the city," Kerina said. "We don't need to satisfy our curiosity that much."

"When have you ever walked away from anything without seeing it all the way through?" I asked.

"There's a first time for everything," Kerina replied. "We haven't stayed alive this long by being stupid."

"The things we do for the Keeper," I said with a shrug. "We have to keep going. We don't know what we're facing."

"That's what I'm worried about." Kerina kept on walking anyway, step by step. "There's another chamber. I see it through the curtain. And power."

"I see a glow," Latika said. She sounded neither excited or scared. Instead she was cold, focused. Every bit the assassin. As long as no vermin jumped out at her, she wouldn't blink or flinch.

I squinted. The glow was faint, but became increasingly stronger the further we went. After a moment, it took shape.

I frowned. What the fuck?

"It's a box," Kerina said. "A sarcophagus drenched in power."

It was a long, stone sarcophagus, longer than me and maybe twice as wide. The glow of power was coming from around the edges of the lid.

"Or leaking power," I said.

"This is a tomb," Latika said. "There's an altar."

She was right. In the light of the power, stood an altar exactly like the ones in every temple I'd ever stepped foot in.

"This is an odd place for a temple," Kerina said.

"It's a long way to come to worship," I agreed. "Although according to the tales, the Alpha of Jintaro had a summer residence here." I rubbed my chin. "I thought we might be headed there."

"That may be where Viva and the others are," Kerina said. She edged back toward the entrance, hand on her knife.

"Stand guard in case this is a trap," I said.

She responded with a curt nod and turned her back on us.

I stepped closer to the sarcophagus, but stopped short of touching it. "If this isn't the place, then why did she want us here?"

"A distraction?" Latika suggested.

"I sense there's more to it than that," I replied. "This place is buzzing with power. Those soldiers wouldn't have known what to look for." I moved slowly around the sarcophagus, my eyes on the stone carvings on the top and down the sides. "If they entered, they would see nothing but darkness. But we see light."

Here, a carved dragon soared, wings spread, neck outstretched. There, another wound along the ground. Beside that, a cat crouched, almost as large as the sand dragon. Whoever did the carvings had either never seen the creatures, or they decided to be imaginative.

"For what purpose?"

I didn't look up, I sensed Latika's eyes on me.

"Because—" I cocked my head and squinted. "There's something we need to see."

"What sort of something?" she asked.

"I have no idea." I almost completed a full circuit when I saw it. Carved into the stone on one of the long sides was a groove. I was no connoisseur of art, but decoratively speaking, it seemed to serve no purpose. It wasn't a part of any creature. Although now that I really looked, two dragons and a tiger faced toward it.

I slid the tip of my finger into the groove. Where I expected it to be smooth, it was slightly rough. I pressed my finger against the stone.

Something clicked.

I froze.

Nothing happened. At least nothing I could see.

I slumped slightly.

"There's another like it on the other side," Latika remarked.

I wanted to kick myself. How had I missed that? "You're right. I thought it was nothing until I saw the one over here." I stopped to think. "I can't reach all the way over."

"I don't think you're supposed to." Latika's voice was tight enough to make my head jerk up to stare. Her eyes were wide, fixed on something straight in front of her. Something I could barely see.

"They're not really there," I told her. "They're just trying to scare you from helping me with this." Whatever *this* was.

I hadn't dismissed the possibility that this might be a bad idea. I sensed this was something important, something I needed to do, but that instinct had let me down before.

"Walk toward me," I told Latika. "Look at me. Focus on my voice. Walk around to the far side."

"I can't," she squeaked. "I can't move."

"I—"

The ground fell away beneath me.

Somehow, I didn't fall with it. I remained stationary, fused in place over a gaping chasm. At least thirty or forty metres deep, the sides were lined with sheer rock. A sparkle of light at the bottom suggested water. Underground lake or stream? Was the water moving?

I forced myself to look away. Up.

"What is it?" Latika asked, her voice high. "You stopped talking to me."

I cleared my throat and swallowed. "Something is showing us our greatest fears." How did it know? It must have gotten inside their heads somehow.

"Kerina," I called out weakly.

"I'm all right," she called back. She didn't sound all right. She sounded just this side of in control. I didn't know what she was scared of, but I knew she saw it. Had the soldiers?

I shook my head and his tongue darted over my lips.

"Latika. We have to do this. We have to fight past what we see. What we *think* we see. There's nothing there, not really."

Involuntarily, my eyes looked toward my feet. Past them. A shiver went through me. If, by some chance, the chasm was real, I could plunge to my death at any moment. I knew I would fall for hours before I hit—

A scream pushed its way up my chest, into my throat. I shoved it down.

I was Bain, captain of the Keeper's bodyguard. Friend, confidant and protector of Dex Breakwater. Protector of Calista. Protector of the Alpha. I would not fall to my death at the bottom of a hole which only existed in my mind.

I forced my way back to the sarcophagus.

"You can do this," I said, half to myself, half to Latika. "Step through them. They can't hurt you. I swear on my last breath, they aren't real. Hades is watching over you, keeping you safe."

"If you're wrong, and I die because I believed you, I will come to you as a pale one for the rest of your days," she said through gritted teeth.

I snorted. "You sound like Kerina."

"Assassins keep their word," she assured me.

Through half lidded eyes, I watched her, face deathly white, step around the air in front of her. She flinched once, twice, then in a rush hurried to the opposite side of the sarcophagus.

"Find the groove," I said.

"I have it," she replied.

"On the count of three." I placed my finger beside mine.

"One."

The ground shifted beneath me, but I didn't move my hand.

"Two."

Latika let out a squeak. "There's more of them."

"Hold firm," I ordered. "Three." I pressed my finger firmly into the groove. Again, I felt a click, but then something more. A vibration which moved from my hand, up my arm into my shoulder. From there, it spread through my entire body.

"The lid is rising, " Kerina shouted.

I glanced up, dropped my hand to my hip and stepped back.

Sure enough, the carved stone lid rose slowly, a hair at first, then steadily more. The glow of power only illuminated an endless darkness inside.

I swore to myself. Latika might not be able to haunt me; I might have killed us all.

"Dex was right," I muttered, although I wasn't sure what I referred to, in particular. Maybe something, maybe nothing. What would Dex do if he were here? I knew the answer to that at least. The Keeper would step closer and look into that endless nothingness until something revealed itself. He was curiosity itself, while I had always been cautious.

Where is that caution now? I asked myself.

"Step back," I ordered. "Back to the tunnel entrance."

Hands out to either side, I stepped back, eyes half on the still rising lid, half on the women I drove toward the door ahead of me.

"This is why you should never open sarcophagi you find in a cave on the side of a mountain," Kerina remarked.

"Good advice," I said over my shoulder. "I'll remember that for next time." If there was a next time.

The ground under my feet shook. I almost missed a step, but caught myself at the last moment. I turned just as the floor beneath me cracked. I leapt to the side as the crack widened.

"Bain—" Kerina and Latika stood on the other side of a widening, jagged slit in the stone.

"Get to safety," I ordered. "Get out of the cave."

Latika half turned, but froze.

"Vermin," she whispered. "Hundreds of them. Thousands."

"No," Kerina snapped. "There are no rats there, only —cows."

Cows?

I shook my head. "Did you say—"

She kept her eyes on the entrance, but threw up a hand. "Don't say anything. I'm scared of cows, all right?"

What could I say to that?

"There's nothing there." Except the gap in front of me, which seemed all too real and steadily growing. I poked at the edge with a booted toe and frowned. Where there should be nothing but air, I found hard ground.

"There are no rats, cows or chasms," I whispered.

I glanced over my shoulder. The lid was half open.

I turned back to the growing crack in the stone. The bottom was as dark as the inside of the sarcophagus. Darker. It wanted to reach up and pull me down, swallow me whole and leave my shattered body on the rocks far below.

"No," my voice was hoarse. "There's nothing there." I swallowed hard, sucked in a breath and started running. If I was wrong…

I ran across the chasm. Where I should have fallen through, my feet crossed solid ground.

"See, nothing to fear," I said as much to myself as to them.

The heartbeat the last word left my mouth, we were plunged into darkness.

No, more than that, nighttime. Stars sparkled overhead. The moon slipped out from behind a cloud to throw silver illumination onto the ground around us.

"What the—" I whirled. The cave was gone. Where it might have been, was a copse of trees.

I blinked.

Blinked again.

"It was all an illusion," Kerina said softly.

"Or this is." Latika stepped over to a tree and rapped at its trunk. "It feels real."

"If it is, then we've lost an entire day," Kerina pointed out. "No wonder I'm hungry."

I rubbed my forehead, where a headache threatened. "This was a distraction," I said. "Something to keep us busy while…"

"While what?" Kerina crouched by a tree where we left our packs and rifled through before she brought out some bread.

"I don't know, but if they went to these lengths to keep us from it, then it must be important."

"Or they want us to think it is." Kerina broke off chunks and tossed them to Latika and me.

"Witches are involved. I'm inclined to think it is." I bit into the slightly stale bread and swallowed. "Knox seemed to think so." The question was, how did we find him and Viva? Could we get there in time, or had this delay made us too late already?

"Judging by the position of the moon, we have a few hours until dawn. We'll get some rest." We would be useless if we were exhausted. "At first light, we'll search for the summer residence."

"How hard can it be to find a residence on a mountain-side?" Kerina asked.

"Precisely. Much easier than finding any cows up here," I said.

She scowled at me. "You'll never let me forget that, will you?"

I responded with a hint of a smile. "I might not, but someday I hope you can tell me why."

I lay down with my pack under my head.

"When we get back to the city, I'll tell you." She lay down near me.

"Deal." I watched the stars for a while.

"I once knew a boy who was terrified of potatoes," Kerina said sleepily.

I snorted. "Really?"

"No," she chuckled, "but I'm sure it's possible."

"Right." Fear didn't always make sense, but I couldn't let it cripple me the way it had twice today. Running across the illusory chasm would haunt my dreams, but it was a fear faced down, at least a little. When this was over, I might find a cliff to climb. Or better yet, keep both booted feet safely on the ground.

23

VIVA

"GET UP, IT IS TIME."

Helene's voice woke me from a fitful sleep.

My first thought was to tell her to fuck off, roll over and go back to sleep. That wouldn't end well for me.

I opened my eyes enough to see Helene in the gloom of early morning. Given how dark the room tended to be, it wasn't much different to the gloom of evening, or the gloom of midday.

It was enough light to see the woman scowl.

"Are you certain I'm ready?" I asked. I pushed myself to sit up, and wiped sleep from my eyes.

"No, but nevertheless, it is time." Helene tossed me a blouse and pants, the same black as hers, and stepped from the room saying, "I expect you in the chamber in ten minutes." She didn't need to say which chamber. As far as she was concerned, there was only one of any importance around here.

"Yes, Hemathea," I muttered. I pushed the blanket aside and rose. While I dressed, I wished I dared to try to get word to Knox, if only so he could know to run if he needed to.

I supposed he would hear about it. Hades willing, it would be soon enough.

It actually came sooner than I expected.

When I made my way toward the stairs, soldiers moved aside for me. At first, I thought they would enter the chamber, but instead, four of them arrayed themselves around the bottom of the stairs. Knox was one of them.

I was so used to him not acknowledging me that his broad smile and wink caught me by surprise.

His companions gave him a knowing look and one even elbowed him in the side.

I raised an eyebrow at them. I didn't suppose it mattered what they thought, but seeing them act that way made me wish I'd given them a good reason to do it. Maybe when this was over.

I looked down at my feet and started up the stairs. Part of me wanted to turn and run.

On the other hand, the soldier's presence might be to prevent me from doing just that, as much as to keep out intruders.

What intruders?

My mind wandered to Bain. If I believed Knox, and I did —mostly—the man was halfway here by now. To help or hinder, who knew? It was too late anyway. By the time he arrived, this would all be over.

I slogged up the steps with all the enthusiasm of a kid entering a classroom to study maths. Actually, that might be better than trying to revive a dead, clearly powerful man, to life.

What could go wrong? I asked myself. Apart from any number of things.

When I reached the top, Helene and Luther stood near the head of the sarcophagus, arms crossed, heads bent together in soft conversation. A sense of urgency filled the room. Was that from them or Comus? Maybe both. If he was in a hurry, it would infect them.

I realised it began to infect me the moment I stepped into the chamber.

"It's about time," Helene snapped.

My mother would have told her to be nice if she wanted help.

I held my tongue, because I knew they didn't need me to have one. They needed my power, not my ability to speak. As for my tongue, I was pretty attached to that. Ice cream would suck without it.

"Sorry," I said, and flashed them what I hoped was a winning smile. "What do we do?"

Apparently I said the right thing. Helene nodded and lowered her arms.

"I will stand at the head. You both stand to either side." She waved us into place and held her hands in front of her. "As one, we will touch Comus's prison. We will draw power from that."

She nodded to a tall stand. An ordinary looking clay bowl stood on top, full to the brim with dried petals.

The smell was so sweet I wanted to inhale it all at once. With that much power I could blow the top off the cave, off the whole mountain.

"Restraint," Helene said firmly. "Between the three of us, we could destroy half a city, but today we must use restraint. A good deal of power, but only a hair of it, directed to opening the prison. Understood?"

I nodded. Suddenly the endless hours moving rice made sense. It was the difference between using an axe to split wood, and a needle to stitch a small wound. The axe would make the wound a lot bigger, and a needle would do fuck all to the wood. Different tools for different uses.

What I didn't understand was why. Surely they could rip the sarcophagus apart with only a small effort? No, there must be more to this than that.

"Follow my lead and let me guide your power," Helene instructed. "Draw and hold."

I did as asked. At Helene's nod, we all placed our hands on the cold stone.

I felt Helene's tug, light as first, then more insistent.

"Refine your power," the woman ordered. "Down to a single strand, no greater than a hair."

I pressed my power down like a fine thread, then rounded it down into a strand like the web of a tiny spider.

"Good." Helene tugged the strand, and one from Luther. She braided them together with a deftness I wouldn't have believed if I hadn't witnessed it myself. She drew more and more power from us, bit by bit, and slid it inside a minuscule crack in the side of the fancy lid.

Once inside, the power slid like a snake, seeking something, flicking this way and that.

"I feel it," Luther said. He sounded excited. "To the left. No, *your* left. There."

"I see it." Helene sounded like a kid who had discovered a stash of sweets, and no one was there to stop her from eating them all.

I considered stopping her, but the slightest tug back on the power was met with a rock wall of resistance. Helene held on so tight I wasn't even sure she was aware of it.

The power snuck into a tiny hole. So small, no one would have seen it with their naked eye, even if they knew to look. There, it found a latch the size of a speck of dust.

Helene wound the power around it and shoved the latch aside.

There was no click, or blast in response.

The ground didn't tremble.

All that came was an overwhelming sense of relief and Helene let the power go.

I took half a step back and shook my head at the sudden surge of power. Instinctively, I held on to it, even while I felt Helene and Luther let go of theirs.

"It is done," the Hemathea whispered. "His prison is unlocked."

"Now what?" Luther asked.

A hint of uncertainty crossed Helene's features. "Now we wait," she said firmly.

"For what?" I asked. They no longer needed me, I could walk away now. I should, but something made me stand my ground. I had gone through enough to be here, I might as well see this Comus for myself.

Helene gave me a look as if she might call for the guards to remove me, but her attention snapped back as the lid moved.

At first it shifted as though a corner was pushed up from underneath. It settled for a moment, then rose straight up so fast it almost struck the ceiling. At the last moment, it stopped, spun in a slow circle and then flew against a wall. It hit with such force, chunks of stone from the lid and the cavern were thrown in every direction.

I threw up my arm, laden with power, to protect my face.

"Oh, sorry about that. I'm out of practice," a smooth voice spoke.

I lowered my arm slowly.

The man who sat in the open sarcophagus was young, but at the same time, not. His skin looked lightly tanned under a sprinkle of beard. The expression in his bright blue eyes was ancient.

"Great One," Helene said in awe. She dropped to her knees.

Luther gaped for a while before he too lowered himself to his knees.

"I suppose you could call me that." Comus, I presumed, swung his legs over the side of the sarcophagus and leapt out. He landed on the floor and staggered with the grace of someone who hadn't used their limbs for a few hundred years.

In spite of that, his body was ripped. I had never seen so many abs on one person before. I barely noticed those though. My eyes went to a cock so big my stomach clenched. Somewhere between desire and the sneaking suspicion he'd tear me in two.

He swaggered toward me, a smile on his lips. He was handsome, with all the arrogance I might expect from a god.

"I presume I have you to thank for releasing me." He spoke with an unfamiliar accent. One hot enough to set panties on fire. If they weren't flooded instead.

Fucking damn.

"No, Great One," Helene said, hasty and loud. "It was me. She—" She nodded in my direction. "She was reluctant."

Comus clicked his tongue, but his eyes didn't leave me.

"Was she now? Well that's a shame, but she's here now. She can witness your reward." He licked his lips as though he wanted to unnerve me and stepped away, toward the other two.

Both looked eager; matching smiles on their faces.

Comus rubbed his chin. Wasn't his beard shorter a moment ago? His hair seemed to have grown as well, at least a finger length.

"My mother, damn her soul to eternity, made this prison for me." He waved toward the sarcophagus. "She knew it would only take those of great power to release me. She," he glanced back toward me, "is Hecate, but you probably know that."

"Helene suggested as much," I agreed.

"Ah." He nodded. "Yes. My father was an Alpha of Jintaro, which technically makes me an Alpha." He rubbed his ever-growing beard.

"I suppose it does." What did they call a half man, half god? A demigod? As far as I knew, they were a myth, but the stories weren't pleasant. Demigods were supposedly bad tempered and power hungry.

Wait— Hemi-theos. Didn't that mean half-god? According to Helene and Luther, we were demigods? What the fuck?

"Yes, you are," Comus replied. "I can sense your thoughts." He turned back to the others. "Once, all hemitheos' magic was combined. My mother made sure it was diluted so a hemitheos only had one ability. She was such a spoilsport." He pouted. "She also had hemitheos quietly killed, so the chance of their being three with the kind of power you have, would be rare."

He smiled. "Anyway, here you all are." He glanced toward the entrance as though troubled by something. He shook his head and his smile returned.

"At any rate, this sarcophagus is special. It kept me alive, and continues to do so."

"Praise the power," Helene whispered.

"Yes." Comus snapped his fingers. "Praise the power indeed. However, in order to keep working, it must be occupied."

Helene's face paled. "But Great One, we sacrificed so much to release you."

He cocked his head for a moment, then barked a laugh. "I

don't mean *I'm* going back in there, dear woman." His gaze went from me to Luther and back again, a satisfied smile on his lips.

"Which one of you two?" he mused.

Both of their eyes widened. "I wish to serve you, Great One," Helene said quickly.

"Oh, goodness, how quickly you throw your companion under the carriage wheels." Comus clicked his tongue again. "Very well."

Luther let out a choked sound as he rose into the air.

"No, Great One, I beg you. I am your most humble servant. I—" With a flick of Comus's wrist, he descended into the sarcophagus. The lid rose up from the floor.

"Please—" Luther sobbed. He put up a hand to keep the lid from lowering down onto him.

I caught sight of his wild, terrified eyes before the lid dropped back into place.

"Don't worry, he's not dead." Comus lowered his arm. "The sarcophagus will keep him alive for as long as I live. I plan for that to be approximately…eternity."

Helene let out a choking sound. "He will be honoured to make the sacrifice for you, Great One."

Comus waved a hand. "Of course he is. Now, as for you two." He rubbed his beard. It was almost to his chin, but seemed to have stopped growing now.

"My uncle, Hades, had a little nickname for me. Lord of the Dead. Isn't that sweet? It's because I liked to kill people and keep their souls from him. Souls make fabulous servants." He eyed Helene.

She took a step back. "I swear to serve you, Great One. You—you promised freedom."

"I did, didn't I?" He examined his fingernails and frowned. "Yes, I did. Freedom from life and all the suffering that comes with it." He pointed a finger toward Helene and she began to shrivel like a grape left out in the sun.

She raised her hands to either side and screamed, even as her hands glowed with power. The glow only lasted a moment before her skin seemed to turn to paper and clung to her bones. Her body fell to the floor with a soft thud. A few heartbeats later a smoky version of herself rose from it.

She still screamed, but it made no sound.

"She'll settle down," Comus said easily. He gave me a warm smile. "So, you weren't as eager to free me. Why did you?"

I shrugged and held onto my power, even though I was sure it was woefully inadequate against him. "They made me do it, and you offered freedom."

"Ah." He held up a finger. "Rule number one: never trust a demigod, especially one trapped inside that for fuck knows how long." He jerked his thumb toward the sarcophagus.

"I don't think they knew what you were." My eyes went to Helene's body.

"That's possible, I suppose," he conceded. "So, you don't want to serve me?"

Was there a way I could respond to that, and not get killed?

"Not particularly," I said honestly. "I've had enough of doing what other people say."

"So, in a way," he said slowly, "I've done you a favour by ridding you of those two."

Helene's ghostly form had stopped screaming and now lay curled in a corner, rocking back and forth.

I wouldn't have wanted that for the woman, even after everything.

"In a manner of speaking, I suppose you have," I agreed.

"Excellent." He smiled brightly. "Then you will owe me a favour in return. I shall call upon you when I need to."

The blood drained from my face. "Uh—"

He held up a hand. "No need to thank me. It will take a while. I need to find my mother first."

"And do what?" I asked carefully.

"Why, kill her of course," he said cheerfully. "And my Uncle Hades." .

"Won't that—"

"Unravel the world and kill everyone on it? Yes, I would imagine it would. Just think how much fun it will be, with all those souls to serve us."

"Us?" My voice broke.

"Yes, you seem like fun; I might let you live. Besides, only a combination of hemitheos power will kill a goddess. As strong as you are, you are only one. With several consorts like you, we could kill all of the gods. Think of the power."

"Don't you have enough power?" I asked.

He sighed. "I am weakened by my time incarcerated, but no, I cannot do it alone." He stepped up to me and placed a finger under my chin.

"I know you must be eager to begin, so am I." He pressed his erect cock to the side of my leg. "But the child of a demigod has diluted blood. Once I kill my mother and my uncle, I will have their power. Perhaps I shall give some to you. Our children will rule worlds."

Wow, I thought Knox was presumptuous. He had nothing on this guy.

My stomach fluttered. I didn't want to take part in any more killing, or locking people away in stone boxes, but I wanted him so badly I wanted to scream. I wanted to beg him to fuck me up against the nearest wall.

My tongue darted over my lips.

He leaned in and whispered in my ear. "This is where you say, yes, Great One."

I snorted. "Whatever you say."

He laughed. "Feisty. I like it. I'm glad they didn't break you. I don't want a woman on her knees like a servant. I want an equal." He gave me a lopsided smile. "Although on your knees while you suck my cock is good too."

He sighed deeply. "I must go now, I need to rest. Remember, while we are apart, that you belong to me. Dream of me. Some day, when I'm ready, I'll come for you." He kissed my mouth, hard and firm.

Then somehow I found myself alone.

That lasted no more than a handful of moments. The sound of booted feet echoed up the stairs.

"What have you done?" The demand preceded the drawing of swords.

I turned and frowned at the soldiers who stood in the entrance, blades bare except for Knox. He wore the same confused expression as the rest of them.

My eyes took in Helene's body and I understood what they must have concluded.

"I didn't touch her," I insisted. "It was Comus. He killed her."

The soldiers looked disbelieving.

"And Luther?" their leader asked. A tall man, he bore a scar down one cheek and a mouth which looked as though he never smiled.

"He's in there." I nodded toward the sarcophagus.

"Open it." The soldiers stepped deeper inside.

"I can't. It takes three of us." Comus ensured I couldn't simply let Luther out.

The leader sheathed his sword and stepped toward it. He tugged at the lid, but it didn't move. He grunted and tried once more before he stepped away.

"Where is the Great One?"

"Gone," I replied, "I don't know where."

"That's unfortunate," the leader said. He nodded to his

fellows. "Take her. She will stand trial for the murder of the Hemathea and hemitheos Luther."

I blinked. "But I—"

It was Knox who gripped my left arm. He gave me a warning look and pulled me toward the stairs.

"I swear to Hades I didn't harm either of them," I said, but I walked beside him without struggling.

"The court of hemitheos will determine that," the leader snapped.

"The what? There's a—"

"I suggest you be silent," he snapped.

I closed my mouth and tried to catch Knox's eyes.

He wouldn't look at me directly.

Did he think I had done what the other soldiers assumed?

I wanted to tell him I hadn't. I didn't. If he was so determined to hold onto his pretence, then I would wait. At least for now. I'd wait until I had time to explain. Hades willing, there would be time.

And Hades.

How long would it take for Comus to be ready to go after him and Hecate? Where did gods and goddesses hide, anyway? They might be in dragon form, for all I knew. Or tadpoles. Hecate might be a speck of dust on the wind, or the petal of a veil flower.

The soldiers marched me down the stairs and toward the front of the citadel. If they took me outside, I could run. I could run now, if I wanted to, but that would make me look guilty. Besides, with the blindfold covering my eyes on the way up, I didn't know the way out. At least, not without blasting a path through the forest, or risking getting wildly lost. Neither option held much appeal.

I blinked as they led me outside into the sunshine. After days in the gloom, I had forgotten how bright the world was, even in the hours after dawn.

Knox released my arm and stepped aside, sword still in hand. "I think she can walk by herself."

"You know what power—" one of the soldiers started.

"She can use it any time she chooses," Knox said. "Whether or not we touch, or even tie her up. This way, she is more likely to cooperate."

"Yes," I said quickly. "I am. I have nothing to hide, I won't be—"

I let out a squeak as Knox lunged toward me. I started to use my power to fend him off, but he stepped past me at the last moment.

The other soldier was caught by surprise, but he managed to bring up his sword and parry before Knox relieved him of his arm. He pushed Knox back and forced him to go on the defensive.

I hesitated, reluctant to use my power in case I hurt Knox, or gave the other soldiers more reason to think of me as a threat.

The soldier pushed Knox back toward an outcrop. Beyond that was a sheer drop.

Before I could react to stop him from plunging over, a knife appeared in the soldier's back and blood blossomed, slick on his black uniform.

"What the fuck?"

"Viva!" Kerina stepped out of the trees several metres from the entrance to the citadel. "There you are."

I blinked. For the second time in as many seconds, I said, "What the fuck? What are you doing here?"

"Looking for you." Kerina was followed by Bain and a woman I didn't know.

"That was your knife?"

The soldier lay where he had fallen and Knox stood close, an eye on him while he still twitched.

"Who else?" Kerina shrugged.

"You dare?" the lead soldier roared. It wasn't clear who he was talking to. Maybe all of us.

"We dare," Bain agreed. "You might be outnumbered, depending on what you say next." He sounded quite reasonable.

"This—woman is a murderer." The man waved toward me with one hand. The other rested on his sword hilt. "She murdered two people in cold blood. Possibly a third."

"I see." Bain nodded. "Would you say she's a threat to the Vault?"

The soldier hesitated, obviously seeing his chance to bring me to some kind of justice slipping away.

"She—"

"Did nothing wrong," I insisted. "There is a very great threat to the Vault. To the world. Comus is—"

"She claims he killed a woman," the soldier said. "However, the real evil is her."

Kerina sauntered toward him, stopped and cocked her head. "You don't look like you'd know evil if it bit you on the ass."

"Kerina," Bain warned.

She shrugged and strode away.

"I believe you," Bain told the soldier. "We will take her into our custody. She will be dealt with by the Keeper. He's been looking for an excuse to execute someone for a while now."

I gaped. "You have to believe me. Comus is—"

"Enough," Bain said softly. "You helped to release him, didn't you? I felt a great presence." he frowned. "It's gone now."

"I did, but I… I didn't know…" Shit. What was happening here?

"You helped release evil into the world," Bain said again.

"I was forced to," I insisted. I inhaled the scent of him. I would blast them all off the top of this mountain. I would—

I would do nothing because then I would be everything they accused me of.

I slumped my shoulders. What do you know, I guess the Covener was right about me all along. I was no use to anyone.

"The others were the ones who did wrong," Knox said softly.

I shot him a grateful look. At least he was on my side. Well, him and Comus, whatever that was worth.

Bain shrugged with one shoulder. "It's not for me to decide. We'll return to the Vault and the Keeper can decide."

The soldier looked uncertain, but lowered his hand and stepped back. He eyed the dead soldier and evidently decided he'd prefer to stay alive.

"Knox, you know the way out?" Bain asked.

Knox's lips twitched, but he nodded. "Yes. Sir."

"Latika, walk in front with Knox," Bain ordered.

The woman nodded and fell in beside the spy, her face expressionless.

Kerina gave me a conciliatory smile and moved into place behind me.

Bain stepped beside me, his expression guarded. He smelled of conflict.

I sent him thoughts of having no sympathy for him, whatsoever. If he wanted to treat me like I was a criminal, then so be it. I wouldn't give him a break.

"Let's get off this mountain," he said, his voice tight.

"Good idea," Kerina said, "before the black tigers get hungry again."

"I'm sure Bain will toss me to them before you all run away," I said.

He shot me a look which clearly said he wanted me to be quiet.

I wouldn't give him the satisfaction. "You're not denying it," I pointed out.

"I'm not throwing anyone to the tigers," he said, "except maybe those soldiers back there."

I looked at him in surprise.

He responded by giving me a faint smile. "Let's get back to the Vault."

The sooner the better. He had some explaining to do.

24

"You're alive!" A voice greeted us as we stepped out of the maze of trees and stones that led down from the citadel.

A man with a lyaer on his shoulder held the reins of a horse. Two girls, younger versions of Latika, held the reins of two others.

"Wesley," Bain greeted the man wearily. "All of you should be in Cape Massin by now."

"Aisha. Erin." Latika greeted them in turn. "You had your orders."

I glanced at her, but the woman's gaze was unwavering.

Kerina muttered something about the girls being in big trouble, but didn't elaborate when I gave her a questioning look.

Aisha lifted her chin. "We tried, Mother, but Erin was certain you needed our help."

Erin scowled at her sister, but didn't try to contradict her.

"I should have you both whipped," Latika growled. She sighed and embraced them. "I'm glad to see you."

"We were about to make camp," Wesley said cheerfully.

"It's as good a place as any," Bain replied. "You two, keep watch." He nodded to Aisha and Erin.

I thought they might argue, but they both seemed pleased instead.

"You keep some interesting company," I said to Bain.

He snorted. "You don't know the half of it." He took me by the elbow and led me aside while the others set up the small camp in the centre of a copse.

"Tell me about this Comus."

He listened while I told him everything which had occurred over the last few weeks. I only left out the details of me and Knox pretending to be lovers.

When I finished, he told me of his journey, although I was certain he omitted details here and there as well.

"Lord of the Dead was also called the Lord of Lies," he said once we were both finished speaking. "I thought he was nothing but a story.

"Apparently not. It seems he has some skill in creating illusions, or making people see things which only exist in the backs of their minds."

"Their greatest fears," I said softly.

"Did he show you any?" he asked.

I made a face. "He suggested some interesting things, but no. As far as I know, everything I saw was real."

"You believe him when he says he's coming for you?" His brown eyes locked onto mine.

"Unless we can stop him from finding Hades and Hecate and taking their power," I replied.

"Then that's what we'll do," he said, as if it was a simple matter. "We'll return to the city and figure out where to start."

"I need to find others like me," I said. "Helene claimed they're out there. The soldier with the scar spoke of a hemitheos council." I stopped and narrowed my eyes. "Would you really have let Dex execute me?"

Bain looked embarrassed, but shrugged. "I couldn't stop him if he insisted, but I would tell him what I sense about you."

"Oh?" I cocked my head and tried to keep from drowning in the depths of his eyes. "What is that?" His scent was heady; sandalwood laced with musk and something else. Something warm, but kept under careful control.

"I sense sincerity," he replied. "I sense a woman whose heart is in the right place. I sense fear of what might come, but determination to stop Comus from destroying the world. Perhaps regret for her part in it, but short of dying, you couldn't have stopped them."

"I know," I replied quickly. "But my curiosity got the best of me as well. And—" I sucked in a breath and inhaled the evening smells of the trees and plants around me. "He promised freedom. He lied about the form of it, but it sounded wonderful."

Bain paused for a few moments. "After all you went through to avoid slavery, you wanted that for everyone else?"

"Exactly." I looked regretful.

Bain grazed my cheek lightly with the back of his hand. "That's not a bad thing to want. For all we know, he could have made it come true and everyone would have lived their days in bliss." The side of his mouth quirked.

"When you put it that way, it seems ridiculous."

"Not ridiculous, just idealistic."

"That's a better word than dumb as fuck."

"Much better," he said with a firm nod.

"What is Dex going to say?"

Bain lowered his hand. "Dex will look forward to the

challenge of stopping an evil demigod from destroying the world. He gets bored sometimes."

I smiled ruefully. "I suspect the next while will be too much excitement for all of us."

"I think you might be right." His eyes lingered on my face for a while and he smiled softly. "Whatever reasons the Covener had for sending you to the Vault, I'm glad he did."

"I'm glad too. Helene would have taken me either way and if she had, I would have been on my way to the hemitheos court right now."

"You wouldn't have let them force you to go," he said.

"Yes I would. I won't be like her or Comus. I won't use my power to hurt people. I will use it to stop him." I was done being a pawn in other people's plans. From then on, I would be the one making plans. They would have to fit in with me, or at least offer viable alternatives to my ideas.

"I believe you," Bain said softly. "I'll do whatever I can to help you." He stepped away from me with reluctance. "We should get some rest," he added in a voice loud enough for everyone to hear. "Although maybe after Kerina tells us all why she's afraid of cows."

Kerina gave him a dirty look, then stuck her tongue out at him.

"That's blatant insubordination," he said, but she seemed amused.

"It is, isn't it?" Kerina replied. "I guess I should take some more training, my discipline is slipping."

I lay down with my head on my pack and pulled a blanket over myself. The last thing I heard was a chuckle. I thought it was Bain, but I wasn't sure.

~

"I'M NOT sure where he came from, sister." The nurse kept his voice low, so as not to disturb the sleeping man. "He staggered through the clinic doors and all but collapsed at my feet. He was as naked as the day he was born." The nurse noticed the expression on the other nurse's face. She looked as though she might peel back the blanket and peek.

"Before he fell asleep, he told me he woke in an alley not far from here. He has no idea how he got there. He claims to have no memory of his name."

"Curious," the second nurse said. "Was he injured? Maybe he hit his head. Or had it hit for him. He wouldn't be the first to have that happen."

"Indeed," the first nurse agreed.

The man under the blanket stirred, but soon lay still again. With his neat beard and bright blue eyes, he might be considered handsome, but there was something about him the man found unnerving. The sooner he was well enough to move on, the better.

"He said he was looking for Hades," the nurse added.

"Sounds like he took a hard blow to the head," the second nurse said dryly.

"Possibly," the male nurse said quickly. "But—"

She quirked an eyebrow at him and gestured for him to continue.

"He seemed serious."

"Drugs?" The second nurse shrugged.

"I guess so. We see when the doctor looks him over." No doubt she'd want blood taken and tests run.

The second nurse nodded. "Hopefully he'll remember everything in the morning." She smiled down at the sleeping man.

"Yes, he may." For some reason, a shiver passed through the nurse. "We should leave him to sleep."

"Yes, we should," she agreed. She looked ready to jump under the blanket with the man.

The nurse shook his head. If she kept him busy, then the he wouldn't have to bother. He could spend more time with other patients. Or with his study into the paranormal. He was close to interpreting some of the ancient scrolls his mother left him. One in particular held his interest. The scroll claimed to show the place where Hades himself rested. That knowledge would bring him acclaim, the world over.

He rubbed his hands together and hurried back to his work.

ABOUT THE AUTHOR

Maggie Alabaster writes reverse harem and, paranormal, sci-fi and fantasy romance.

She lives in NSW, Australia with one spouse, two daughters, one dog, and countless birds.

Sign up for my newsletter! Sign Up!

Join my reader group! Join here!

Follow me on Bookbub! Click here to follow me!

Check out my website- www.maggiealabaster.com

ALSO BY MAGGIE ALABASTER

Ruck Boys

Filthy Ruck

Hard Ruck

Twisted Ruck

Sparrow and the Mafia Kings

Possessive

Ruined

Corrupted

Pucking Dark Hearts

Pucking Hearts Collide

Pucking Forbidden Hearts

Pucking Hardened Hearts

Dusk Bay Demons

Puck Drop

Breakaway

Power Play

Brutal Academy

Book 1 Heartless

Book 2 Cruel

Book 3 Vengeful

Court of Blood and Binding

Book 1 Song of Scent and Magic

Book 2 Crown of Mist and Heat

Book 3 Sword of Balm and Shadow

Book 4 Whisper of Frost and Flame

Dark Masque

Book 1 Bait

Book 2 Prey

Book 3 Trap

Saving Abbie

Book 1 Pitch

Book 2 Pound

Book 3 Session

Book 4 Muse

Book 5 Rhythm

Book 6 Encore

Novella Venomous

Saving Abbie books 1-4

Saving Abbie books 4-6 + Venomous

Ruthless Claws

Book 1 Ivory

Book 2 Crimson

Book 3 Elodie

Harmony's Magic

Book 1 Summoned by Fire

Book 2 Summoned by Fate

Book 3 Summoned by Desire

Shifter's Vault

Book 1 Discarded

Book 2 Deceived

Book 3 Disgraced

My Alien Mates

Book 1 Star Warriors

Book 2 Star Defenders

Book 3 Star Protectors

Academy of Modern Magic

Book 1 Digital Magic

Book 2 Virtual Magic

Book 3 Logical Magic

Complete Collection

Summer's Harem

Book 1: Shimmer

Book 2: Glimmer

Book 3: Flicker

Complete collection

Short reads

Taken by the Snowmen

Jingle All the Way

Also by Maggie Alabaster and Erin Yoshikawa

Caught by the Tide

Book 1–Pursued by Shadows

Book 2 Pursued by Darkness

Book 3 Pursued by Monsters

9 780645 289107